# TELL IT
## TO THE
# MARINES

By Jack Lewis

CHARGER BOOKS

# TELL IT TO THE MARINES

A Charger Book
Paperback Library edition/August 1966
Charger Books edition/August 1983

This book may not be reproduced in whole or in part, by
mimeograph or any other process, without permission.
For information address: Charger Books, Incorporated,
34249 Camino Capistrano, Capistrano Beach, CA 92624

ISBN 0-937752-04-5

Library of Congress Catalog Card Number: 83-071708

*Printed in the United States of America*

*Any similarity to persons, places or incidents is highly plausible; only the names have been changed to avoid court-martial.*

# DEDICATION

This book is dedicated to numerous persons — and to a single premise.

First and foremost, it is dedicated to Donna, who didn't realize the Marine Corps is composed of characters until she married one.

It is for General Christian F. Schilt, USMC (Retired), one of the Old School; a true officer, a dedicated gentleman and, above all, a human being.

It is gratefully dedicated to Colonel Richard R. Breen, USMC (Retired). Without his gentle persuasions, I still might be wearing green instead of making it.

It is dedicated to the officers and men of the 1st Marine Aircraft Wing, past and present.

And finally, it is dedicated to the premise that rank and brains are not necessarily synonymous.

# CHAPTER 1

**P**ROPERLY DRESSED in full uniform including blouse and field scarf, First Lieutenant Joseph Wingate McCorkle, United States Marines Corps Reserve, was uneasy. In fact, he was downright self-conscious. Everyone else in the Officers Club was wearing the green herringbone utility uniform peculiar to Marines. Blushing in spite of the awareness that he was correct, he realized he was in the position of a man in a tuxedo who has just learned he is the guest speaker at a hobo convention.

Glancing about the club, it was simple to tell those who had just returned from those who were bound for the war. The difference was in the dirt. Those who had arrived from Korea wore dirty dungarees. Those bound for Korea had clean ones.

McCorkle attempted to appear casual as he sipped his beer. According to The Book, he was the only one who belonged; one was not supposed to appear in Officers Clubs in dungarees. How was it possible to feel wrong, out of place, when The Book said he was right?

There was no one in the room he knew. The other newcomers had arrived by ship that afternoon, while he had come in by plane barely two hours ago. Now, eyeing the two distinctive groups in the room, he noted another method of telling the neophytes from the veterans.

Some of the latter group were going home, others were here only for a few days' Rest and Recreation leave.

"This here R'n R's the bat's balls," one of the officers at the nearby table roared.

"Better we should call it A'n A," one of his cohorts shouted back. "Ass'n Alcohol!" There was a wild clatter of laughter.

1

Grouped in a corner, caught up in a camaraderie born of the unknown, the new arrivals were strangely quiet, staring into their beers, saying little even to each other, each wondering what lay ahead. But even this group had cast questioning glances at McCorkle, surveying his comparative splendor with jaundiced eyes.

The club at this former Japanese air base was unlike anything McCorkle had ever seen. It consisted of a single gymnasium-like room with a high ceiling that was lost in tobacco smoke and darkness. The lights were dim, while the wide, high windows and even sections of the walls were hung with yards of buff-colored raw silk. At one end of the room was an unoccupied bandstand flanked by unlikely Grecian columns, while one entire wall was taken up by a bar. Behind this bulwark, quick-moving Japanese bartenders concocted drinks, decapped quart bottles of rice beer and loaded the trays of the half-dozen Oriental waitresses.

In the far corner a juke box, red and glaring in the dimness, blared a Japanese tune, while a group of veterans hunched before the machine bawled their hastily paraphrased words to the song.

> "...I ain't got no yo-yo,
> An' I don't like your no, no..."

A bearded young lieutenant turned to pinch one of the Japanese waitresses, but she whirled expertly out of reach, still smiling jadedly.

This, the sign over the operations building at the air strip had stated in bold Oriental script, was

*Itami Air Base, Japan*
*The Gateway to Korea*

It was through Itami that most of the replacements passed on their way to respective units of the 1st Marine Division and the 1st Marine Air Wing.

A heavy hand fell on his shoulder. McCorkle started, glancing up, then leaped up to attention, ignoring the table that teetered from his knee, sloshing beer over its surface. Although the bulky figure before him was swathed in a stained trench coat, the gold leaf of a major twinkled on his dungaree cap.

"You're McCorkle." The major's tone was positive, but his expression was dubious as he inspected McCorkle's carefully pressed uniform.

The lieutenant nodded, his voice catching in this throat. "Y-yes, sir," he stammered, wondering how the other knew his name.

"You're my relief," the other stated. "I'm Lawrence."

"Yes, sir," McCorkle repeated, not knowing what else to say. He was coloring again under the inspection, but he extended his hand and Lawrence enveloped it in wide, bulky fingers.

"I came over to fly you back," the major explained. "Come on. I'll help you pack."

McCorkle gulped, trying to hide his confusion and awe. "But I thought..."

"I cleared it all the way," Lawrence declared briskly, waving at McCorkle's uniform with disapproval. "But you can't wear that!"

McCorkle colored perceptibly as he glanced at the major's frayed, dirty trench coat then to his own comparative elegance. But before he could respond, Lawrence had him firmly by the elbow, guiding him toward the doorway, ignoring the amused glances.

"That's right, Lawrence," someone bawled, "Don't let him get away!" McCorkle quickened his step, not looking back.

Ten minutes later, wearing dungarees that still were stiff with newness, McCorkle was on the rear seat of a jeep with the major. Having this officer who outranked him arrive to personally fly him to the battle zone seemed a special honor, but the major's urgency, his rush to be off, held something secretive, even alarming.

As they sped along the narrow roadway, a sign at the edge of the pitted paving was picked out by the headlights and McCorkle craned his neck to see it.

*Drive With Care!*
*The Man You Hit May Be Your*
*Relief!*

McCorkle knew little about airplanes but he recognized wreckage. He shuddered at the sight of the antiquated torpedo bomber, its paint peeling, fuselage still wearing the poorly-healed scars left by Japanese shrapnel nearly a decade earlier.

"This is what you're flying?" he asked dubiously. Lawrence nodded cheerily.

"Not exactly. It's too old to fly. It sort of skips across the water, but

3

it was all I could get. It's carried on the Government's books at $2. One for the engine, one for the fuselage."

"I don't think I want to go tonight, sir," McCorkle declared.

"What'cha mean?"

"I...I don't feel so good," he stammered lamely. He was remembering a conversation overheard at the club. Two pilots had mentioned that there was only one of these old torpedo bombers left in the entire Far East. If one had even a basic knowledge of arithmetic, this had to be it.

"What happened to the others?" one of the pilots had asked over his beer.

"Just got tired of flying," had been the shrugged reply. This plane was weary, too. Judging from its appearance, it had been weary for at least ten years.

"Now you wouldn't let me come clear over here to get you, then fly back alone, would you, lieutenant?"

McCorkle nodded miserably, eyes still on the dilapidated aircraft. "I...I heard some talk of a typhoon."

"No sense of adventure," the major snorted. "That wind'll miss us by a hundred miles. Besides, you'll feel better when you get up there in the fresh air."

"Fresh air, sir?"

"One of the panels in the canopy is cracked. Lots of fresh air."

Still seeking an out that could not be construed as rank disobedience, McCorkle was shoved up onto the wing and into the rear cockpit, while the jeep driver stowed his gear in the belly compartment.

Moments later he was clutching the frayed safety belt across his lap, as the plane roared down the runway and lifted falteringly into the air. The engine missed once and the craft started to nose down. Then it caught, settling into a troubled drone.

Leaning back, the wind whipping across his face, McCorkle pondered whether he could blame his mother for being aloft in this tired monster. After all, it *was* her fault.

He should have had sense enough to protest, he realized, but his greatest problem was the fact that his mother had been frightened by a master sergeant who, by coincidence, happened to be his father. As a result of that union, he had been brought up under strict, stern and sometimes harsh standards of discipline. Until he had left home, he never had made a major decision for himself. These had

4

been made for him by his father. As a result, he had developed a respect born of fear, not so much for rank as for experience. That, he knew, was why he had felt uncomfortable before the Korean veterans in the club earlier; it was why he had not argued with the major about this flight.

And the urge to escape such standards might well have been his reason for being here now. He was four years old when he had wandered away from his mother in a department store and had been rescued by a Marine recruiting sergeant resplendent in dress blues.

From that moment, the Marine Corps had been an obsession even over his father's objections. Although a midwestern farmer by economic requirement, the senior McCorkle still lived in his own past glories. In the days before World War I, he had served with the cavalry, chasing Pancho Villa through the Mexican mountains with John J. Pershing. As a result of this action, he had been awarded some minor medal, which had come to be one of his most prized possessions.

The younger McCorkle had lived with that medal, came to be awed by it, and eventually rebelled — silently to be sure — against its influence upon his life. But in spite of this rebellion, the awe was still there for any man who had a medal, anyone broad in military experience.

When college had come, he had told his parents he could avoid the draft and complete his education by enlisting in the Marine Corps Platoon Leaders Program. This meant two summers of training followed by a commission as a second lieutenant. It also meant three years' active duty at the convenience of the Marine Corps, but this he neglected to mention in campaigning for the necessary parental signatures.

Through all of his earlier life, McCorkle had been frequently defended or backed by his mother against his father, but she invariably had lost these bouts. As a result, the youth had subconsciously come to think of her as a loser. In this instance, though, her reasoning had won, when she had pointed out that no McCorkle ever had been drafted. Still grumbling over his son's lack of allegiance to the Army, the older McCorkle had signed.

During the two summers of training at the Marine Corps Schools at Quantico, Virginia, McCorkle had been made a sergeant and had treasured these minor indicators of rank and responsibility. Some of his contemporaries in this program, self-admitted draft dodgers, had sneeringly accused him of being "shot in the ass with the Corps." He had not bothered with denials.

He fully realized that, with his skinny frame, the straw-colored hair that tended to part in a dozen directions even when clipped to skin level, and a nose that was slightly larger for his face, he was not a likely candidate for recruiting posters. But commanders, he felt, were selected for their brains. He would remedy these physical inadequacies through knowledge. As a result, his marks were high and training officers were impressed enough that they were inclined to overlook the seeming lack of self-assurance, the fact that McCorkle was inclined to blush each time he was addressed by a superior. There were even those who secretly felt such a reaction was their just due.

After graduation with a degree in journalism and his newly-signed commission, he had inquired about the active duty contract, but the Corps was long on lieutenants at that precise moment. Still, he had kept his uniforms pressed, polished his cordovan brown shoes each week in a frustrated display of duty conscience and had subscribed to the *Marine Corps Gazette*. He also had begun the study of advanced tactics through a mail order course offered by the Marine Corps Institute.

With his new degree, he had made for California, knocking on the doors of newspapers and publicity offices until eventually he had landed a job at Metro-Goldwyn-Mayer as a studio messenger. Any dreams of glamor in such a job had been dispelled rapidly. His greatest claim to fame had been the fact that he once had been called upon to deliver a cup of coffee to Clark Gable's dressing room.

When the Korean War had broken out without warning, he had received the telegram ordering him to report for active duty. After passing the physical examinations at Reserve Headquarters in Chavez Ravine, he had reported somewhat dazedly for classification. The non-commissioned officer had leafed through the Marine Corps Manual until he had found an appropriate passage.

"Okay," the sergeant told him, "you are a Motion Picture Production Officer. Your Primary MOS will be 4602. Secondary MOS is 4302, Informational Services Officer." He looked up sadly, shaking his head in disgust. "You got yourself a soft touch, lieutenant."

"What's an MOS?" McCorkle wanted to know uncertainly.

"Military Occupational Specialty."

"But I don't know anything about producing motion pictures," McCorkle protested. "I was a studio messenger. That's all."

The sergeant sighed his frustration, then flipped through the thick volume as a matter of courtesy before shaking his head.

"There ain't no MOS for studio messenger, an' The Book ain't never wrong!"

A gush of water full in the face jerked McCorkle out of his thoughts. The lights of Japan had not yet faded in the darkness as the storm struck.

The ancient aircraft bucked about like a cork in a washing machine, as Major Lawrence's unconcerned voice came through the earphones clamped over the lieutenant's utility cap.

"You still back there?" the major asked soothingly. It was difficult for McCorkle to answer. His superior had grossly understated the matter of the crack in the canopy. One section was completely gone and torrents of rain beat through the opening to lash his face. When he attempted to shrink away, this deluge seemed to track him about the narrow confines of the cockpit.

"You said we'd miss this," he gulped miserably into the microphone, his usual meakness missing.

"Never trust a weather forecaster, son," Lawrence's voice advised amid a crackle of static. "They'll screw you every time. They said we had a fifty-fifty chance."

"You knew!" McCorkle sought unsuccessfully to keep the panic out of his tone as the plane dropped for a moment like a runaway yo-yo, then settled into level flight.

"But those characters lie so much about their weather. Comfortable?"

There was no way of replying without risk of general court-martial.

McCorkle had no way of judging the interval of misery before Lawrence's voice crackled again in his earphones, this time directed to someone on the radio net.

"Awaiting landing instructions," the major concluded.

"This is Oxbow Home," a bored voice returned. "This is Oxbow Home. You will take a bearing of one-two-four degrees and hold for three minutes. At that time, make a one-eighty and report to me."

"Dammit, it's dark up here. Let's get this turkey down," Lawrence urged.

"We're clearing a flight of transports off the strip," the filtered voice stated unconcernedly. Those would be the planes bound for Itami to airlift the replacements to Korea the following morning. One would be the aircraft he should be awaiting now, McCorkle realized, instead of being buffeted about in the night.

"Roger," Lawrence snarled and McCorkle felt the shift of his own weight as the craft swung to take up the assigned bearing. Although it was dark all around him, he saw the sudden glow of a match through the panel of heavy plastic that separated him from the pilot's compartment.

Maybe a smoke would help his own nerves, he thought, reaching for the pack of cigarettes in his jacket. The pocket of the canvas-like blouse was filled with water and he gave up the idea.

"Last time I let one of those idiots plot my course, I was twenty miles back of the enemy lines in a war surplus kite before I realized some bastard was shooting at me," Lawrence announced through the earphones.

Surplus kite! What the hell does he call this? McCorkle asked himself with a savageness of thought that surprised him.

Another match glowed in the cockpit ahead. Maybe the major wasn't as calm as he appeared, if he couldn't even keep his cigarette lighted. Moments later, Lawrence's voice snapped in his earphones, asking for landing instructions. The controller, more bored than before, reported transports still were taking off in the storm.

"Look, dammit," Lawrence growled, "I don't have any instrument lights and I'm watching the compass with matches. I only have two left."

"What's your position?" the radioman wanted to know.

"Hell, you tell me!" Lawrence snarled. "You've been calling the plays, so get me down from here."

There was a moment's silence before the major's voice sounded again: "McCorkle?" He was answered by silence. "McCorkle, dammit, you can't faint; it ain't Marine!"

# CHAPTER 2

**A** CHILL RIPPLED along McCorkle's spine as the jeep raced along the blackness of the road. It was more than the wind and driving rain that clawed at him. It might have been the recollection of that feeling of helplessness as they had flown up there in the night without instruments. Or it might have been a feeling of shame at having Major Lawrence believe he had actually fainted. But the truth was that he was not certain he hadn't.

For some minutes there had been confusion on the radio net as the controllers had attempted to determine exactly where the plane was supposed to be. Then had come the blind landing in the storm. Now it all seemed dim and unreal, a nightmare in which the incidents had run together without reason.

As the vehicle charged into the driving rain, the dimmed headlights failed to show more than suspicious evidence of a road and the driver hunched over the wheel was seemingly guided only by instinct.

At the air strip, when they had landed, he had made out the dim shapes of several types of aircraft lined up abreast. In the operations shack, a box-like metal-walled structure, night fighter pilots were checking in and out in spite of the weather.

Now McCorkle caught other glimpses of the base. At each side of the roadway were occasional drifts of snow and, beyond, rows upon rows of pyramidal tents. Most were dark, but slivers of light shone between the flaps of a few. One section was made up of steep-roofed metal huts. These, too, were dark. A quick view of a sign indicated that most of these were occupied by supply functions.

Suddenly the jeep skidded to a wavering halt and McCorkle was nudged by the dark figure beside him.

"This is it," Lawrence volunteered from somewhere within the dark folds of his parka. He slid out of the vehicle and reached for the lieutenant's gear, while McCorkle fought the bulk of his own coat and struggled out over the seat. The driver sat impatiently racing the jeep's engine, making no effort to help with the two seabags. The private sat with a foot on the gas, making it plain he wanted to be off.

"Park it around in back," the major shouted at him. "The Chief of Staff's looking for a new vehicle, again!"

The driver nodded, mumbling something unintelligible behind the shriek of the wind and the rattle of icy rain. Wearing only a wet trench coat over his dungarees, McCorkle was stiff with cold as he reached for one of the heavy bags, but the major already had one on each shoulder and was leading the way toward the gray, billowing tent that faced upon the muddy roadway. With a clash of gears and an insolent spinning of wheels, the jeep lurched into the darkness.

McCorkle, confused, stood for an instant staring at the major's broad back as the latter made for the tent. He should have made that driver carry in the baggage, he thought with disapproval. Or maybe he's trying to show me something; that he doesn't really believe I fainted. He hurried to catch up, still pondering.

Suddenly the silence of the night was shattered by the roar of a heavy caliber weapon. Frightened, reacting to his recent combat training, McCorkle sprawled belly down in the mud, clawing at the half-frozen dirt with cold-numbed fingers.

"Dammit!" a voice roared in outraged complaint from somewhere beyond the canvas wall. There was another crashing report from the forty-five followed by a string of curses.

The major waited patiently as the new lieutenant rose to his feet, shaking the mud off his hands and trying to brush his clothing. Then he jerked open the door to the tent and nodded McCorkle through. The panel was fashioned from old ammunition cases, the Government stencil marks still visible in the weathering wood.

"Quillan," the major snarled. "Put down that damned gun!"

Within the tent — a partition divided it in the middle — a single dancing light bulb illuminated the front section. At one side of the patchwork of ration crates and ammo boxes that formed the wall was an opening covered by an issue blanket. This was thrown aside abruptly and a master sergeant staggered heavily into the circle of light. Dangling loosely from his fingers was a forty-five caliber service automatic. It was still cocked and he hoisted it for emphasis.

"This is my pistol," he quoted with an obscene gesture toward his groin, "and this is my gun. One is for shooting, the other's for fun."

"Where the hell you been, skipper?" he demanded on a fresh breath. "All hell's broke loose. That damned rat's been runnin' wild. Henry's out there, hangin' onta the side of th' tent t'keep it from blowin' away, and the Chief's roundin' up every jeep on the base, tryin' t'find ours!"

Frank Lawrence, shrugging out of his parka, shook his head and scowled at the six-striper. "I take off for a day and the whole outfit panics. How much time you got in the Corps, Quillan?"

The question apparently was part of a ritual; a private joke between the pair. Quillan straightened abruptly, bracing his shoulders to glare at this field grade officer as he replied in a hoarse monotone. "Twenty-seven years, eleven months an' fourteen days, sir." He hoisted the forty-five. "Long enough not to call an automatic a gun, sir."

"Almost twice as long as I've been in," the major mused in mock sadness. "Why aren't you twice as smart?"

"I am," the other replied. "The brass just don't admit it." He hiccuped gently and lowered the hammer of the automatic with a practiced flick of his thumb, while McCorkle shrank in horror.

Master Sergeant Quillan was in his late forties, his close-cropped hair streaked with white. His heavy face was a deep Irish-whisky red and his blue eyes were ringed with an alcoholic pink. Beneath the loose folds of his dungaree jacket was a barrel chest that still suggested power despite the misuse of his body. Evidence of a sizable spare tire overhung his web belt. The man was drunk. Dirty, stinking drunk!

"What've you been drinking?" Lawrence demanded blandly, then added: "I amend that. Whose booze have you been tapping?"

"Yours," was the unconcerned answer. "It seemed to be goin' sour. Didn't want it t'go ta waste."

Major Lawrence lifted a dirty towel from the back of a canvas chair and handed it to McCorkle without looking at him. The latter studiously wiped his hands clean of mud, then began to dab at his trench coat and dungarees, trying to recall whether he ever had heard of liquor turning sour. In the light from the dancing bulb that swung with each new blast of wind, he covertly studied the pair.

Lawrence, wearing regulation Marine Corps dungarees — time-faded green twill trousers and jacket — stood five feet ten inches and was approaching forty. Pinned to his dungaree jacket above the left pocket were the wings of a Naval Aviator, an outright violation of uniform regulations since the wings were meant for more formal display.

He had thinning brown hair with the suggestion of a curl and a manner that seemed unshakable even in the face of the familiarities of this master sergeant. Along one cheek was an almost invisible scar left by Japanese shrapnel at Guadalcanal, if the stories about him were dependable.

"Top, this is going to be your new boss," the major declared, waving a vague hand in the direction of the bespattered new arrival. "First Lieutenant McCorkle."

Quillan squinted at him through the light for a moment, obviously judging him. Uncomfortable, McCorkle felt the redness of a blush creeping up his neck and this irritated him. Lawrence should be calling the MPs to haul this man away instead of making introductions. Then the sergeant took a step forward, extending a fist. The forty-five was in it and McCorkle cringed visibly as the bore was centered momentarily upon his belt buckle. The sergeant quickly shifted the weapon to his left hand, while he shook the newcomer's cold fingers.

"Welcome aboard," he said thickly. "How do you feel about colonels?"

"Huh?" McCorkle took an awkward step to the rear and nearly tripped over one of his seabags. Quillan closed upon him, relentlessly seeking an opinion.

"Colonels. Like our Chief of Staff. He's tryin' to steal our jeep again!" There was indignation in the tone.

"I haven't briefed him, Top," Lawrence put in gently. "See if you can scrounge up some coffee. And get Henry in here to make up that spare bunk."

"But if th' kid quits hangin' onta the side of this tent, th' whole damned thing'll blow away," the master sergeant protested.

"Let it. We'll all go over the hill," the major agreed nonchalantly, then added: "In our jeep."

Shrugging, the sergeant turned to face the side of the tent, roaring, "Henry! Get your ass in here! *Poli poli!*"

There was a boyish soprano shout from somewhere outside, and the master sergeant, satisfied, turned to push his way past the blanket that divided the tent.

McCorkle slipped off the muddy, water-logged trench coat and dropped it across the seabags. He was dazed by the rapid succession of happenings, groping for some shred of reality.

"Who's Henry?" he asked, tone uncertain in spite of his effort. Lawrence was watching him with quiet amusement.

"Our houseboy. We picked him up in some ruins in North Korea before the gooks ran us out. He's been with us ever since."

"But how long's he been out there in the rain? He could die of exposure."

The major shrugged. "Call him a field expedient. In a war, you have to make up your own rules." He glanced up at the billowing, snapping canvas overhead. "Besides, he enjoys showing how useful he can be. Can you think of a better way than for him to keep a roof over our heads?"

McCorkle obviously had no rebuttal and Lawrence went on: "These damned tents were declared surplus by the Army in the War of 1812." There was a touch of the professional bitterness all Marines reserve specifically for the Army. "That's how the Marine Corps got them."

"And the jeep?" McCorkle's tone was even more uncertain. "What about that? And the Chief of Staff?"

"It's our vehicle," the major decreed flatly. "We stole it fair and square from the Army and the Chief's had his eye on it ever since."

"You...you mean he knows it's stolen?" McCorkle's voice rose in astonishment, but it only brought another shrug.

"Possibly not. We gave it a fast paint job. Then we took my serial number and Quillan's, added them together, then divided the total. That's the number we painted on the hood. But it's the best damn jeep in Korea and the Chief wants it."

"Lo, maja, suh," a thin voice piped behind him and McCorkle turned, startled at the small, pinched face staring at him from the folds of the camouflage poncho.

The Korean boy was less than five feet tall and the waterproofed material hung on him like a fallen circus tent. A torn utility cap with the single stripe of a private first class stenciled across the visor was balanced on his ears at a twisted angle. He had the look of a homeless gnome.

"Hello, Henry." The major's tone was kindly. "Blow up any generals while I was away?"

The boy grinned shyly, shaking his head. "Not t'day, suh."

Lawrence eyed McCorkle speculatively as he explained, "Some idiot down in Intelligence is certain Henry's a spy just because we picked him up in North Korea before we had to bug out of there."

McCorkle felt a wave of objections sweep over him at the major's choice of words. Bug out: Slang for retreat. Didn't he know that Marines never retreat? A strategic withdrawal, yes; retreat, *never!*

"Tell me, Henry," Lawrence asked, "are you really a spy?"

The boy nodded enthusiastically. *"Hai.* One of th' best, suh."

Good Lord, was McCorkle's shocked realization, the kid speaks English with a Texas drawl!

"Quillan, get the hell out of my bourbon and bring on that coffee!" the major shouted, turning toward the blanket-covered doorway.

"I think I got that damn rat cornered!" came the muffled reply. The forty-five automatic roared, followed by a repetition of the earlier string of oaths.

"Quillan lacks imagination in his swearing," Lawrence explained with sympathy, pretending not to notice the tense pose McCorkle had assumed, ready to dive for the floor.

An instant later, the master sergeant shouldered aside the blanket, a steaming cup in each hand, a bourbon bottle tucked cozily between his elbow and body.

"Did you ever get the coffee pot washed?" Lawrence asked.

"Never wash a coffee pot," Quillan insisted, shaking his head. "It ruins the character of the stuff for months." As he handed each of the officers an aluminum canteen cup, he glanced at McCorkle suggestively. "Thought a spot of the major's bourbon might help warm you up, lootenant."

"No thanks." McCorkle shook his head. "Not now." But the sergeant already had twisted the cap off the bottle and was sloshing a liberal shot into the black, evil contents of the cup.

"Gotta watch out for rat bite around here," he muttered. Lawrence pushed his own cup forward and Quillan tilted the bottle even more liberally.

As the two officers raised the cups to their lips, the master sergeant turned to another cup on the open field desk and drained the remainder of the bourbon into it. He glanced up to see McCorkle staring at him. As he raised the cup in salute, he nodded meaningfully.

"Coffee keeps me awake," he confided, then took a long gulp of the liquor, licking his lips with relish.

"Henry, this is Lieutenant McCorkle. He's your new father," the major told the Korean boy.

"Me?" There was a strangled note in the younger officer's tone. The Korean appraised him shrewdly as the major nodded.

"Every new man who joins this section takes a part in Henry's education," he explained expansively. "We're Americanizing him. In fact, he's a pretty good Marine." He glanced at the boy for confirmation. "Aren't you, Henry?"

"Hell, no," the boy snorted. "I'm a spy!"

"Knock off that crap and say hello to the lieutenant," the major ordered sternly. At first the boy hesitated, then moved forward and extended a small brown hand from beneath the poncho. As McCorkle gripped the cold fingers, Henry's hard heel came down sharply upon McCorkle's foot. Pain lanced through his foot, causing him to gasp in agony.

"S'cuse me, suh," the boy drawled proudly.

"Little bastard!" blurted the new officer.

"Hold it!" Lawrence ordered with disapproval. "He doesn't understand." He turned to Henry, speaking severely.

"Boy, I told you to forget that. Just because someone stepped on you and said 'excuse me' doesn't make it a standard American custom."

"Ah know," the boy agreed cheerfully, "but ah learn a lotta new cuss wohds. Listen: Duhty li'l bastard! Li'l gook sonuvabitch! Goddam...'

"What the hell's with this kid, Top?" the major demanded accusingly of Master Sergeant Quillan. "You're supposed to be in charge of discipline."

"Goddam Korean brat! Duhty gook spy!" the boy continued with relish, pridefully tasting each word to roll off his tongue.

"Spare th' rod an' spoil th' child," Quillan quoted with a sigh. "But lay a hand on 'im, an' some enemy propagandist'll make an inter-

15

national incident of it. Maltreatment of the indigenous labor. Child beating."

"International incident be damned," the major snarled, whirling back to the Korean lad. "Get that poncho off, kid. I'm going to teach you another grand old American custom like washing your mouth out with soap!"

The boy cut short his monologue, staring at the major in hurt surprise. "Yuh don't like? I don' learn Engliss good?"

"Get that poncho off so I can whale holy hell out of you!"

"But you said he didn't understand," McCorkle put in weakly. "Maybe he doesn't know what the words mean."

"I'll make him understand!" the major raged. "No kid of mine's going to turn into a juvenile delinquent on my last night in camp!"

As the boy came hesitantly out of the folds of the poncho and allowed it to fall in a wet heap at his feet, a five-pointed star pinned to the breast of his cut-down dungarees glinted in the yellow light.

"Who're you?" McCorkle asked in as kindly a tone as he could muster, bending to look at the emblem obviously cut from the bottom of a beer can. "The Durango Kid or Tom Mix?"

"Neithah," the boy replied with grave pride. "Ah'm an honorary Mohrine. One of Pres'den' T'uman's Poleece Fohce!"

"Quillan, are you responsible for this?" Lawrence demanded grimly. "Is this your idea of humor? Debasing your Commander-in-Chief?"

"Not me, major," the master sergeant replied over the lip of his canteen cup. "I'm a Democrat, myself. Or I was till this police action come along." He hiccuped gently. "But most the men on the base're wearin' the same thing."

"Bet your sweet ass the general hasn't heard about it!" Lawrence muttered, somewhat chastised by this news. "It's...it's disloyal!"

"Oh, I don't know," Quillan countered. "The Ole Man's driver tole me the boss has one with Chief of Police hammered inta it. He just don't wear it around in public."

"And I told you to take down that sign." The major pursued a new tack, waving at the wall above the cluttered field desk.

The partition was well blanketed with photographs of Marine personnel, newspaper clippings bearing more pictures of men, officers and aircraft. Amid this montage was a hand-lettered sign reading:

*Informational Services Section*
*First Marine Aircraft Wing, FMF*

And in slightly smaller letters were the bold words:

*This Propaganda Section Is Second*
*To None...Including Joe Stalin's!*

"Take it down," the major ordered shortly. "The President apologized for saying it."

"Aye, sir," Quillan acknowledged grumpily, "but I'm still gonna vote Republican."

There was an urgent nervous rap at the door. McCorkle started to turn, but Henry was quicker, seeing an escape from the threatened discipline.

As the boy unhooked the board door and swung it back, a stiff, youthful figure marched indignantly into the circle of light and cast back the hood of his wet parka.

He was no more than twenty-five, his hair was blond and carefully combed, and there was a thin, intense excitement in the set of his eyes. But to McCorkle, he represented security; a thin segment of sanity wedged into the realm of madness he had experienced ever since Lawrence had approached him in Itami. Pinned to the newcomer's utility cap was the small silver cross of the Navy Chaplain Corps.

"I want that shooting stopped!" the chaplain announced coldly, sweeping the group with his gaze: "What kind of heathen would interrupt a man's meditations on Sunday night?"

"It was a rat," Quillan explained defensively.

"Rats don't shoot," the chaplain declared, glaring at the sergeant. "There's something else. I understand you had something to do with erecting the street markers around this base."

"Me, padre?" Somewhat sobered, Quillan was doing his best to display innocence.

"Was it your idea to have my tent located at the intersection of Bourbon Street and Cat House Alley?" The chaplain's tone was one of hurt rather than anger now.

Quillan shook his head stubbornly. "I just helped with the names. I didn't tell no one where to put 'em up."

"I want it removed." The chaplain whirled back to Lawrence,

shaking a finger at the Korean boy trying to hide in the shadow of the major's bulk. "And I want something done about this orphan. I caught him stealing the plywood for my new altar and he told me to go soak my head in a urinal!"

"Henry, did you say that to the chaplain?" Lawrence asked sternly, glaring down at the boy.

Henry shrugged with a complete lack of concern. "Yes, suh. Aftah he called me a filt'y li'l heathen."

"You called him that?" Lawrence demanded incredulously of the chaplain. "Don't you have respect for any religion besides your own? What kind of chaplain are you?"

The man beneath the silver cross retreated a pace. He had come to protest, not to defend himself. Chaplains are not supposed to be on the defensive.

"You don't understand," he explained uncertainly. "I was upset. Certainly I respect his religious affiliation." He glanced at the Korean as though doubting he had any. "It was only a figure of speech." He took hold of that phrase like a life preserver, repeating it more loudly for emphasis. "That's all. Simply a figure of speech."

With that, he turned and fled into the rain, and Henry hooked the door against the wind that seemed to be dying.

For a moment there was a lull in the conversation. McCorkle welcomed it, realizing he was at least two climaxes in arrears. However, he found himself feeling a bit sorry for this youthful chaplain. The man hadn't had a chance against such obviously well organized opposition.

Henry, dragging the wet poncho in his wake, disappeared behind the blanket curtain. Quillan tried in vain to wring a few more drops from the empty bourbon bottle, then heaved it into a rusty oil drum beside his field desk. Lawrence stared thoughtfully into his coffee as he said, "You'll meet the rest of the crew in the morning. Two of them'll be coming down from the front if the rain lets up.

"They have to be pampered a little to get the best out of them," he added, "but you'll do fine."

McCorkle took a long draught of the spiked coffee and gagged. Quillan was right. Either the bourbon was turning sour or this was the worst coffee he had ever tasted.

"This stuff has character," he offered, nodding to the cup.

"We scrubbed the pot," Quillan defended. "Worked on it some

last week."

"I saw," the major chided. "You cleaned up one spot on the front to weld a hole."

"How far is the front?" McCorkle asked. "It seems pretty quiet."

"About two hundred miles."

"Two hundred miles!" There was surprise and dismay in McCorkle's tone.

Lawrence studied him with a sorrowful, knowing gaze. "You'll have all the fighting you want just keeping those idiots in Washington out of your hair and the Chief-of-Staff out of your jeep."

"B-but do we rate a vehicle?" McCorkle asked cautiously.

"Out here we rate what we can get. And that jeep's a sort of status symbol to this outfit. If you lose it, the whole mob loses face. Besides, it beats hell out of walking."

"Yes, sir," he agreed glumly. From the other side of the partition, there were irate mutterings in an Oriental tongue.

"What is it, Henry?" Lawrence called.

"Tha' damn rat," the Korean complained from beyond the blanket. "It's tryin' t'get in bed wi' me!"

"My God, a queer rat," muttered Quillan. He began to rummage on top of the cluttered field desk.

"Quillan, you fire that forty-five again and I'll have you fighting rats in a foxhole," Lawrence warned calmly. "Go to bed and we'll give you a rabies shot in the morning."

Muttering beneath his breath, Quillan disappeared behind the curtain. Lawrence turned to glance at his relief. "More coffee?"

McCorkle shook his head. "No, sir." He hesitated before he asked: "How long since that pot's really been cleaned?"

"About the time Christ was a corporal. Quillan uses it as an excuse to stick to booze."

McCorkle glanced toward the door. The wind had died as had the rattle of rain upon the canvas. "Think I'll relieve my kidneys," he said delicately. "Where's the head around here?"

"There's a pisser about two hundred yards from here," Lawrence told him, ignoring his apologetic tone, "but the officers' crapper's damn near a quarter mile. It pays to get on a schedule in this outfit."

"Which way?" McCorkle asked, rising and starting to squirm uncomfortably.

Lawrence seemed to ignore him, glancing instead toward the rear of the tent. "Henry?"

"Suh?"

"That rat still bothering you?"

"Yes, suh," came the muffled reply.

"Then haul your can out of there and show the lieutenant where the pisser is," Lawrence ordered sternly, raising his cup to sip from it. He ignored the childish groan of protest. A moment later the Korean lad came staggering through the curtain, pulling on his pants and blinking his eyes. He glanced at McCorkle with a hint of hostility as he stuffed his over-long shirttail under his belt.

"Move," Lawrence ordered with no hint of compassion. McCorkle started to protest, to say he could find his own way, but decided against it. As the boy moved past him, shoving open the door and holding it, McCorkle dutifully followed him.

The heat inside the tent had long since dried the mud on the young officer's dungarees, but it was still chilly as he stepped out the door of the tent. It was growing light and the rim of the sun was beginning to herald a full scale appearance on the sea beyond the small semicircular harbor.

Not a breath of air stirred as the grayness of the water began to hint at blue in the suggested light. The harbor was nearly ringed by hills, but below the crest where he paused, the land fell away in a gentle slope to a small village less than half a mile away. Beyond the buildings, fishing boats were drawn up on the white sand beach. The huts were small and square with crude mud walls, small windows and roofs of rice straw.

Between the village and the edge of the base was a high barbedwire fence that ran as far as he could see in either direction. The only visible break in the wire was at the roadway that ran down the hill through the encampment and into the village below. Overlooking the entry point was a small sentry box, and as McCorkle watched a Marine wearing a camouflage-covered helmet, rifle slung over his shoulder, stepped out and paused to look about, yawning his boredom.

In the opposite direction, gracing most of the top of the mesa-like hill were the rows upon rows of pyramidal tents and a few larger hospital tents. It was one of the latter that his new outfit used as an office.

On the other side of the muddy road were the evenly aligned rows of sheet metal structures, most of them windowless. Near the far end was a larger, low building of raggedly octagonal design. A flagpole before it marked this as Wing headquarters. All of these structures had their metal plates coated with zinc, but rust was beginning to streak through.

The air strip below, running parallel with the upper end of the bay, was hidden by the tents; but he could hear the first growl of jet engines being started, then their full-throated roar.

Standing there in the mud, breathing frost in the morning cold, McCorkle realized he was standing at attention. He was at attention before his own fears, his lack of confidence.

Thinking about Lawrence, he realized there was something definitely wrong with the major's approach. As a career officer, he elected to sleep in the same tent with an alcoholic sergeant and a Korean. One of the basic rules was that officers did not fraternize with enlisted men. Familiarity could only breed contempt.

But there was more than that. There was a curious, unspoken friendship between Lawrence and the men he had met. In spite of the banter, there was respect for the major and his rank.

McCorkle's fear was born of the realization that he would be expected by these men to live up to the image established by Lawrence, the image born of that old dread: Experience. And chances were that everyone in the outfit, including this Korean waif, knew more about the Marine Corps and its workings in combat than he. They would be waiting for him to make mistakes; they would be expecting it and it was this dread that gripped him.

"Jeez, lootenant," Henry whined, "Ah'm freezin' mah ass."

McCorkle glanced down at him, trying to appear stern in the face of the boy's scowl. "Where's the head?"

The boy motioned toward the rim of the hill, then moved in that direction, stepping gingerly to miss the interspersed mud puddles. A few moments later, the boy motioned toward an odd-looking trough that had been erected between a pair of weathered timbers. It obviously had been cut from one of the canisters that protects artillery shells or rockets and a pipe led downward to be buried in some underground tank.

"There," the boy announced.

Self-consciously, McCorkle stepped up to the trough and began to fumble with the brass buttons of his dungaree fly.

As he started to re-button, there was a sharp crack from somewhere nearby and he heard the high-pitched shriek of a ricocheting bullet.

"Sonuvabitch!" the boy cried and turned, stumbling as there was another shot. McCorkle, panicked, turned wildly and started to run after him but ran into the boy. Henry pitched headlong into the mud, skidding loosely through a puddle. McCorkle, without thinking, glanced about, saw another bullet kick up water only a foot or so from the still form, then hurled himself on top of the lad. Wallowing frantically, he was trying to force the boy down into the sticky mud as he heard another shot, then heard shouts of surprise and frustration.

There was the sound of a racing jeep engine, then other shots, these not far away.

"There he went," someone bawled. "Th' bastard just went over th' hill!"

He waited for a moment, still expecting another bullet, before he slowly sat up. He hesitated, feeling nauseated, then grabbed the Korean boy's limp shoulder and turned him over. In the dim light, he could see no sign of blood, but the boy's eyes were closed and he seemed to be having trouble with his breathing.

"Henry!" he said urgently, shaking the boy with one hand, trying to wipe the mud off the lad's features with the other.

"What happened? Is he hit?" He glanced up to see Lawrence staring down at him, feet wide spread in the mud. In his hand was a carbine. A few feet behind him, staggering, but his forty-five in his hand, was Quillan.

McCorkle still confused, shook his head, saying nothing. It was more of a shrug. Lawrence knelt beside him and began to shake the Korean boy.

"Is he hurt?" Quillan wanted to know, skidding to a stop.

"I don't think so," Lawrence returned. He glanced up at the master sergeant, then scowled. "Put away that goddamn pistol before you shoot us all!"

Quillan hesitated, then lowered the hammer and stuffed the automatic into his rear pocket. At the same moment, Henry groaned and began to struggle. An instant later, he sat up, shaking his head and glaring at McCorkle.

"Y'tried t'drown me!" he accused, digging his fingers into the mud pack on his face.

"I fell on you," McCorkle defended.

"That's enough," Lawrence snarled, rising and dragging the lad erect. He shoved him toward Quillan, who staggered rearward to avoid this muddy mess. "Get him cleaned up, Quillan."

"Aye, sir," Quillan gingerly grabbed Henry's wrist and began to drag him away, while the boy still muttered in Korean, twisting to cast a backward glance at McCorkle.

A hundred yards away, security guards were still wandering about, rifles ready, looking for signs of the sniper. McCorkle took this in as the major stared at him thoughtfully.

"What happened?" Lawrence wanted to know.

McCorkle waved vaguely toward the makeshift urinal. "I'd just finished," he explained uncertainly, "then the shooting started. We both started to run and I fell on top of him." Self-consciously, he glanced down at the mud and wetness that again covered the front of his dungarees, wondering whether he really had been finished at the trough. His kidneys now felt strangely empty.

"You sure you just fell on him?" Lawrence asked sharply and McCorkle looked up in puzzlement.

"W-what?" Then he added, "sir?"

Lawrence's voice was hard, almost to the point of cruelty. "Look, mister, let me explain something to you. If you threw yourself on top of that kid, trying to save him, you were running the chance of wasting your life and the Marine Corps doesn't pay you for that kind of heroism.

"These kids out here were born to die. Even when there's no war, more of them probably die than live. It's their way of life." He waved a vague hand at the surrounding area. "Right around here, within ten miles, there are probably a couple of thousand orphans. Some of them probably froze to death this winter, some more starved, and the rest probably stole enough from us to trade it for food. But some of them won't make it through this next winter."

"Wha-what're you trying to tell me?" McCorkle asked in confusion.

"I'm telling you not to get emotionally involved with any of these kids. You're not their savior. There's damned little that you can do to help them. Leave that to the proper agencies, whoever the hell they are. You start taking on the responsibility personally for every orphan in Korea, you'll go off your rocker. So build a wall around your sense of responsibility and start getting your religion out of the Marine Corps Manual." There was a harsh edge to Lawrence's voice now, a note that was in strange contrast to his normal relaxed manner.

"Y-you haven't gotten emotionally involved? With Henry?"

"I've tried to keep it a clean deal," Lawrence insisted. "We've helped one. He's it. We can't help them all." But the note of nastiness was gone. In its place was a defensive tone.

McCorkle shuddered suddenly at a swift breeze, but it was more than the cold. A strange unpleasant smell assailed his nostrils. Uncontrollably he gagged at the odor from the rice paddies, fertilized with human excrement. The rain had thawed them, releasing the odor, mixing this unpleasantness with his experience.

As he retched, muscles of his stomach jerking in spasms of revolt, there was a sardonic chuckle from the major.

"That gawdawful smell," McCorkle gasped.

"Son," the major's weary voice confided, "that's Spring!"

# CHAPTER 3

THE DRIVER and the sergeant glanced about the forward end of the tent until the latter spotted the neck of the bourbon bottle protruding from the trash. He lifted it out, noted its emptiness with a grimace of disgust, then tossed it back.

"Well, at least he ain't against booze," the sergeant noted, still scowling. "What kinda guy is he?"

The driver shrugged. "I don't know. I ain't heard him say a half dozen words."

"That's the sneaky kind. Never know what's goin' on in his head," the sergeant complained. "We spend all this time straightenin' out one officer, so they trade him in for a lootenant!"

"Give him some time to learn the ropes," the jeep driver insisted.

"It ain't the ropes," the officer fretted. "It's them bars on his shoulders. There ain't no such thing as a good lootenant. They're all captains, at least, b'fore they relax enough t' knock off the chickenshit."

"Come on. Let's get down to the mess hall an' rumble up some chow."

"Hell!" Sergeant Shade was still showing his disgust and wouldn't be denied this pleasure. "They've been closed down for two hours!"

"I know the mess sergeant."

The slamming of the wooden door awakened McCorkle, who came out of his blankets, squinting at his watch. It was nearly nine o'clock. He scrambled to his feet, shivering against the cold, and grabbed his utilities off a nail in the framework above his bunk. Henry sat up on his cot, rubbing his eyes and yawning.

"What time does reveille sound around here?" the lieutenant asked softly, puzzled at the lack of activity. The boy paused, mouth still open, to eye him with suspicion.

"Re-veille?" he repeated slowly, testing the syllables on the tip of his tongue. "Whass that? More a' that Stateside crap ah'm alla time hearin' about?"

"Reveille!" McCorkle snapped at him. "Time to get up. It's a bugle call!"

The boy replied with solemn disdain, nodding. "Stateside crap, sure 'nough,"

There was a stirring among the blankets on the other side of the tent and Lawrence's tousled head slowly emerged.

"Goddamit, doesn't a short-timer rate any privileges?" he demanded grumpily, glancing at his watch. "It's only nine o'clock."

McCorkle, with one leg through his trousers, stumbled and fell across the bunk. "But reveille," he stated uncertainly. "It must have gone three hours ago!"

The major snorted his opinion of such nonsense. "This is a combat zone. Besides, the general's a late sleeper and he hates the sound of a bugle at dawn." He ignored the fact that McCorkle still lay across the bunk, pants half on, absorbing this with disbelief.

"I need a drink," Master Sergeant Quillan announced abruptly, his tone muffled beneath the blankets. "Henry, fetch me a shot like a good lad."

"Nevah' 'oppen," the Korean announced. "Yuh drank it all las' night."

Quillan, hair pointing in all directions as though he had been tilting against dream windmills, eyes red with hangover, slowly materialized from the mass of blankets. "Whatta helluva'n outfit," he grumbled.

Combat boots in one hand, utility jacket in the other, McCorkle ducked through the blanket that served as the door to the office. He came up abruptly, eyes bugging, mouth open at the sight half a dozen feet before him.

The back side facing him was a girl's. As she swung toward him, she smiled, showing rows of even, white teeth, flashing black eyes.

"Good morning, sir. I am Jane," she announced in formal but excellent English. She wore a Sears, Roebuck cotton dress, petite

Oriental rubber shoes and in her hair, a bright yellow ribbon. She bowed from the waist as she spoke, delicately balancing a steaming cup of coffee.

This was more than McCorkle could take. "Major," he howled, "there's a *woman* out here!"

"Excuse me, sir," the girl said unconcernedly. "Sergeant Quillan's coffee will get cold."

She dodged past him and disappeared into the makeshift boudoir with the canteen cup. An instant later, Lawrence appeared in his shorts, the rest of his clothing over his arm.

"Wha-what's she doin' here?" McCorkle stammered, trying to ward off acute shock.

"She's an employee," the major explained, stifling a yawn behind his ragged undershirt. "Halloran pays her."

"Halloran?"

"The driver who drove us from the plane."

McCorkle shook his head, still blushing at his sudden exposure to womanhood. The major was so matter-of-fact, as though the driver's name should explain all.

"Halloran was assigned to us as a clerk-typist. He couldn't find three given keys on a typewriter, so he hired the girl to do his work. It was either that or be transferred back to Motor Transport as a grease monkey and he's allergic to grease."

McCorkle shook his head again.

"If we packed him off to the motor pool again, we'd just get some other character who can't type. This way, we get an efficient typist and a driver of our own for the same price."

The Korean girl came back into the room and moved to the oil stove in the center of the floor, pouring two more canteen cups half full of coffee from the huge, unscrubbed pot, then turned to the two officers, presenting the major with his first. Turning to McCorkle, she looked him up and down gravely and finally nodded approval.

"You have sexy eyes, lieutenant," she declared with a thin accent.

"Huh?" McCorkle almost dropped the accepted cup, coloring again.

"Dammit, Janie," the major protested. "You've been reading those confession magazines again."

He glanced at the lieutenant with an expression of apology. "Don't mind her. She'd like to be a nymphomaniac, but doesn't quite

27

know how." Lawrence glanced at his wristwatch. "Drink up, we'll grab a fast shave and go see The Man." The major's expression became more stern as he judged the younger man. "And remember, he'll try to brainwash you. He wants our jeep!"

The Chief-of-Staff had his office in the strangely shaped structure, which Lawrence sneeringly referred to as the Rice Paddie Pentagon. The sprawling structure of sheet metal promised to be cold in winter and miserably hot in summer. The major explained that all of the Wing Staff Sections, with the exception of Informational Services, had offices here so that the commanding general had immediate access to his advisors.

"But we're outcasts," Lawrence added. "They stuck us down there near the flight line on the pretext that we should be close to the planes and be able to report the news as soon as the pilots come back from missions."

"That makes sense," McCorkle had to agree.

"Not really. Ninety-five percent of our stuff has to be air mailed to Washington. It takes a week to get there, then spends weeks in someone's basket before it gets processed, cleared for security, and released.

"But it has its advantages," he added. "We can always take the phone off the hook when we don't want to be bothered."

McCorkle offered him a sidelong glance to determine if he meant it and decided he did.

As they dismounted from the jeep and Lawrence told Halloran to wait, McCorkle gazed upon the scene spread out before him. He could see now that bits of lumber, probably of American military origin, had been used in some of the structures in the village under the hill. There were people thronging the narrow streets now and in the bay beyond, blue and dotted with whitecaps, the fishing fleet was under full sail.

On the outskirts of the village, the flat land had been divided into squares, each enclosed by dikes. These rice paddies now were barren except for water from the melted snow and an occasional lonely length of straw sticking above the muddy surface, missed in the last harvest.

"Is that where the girl lives?" he asked, nodding toward the cluster of ugly mud huts below.

"Yeah, but don't even think about it," Lawrence warned knowingly.

"About what?" McCorkle's tone was defensive.

"The village is out of bounds. Especially after sundown. There's a policy against playing footsie with the native girls."

"That isn't what I had in mind," McCorkle protested formally.

"Neither did I when I got here."

As they moved toward the door of the headquarters structure, McCorkle realized that the barbed wire surrounding this base probably was meant as a hindrance to nocturnal fraternization.

The adjutant, Gunner Max Schmake, eyed the new officer over the rims of his bifocals as the major made introductions. Schmake was a small, round man, a commissioned warrant officer with more than thirty years' service, who no longer looked like a Marine. Time, good booze and a desk had taken the starch out of his spine, but not out of his voice.

"Oh yeah," he acknowledged graciously. "The Chief's been buggin' me to find out when you'd be around. Something about a jeep." There was a note of malice in his tone. It was nothing personal, but a general attitude he applied to all junior officers. But McCorkle could hardly know this.

"Any word on my orders?" Lawrence wanted to know. The gunner turned pale eyes upon him, lip curling a trifle. He didn't like majors either.

"They're over in G-1," he said, then added pointedly, "That's military for Personnel, son."

The relaxed smile slowly faded from the major's lips and his shoulders straightened. He turned to McCorkle almost in apology. "Lieutenant, would you step into the passageway. There's something I have to take up with the gunner."

McCorkle looked from one to the other, wondering, then nodded and went through the door, pulling it shut behind him. The panel, cut from rough lumber, was a poor fit. He couldn't help overhearing.

"Gunner, I'm leaving, but we'll no doubt be seeing each other again," Lawrence said slowly. "So I think there's something we'd best get straight. I outrank you. I am a major in the United States Marine Corps and the next time you call me 'son' in private or in public I'll have your ass and I don't give a damn if you were in the Banana Wars with Smedley Butler!"

There was a moment of strained silence before Schmake's strangled voice was heard. "I'll be damned!"

"And don't swear at me either," Lawrence warned. "Now, are

those orders all signed, sealed and ready for my hot little hand?"

"They're ready, but you'd better wait," Schmake warned, now much less certain of himself. "The Chief'll want to talk to you, too." As an afterthought, tone slightly surly, he added, "sir."

"It'll only take a minute," Lawrence said, swinging the door open. His back was to Schmake but there was a smile of satisfaction on his lips. "I'll just whip over there and pick them up while we're waiting." He jerked his head at McCorkle to indicate he could reenter the office, then disappeared down the hallway. Warrant Officer Schmake turned his brooding eyes back to the thin young man framed in the doorway.

"Hollywood Marine, huh?" It wasn't a question. It was meant as an open insult, the backlash of having just been chewed out by a superior.

"Wh-what?" McCorkle tried to hide his embarrassment and the beginnings of anger, feeling his face growing red. There was no use in explaining about the classification clerk back in Chavez Ravine. Schmake looked as though he, too, had learned to read out of the Marine Corps Manual.

"Hollywood Marine," he repeated. "Don't know what good you'll be to us out here. This ain't no movie set, son. This is a goddamn war!"

McCorkle inhaled, releasing the breath slowly, looking away. He clenched his fists, aware that his hands were shaking.

"Max!" a voice roared somewhere down the hallway. "Where the hell's that new camera clicker?"

As if operated by strings, the dumpy little man snapped up from behind the desk, straightening his uniform and his dignity.

"Coming, sir! He's right here, sir!" Schmake called.

There was still a note of awe in the warrant officer's voice as he waved McCorkle toward the passageway. He was irritated, too, at Lawrence. It was a fact known throughout the Marine Corps that you never screwed around with a WO; they knew too many people, had worked for too many generals. They were dangerous. They had time and experience and, by damn, you respected them. That was the way it was supposed to be. But as he led the way down the corridor, Schmake's back was straight, his shoulders back. There was a renewed swagger in his walk.

He pushed open the door to the Chief-of-Staff's office, waved McCorkle through, then followed to stand at the side of the room, still straight-backed and soldierly, as Colonel Dade turned from his wall map to glance first at McCorkle, then at him.

"What's the matter with you?" the Chief growled, giving Schmake a second glance. "You look like you've got a boil on your ass."

The starch went abruptly out of Warrant Officer Max Schmake's spine and he dissolved — again a slave to the demands of his immediate superior, General Administration.

The colonel turned on the young lieutenant, glowering. Hell, much more of this and they'd have to start serving Pablum in the Officer's Mess.

McCorkle stood stiffly before the makeshift desk, eyes straight ahead, thumbs along the seams of his trousers, feet pointed outward at the forty-five-degree angle recommended by the Landing Forces Manual. Dade looked him up and down, puzzled.

"At ease, lieutenant," he growled. McCorkle's shoulders sagged an eighth of an inch and his eyes swiveled to meet those of his commander.

"Thank you, sir," he said formally, voice a trifle thin. The colonel, like Schmake, was a small man; not quite so heavy about the middle and he boasted a better haircut. He was clean shaven, but his hair was combed in such a fashion as to hide its thinness in front. McCorkle noticed these things as the colonel continued to stare.

"You're McCorkle?"

"Yes, sir. First Lieutenant Joseph Wingate McCorkle, oh-four-six-five-one-four, United States Marine Corps Reserve, reporting for duty, sir." The last words were a bit breathless.

"I know you're reporting for duty, lieutenant. I can read your orders." He reached to his desk, picking up the smoldering stub of a cigar and ground it into the ashtray in a gesture of frustration. He turned his eyes upon Schmake.

"Where the hell's Lawrence?"

"At G-1, sir. Picking up his orders." the gunner replied.

"Get him in here. We'll settle this jeep matter here and now!"

"Aye, sir!" the adjutant snapped and whirled to bolt for the door.

The colonel paced back and forth across the floor behind his plywood desk, pawing unconsciously at his jacket pocket in a futile search for a fresh cigar. Irritated at this failure, he paused, feet wide-spread, to glare at McCorkle.

"I only hope to hell you're an improvement over the man you're relieving."

"Major Lawrence appears to know his business, sir." McCorkle was coloring again and he could not keep the defensive note out of his tone. "He seems to be respected by his men."

Dade snorted his derision, half closing one eye to glare in a poor imitation of Wallace Beery portraying a Marine.

"Men!" he snorted again. "That bunch of misfits!" He shifted his questioning gaze to Schmake who had stepped back into the office. "Where's Lawrence?"

Max shook his head, eyeing the floor. "He's gone, sir. Picked up his orders from G-1, and he just took off for Itami on one of the troop carriers."

"That's desertion!" The colonel slammed a fist down on his desk in a show of anger. "Get him back here!"

"Yes, sir." Max scuttled for the door again.

"No, wait." The colonel was suddenly thoughtful, staring at McCorkle with all the aplomb of a barracuda observing a mass baptism.

"Sir?" the warrant officer asked on a note of confusion. The sudden insistent sound of a buzzer added to his consternation and he waved to it vaguely.

"Let him go," the colonel said quietly. "There'd only be more trouble if we brought him back." His eyes were still on the lieutenant, who had come back to attention. "McCorkle, you have a jeep and..."

The buzzer sounded again, this time in a series of short indications of irritation. The colonel looked toward it.

"Sir, the general," Schmake suggested.

"I hear it," the colonel half snarled, swinging toward the door at the far end of his office. Then he paused to glare at McCorkle as though this interruption was his doing.

"We'll talk about this again," he promised. "Soon."

Schmake held the door open for McCorkle. then paused to look up at the young officer as the panel closed behind them. McCorkle was frowning. In fact, he was angry and puzzled.

He had expected Lawrence to be around for several days, at least, checking him out in his duties. The thought of the major simply deserting him in the face of his first crisis didn't make sense. Or perhaps it did.

Schmake was expressing his own puzzlement as he said thoughtfully, "Lawrence left a message for you, son."

"What?" McCorkle was seeking hope, a savior.

"He said to tell you he don't like good-byes," Schmake said slowly, frowning and looking away. "He figgered you'd make out okay, but you're to look after th' kid. What kid's he mean? That silly-assed driver?"

"I suppose so," McCorkle lied. He had found his hope in those few words, and his faith in the major had been restored. The night before, when Henry had been knocked out, Lawrence had been deliberately treating the boy with anger, attempting to build a new image in the boy's mind. Perhaps he felt it would be better for Henry to dislike him at the time of his departure than to hold any feelings of love for this strange man who had helped him.

And Lawrence had no doubt been lying to himself the night before, McCorkle suddenly realized, when the major had warned him about becoming emotionally involved with any of the orphans. He had simply been showing his own frustration at his own involvement.

"You do what he says," Schmake suggested mildly, wondering at the sudden smile on the junior officer's lips. "That driver damn near ran down the general a couple weeks back. Hadn't been for Lawrence, he'd be sittin' behind barbed wire. You'd better take care of him, you hear?"

"I'll take care of him," McCorkle promised. But he wasn't thinking of the driver.

# CHAPTER 4

"**H**ALLORAN! Get that damned jeep 'round in back an' put that tarp back over it," Master Sergeant Quillan ordered, pushing away from his desk.

"But the Chief-of-Staff didn't take it," argued the driver. "Why all the excitement?"

"His decision just got delayed," Quillan stated patiently.

"But that's how we've been hangin' onto it ever since he seen it. By delayin' action."

"The Chief's told every officer on this base he's gonna get that jeep. Just because we still have it ain't no reason to embarrass him."

"My Gawd, Sarge, you been readin' some of them psycho books?"

"Move that jeep!" There was warning in Quillan's gravel voice.

"Sure...sure." Halloran's reply was casual, but he was hurried as he made for the door.

"Where'd you hear about what happened in the Chief's office?" The speaker was a boy trying to look like a man. The degree of success was dubious. He was heavy-set and wore an 1870 cavalryman's hat, the front brim turned back against the crown and held jauntily in place by a bronze Marine Corps emblem. His combat boots were too large, laced only half-way up and the strings dangled loosely over his instep. His name was Handley.

Quillan eyed him. "Henry told me."

Handley's lips twisted in a grimace of dislike. "That damned kid."

"Henry's awright," Quillan said gruffly. "He feeds a lotta good dope."

"Maybe," the other said seriously, "but what the hell's he feedin' other people? He's a damned North Korean, ain't he?"

"He's a kid, Handley," Quillan answered slowly. "So you don't like Koreans, North, South or in-between. That's your business. But Henry's still a kid, so just let him be one."

"He's a goddam spy," Handley insisted stubbornly. "Even he admits it an' one of these nights, you'll find yourself coughin' up your own bayonet if you don't watch him!"

"That's all," Quillan dismissed him shortly and turned back to Halloran, who had paused at the door to listen. "Get that jeep moved b'fore I put you in gear!"

The driver, scuttling through the opening, almost bowled over McCorkle. The three enlisted men exchanged glances, wondering how much of their conversation had been overheard, but the officer was smiling. Henry and Jane, trailing a few feet in his wake, smiled, too.

"They've been pointing out some of the local landmarks," McCorkle explained. "We have a beautiful view of the bay."

"Yes, sir," Quillan agreed without enthusiasm. "Some more of your motley crew is on the way over."

"Fine," McCorkle said, glancing warily at Handley. What had the Chief-of-Staff called Quillan and the others? Misfits? "I'm going to clean up a little, Top." He seemed at ease for the first time since arriving. "Can you step back here for a moment?"

Quillan followed him into the rear of the tent and stood waiting expectantly. McCorkle's smile was gone, replaced by an uncertain frown.

"What was going on when I came in?" he asked softly. "The discussion of Henry?"

"Nothin' to worry about," Quillan explained soothingly. "It's just that Corporal Handley out there had a brother killed durin' the Inchon landin'. He don't like Koreans. He don't trust Henry."

McCorkle pondered for a moment, his frown growing deeper. "The boy *is* a North Korean," he ventured.

"He's still a kid," the other defended. "Handley's sorta like a feller I knew back home once. Confused, you might say."

"Confused?"

"Well, this here feller was against just three things, he always said: Niggers, Jews an' racial prejudice."

There was a sudden stir in the forward half of the tent. Without a word, Quillan ducked past the curtain, leaving McCorkle to ponder his philosophy.

"Sarge, all hell's gonna break loose," a new voice decreed. "That boy chaplain caught us borrowin' some of th' copper tubing outa his stoves last night. Said he'd be over here first thing this mornin'."

"Good Lord," Quillan said disgustedly. "What kinda Marines are you? You can't even steal right!"

"But what right's a chaplain got to be suspicious?" the voice demanded indignantly. "The man's got one a' them split personalities. He's s'posed t'be all fulla goodness an' light, showin' faith in his feller man. He ain't s'posed t' go wanderin' around in th' dark with a forty-five 'n his hand. He might hurt hisself!"

"Or one of us!" another voice put in.

McCorkle stepped into the room and surveyed the array of manpower. Even at a quick glance, it showed little promise.

Besides Quillan, the two Koreans and Handley, there were two others, a fuzzy-cheeked buck-toothed teenager with straw-colored hair and an older man, a technical sergeant with dark hair, clean uniform and a carefully waxed and groomed mustache that stood out a full two inches on each side of his upper lip.

"What's this about tubing?" the lieutenant asked with a show of sternness.

"It's for our photo lab," Quillan put in quickly. "We've had to rebuild it since we moved the base."

"Did you have to steal it?" McCorkle was a bit less sure of himself. "What about Supply?"

The technical sergeant stepped forward, heels together, shoulders back. "There's a shortage of tubing, sir. And if you know about chaplains, they get special preference for everything. You can lose a war, but you'll have a church when it happens."

McCorkle looked this man up and down, wondering vaguely what the Uniform Code of Military Justice had to say about sacrilege. The sergeant thrust out his hand.

"Technical Sergeant Shamley," he announced. "Paul L., fighter-writer."

"Lieutenant McCorkle."

"And this is Sergeant Shade," Quillan stated, motioning forward the youth with the cheek fuzz. The buck sergeant stepped out of the loose formation, grasping the officer's fingers, flashing a mouthful of horse-sized teeth.

"Welcome aboard, skipper," he said breezily "Bob Shade, late of Salt Lake City. At your service."

McCorkle stiffened at the familiarity, staring at the sergeant's chin. "Sergeant, when did you last shave?"

Shade's jaw dropped and he hastily drew his hand from the officer's clasp, running his fingertips across his chin.

"'Bout four months ago, sir," he said, a defensive note entering his tone.

McCorkle's eyes were still on the youngster's chin as he said firmly, "You will shave every day, unless you consider yourself too immature to grow a beard. If you're that young, you are too immature to be a sergeant!" He was pleased at the sureness in his own tone.

"Aye, sir!" the youth snapped. "Right away, sir. May I be excused?"

"You are dismissed." McCorkle turned to Handley, last of the trio. Seeing signs of danger in the officer's appraisal of Shade, Handley had removed the cavalryman's hat and was attempting to hide it behind his back.

"Corporal Handley," Quillan announced, looking the man over regretfully. "Our radio correspondent." Handley started to speak, but the section chief cut him short, "He figgers that since he ain't in front of a TV camera, it don't matter how he looks."

Handley cast the top sergeant a look of gentle reprimand. "But you know how it's been with me, Sarge."

"Yeah, I know, but you get your tail down an' draw some new clothes b'fore we declare you a public health menace!"

"But they'll make me pay for them," the corporal protested in deep, well-rounded tones.

"What else is there t'do with your money? You think you can play the horses around here?"

Handley brightened at the possibilities. "It's something to work on."

McCorkle stared. The light exchange of banter between the master sergeant and the lesser ranking men disturbed him. There was an element of contempt, vague but unmistakable.

But with Handley there was something more. The words of banter were there, but there was a lack of feeling in his words. It was as though he spoke well rehearsed lines that had been repeated so often they had gone stale on his tongue.

Listening to the corporal, McCorkle had recognized the tones of education in his voice, yet it was as though he was trying desperately to hide amid mediocrity. By adopting the same attitude as the others on the surface, he became a chameleon, emerging as a part of the overall camouflage.

"Go get those clothes before we scrub you down with G.I. brushes and a bucket of sand," Quillan growled, eyeing the corporal balefully.

"I've been waiting three months for them to get in boots in my size. I've stuffed so much paper in the bottoms of these I'm creating a paper shortage," the corporal complained, slouching away.

Between Handley and the door stood Henry. The corporal growled deep in his throat, hunched his shoulders and bore down upon the boy like a lineman out to destroy the opposition, but Henry stepped nimbly out of the way. There was no change in his pinched expression as the door slammed behind the corporal.

Quillan heaved a sigh. "He's a good lad, lootenant. Lotsa talent, but he's still a little bitter."

"His brother, you mean?"

"That an' more maybe. He was doin' ninety days' active duty, trainin' Reserves at Camp Pendleton, when this shoot-up started. When they sent th' Division in for that Inchon landin' they'd gathered up every loose body they could lay hands on. Handley went wadin' ashore with th' others, mutterin' as how his ninety days' orders was up an' they couldn't do this to him."

"What about his brother?"

"He was a Regular buck sergeant. Handley was there when he got it." Quillan glanced at Henry. "He claims that patrol was lured into a trap by a young Korean kid."

McCorkle glanced at Henry, too, taking in the tight features, the turned down mouth and the bright eyes that reflected veiled suspicion.

He had asked Henry to show him about the base, thinking that he might have a chance to explain to the boy how Major Lawrence really had felt; that the officer had not deserted him as he probably thought, but had felt it would be better — emotionally, at least — if there was no parting scene.

McCorkle had discussed it first with Quillan after his interview with the Chief-of-Staff and the news that Lawrence had taken leave so unceremoniously, asking if the master sergeant felt it would not be a good idea for him to talk with the boy.

"I don't know, skipper. I don't know nothin' about that child psychology, but there's one thing you gotta figger."

"What?"

"This ain't th' first time this has happened t'the kid. He's seen lotsa men come'n go. You make th' thirty-seventh man so far an' there'll probably be plenty more b'fore this rat race's over. You'd think maybe he'd be gettin' used to it by now."

"But I felt that Major Lawrence was something rather special with the boy," McCorkle suggested with slow stubbornness. Quillan leaned back and sighed, staring at the young officer thoughtfully.

"Or maybe it was a case of Henry was somethin' special with him."

In spite of the master sergeant's thoughts, McCorkle had tried to approach the matter of Lawrence during his tour with Henry and Jane. He had waited until the girl had gone a few yards ahead before he had broached the subject, picking his words carefully, seeking a touch of delicacy. Henry's reaction had been a shrug, while he had stood glaring out across the harbor below.

"He hadda go," Henry explained philosophically. "He tole me one time it don't pay fo' no one to get too frien'ly wi' no one else, 'cause in th' Marines, sometime yuh gotta go."

McCorkle had stared down at the boy's features, seeing the mask that had been placed there with time, terror and hurt. It had been Lawrence who had said something about putting a wall around your emotions so that the Korean orphans couldn't get to you; but it seemed to be Henry who had taken the advice. His shell was hard and brittle far beyond his years. No doubt, he had been hurt; wars do that, particularly to children, but he had found the most obvious means of not being hurt again.

He turned and looked up at McCorkle, no hint of emotion or grief showing in his expression, in his eyes.

"What else yuh wanna see?" he asked on a cold note, seeming to resent the fact that this newcomer had attempted to meddle in his affairs.

"I've seen enough," McCorkle had said, not knowing exactly what he meant by the statement.

Now, standing in the tent, staring at the boy, seeing the same hardness in Henry's eyes, he shook his head and looked back at Quillan, waving his hand to the others in the tent. "Is this all the men we have in this outfit?"

"The rest'll be comin' down from our other bases one of these days. Fact, Ashdon an' Taylor're due down from th' front lines t'day, if they kin find a plane comin' this way."

"Who're they?" the lieutenant asked cautiously, trying to ignore Henry.

"Motion picture cameramen," Shamley put in, distaste coloring his words. "Don't ever get'n th' open with them two. They'll get you killed!"

"Take it easy, Shamley," Quillan soothed. "They ain't really that bad."

"They're a pair of medal-happy DeMilles," the five-striper growled. "They'll do anything to get a few feet of film, an' they don't care who gets hurt."

"Look at Ashdon." He was addressing McCorkle. "He was in th' Navy last war. Volunteered for Underwater Demolition School an' was in the sixth week of trainin' b'fore they found out he couldn't swim. Now is that normal?"

"It sounds as though it might take talent," McCorkle replied judiciously.

"Talent, hell! He's crazy and Taylor's damned near as bad!"

"Don't you have work to do?" Quillan interjected roughly. Shamley turned to him, nodding.

"Yeah. Thirty rolls of film to develop. I better get at it."

"How soon can we see some contact sheets?" McCorkle wanted to know. He suddenly realized that this was supposed to be an operating Information Section. Until now, he had seen few signs of effort.

Quillan and Shamley exchanged uncomfortable looks and Henry, still slouched near the door, chuckled discreetly. As the officer threw the boy a questioning glance, the technical sergeant made for the door and disappeared.

"It wasn't our work Shifty was talkin' about," Quillan explained with slow caution. "It was his own."

"His own what?"

"He's set up a little photo business on the side," the master sergeant explained delicately. "Prints pictures for the troops with their own cameras. They get better service'n they can get from the Korean shop in the village an' he's cheaper."

McCorkle searched the vague files of memory. There was some

regulation to cover this situation, he was certain.

"He's using Government equipment for personal gain," he accused slowly.

Quillan, reddening, shifted uncomfortably but shook his head in a show of stubbornness. "He buys his own paper'n stuff. He has receipts for the stuff his wife sends him from th' States. He just uses our darkroom."

"It...it's against regulations." The point had to be made even though McCorkle was uncertain of himself. Had Lawrence known of this? The answer was quick in coming.

"Lootenant, regulations are in how you interpret 'em. There's no rule against a serviceman workin' his off-duty hours back in th' States. Out here, a man's gotta pick up a spare buck where he finds it." He shook his head slowly, looking the officer in the eye, as he went on in the same dispassionate tone.

"This ain't your Marine Corps Schools and it ain't Henderson Hall in Dee Cee. This is Korea an' we gotta make allowances."

McCorkle, pink with anger and embarrassment, started to speak, but Quillan cut him off.

"It's pretty simple, sir. How well you get along with th' brass over there in the Rice Paddy Pentagon's gonna depend mostly on how well these men do for you. You can't order one of these kids to write the best story or take the best picture he's ever done. He hasta wanta do it. He hasta wanta do it for you."

Face red, lips compressed, McCorkle stared at the master sergeant. He was being blackmailed, he realized, but what was he to do about it? There was truth in what he had just been told.

"Lieutenant?" It was the Korean girl, who sat before her typewriter, staring at him through brown, cow-like eyes. McCorkle had forgotten that she and Henry were listening.

"What is another word for sexy?" she asked softly. McCorkle gulped, growing even redder above the collar. He glanced at Quillan, expecting him to laugh, but the master sergeant was pouring coffee, pretending he hadn't heard. Perhaps he realized he had been out of bounds.

"I don't know," McCorkle grated. "I'm busy."

"But I'm writing a poem," the girl pouted. "About your sexy eyes."

"Good Lord, Quillan," he asked lamely, turning toward the top sergeant to gesture his confusion. "What kind of outfit is this?"

"The best damned outfit in the Marine Corps, lootenant," was the grave reply expressed over the lip of the steaming canteen cup. "Unusual, I'll grant, but the best."

There was a rap at the door and both men swung toward it. The chaplain stood there. He looked even younger than he had the preceding night.

"Lieutenant," he declared formally, "I have to talk to you."

McCorkle glared at him, wanting to take his wrath out on someone. The chaplain was even younger than he, probably less experienced.

"About that copper tubing?" he demanded.

"That can wait," the chaplain stated gravely.

"We needed that tubing for our photo lab," McCorkle declared.

"You've been brainwashed," the chaplain suddenly declared. "They're building a still. They're using it to mix up that four-hundred-proof raisinjack!"

"There's no such thing as four-hundred-proof booze!"

"Do you want to bet?" was the baleful challenge from the man of the cloth. "But that's not why I came."

McCorkle had turned to glare at Quillan, seeking an explanation, but the master sergeant was hiding behind his coffee cup.

"Major Lawrence is dead," the chaplain said quietly. There was a moment of silence. Then Quillan slowly lowered his cup, staring blindly at the chaplain. There was a little cry from Jane, a sound of hurt. Henry didn't move from his post near the door.

"He was headed home from Tokyo," the chaplain explained softly. "The plane crashed on take-off."

Quillan slowly set the cup on the corner of his desk and crossed himself. McCorkle turned toward the door and noticed that the Korean boy, still silent, unmoving, had eyes that were bathed in tears. Drops of salt were starting to course down his cheeks.

The chaplain glanced about, shuffling unconsciously. "I thought you'd want to know," he said uncomfortably. He was saying other things, but McCorkle didn't hear. Instead, he walked stiff-legged across the floor and flung open the door, stepping out.

The sun was gone. In its place were black, low-hanging clouds. Far off was the rumble of thunder. In the village below there was no sign of activity. The boats were no longer visible in the harbor and the sea was black and foreboding.

His first thoughts were of himself. Before, he had been inclined to think of Lawrence as a disturbing influence. He had seen evidence of the loyalty between the major and the troops and it had been disturbing. It had left him wondering how, with his lack of experience, he could ever call upon them for the same kind of loyalty. That had been bad enough. This would be worse. Before he was replacing a man. Now, he realized, he was replacing a ghost; perhaps even a legend. And he knew he wasn't up to it. For a moment he was engulfed in a feeling of loneliness, realizing the gulf that stood between him and the others.

But a new realization also was born in him and there was a feeling of wonderment. He suddenly realized that he had felt some of the same affection for Lawrence as the group in the tent. There had been something about the man that instilled confidence. How, in only a few hours, could he come to have this feeling? Was it the closeness during the flight through the typhoon; facing the same dangers together?

As he stood there, it began to rain, but McCorkle hardly noticed.

There had been a great deal of talk about emotional walls and he had tended to think of people in the Marine Corps as machines; either they were efficient or they were not. At first, he had thought of Lawrence as the inefficient type, one that needed repair and oiling.

The *Marine Corps Manual,* McCorkle thought, was the book of instructions for operating the entire organization; if some cog in the machinery failed to act or react as the Manual outlined, it was inefficient and either needed repair or replacement. McCorkle was particularly inclined to view those senior to himself in that light, realizing at the same time that he was only a minor cog.

But in the few hours he had been in Korea, he also had learned that Lawrence was two people. On the surface, he had been assured even to the point of brashness; his approach to life and war had seemingly been too relaxed; it was as though he had been a badly worn cog, resulting from too much production of war and things military.

Instead, he no doubt had been a human being, the type of person who had his own problems, and who came into the troubles of others, reacting toward them. And in that moment, McCorkle knew that he wanted to be like Lawrence. It would be a tough act to follow.

"I liked that silly-assed bastard!" he murmured to himself, looking up at the black sky. In spite of the disrespect, he meant it. He hoped he could be like Major Lawrence.

# CHAPTER 5

"**A**S LONG AS I am a lieutenant colonel and you are a first lieutenant, I am never wrong!" snarled Colonel Barrymore.

"Bu...but, sir..." stammered McCorkle.

"Get that thing the hell over to G-2," the lieutenant colonel ordered, then added, "Get out of my sight!"

"Y-yes, sir!" McCorkle, red-faced and perspiring, did a stumbling about face and made for the door.

In the narrow, unlighted passageway, he glanced up and down, still in a state of minor shock, uncertain as to his next move. The walls of rough lumber and corregated metal offered little inspiration. Gunner Schmake stuck his head out of his tiny office.

"What the hell was goin' on in there?"

"I told a lieutenant colonel he was wrong," McCorkle said ruefully.

"About what?"

McCorkle waved the document in his hand. "The daily report to the Navy Press Section in Tokyo. The Operations Section is supposed to clear it, but now Colonel Barrymore tells me to take it to Intelligence."

Schmake surveyed the younger man with sudden interest. "Step in here, son. Let's figger this thing out."

McCorkle followed Schmake into the office and the latter closed the door, unable to hide the strange glint behind his glasses.

"Don't you know better'n to trust a man with tailored dungarees?" As he spoke Schmake pulled a fat volume from his desktop and started to search through it.

"Lieutenant Colonel Barrymore?" It was true. He did wear carefully tailored and pressed utilities.

The little warrant officer snorted his derision. "Barrymore, hell! His real name's Baronofsky, but he doubled for John Wayne in a Marine picture once. He got so shot in the ass with the Hollywood thing that he had his name legally changed. It played hell with all the paper work back in Dee Cee, too. Hadda change all his records to J.E.L. Barrymore. Had clerk-typists workin' nights."

"J.E.L.," McCorkle mused. "What does that stand for?"

"Just the initials are on the record, but rumor is that he went all out. That they really stand for John, Ethel an' Lionel."

Recalling Schmake's run-in with Lawrence, McCorkle listened warily. Officers were supposed to display loyalty, not run down their superiors no matter what their personal feelings. He tried a tentative question.

"Didn't the Corps frown upon all that?"

"Any man has a legal right to change his name." The warrant officer scowled, then shrugged, still leafing through the well-thumbed pages. "Even to Barrymore."

"They couldn't have been too unhappy, if they'd kept him there in Headquarters all these years."

"Certainly not." Schmake agreed a bit too easily. "After all, he was somethin' of a hero back in the Late Great Hate. An ace, in fact."

"Oh? How many Japs did..."

Schmake interrupted coarsely. "That's the rub. He was a Japanese ace. He crashed six of ours!"

"Gunner," McCorkle asked solemnly, "did this man spit in your mess gear somewhere along the way?"

Max shook his head. "I just don't trust a man in tailored dungarees, like I said. They're all politicians. Parade ground soldiers you can't find when some bastard's shootin' at you." He glanced at McCorkle. "Maybe I don't look like it now, son, but I've been shot at."

McCorkle's mouth twitched at the use of the youthful term, but Schmake seemed not to notice. Out of the pile of rubble he had created on his battered field desk, he pulled forth a sheet of yellowing mimeograph paper. He shoved it toward the lieutenant.

"This is the order. Operations will clear your dispatches, not Intelligence. Take this back an' show it to Barrymore."

McCorkle hesitated, then shook his head cautiously. "I...I'd rather not."

Schmake raised an eyebrow. "You afraid of him?"

This time, McCorkle nodded, feeling uncomfortable under the jaundiced scrutiny. "Have you ever had him come down in the middle of your back?"

"Unlike some I know, he don't screw around with warrant officers," was the pointed reply. "What he does best is pull rank on junior officers." He tapped the signature at the bottom of the sheet. "But how can he argue with an order signed by the commanding general?"

McCorkle was panicked by the fleeting notion that he suddenly was in the midst of a No-Man's Land, waiting for a battle to begin. But he wasn't certain on which side he was supposed to be.

"But if he just came from Washington, he may know something we don't." There was caution in his tone. "Maybe some command decision back there that supersedes this order."

"If there was, he wouldn't know about it," Schmake sneered. "If he ever did anything but go to cocktail parties an' brown nose, I never heard.

"Why'd you think they kept him back there in Henderson Hall? Anytime you find a man spendin' that long in Headquarters, it's 'cause they're scared to turn 'im loose in th' field!"

McCorkle surrendered. "I'll show it to him, but first I want the G-2 people to tell me they aren't supposed to sign it."

In the dim room where Intelligence labored amid seemingly senseless maps and graphs, it took less than a minute to learn Schmake was right, but McCorkle was no less uneasy as he pushed through the door to the office where Barrymore sat running a thumb along the starched, carefully creased trousers of his utility uniform.

"You're back?" There was a haughty note in the colonel's voice and McCorkle could only nod, the perspiration starting to pop out on his forehead. He handed the other the yellowing order, retaining his news dispatch.

Barrymore eyed the aged sheet of paper, as blood began slowly to creep up his neck, flushing his face. Finally, he tossed the paper onto his desk and swung his chair to stare at the lieutenant through slitted eyes.

"Lieutenant, this only proves you're wasting your time," the colonel said in a quiet voice that contradicted the redness of his face. "If you're going to go around trying to prove me wrong, you'll never make it!"

"I...I'm not trying to prove anything, sir," McCorkle insisted on a note of stubborn misery. He waved the dispatch in a vague gesture of confusion. "I have to get this signed. The Intelligence officer said it was up to you."

"I don't care what he said." Barrymore's voice rose in irritation. "I'm senior to him."

"Sign the dispatch," a voice said crisply from the doorway. "The lieutenant has some business with me." McCorkle saw the startled expression on Barrymore's face and turned. The squat figure of the Chief-of-Staff loomed in the entrance. Behind him was the bulk of Max Schmake.

"Or doesn't the commanding general's signature on an order mean anything to you?" The Chief took a threatening step into the room.

Barrymore had risen to his full five feet five inches in his built-up combat boots and was standing at attention. If he had really doubled for John Wayne, McCorkle realized, it had to be while sitting down.

"No, sir," Barrymore protested uncertainly. "It was just that..."

"Sign the man's dispatch," the Chief repeated brusquely.

"Yes, sir." Barrymore turned to his desk, pawing through the stacks of papers. McCorkle, still holding the dispatch form, stepped forward. Barrymore snatched the paper away and fumbled for a pen. McCorkle supplied that, too, and won a guarded but dirty look for his promptness.

Barrymore handed back the signed form and McCorkle was in the midst of a military about face, when the Chief's voice caught him with his left foot in mid-air.

"McCorkle. About our jeep."

The lieutenant slowly put his foot down, completed the turn and remained at attention, staring past the Chief's left ear. "Yes, sir?"

"You have a jeep," Colonel Dade said slowly, "and I intend to have it. I'm driving a relic of World War II and it's going to be junked. I'll be damned if I'll walk, while you and that crew of yours ride."

Barrymore was attempting to stifle a smile, happy to have the Chief-of-Staff's ire directed elsewhere. Schmake was looking at his feet, avoiding McCorkle's eyes.

"Yes, sir," McCorkle replied dutifully. "Does the colonel want it tonight or can it wait till morning?"

"What's that?" Surprised, he had expected a battle.

McCorkle was braced so stiffly that he could feel his Adam's apple bobbing against his chin. "I can have it washed and delivered first thing in the morning. I'll be happy to have it off my hands."

"What're you talking about, lieutenant?"

"The jeep, sir. I'd rather not be involved." McCorkle's face was growing red, as though holding his breath and talking at the same time.

"Involved in what?" The Chief's tone was one of irritation but there also was a note of wariness.

"I have no desire to be in possession of stolen Government property," McCorkle gulped.

Colonel Dade's eyes widened and he turned to look out the window. His shoulders twitched several times before he asked guardedly, "Stolen property?"

"I thought the colonel knew. That jeep was stolen from the Army, then painted with Marine Corps colors and a fake serial number. But I don't imagine they'll bother you."

*"Who* won't bother me?"

"The CID, sir. Criminal Investigation. A colonel would be above suspicion."

"No you don't!" The colonel whirled to stare searchingly into McCorkle's eyes. "You're not foisting stolen gear off on me. The Army'd love that. The Chief-of-Staff caught with a stolen jeep!" He shuddered violently at the thought.

"As the colonel says, sir."

"You can keep that jeep, lieutenant," Dade said softly. "If you get caught with it, you do the explaining. But you're not passing trouble on to me."

"We can turn it back to the Army, sir," McCorkle suggested thinly.

"Are you crazy, boy?" the colonel roared at him indignantly. "Stealing from the Army's an honorable source of supply. Getting caught's the crime. You think I'd turn it back and let them know we stole it in the first place? You talk like a damned boot!"

"Yes, sir," McCorkle agreed, sounding like a boot recruit.

"Gunner," the Chief-of-Staff said, "have one of your runners hike McCorkle's dispatch over to Communications and get it sent."

"Aye, sir," Schmake returned. He took the paper from the officer's fingers and went through the doorway, casting a wolfishly cheerful backward glance. Slowly it dawned upon McCorkle that Max was after Barrymore's scalp and had used him as bait.

"McCorkle, you come with me. The general wants to see you."

McCorkle had started to relax but came back to attention. Trouble. He'd been here for weeks and hadn't even seen the general. Now he was being summoned at nine o'clock at night.

"Carry on, Barrymore," the Chief ordered tightly and turned on his heel. McCorkle clung to his shadow, not daring to look back. Barrymore didn't have a jeep.

And there was the queasy feeling in the pit of his stomach. Could the general have heard of his insubordination regarding Barrymore? The Chief had seemed to defend him there. Or was the matter of the jeep being carried a notch higher? Had the chaplain lodged an official complaint?

The first thing that struck McCorkle was that he didn't look at all like a general. He looked more like a German butcher. He was in his fifties, face cut by wind wrinkles from that era when only a flimsy windshield protected pilots from the elements. He was totally bald, and behind the huge desk, his figure hunched against this bulwark, the green uniform seemed too large for him. He had all of the grace of a huge misplaced frog.

But, as he rose and extended a hand, McCorkle saw that the forest green uniform was a perfect, tailored fit. But the handshake afforded him little confidence. Something was about to happen.

"Happy to meet you, lieutenant," the general declared, wrinkled face splitting in a warm smile. He sounded as though he meant it. "Sorry I haven't had time to call you in before." He gestured to the baskets of paper before him. The motion suggested distaste from a man who was accustomed to campaigning. "But this."

"I'm sorry, too," McCorkle muttered dutifully, staring at the single blue ribbon with the sprinkling of white stars the general wore a quarter-inch above his left breast pocket. The Medal of Honor. Suddenly he looked less like a frog.

"Have a seat," the general said easily. "How's everything in your section?"

McCorkle hesitated for a moment. He stared at the general and was surprised to find that here was a man unlike the others. Not like the Chief, Barrymore, Schmake. Perhaps that was why he was a general. He seemed genuinely interested in something besides his own rank. McCorkle took a deep breath and plunged before his vocal cords could freeze.

"General, I want to go home!"

There was a sharp intake of shocked breath from the Chief-of-Staff standing behind him. The general scowled. McCorkle knew he had been too brave and the tell-tale perspiration leaped out along his brow.

"You what?" The general's voice was strangled in disbelief.

"And you might as well send the rest of my crew, too," McCorkle went on, rushing his words, trying to get them out ahead of the fright that was growing within him. "They're wasting their time here."

The general lowered himself slowly into his seat. The Chief exhaled in a long, defeated sigh.

"You'd better explain yourself, lieutenant," the general suggested with troubled formality.

"We can't get film, sir. W-we can't get parts for our cameras." With the general's eyes upon him, McCorkle knew he was starting to blush. Inwardly he was squirming, realizing he had gone too far. The frown across the desk from him was growing heavier. "Most of the stuff we have is junk left over from World War II. I see no sense in sending men to the front to get hurt or killed without reason."

The general, still scowling, glared over his shoulder to the Chief-of-Staff. "Do you know about this?"

"He's right, sir," Dade agreed, his voice defensive.

"Why hasn't it been straightened out?" the general demanded. "Or why wasn't I told?" McCorkle slowly exhaled, allowing his shoulders to sag a bit.

"We've sent dispatches to Headquarters, Marine Corps," the Chief said defensively, "but they're all stopped at Pearl Harbor. They tell us to go to the Navy. The Navy refers us to the Army and the Army sends us to the Air Force.

"And the Air Force laughs at us," he concluded somewhat miserably. "They say they're not going to supply us with the material to publicize a competing service."

In that moment, McCorkle, too, was feeling miserable. It occurred to him that he had achieved what was probably a Marine Corps first. He had put two superior officers' feet to the fire all within a twenty-minute period. First Barrymore, now the Chief-of-Staff. Neither would be likely to forget.

The general grunted. "Great thing, this unification of the services." He wheeled suddenly back to McCorkle. "Lieutenant, how would you like to go to Tokyo?"

McCorkle hesitated, his eyes upon the little blue ribbon with the seven stars that graced the general's chest. "I was hoping to get to the front, sir."

"Hell!" the general growled. "That's the easiest place in this war to get, but not everyone can get to Japan."

"I'd still like to go up where they're fighting." He was certain he could feel the Chief's breath on the back of his neck. The front might be safer.

"What are you?" the general demanded. "Some kind of a nut? Those bastards're shooting at each other!"

"I—I know, sir," the lieutenant stammered, but his eyes still were on the blue rectangle of ribbon and the general caught the look. He glanced down at the token on his chest, suddenly understanding.

"You can get into the war, later," he promised gruffly. "But tonight you make a list of everything you need. I'll sign it in the morning and there'll be a plane ready."

The general cleared his throat for emphasis. "And you can state in the last paragraph that if we don't get that gear, I'm sending you and your mob of outcasts over to work for them. That ought to shake hell out of somebody!"

"Yes, sir." Realizing he had been dismissed, McCorkle did an about face.

"What about those new planes?" the general asked the colonel. "Why aren't they assigned to squadrons and in the air?"

Dade was still on the defensive. "There are the property transfers. A bit more paper work to finish."

"Screw the paper," the general growled. "Do it after the war. That's why we have peace!"

# CHAPTER 6

"**I**F THEY ever built him a two-hole crapper, he'd shit his pants trying to make up his mind which hole to sit on!"

Quillan, who seemed to know everybody in the entire Marine Corps, had been expounding elegantly upon the inabilities of Lieutenant Colonel J.E.L. Barrymore.

The master sergeant, McCorkle realized, was slightly drunk, an indication that the chaplain's copper tubing had been put into operation. He didn't know where the still was located; he didn't want to know, since such knowledge would call for action. Still, he couldn't help wondering how Lawrence would have rationalized away such a situation. There probably would be no rationalization involved. He would approve. This realization caused McCorkle a twinge that no doubt could have been diagnosed as jealousy had he been willing to acknowledge it.

With Quillan's aid, he had just finished compiling the list of needed photo supplies, when Sergeant Shade and Corporal Handley appeared out of the darkness. Shade had shaved and looked squared away, McCorkle noted, but the corporal still looked as though he had slept in a dung pile.

"Where's the coffee pot?" Handley asked Quillan, glancing toward the top of the oil stove.

"In th' back room. We scrounged a hot plate. Henry, get him some coffee."

The Korean boy looked up from his hangnail and stirred, but Handley shook his head. "I'll get it myself."

He disappeared into the rear half of the tent, then there was a crash, the rattle of metal on metal and the slosh of liquid.

53

"Little gook bastard!"

The corporal came through the curtained doorway clutching a wooden box about the size of a whiskey case, but marked with Oriental characters.

"Goddammit," Shade rattled fearfully, "take it easy. That's dynamite!"

There was a wild scramble for cover, Jane disappearing beneath her desk, while Quillan dived behind Shamley's bulk, holding him as a shield while the tech sergeant bawled his unwillingness.

Blithely, Handley threw the case at Shade, who caught it and went to his knees, lowering the explosive package gently to the floor.

"Hold it!" McCorkle shouted, but Handley seemed not to hear. Instead, he whirled upon Henry, who took a step to the rear and tried to run. He was in a corner and there was no escape. One of the corporal's open hands caught him on the side of the head, exploding loudly, and Henry's face twisted in pain. Handley's other hand tightened on his shoulder, finger twisting into the flesh, shaking him.

"I'll kill you!"

McCorkle, reacting, caught Handley by the wrist, jerking him about. Henry made for the door, the corporal after him, but Quillan was suddenly between them, grabbing Handley by the shoulders, holding him at arm's length.

"Tell it!" Quillan snapped. "Why?"

"Dirty sonuvabitch was tryin' to blow us up!" Handley snarled. "He set that hot plate on top of that dynamite and turned it up full bore. He was..."

"That's enough!" Quillan declared, turning upon Shade. But McCorkle was already staring down at the box between the buck sergeant's knees.

"Is that dynamite?" There was an audible shake in his tone but it demanded an answer nonetheless.

Shade slowly rose, standing at loose attention. "Yes, sir," he agreed. "Chinese dynamite. Found it in a cave up front. We was gonna use it on the Fourth 'a July t'show Henry how we celebrate it back home."

"Try to Americanize the bastard," Handley put in, "and all the time he's out to kill us!"

"Where were you keeping it?" McCorkle was eyeing the strange characters on the box, wondering whether Henry read Chinese.

Shade hesitated, then stiffened a bit more. "Under the lieutenant's bunk, sir. It seemed a safe spot."

"Well, get it out of here," McCorkle told him softly. It wasn't self control. It was awe at the realization that he had been using dynamite for inner springs.

"Aye, sir." The sergeant picked up the wooden case and pushed through the door with it. McCorkle turned to Handley and Quillan.

"Did Henry know what was in that box?"

Quillan shook his head. "I don't think so, skipper."

"But you're not sure," Handley growled sullenly. "You still won't be sure the day he blows us all to hell in little bits."

"No one spoke to you." Quillan took a threatening step toward him.

"I'm speaking to him now." The quaver was gone from the officer's voice and both men looked at him. Handley's expression was suddenly uncomfortable.

"Henry is a twelve-year-old boy," McCorkle stated slowly, "that makes him a minor and I'm certain there's something in the Book about molesting a minor." Handley's face held a hurt, puzzled look, but McCorkle went on coldly, "If you ever lay a hand on him again, I'll lock your ass up so tight the Red Cross'll need tweezers to get your mother's cookies between the bars!"

"Yes, sir." Handley looked sullen, evading the officer's eyes.

It had been a restless sleep and McCorkle came out of it with a start, body stiff and trembling beneath the blankets. There had been a dream but he couldn't remember what it had concerned. He held his arm up to glance at the luminous dial on his watch. A little after three.

He had been alone in the tent when he had decided to find his bunk. Handley had cleaned up the mess created when he had knocked over the coffee pot and hot plate, then had departed, shoulders hunched and not speaking. Shortly after, Quillan had said something about checking some photos in the photo lab, but it was obvious he was more interested in a drink and was headed for the hidden still, if there really was one.

McCorkle had sat alone at his desk, rechecking the list of equipment and wondering what had become of Henry. The boy had simply disappeared into the night after the set-to with Handley and had not returned.

Listening now, ears strained against the wind on the creaking canvas, there was no sound of Quillan's familiar snoring. He must still be out.

Thinking back to the manner in which he had handled Handley, he decided it had been handily. He had handily handled Handley. The thought had ideas, but he decided to reject it.

Actually, recalling the incident, there was a degree of satisfaction. He had faced a crisis, minor, true, but he had bested it. There had been no doubt in anyone's mind that he meant business; that when he gave an order, he expected results. But what had triggered this reaction? Was it simply the sight of seeing the corporal mistreat the boy? He wished he knew and it troubled him in his state of semi-awakeness, being blown out of proportional importance by the darkness.

McCorkle pushed himself up on one elbow, staring into the darkness toward Henry's bunk.

"Henry? Are you here?"

There was no sound for a moment, then a stirring.

"Henry?"

"Yes, suh?"

"I just wondered whether you were here. I waited for you to come back." He waited for the boy to say something. "Don't worry about Handley. He won't bother you any more. You understand why he's the way he is, Henry?"

"I unnahstan'."

McCorkle sat up, pushing back the blankets. This was as close to the boy as he had ever gotten. Usually there was the impression that Henry was trying to prove himself as tough and cynical as the Marines surrounding him.

"Henry, do you ever get homesick?" McCorkle asked quietly, still staring into the darkness. A cold wind was whistling through the pores of the tight-knit canvas and he shivered, waiting for an answer. Only silence.

McCorkle lay back on the thin mattress to stare up into the night, frowning. There were hundreds of orphans throughout South Korea like Henry; perhaps thousands who had been unofficially adopted by troop units, saving them from the rigors of life in orphanages. But what was to happen to these kids when the war was ended and the troops pulled out? True, they could always be turned over to orphanages, but by that time the damage would be done. The boys would have become used to another way of life, another level of living. Spoiled, actually, by the adulation of the Americans who sought in some small way to impart the kindness and generosity here that they would be spreading among their own kids or younger brothers and sisters back home. But what effect would this mass rejection have upon these orphans when the GI foster fathers were ordered away?

Muffled words from across the room interrupted McCorkle's ponderous train of thought.

"Lieutenant, sir. Dog. You hava—yes?" Henry asked in pidgin English.

McCorkle sat up, staring into the dark void, frowning at the strange question.

"Not any more, Henry. But I had one. A good one. A German shepherd. But he died."

The officer sat there, cold in his undershirt, goose pimples popping out to cause him to shudder. There was nothing but silence as he sat there, waiting for the boy to speak again. Finally he did.

"I hadda dog. Little dog. Black. Some brown, maybe."

"What happened to him, Henry?" It was a strange conversation, but it was a conversational wedge and McCorkle drove it in.

"Communists," the boy said simply. "Communist soldiers kill. Eat. One soldier make winter hat out of skin. Alla time they laugh. Laugh!"

As he spoke, his words ran into each other, the vocal sounds rising in pitch to the edge of hysteria. McCorkle could feel the hatred there in the tent, filling the darkness.

There was silence and the officer sat quietly, the cold forgotten, waiting for the boy to go on, but words didn't come. Instead, he caught the sound of muffled sobs from deep in the boy's sleeping bag. He remembered his own feelings after his dog had been injured by a car and his father had shot it. There suddenly was nothing to say. He sat there, the sobs rasping at his ears, until he threw blankets aside and slid his feet onto the rough board floor.

Crossing in the darkness, he kicked the corner of a locker box and swore under his breath. When he reached the canvas cot, he sat down on the edge of it, reaching out, groping, until he felt the shaking form beneath the padded folds of the bag.

Henry choked, trying to cut off his sobs, when he realized McCorkle was there. Instead, the sounds jerked their way out of his throat, making little strangling noises.

"Listen to me, Henry!" McCorkle's tone sounded harsh in his own ears. It might have been caused by the lump in his own throat. "Sit up, dammit, and listen to me!"

There was movement, the sound of a struggle within the bag, then the rasp of the zipper as the boy obeyed. McCorkle could feel the boy's hot, moist breathing on his bare arm as he sat up, the sobs still coming from his throat. He reached out to put a hand on the boy's thin shoulder.

"Listen to me! Tomorrow we'll go to the village. We'll buy you another dog. A little one. Black and brown."

There was a moment's silence before the boy said thickly, "Th' majah was gonna get me a dog. But I guess he fohgot." There was no accusation in the tone. Only sadness, and McCorkle couldn't tell whether it was for the dead Major Lawrence or for the forgotten promise.

"We'll get you a dog, Henry," he promised sternly. "It won't be the same one you lost, but it'll be a cute one."

The sobs died a bit, suspended there in the blackness. Henry seemed to be holding his breath, waiting for McCorkle to speak. "Now can you go to sleep?"

"Yes, suh."

McCorkle started to rise, but the boy's arms were suddenly about his neck. They weren't dry, muffled sobs now. They were the tears of a small boy, crying for more than a dog. He was weeping for a lost family, perhaps a lost way of life. He was allowing his loss, his frustration, his confusion to leak out through the tears.

McCorkle sat there for a long time, allowing the tears to soak into his skivvy shirt, patting the boy gently on the shoulder, rocking him back and forth.

Neither of them said anything more. They didn't have to.

# CHAPTER 7

**H**ENRY'S BUNK was empty when McCorkle awoke, the patched sleeping bag neatly rolled up on the bottom of the cot, the extra blanket beneath it. As he dressed, he heard movement and vague murmurings in the outer office.

When he ducked through the curtained doorway, he found Quillan at his desk and Technical Sergeant Ashdon shaved, shined, showered, packed and ready to depart.

"Where's Henry?" McCorkle asked Quillan.

"Raidin' the mess hall. We're outa coffee."

"Send someone down to the village to try to buy a dog," McCorkle ordered. "A black one. Some brown."

Both of the sergeants were staring at him, but McCorkle made no effort to explain. Quillan shook his head.

"Skipper, how many full grown dogs have you seen around here?"

The officer thought about it for a moment, then shook his head. "I haven't given it much thought."

"Well, these Koreans like dog meat," Quillan explained. "You may be putting in a tall order. One we can't fill."

McCorkle turned to eye Ashdon in his uniformed splendor. "Where're you going?"

"With the lieutenant, sir," Ashdon replied crisply. "Sergeant Quillan figgers you might need a guide to get around Tokyo."

"Henry says this is all a reward for puttin' Barrymore in his place," Quillan put in smugly. "An' thanks for savin' our jeep, skipper."

"When did Henry tell you this?" McCorkle wanted to know.

59

"This mornin'. He picked it up somewhere last night."

"I'd rather we didn't have that jeep," McCorkle stated coldly. "It only means trouble. And I certainly did not put Lieutenant Colonel Barrymore anywhere." He turned to Ashdon. He had only met this man once, when the latter had been between trips to the front. He was short, heavy, rosy-cheeked and didn't look at all like a man who thrived on danger as Shamley had insisted. "How well do you know Tokyo, sergeant?"

"I can find my way around, sir."

"You should see some of the things he finds around," Quillan leered. "Built like reject battleships. That's why I picked him to go with you." But he was frowning over the officer's lack of concern for the jeep.

McCorkle's eyes lingered on the three rows of campaign ribbons that colored Ashdon's chest. One was the Navy Good Conduct Medal. "When were you in the Navy?"

"Double-Yew, Double-Yew Deuce."

"He was in Underwater Demolition," Quillan put in informatively.

"But only for six weeks," Ashdon hastened to explain. McCorkle already knew the reason. He didn't question beyond; it might actually be true that the sergeant couldn't swim.

"Where's that requisition for the gear?"

"All typed up in the smooth, sir, an' gone down to the general for signature. It'll be back in a minute." The ancient master sergeant elevated his battered visage to look at the officer. "An' Henry told us what the general said about sendin' us all to Tokyo if we don't get the stuff. Think you can arrange that?"

"No, I don't think I can arrange that!" McCorkle snapped. "Let's see that list again."

Quillan handed him the rough draft they had prepared the previous night and McCorkle ran down the list, noting with satisfaction that nothing had been forgotten. But at the last notation, he paused. It had been added.

"And two dozen one-gallon jugs?" he questioned, staring accusingly first at Quillan then Ashdon. "Should I bother to ask why those?"

"Certainly, sir," Quillan lied. "They're for photo chemicals."

"I'm surprised you didn't want to go get this stuff yourself," McCorkle commented with a trace of bitterness. He knew the jugs had

60

something to do with the hidden still, but couldn't prove it. And the idea of being made a party to the bootlegging operation rankled.

"I know all about goin' after gear," Quillan agreed cheerfully, "but there's things here t' be done."

"In your case, it was beer, not gear, an' after two weeks we hadda come after you," put in Ashdon. "Incidentally, skipper, don't ever let him talk you into sendin' him t'Japan for anything, or you'll likely never see him again."

"Never mind," Quillan warned, glaring at Ashdon.

"You were over the hill?" McCorkle asked the master sergeant, tone heavy with doubt.

"Not that," Ashdon added hastily. "He just got a little drunked up an' thought all them Japs was gonna try a banzai charge ten years too late. He cleaned about twenty of 'em b'fore the Nip cops broke it up. They had a list of charges against him that reads like what they'd've read off if the surrender'd been on their ship 'stead of ours. He can't go back!"

Further questions would only have given the conversation a degree of dignity. At that point, Halloran came through the door with a large brown envelope in his hand. He extended it to McCorkle.

"The general's signed it," he said simply. McCorkle waved to the door, then to the small bag at his feet.

"Lead on," he ordered with abnormal stuffiness. Halloran glanced at him in surprise, then dutifully picked up the bag and pushed through the makeshift door, Ashdon behind him. McCorkle cast Quillan a final wary glance, wondering whether it was safe to leave him in charge, then followed.

In the valley below, the dikes had been repaired, the rice planted and the green shoots were beginning to show above the water level that flooded the fields. Several Koreans were bent double, separating the weeds from the crop, one green sprig at a time.

As he scrambled into the jeep, McCorkle looked down upon the bent backs, wondering about the true feelings of these people, whether they really were interested in any battle other than that of grubbing a living from the soil.

It was possible, he realized, that some were enemy guerrillas, farming by day, raiding by night. Less than a week before, an Army motor convoy had been ambushed only a dozen miles away. And the sentries at the air strip were constantly filing reports, most of them unverified, of dim figures attempting to creep into the plane park at night, supposedly to sabotage the aircraft.

And Henry, he realized, was developing into a problem. How much animosity there had been on Handley's part before he had arrived he did not know, nor did he have any idea how Major Lawrence had gone about keeping it in check. But he was certain that the incident of the dynamite would no doubt plant seeds of distrust in more minds than one.

There was an established Catholic orphanage run by an aged French priest less than five miles away, but he probably would have to fight Quillan, Shade and others of the section if he even suggested this might be the best place for the boy. McCorkle tried to tell himself that this might be the best solution, realizing at the same time that he would never be the one to institute such a move. Not after seeing the boy, crying there in the dark, his soul stripped bare. And he realized that Henry hadn't been crying over a dog. That had only been a convenient object upon which he could center his emotions, shutting out for the moment, at least, all of the other horrors that had made up his few years.

Five minutes later, they dismounted from the jeep at the air strip, where a plane was warming up, propeller turning with asthmatic protests. McCorkle glared at the aircraft, a bunglesome, war-battered hulk that held a far too familiar appearance.

"It's your plane, skipper," the driver assured him with an understandable nod of pity. "They was gonna send the general's Beechcraft, but it's due for a check. This here's the only ship available."

"Where'd you hear all this?" McCorkle asked suspiciously.

"That leaf colonel, Baronofsky, was..."

"Colonel Barrymore," McCorkle corrected shortly.

"Yes, sir. Him. He was tellin' somebody you'd hafta use this ole turkey. That was when I was pickin' up your orders an' that requisition."

McCorkle looked again at the ancient torpedo bomber, the same scarred veteran in which he had made that ill-timed flight across the Sea of Japan. And when he thought of Major Lawrence and his attitude in the face of that danger, he realized how much had happened, none of it particularly good, since that night they had flown through the edge of the typhoon.

"Lieutenant," Ashdon asked delicately, "would you mind lettin' me carry my own orders?"

McCorkle turned questioning eyes upon the sergeant, who shuffled his feet uncomfortably, glancing at the driver who was loading their bags into the belly compartment.

"Just in case we hafta parachute," he explained lamely. "It's hell to try to get around without orders."

McCorkle continued to stare, attempting to appear disapproving rather than in agreement, until Ashdon shrugged and started to enter the aircraft. McCorkle followed reluctantly.

The laboring, protesting, old torpedo bomber made it into Tokyo's Haneda International Airport after popping only a dozen or so of its vital wing rivets in the down drafts over the Sea of Japan.

With the curtain of dread still shrouding his mental curses for Colonel Barrymore, McCorkle crawled from the bomb bay of the plane, where he and Ashdon had been crowded with their gear during the trip.

Ducking clear of the propeller blast, he turned to look back at the pilot, who was grinning through the plastic cockpit canopy. McCorkle started to signal his appreciation, then froze, hand suspended loosely in the air.

"He's only a sergeant!" he muttered aghast.

"One of the best damn pilots in the Corps, too," Ashdon agreed primly. "Used to be a master sergeant till he got busted."

McCorkle looked at the underling with a mixture of emotions dominated by uncertainty. "For what?"

"He was buzzin' a hangar an' got caught at it," was the matter-of-fact reply.

"They took three stripes just for buzzing a hangar?"

"But he was doin' it from the inside," Ashdon explained gently.

Whatever reply McCorkle might have been able to muster was cut off by the broken roar of the old bomber's sickly engine. He turned to watch as this aging mechanical warrior lumbered down the runway, then he turned to follow the sergeant across the concrete ramp.

Although utilized by commercial airlines from over the globe, the entire airdome still was under the control of General Ridgeway's United Nations forces and the uniforms of a dozen friendly nations were clustered near the entrance to the administration building. Inside, the uniforms were packed shoulder to shoulder; men going to Korea, others bound for home. The area was in turmoil with harried officials of the Military Air Transport Service attempting to maintain a degree of order while they sorted out the various priorities for air travel.

"What now?" McCorkle asked as the tech sergeant paused just inside the stripped-down lobby.

Ashdon consulted his wristwatch. "First, we'll go over t'the Army Finance Office and change some Mickey Mouse money into *yen*. Then you can order a car." Mickey Mouse money was the term popularly applied to the red and purple scrip issued to troops in place of United States currency. This system was supposed to keep greenbacks from getting into the hands of Communist sympathizers, who would, in turn, transport them behind the Bamboo Curtain via Hong Kong or other outposts to ultimately be used to pay for Red arms.

"I order a car?" McCorkle asked dubiously and Ashdon returned a sturdy nod.

"Hell, man, you're a lieutenant an' we're on official business. They can't expect you to roller skate down the Ginza."

Slightly confused and a bit suspicious of this show of confidence, McCorkle followed him to the Finance Office, where each exchanged $50 for the *yen* notes that bulged their pockets with the ratio of three hundred sixty to one American dollar.

Then McCorkle used the office telephone to call the Army motor pool and order an official sedan.

"What's your rank, bud?" a grudging voice at the other end of the line wanted to know.

"First Lieutenant, United States Marine Corps," McCorkle replied, recognizing a note of uncertainty in his tone in spite of Ashdon's steady gaze. The answer brought a raucous laugh grating through the receiver.

"Hell, mister, we got first looies around here we ain't even counted yet, an' we ain't even got enough cars t'go aroun' for the colonels. What'cha tryin' t'pull?"

Ashdon had stepped closer, catching some of the reply through the earphone loosely held to McCorkle's ear. He made signals which the officer failed to understand.

"You gotta give him hell, skipper," Ashdon whispered loudly. "These rear echelon pogues'll run you around all night 'less you give 'em th' word."

McCorkle nodded, then turned so that he didn't have to see the sergeant watching him, gauging. He took a long breath, then deliberately attempted to lower his voice an octave.

"And what are you trying to pull?" he demanded as brusquely as he could make it. "What is your name, rank and serial number?"

There was a long silence before the voice came over in a subdued, more respectful tone. The change in attitude surprised McCorkle. It also gave him a moment of delight. "Sorry, sir, but we just ain't got no vehicles available. Not even a bicycle."

"I am here as a personal courier for the Commanding General of the First Marine Air Wing," McCorkle announced coldly, taking full advantage of the dispatcher's wariness. "You'll certainly find a vehicle for him!"

There was another long pause and the empty sound of a hand being held over the mouthpiece while a conference went on at the motor pool. Then the voice, still respectful, said: "Car'll be there in five minutes, sir." There was a pause. "Sorry, but I won't be able to give you nothin' but a Jap driver."

If there was threat in that last statement, it went unidentified. Instead, McCorkle was concentrating upon the expression of approval on Ashdon's face as he hung up. And he could not help a small smile of satisfaction at the realization that he had made a small gain, had placed another brick on the wall of command presence which he realized he lacked.

He stood there with his hand on the telephone for a long moment, wondering whether he could take this man into his confidence, whether he could allow his concern to be known without it being transmitted to the rest of the section when they returned to Korea. Ashdon usually was more quiet, less boisterous than the others in spite of Shamley's accusations that he was medal happy.

"Sergeant," he said finally. "I need some answers." Some of the approval went out of Ashdon's expression, replaced by wariness.

"Yes, sir?" The tone was respectful but committed nothing in the way of cooperation. McCorkle frowned, not knowing quite how to ask the question that had been haunting him.

"It's about this Korean boy," he said looking down at the telephone. "Is there any chance that he could be a spy? That he deliberately tried to blow us up?" He glanced up and found the leeriness still in the other man's face. "You aren't around him as much as Quillan and some of the others. That might make you a bit more objective."

Ashdon thought about it, frowning thoughtfully. He took his time in framing a reply.

"I was there when we found him," he said slowly. "He was nothin' but a scared hunk of humanity there in that bombed out buildin', hidin' from everything includin' daylight. His mother an' father were there, too, both dead. Even after we got him cleaned up some an' fed him, he was still in shock for weeks."

Ashdon offered a grimace, as though he found the mustering of thoughts on the subject painful. "I'd say he's still scared. A couple weeks b'fore you came, one of our planes came back in with a hung bomb. When it hit the runway, the egg shook loose an' went skippin' down th' strip till it exploded. When he heard that, I thought th' kid was gonna dig a hole through the board floor. Took him days t'get over that."

McCorkle glanced at his watch. "We'd better get outside so that driver can find us."

Standing on the curb in front of the building, he had another thought. "About that bombed building where you found him and his parents. Which side did the bombing?"

Ashdon offered a shrug. "I don't even think Henry knows, or if he does, he won't say." Then he added carefully. "But I suspect it was our side."

# CHAPTER 8

THERE WAS A bearish clap on McCorkle's shoulder that almost drove him to his knees.

"Well, a man who looks like he's waitin' for a car!" A gruff, jovial bass blared only inches from his ear. As he turned, his eyebrows elevated in surprise. It was the pilot of the torpedo bomber, who stood in flight suit, hard helmet and one of the most gigantic handlebar mustaches McCorkle had ever seen.

The man's thick eyebrows were ragged and bushy, an unlikely contrast to the trimmed, well-waxed efficiency of the spiked hair that stood out a full three inches on each side of his nose, seeming to divide his face into two segments. It was obvious he was unaware or simply ignored the tradition that an enlisted man never lays hands upon an officer, McCorkle told himself, but what could one expect of a man who buzzes hangars from the inside?

"I thought you just took off," he offered somewhat lamely.

The sergeant offered a dour shake of his head. "Not quite. The old beast quit on me right at the end of the runway."

"You mean it won't fly?" McCorkle asked, that familiar sensation of illness beginning to take form in the pit of his stomach.

"Hell, skipper," the other growled, "it won't even start. They're gonna work on it tonight. They get it done, you two kin fly back with me tomorrow morning."

"We'll see," the officer promised, in an unconvincing murmur, mentally seeking an escape route. That machine was little more than a flying coffin, obviously made even more dangerous by this busted sergeant at the controls.

"Did they ever get the lights fixed on that instrument panel?" he asked as an afterthought.

"What instrument panel?" was the cynical demand. "Nothin' has worked on that plane, includin' the wings, since the Battle of the Coral Sea!

"That was Double-Yew Double-Yew Deuce," the flying sergeant added with just a trace of arrogance, staring critically at McCorkle's hairless upper lip.

McCorkle stiffened, feeling the warmth in his cheeks as he blushed in spite of himself. "Yes, sergeant, I know," he replied grimly.

"This is Jack Sales, sir," Sergeant Ashdon put in hurriedly. He had heard the barrier building up in the officer's tone and now sought to keep it from growing any higher. "Peon Pilot First Class. Jack, this is my boss, Lieutenant McCorkle." There was a warning in his tone.

And at that offbeat note, the flying sergeant straightened to a position of loose attention; now his hand went to the edge of the hard hat in a vague gesture of salute. McCorkle returned the dubious gesture of respect with correctness and precision, but he still could feel the warmth that colored his neck.

"Happy to have been your pilot, skipper," Sales declared with sudden warmth, then thrust out his hand. "Any time you need someone to ferry you around, jest send word. I ain't doin' nothin' else, 'cept tryin' to keep out of Colonel Barrymore's way."

"Colonel Barrymore?" McCorkle was unable to keep the sudden interest out of his tone. "You know him well?"

"We've met," the pilot admitted sagely. "But it's a long, extremely unpleasant story. Can I catch a ride into town with you? No reason for me to hang around here. I'd only cringe at the amount of balin' wire they'll use to put that turkey back in one piece."

"Fine," McCorkle agreed a bit expansively. He suddenly was feeling less unkindly toward this sergeant pilot. Actually, he was intrigued with what he might have to say about the lieutenant colonel. As the green Army sedan, old and full of rattles, pulled up, the three piled their luggage in the rear seat, then settled themselves amid it.

Three hours later, it occurred to McCorkle that he had been had by the dispatcher whom he had threatened. It was not until then that Sales and Ashdon, using their combined knowledge of pidgin English and bastard Japanese, had learned that the civilian driver was hopelessly lost. Although he lived on the outskirts of Tokyo, not far from the air field, he had only recently come to work for the Army as an indigenous employee. He didn't know the city at all; few Japanese, McCorkle learned much later, know the sprawling intricacies of Tokyo's street system outside of the particular boroughs where they live. They often are born, live their entire lives and die within a few bustling, crowded blocks.

Two hours and a half a dozen Japanese police officers later, they finally found the huge, stone-columned structure that housed the headquarters of the Commander, Naval Forces, Far East.

Instead of overlooking the beauties of Tokyo Harbor, as he had imagined it should, the body of water closest to the imposing structure was a narrow, deep and rather odorous drainage ditch on the opposite side of the cobblestone street.

As the lieutenant crawled stiffly from the rear seat and attempted to brush the creases back into his rumpled uniform, the squat, middle-aged Japanese driver began talking in rapid-fire syllables, addressing Ashdon and Sales as he waved vaguely at his surroundings.

The former leaned close, listening, nodding sympathetically and offering an occasional comment in his halting Japanese. Finally, the driver seemed satisfied. He smiled, bowed once to each of the three Marines and returned to the vehicle. As he drove away, the sergeants joined McCorkle, who waited impatiently before the Marine sentry guarding the huge open archway of the headquarters structure.

"What was that all about?" the officer asked grudgingly.

"He wanted to know how he was going to find his way back to Haneda."

"What did you tell him?"

Ashdon shrugged. "Told him to just take off. When he's missin' long enough, someone'll decide he's gone over th' hill with a piece of Government equipment. The MP's'll find him an' escort him back."

McCorkle shook his head in a sigh of defeat. This organization was no place for anyone with a sense of efficiency. Less so for a man with a sense of honor.

With their credentials checked by the sentry, the three signed the log and were directed to an upper floor, where a Marine lieutenant colonel shared an office with two sergeants.

"I know a bird colonel about my size," Sales declared, as they paused outside the door. "Maybe I can borrow a spare uniform from him." He raised his hand in open palmed signal, staring meaningfully at Ashdon. "See you aroun' th' campus. The Nichigeki about eight?"

Ashdon nodded, glancing at McCorkle as though for approval. "As long as I'm showin' the skipper the town, that sounds like a good stop for a beer."

As Sales sauntered away, his hard hat dangling loosely from his fingers, McCorkle stared after him, puzzled. "He's really going to borrow a uniform from a full colonel?" he wanted to know.

"I reckon, if he says so," was the laconic reply. "After all, we're a long way from Henderson Hall. We gotta sorta stick together an' share our resources."

Entering the office, the lieutenant and his sergeant stood before a high counter, where they went ignored for several minutes, while the occupants concentrated upon the cribbage game. But the moment that Ashdon mentioned the general's name in an overly loud tone, the light colonel and both sergeants looked up as one.

"What's this the general wants?" the senior officer demanded warily, peering from beneath a few wisps of hair. McCorkle noted that his face and hands were a pasty white, proof he rarely ventured from his catacomb; the mark of a true supply officer.

"It's all right here, sir," McCorkle told him with weary respect, holding aloft the crumpled Speed Letter. The colonel rose to accept the supply request and stare down at it for a moment, his gray face growing a scowl. Then, as though in disbelief, he called for one of the sergeants to bring his glasses. A few seconds later, he glanced up, squinting at McCorkle through the thick lenses.

"We can't give you all of this stuff," he protested indignantly. "Marine aviation's supposed to receive all its supplies from the Navy. That's the way the Book reads."

"Perhaps the colonel would like to contact the general by radio," Ashdon suggested gently. "He's been readin' your Supply Manual here of late, an' we get the impression he thinks it's lousy readin'. In fact, he don't even believe most of it."

McCorkle took a step rearward, recalling Barrymore's reaction in a similar situation. This lieutenant colonel glanced at him as though wondering whether he was going to stand for the sarcasm in the sergeant's tone. McCorkle looked away, but the staff officer proved only to be stubborn.

"You people over there in Korea can do anything you want," he declared accusingly, "but we are bound by regulations." He waved the requisition. "I don't have the authority to issue this to you."

"Then who does?" McCorkle asked suddenly. He realized he had been allowing Ashdon to do the ground breaking. He had to show that he was in charge of this project.

The lieutenant colonel thought for a moment, frowning. "I would say Colonel Smith-Smythe. He's the G-4. I suppose he could take the responsibility, if he chose."

"And where is the colonel's office?" McCorkle asked, the sudden touch of grimness in his tone covering any misgivings.

"Straight down the passageway. The door at the end." The promptness of the supply officer's reply made it obvious he was happy to be able to pass the buck. When a general sent a personal envoy for something, it was not good to be the man who offered the final refusal. "He can make the decision." He shoved the document toward McCorkle as though it was suddenly hot to the touch.

The full colonel's name was on the door at the end of the corridor, but the office was unoccupied except for a corporal who lurked behind a typewriter. He looked up, blinking at the interruption as McCorkle and Ashdon knocked, then entered.

"Where's Colonel Smith-Smythe?" Ashdon asked him, gesturing toward the empty desk at the end of the room.

"Some kinda staff meetin'. Least, that's where he said he was goin'." The corporal's tone indicated that the colonel was probably at a cocktail party or on the golf course.

"When's he due back?" the sergeant asked. This brought a shrug and a glance at the clock on the wall above the larger desk.

"It's near sixteen hunnert," the corporal explained. "He may not be back at all."

"Bankers' hours yet," Ashdon growled, glancing at McCorkle, who still clutched the paper bearing the general's signature. "This is Lieutenant McCorkle. He's representin' the Commandin' General of th' Wing."

The corporal, a thin, gangling youth barely out of his pimples, came to his feet, seemingly impressed with the introduction. "Is there anything I can do, sir?"

"Not unless you make the decisions around here." The officer wearily extended the supply order and the other took it, frowning down at the extensive list of wants.

"Maybe th' supply people down the hall could help you," the corporal suggested doubtfully.

"They sent us here," Ashdon explained disgustedly and the corporal nodded his understanding.

"They usually do. Why not step down th' hall for some coffee, while I try t'get Colonel Ess-Ess on th' phone and tell him you're waitin'?"

"That would be nice," McCorkle agreed.

The coffee was a welcome relief from that made by Henry and was nearly passable. McCorkle noted that the coffee urn was scrubbed to a bright shine, probably a daily ritual for some private or seaman last class. In this small room off the corridor, he and Ashdon leaned against the makeshift coffee bar, enjoying the aroma from the steaming white mugs.

"I don't know whether we're making progress or not," McCorkle pondered, staring into the thick black brew.

The technical sergeant looked at him with an amused smile. "Some of these people can get so frustrated with all th' red tape that they finally figger it's easier t'do nothin' than t'fight it," he philosophized. "Now an' then, it takes a little shock power t'shake 'em outa that lethargy an' get 'em back to fightin' th' war." He glanced at his watch. "We'd better get back or that meathead'll be lockin' the door and blowin' th' joint."

The corporal was just hanging up the telephone and still had the Speed Letter in his hand. He cast a sorrowful glance at the pair as he shook his head.

"Nothin' you kin do t'night," he decreed. "The colonel ain't comin' back. Said he's already late for some social doin's over at th' Imperial Hotel."

"When will he be back?" McCorkle asked, his frustration reflected in the pointedness of the question.

"He comes in about oh-nine hunnert. Tole me t'leave this in his basket an' he'd look at it in the mornin'. He didn't sound too enthusiastic, though."

"Thanks for all your help, buddy," Ashdon replied sarcastically. Either it went over the other man's head or he chose to ignore it.

"That's why we're here, sarge," he replied cheerfully, covering his typewriter and reaching for the light switch. "Always ready to back up the Fleet Marine Force."

"Yeah? Into what corner?" the sergeant growled.

As the officer and sergeant sauntered down the passageway, most of the other doors now were locked, the lights within no longer burning. Ashdon paused and McCorkle turned to him questioningly.

"Lieutenant," Ashdon began dubiously, "I don't want'cha t'think I'm like some other folks we know, but this runaround might seem less frustratin' if we had a drink."

"Several," was the grim agreement.

# CHAPTER 9

**M**cCORKLE STOOD at the bar, nursing a drink and watching the Japanese combo struggle to translate American jazz into the local musical idiom. Sipping at the rice beer, he was blaming himself for allowing Ashdon to take the lead in the effort to get supplies that afternoon. It had been his assignment and he should have been the one to carry it out. Instead, it had been easier to allow the sergeant to make the contact, do the arguing. He glanced at Ashdon, huddled with the two girls, whispering in undertones, then attempted to pretend he hadn't noticed.

One of the girls, a solid, stolid post-teenager with a front tooth of gold, stared at him critically, then turned back to the sergeant to wrinkle her nose in a show of derision. "But he's 'n officer," she protested in a stage whisper. "I don' wanna go wi' officer. They alla-time stingy boys."

"Listen to me, Suki," Ashdon ordered shortly. "Just remember that he don't act like that kinda officer. He don't even think that way!"

The girl turned to survey McCorkle more closely, showing only minor interest. "Z'at so," she hissed thoughtfully. "Wha' does he think like?"

McCorkle wondered rather vaguely whether he was being complimented or slandered by the sergeant, but it was a technical question and Ashdon brushed it aside impatiently. "Hell, I don't know. A lotta people, prob'ly includin' a two-star general, are workin' nights t'figger that out."

"He looks sorta nice," the girl conceded, still staring at this man of mystery. As for McCorkle, his show of unconcern was only a cover for rank embarrassment. This had been a mistake, one of his own making. Ashdon, he realized, was drunk and he should get out of here before the familiarities progressed any farther, except that he didn't know where the hell he was.

"Then quit standin' there," Ashdon urged the one called Suki, his arm encircling the other girl's thin waist, hand creeping toward the round of her bosom. "Let's let lechery leap!"

The huge quantities of rice beer which he had been downing, bottle for bottle, with the sergeant had created a glow for McCorkle, too. He was verging upon drunkenness, but he realized it. He realized, too, that he could not afford to make an ass of himself in front of an enlisted man. It wasn't done.

"We gotta ge' outta here," he slurred. "Gotta fine some place t'sack out."

"Yes, sir," the sergeant agreed owlishly. "An' I know jess th' place, but we gotta find Jack Sales firs', less we wanna swim t'Chosin wi' alla that camera gear on our backs."

McCorkle gripped the edge of the bar, stiffening to keep from swaying. The attempt was not entirely successful. "He said so'thin' about meetin' us later," he recalled. "Some place called th' Nickodemus."

"Th' Nichigeki Music Hall," Ashdon prompted. "He's prob'ly doin' the las' show there now."

"What?" There was puzzlement in McCorkle's tone, but Ashdon preferred not to hear.

"We'll take th' girls along," he decreed, glancing over his shoulder to the one with the glaring gold tooth. "We'll gather in ol' Sales, hava few brews, then get set up. I know jess th' spot."

"Her?" McCorkle frowned, staring past the sergeant's bulky shoulder at the yellow metal flashing signals in the dim light. It occurred to him that, under the right conditions of lighting, the girl could send Morse code messages simply by opening and closing her mouth at the correct intervals.

"She's a lotta kicks, skipper," Ashdon insisted staunchly, as though introducing a time-worn maiden aunt. "Name's Suki."

"No it ain't," the girl cut in, pouting over the gold tooth. "Tha's my Monday name. This is Tuesday. I'm Mitzi."

McCorkle leaned closer to stare at her, still frowning. "An' what happens at midnight, m'dear," he asked with a grandeur fostered by alcohol. "Does your tooth turn into a gold'n pumpkin?"

"No, it don't," the girl declared, staring at him in exasperation.

"At mi-night, it's Wednesday. An' after that, my name's Betty."

"Never mind, skipper," Ashdon chided gently. "It's a li'l game w' some of these broads. B'sides, it keeps the local vice squad confused.

"You'll like Suki," he promised. "She already thinks you're great."

"Mitzi," the girl corrected angrily, stamping her foot.

"Sure, sure," McCorkle agreed amiably, guardedly clutching the edge of the bar. He realized that the dubious protective facade of officer and gentleman had been damaged; there was the rationalization, too, that he had gone too far now to return to the womb of respectability, but he fought accepting it. "But I gotta get in a sack. An' soon." He could always escape in slumber.

"That's th' gen'ral idea," the sergeant agreed on an evil note, leading the way across the dance floor to the entrance. McCorkle followed, glancing about self-consciously to determine whether anyone noted that he was being led by an enlisted man. No one looked in his direction in spite of the scattering of uniforms.

In the street below, they found one of the small, compact, poorly used Japanese taxicabs and all piled into the cramped rear seat. While Ashdon pinched and kneaded the girl on his lap, the one who called herself Mitzi clung to McCorkle, openly disappointed at his reluctance to follow the sergeant's example.

"Whassa mattah you, lootenant?" she wanted to know, turning her head to smile at him. "You don' ack like no Marine I know b'fore. You don' even try t'police a li'l feel."

"The term is 'cop a feel'," Ashdon corrected her painfully. "Don'tcha even try to remember th' English we teach you?"

"You tole me 'cop' was slang an' wasn' good Engliss," the girl insisted, still eyeing McCorkle hopefully, but he had retreated into the corner of the seat. He pretended to watch the street lights and strange neon designs that flashed in a kaleidoscope of color and action, while the driver whirled the little vehicle through hordes of evening traffic, constantly leaning on his klaxon-like horn.

The driver brought the laboring cab to a crunching halt before a huge European-style structure that was at least eight stories in height. As they crawled through the low door held open by the bowing driver, McCorkle reached to his breast pocket for money, but Ashdon already had his hand filled with *yen* notes, arguing in pidgin English over the fare.

As the lieutenant started to cross the sidewalk to the brilliantly lighted marquee advertising a Japanese movie, Ashdon grabbed his elbow to halt him, offering a shake of the head.

"This ain't it, skipper," he explained briefly. "It ain't no movie. We gotta take th' elevator." The two Marines and the pair of Japanese girls, all rumpled from the close contact in the diminutive cab, were the only passengers in the cage as it carried them along on creaking cables. Several times the elevator came to a near halt, then seemed to recover and continued aloft, while McCorkle stared upward, eyeing the escape hatch in the top of the enclosed cubicle.

The tall, thin girl had Ashdon's arms clamped about her, but each time one of his hands crawled higher, grasping hungrily for her bosom, she pushed it sedately away from her breasts, casting embarrassed, apologetic glances at the officer. McCorkle pretended not to notice, but the one called Mitzi on Tuesdays thought Ashdon's frustrated attempts humorous and kept poking McCorkle in the ribs to direct his attention to the other pair. Instead, the lieutenant continued to inspect the grilling in the top of the flimsy cage, feeling the color rising above his collar and into his face. Mitzi must have noticed this, too, for she began to giggle even more strongly.

At the top floor, the car shuddered to an uncertain halt and the four moved into a narrow corridor. It was dimly lighted and somewhere close by McCorkle could make out the tinny measures of music that was even worse than the music of the dance hall they had just left. This group played in a rhythm and tempo that made the tune virtually unrecognizable.

"He'll be backstage," Ashdon ventured knowingly as he whirled and made for a heavy sheet metal door facing upon the corridor. The two girls fell in behind him, as though old hands at this odd game of follow the leader. McCorkle, uncertain, somewhat groggy from the close confines of the elevator, followed without protest.

An instant later, a blast of cold air hit him full in the face. As the metal door snapped shut behind him on a clanging note, he found himself on an open roof. The theater must cover only a portion of the building's top floor, he reasoned, squinting until he could make out the walls of the last story looming above him in the star-studded darkness. The metallic sounds from the orchestra still assailed his ears, but they were muffled now.

Indian file, the four crossed the open roof under Ashdon's seemingly practiced leadership, then McCorkle was blinded by a sudden glare, as another door was abruptly opened. The rice beer starting to wear off in favor of a hangover, the wild, disjointed beat of drums throbbed against his aching temples.

As he stepped through the doorway, still blinded by the harsh light, he stumbled and fell headlong into a mass of quivering flesh. There was a surprised grunt, recognizable as being feminine, as he fought to right himself, arms and legs flailing wildly. A pair of strong hands suddenly grasped him firmly beneath the armpits and set him upright.

"Thank you," the officer muttered in apology, then shrank back in horror. He was staring head-on at a pair of huge, balloon-like breasts that were precisely at eye level. He shook his head, still blinking against the brightness, unwilling to believe what he was seeing, but he had been right the first time.

The huge Oriental girl, nearly six feet tall and perfectly proportioned, was standing on the six-inch beam that ran along the rear wall. It was she who had helped him recover his balance; except for a sequined G-string and a revolting headdress suggesting a Sioux warbonnet, she was totally naked.

Then the tinny music, the double beat, began to make sense to McCorkle. He was in a burlesque house. Backstage in a strip joint!

Feeling the blood rushing up his neck and face in a scarlet wave of embarrassment, McCorkle took another step backward, seeking escape, muttering vague, jumbled apologies to the girl, whose blue-black hair hung nearly to her waist. She noted his expression of abject panic and began to chuckle, the twin globules of flesh vibrating in what should have been a delightful manner. Terror-stricken, McCorkle whirled, looking for sanctuary.

Ashdon and the two Japanese girls were standing in the wings, staring out to the runway. He rushed toward them, then paused, staring over the sergeant's shoulder.

The mood of the music had changed and the Japanese orchestra no longer was attempting to copy the current juke box winners. Instead, the tune was typically Oriental. On the stage, a nude girl bearing a curved samurai sword was making war apparently upon an equally nude woman, who wore what appeared to be the mane of a lion.

McCorkle was hardly new to burlesque. There had been dingy, ill-kept theaters in Minneapolis, Chicago and Kansas City during his college years. These usually had been visited in company with other students after football games or other respectable jaunts, but those others never had been like this, he reflected. With members of the vice squad invariably in the audience, the performers were forced to keep their bosoms covered, their G-strings large and their acts sterile.

Ashdon shook his head, turning to glance at McCorkle, frowning with a hint of worry.

"I thought maybe he'd be on th' other side of th' stage," he explained. "In th' other wing, but I don't see him."

"Sales?" McCorkle asked vaguely. "What's going on here, sergeant? I'd like to know."

Ashdon shook his head again, still frowning. "Nothin' t'sweat yourself over, lieutenant." The suddenly formal note was not lost upon McCorkle, as the sergeant continued. "It's just that he has some mighty funny hobbies when he gets sorta tanked up."

McCorkle glanced over his shoulder at the dozen or so nude Japanese women behind him in the wings. One of them had removed her G-string and was nonchalantly selecting another one — a bright shade of red — from a stand near the door through which they had entered. He quickly averted his eyes, staring again at the two women on the stage. With his eyes used to the light, he could see beyond the footlights and make out Caucasian faces as well as the glittering brass ornaments of army uniforms and the parallel white piping on Navy dress blues.

"I'd better check aroun'n see if I c'n locate him," Ashdon muttered. He didn't wait for McCorkle's approval, but turned and moved away, flanking the group of strippers to make his way behind the back drop of the stage.

Mitzi nudged him in the ribs and McCorkle glanced down at her smiling face. The gold tooth in the front of her mouth seemed to gather the light, reflecting it.

"You like?" she asked enthusiastically. McCorkle hesitated, then waved a vague hand toward the stage.

"What are they supposed to be doing?" he asked meekly.

"Thass *kabuki shibai*," the girl explained on a proud note. *"Ichibon* curture."

"Curture?" McCorkle echoed in his puzzlement.

"Curture," she agreed positively. "Rike Shakespeare."

"Culture, you mean."

She nodded her head, disturbed at his lack of understanding. "Thass what I said. Curture."

"But what's it all about?" he wanted to know.

"Iss an ole, ole story 'bout a samurai who srays a rion," the girl explained.

"Slays a lion?" he asked, wanting to be certain in spite of the obvious. "Is this the way it's always done?"

"No, no," the girl protested. "Not rike tis. But they do this way to make gee-eyes happy-happy."

McCorkle looked again. The girl wearing the lion head piece was shaking her head in a wild rotating motion that caused the long tail attached to the mane to rotate in a strange circular motion. He noted, too, that her breasts were rotating, but in opposite directions.

"You're right, of course," he agreed somewhat gloomily. "That's real culture."

"Suah." Mitzie agreed, flashing the gold tooth at him for emphasis. But McCorkle no longer was paying attention. Eyes shaded against the light, he was staring past the performers to the opposite wing, where he could see Ashdon. The sergeant stood there, glancing about, then he spoke to another naked dancer and McCorkle could see her shake her head with a shrug. Ashton turned and disappeared into the darkness beyond.

Five minutes later, the sergeant was at McCorkle's shoulder. "Couldn't find him," he muttered.

"What makes you think he's here?" McCorkle asked, causing the sergeant to nod his head.

"He's here," he promised and there was a glum note of foreboding in his tone that caused McCorkle to look at him more closely. The worried frown still wrinkled his forehead.

There was a sudden crash of cymbals and rattle of drums and the officer turned in time to see the girl with the sword slay the lion. The girl in the lion's mane dropped to the floor for a moment, while the female samurai went through the motions of declaring victory. Then as the music died, there was polite applause from the audience. It was obvious that the military audience didn't care much about culture. A moment later, the lion rose and both of them scurried toward the wing where the Marines stood. McCorkle gave way, but the lion girl brushed past him, pressing her breasts against his chest, while he, in turn, backed against Mitzi, trying to avoid the contact.

The orchestra suddenly struck up a tune that McCorkle recognized after a few moments of concentration. As the dubious strains of *You Must Have Been A Beautiful Baby* echoed lustily if not beautifully against the walls, Ashdon uttered a groan.

"Oh, oh," he muttered, staring out over the stage. McCorkle looked, too, but all he saw was the huge Japanese girl with whom he had made initial contact. Now minus the Indian war bonnet, she stepped onto the stage and began to dance slowly, sensuously to the music.

"What's that mean?" McCorkle asked in confusion, wanting Ashdon to interpret his two syllables.

"That's his song," Ashdon explained, not looking at the officer. McCorkle looked at Mitzi, then to the latter girl, seeking further explanation, but both of them were staring expectantly toward the stage. Suddenly, his own attention was drawn back to the spotlighted area by a sudden roar of approval.

Closest to him, leaning against the corner of the painted scenery, seemingly bored, was the Japanese girl. In her position, one hip thrust out from her body, weight on one foot, her show of nonchalance could best be described as shocking.

But that was tame compared to what the unnerved, perspiring lieutenant beheld in the center of the stage. Outlined in the glare of the overhead spotlight was a nearly nude man with a large tattoo inscribed over his chest and belly. A spike mustache protruded jauntily from each side of his red, sweat-glazed face.

Except for cordovan brown shoes and socks, he wore nothing except faded Marine-green shorts that were in danger of falling over his narrow hips. And with each exotic beat of the music, he twisted and turned with practiced but sensual dignity. Each flexed muscle in his chest and stomach reacted upon the tattooed figure of the nude dancer impregnated into his skin. She seemed to be dancing rather than he.

McCorkle stared in an open-mouthed awe for several seconds, unable or unwilling to accept what he was seeing.

"Take it off!" Someone was shouting from the audience and the demand was immediately followed by other loudly voiced bawdy suggestions. It brought McCorkle back to reality.

"Get him off of there!" he hissed into Ashdon's ear. The sergeant turned to stare at him cynically.

"What do you suggest?" Ashdon asked with cool tone. "Go drag him off bodily?"

"But we have to get him off!" McCorkle insisted, then a new thought struck him. "You knew he was going to do this," he declared accusingly.

"I told you he has some strange impulses when he drinks," the sergeant conceded.

"You called it a hobby!" McCorkle declared, forgetting to keep his voice down. This brought a glare of disapproval from the man in the middle of the stage. Behind them, the two Japanese girls were giggling at the exchange between the pair. McCorkle glanced over his shoulder at them and was surprised to see that what must have comprised the entire cast had gathered in the wings, staring past them at the flying sergeant. Most of them were grinning, while others appeared almost jealous.

"He's making a damned fool of himself," McCorkle declared, lowering his voice in view of the audience of performers.

"He's makin' a double-cheeked ass outa himself," the sergeant agreed, making no move to correct the impression.

"Take it off, sarge," a brash American voice shrieked from the audience.

*"Hai, hai!"* echoed a shrill Japanese tone. "Take off! Take off!"

"Go, man! Go! Go! Go!"

There were other shouts of encouragement in the lyrical tongue McCorkle recognized as Japanese. His eyes were on the sergeant in the middle of the stage. What the hell does he do as a climax? he wondered wildly.

Suddenly, Ashdon stiffened, blocking McCorkle's view, as he stared out over the heads of the audience. Then he whirled.

"Move out!" he cried. "It's the fuzz!"

Staring beyond the shaft of brightness that outlined Sales in the middle of the stage, McCorkle could make out the bullet shapes of several white-painted helmet liners. Military police. Darker shadows, dressed in studious black uniforms, must be Japanese police.

Suddenly a whistle shrilled at the rear of the theater. The music died a strangling, discordant death and Sales halted in mid-grind, staring.

"Don't nobody move!" a gruff voice called from the rear of the audience. "It's a raid!"

The declaration was repeated in Japanese by one of the local officers, and there were cries of derision and anger from the Oriental customers. Then the lights went out.

"Skipper!" Ashdon's voice hissed with urgency amid the melee of clattering high heels, police whistles and shouts of outrage. "Get the girls out on the roof. I gotta get that maniac!"

McCorkle plunged his hands into the darkness before him, then withdrew them as though burned. His fingers had firmly grasped a heaving bare breast instead of the thin arm he sought. There was an intake of surprised breath in the blackness, but if anyone swung at him, the blow went astray amid the bedlam.

After careful groping, he got each of the girls gingerly by an elbow, drawing them close. "The roof," he muttered, wondering whether either understood amid the noise. He wasn't even certain he had the right girls. "Let's get to the roof!"

He became completely disoriented amid the shoving press of nude bodies, but he managed to cling to the two Japanese, as they joined the rush, and a moment later, pushed through the door through which they had entered. Confused by the pressure of warm nudity and the tantilizing mixture of perfumes, he had followed the pair more than he had led.

On the roof, trembling now, McCorkle released his hold on the girls. They stopped in their tracks, turning to stare at him with obvious glee, while he sucked huge draughts of cold, crisp air into his paralyzed lungs.

An instant later, Sergeant Sales, still clad in his baggy shorts, was catapulted through the doorway. Ashdon followed by a scant pace before the door clanged shut.

Sales, shuddering at the sting of the cold air upon his perspiring nakedness, cursed, then turned to Ashdon, not seeing the officer. He rocked drunkenly back and forth on his heels.

"You loused up my finale, you bastard!"

"I just kept you from gettin' your silly ass locked up in a Nip jail. Why d'you hafta pull this every time you get your hide fulla *saki?*"

Sales straightened to pretend indignation. "Hell, you think I'd do it sober?

"Besides, I'm only imparting a little culture to a defeated people. There ain't a broad in the whole damn place knows as much about sheddin' as my Aunt Tessie."

"Yeah?" Ashdon snarled. "Where's she playin'?" Before the pilot could frame a reply, Ashdon glanced anxiously toward the heavy metal door, then to McCorkle, who was totally sober by now.

"What're we gonna do, skipper? Throw him to the wolves?" He jerked an unsympathetic thumb toward Sales.

"Huh?" The officer was uncertain as to why his opinion was being sought.

"Those MPs'll be out here. If they spot Sales, they'll lock him up. But you might be able to dazzle 'em with your bars."

"Or get us all hauled in," McCorkle shook his head. "I don't want to get involved."

Ashdon shrugged noncommitally. "Okay, we'll let 'em have him. It's his own damn fault." But there was disappointment in his tone.

McCorkle glanced at Sales, who stood with his back to him, shoulders sagging, then back to Ashdon. He suspected he was being used, but he recalled the Chief-of-Staff's wrath when he had suggested turning the stolen jeep back to the Army. Such a move would be sacrilege. Was stealing a prisoner from them any different? And there also was a matter of loyalty that had been pounded into him for hour after hour at OCS.

"Wait," he ordered, stretching to his full height, taking a deep breath of surrender. "Get him over there out of sight. In the dark. Move!"

Sales might have debated his decision, but Ashdon gave the pilot an ugly shove that sent him careening into the shadows. It was none too soon. As the sergeant grabbed the thin girl and followed Sales, the door squeaked open and two Army policemen looked out, then stepped onto the roof, their white helmets contrasting with the darkness.

"What're you doin' out here, lieutenant?" one demanded suspiciously, glancing at Mitzi, then back to the officer. McCorkle was shaking, but he drew a protective arm about her shoulder and she cuddled cooperatively in the hollow of his elbow.

"Looking at the moon," the officer replied, trying for just the right degree of hauteur but failing. His voice sounded thin and high pitched. There was no moon, but he had to pursue it. "Is this your regular beat? Across the rooftops?"

The MP's must have mistaken his tone for coldness. One a sergeant, the other a private first class, they touched the forward edges of their helmets in salute.

"You didn't see a naked Marine come through that door, did you, sir?" the sergeant asked, glancing about furtively.

"I am a Marine, but I'm hardly naked." As his voice came down an octave, McCorkle gained confidence. "What is your name, sergeant?"

This question, aimed specifically at putting the other on the defensive, dissolved some of the MP's arrogance and he took a step backward, saluted again. "Nothin' t'worry about, sir. Justa case of indecent exposure. Some Marine drifted in here an' took the act away from the girls." The other was already drifting toward the door.

As the door clanged shut behind the soldiers, there was a vague stirring in the far corner of the roof, then Ashdon and Sales emerged from the protective shadows with the thin girl.

"You did that like you've been battlin' cops alla your life," Sales muttered thankfully. "An Academy Award performance. Better'n mine even."

McCorkle ignored the compliment, still a trifle confused at his own daring; surprised at its success. "Let's get out of here."

"I can't lootenant," Sales declared sheepishly, waving a hand in the direction of the stage door. "That colonel's uniform's still in there. His name's sewed in the linin', an' that could cause all sortsa embarrassment."

"Embarrassment to whom?" McCorkle demanded with stern correctness.

"To him," was the surprised reply. "What would happen if them cops found a colonel's uniform in a stripper's dressin' room. 'Specially if the colonel wasn't in it?"

McCorkle glanced at Ashdon, nodding. "Better get the uniform, sergeant." Ashdon shuffled his feet uncomfortable, looking at the door, then at his commander.

"They're lookin' for a sergeant in there, skipper," he reminded delicately.

McCorkle considered, realizing that the chore had returned to him. "What kind of fellow is this colonel?"

"He loaned me his uniform, didn't he?" Sales demanded defensively.

"Okay," McCorkle surrendered, not liking it. "Stay here. I'll be right back."

"In the room with the star on the door," the pilot instructed.

McCorkle waved the others back to the cover of the shadows, then braced his shoulders and turned to the door. As he pulled it

85

open, the blast of sour brass again assailed his senses. The show had been interrupted only temporarily and there was another Oriental under the spotlight, tossing segments of her attire to the squealing audience.

Still cautious, he ventured through the backstage area until he spotted the door with the huge gilt star. There was no reply to his hesitant knock, so he pushed open the door.

Under the single light bulb, he found the statuesque stripper who had been in the wings. She stood with a green blouse, colonel's eagles on the shoulders, in one hand. In the other, she held a slightly rumpled pair of trousers.

She glanced inquiringly at McCorkle, as blushing, he reached for the uniform. The girl was even minus her G-string now, and he averted his eyes.

"I din' know Jack wassa colonel," the dark brunette said conversationally. "Tell 'im he doessa lovely strip!"

# CHAPTER 10

**S**ALES WAS little the worse for wear as a result of the night's escapade, or he may still have been a trifle drunk. Ashdon, squinting at him in the light of the new dawn, tried to determine which was the case, but decided it was too much effort with his hangover. He dropped back onto the Japanese mat. It was easier to let him talk.

"Yes, sir, Ash, there I was: Fat, dumb and secure, sittin' at El Toro, figgerin' I'd while away the rest of this clambake in the confines of Southern Cal. That was till I made a grave social error.

"I was on twenty-four hours, then off forty-eight, with the Air-Sea Rescue outfit. Everybody else that came through was bound for Chosin, but me. With all that free time, I even had my eye on a gas station to rent.

"But I was hangin' around one mornin', when the phone rang an' some character said he was from *Life* Magazine. He was doin' some sorta story on beach livin', an' this woman he was interviewin' had mentioned that one of our 'copters flew up an' down th' beach every mornin' an' evenin'. He wanted to know if I'd come down with a 'copter so he could take some pictures for his story.

"I'd just got off duty an' wasn't doin' anything, so I told him I'd be right along. I called the Information Office an' some sergeant answered. I told him what I was gonna do in the name of public relations, so he volunteered to go along."

Sales pushed himself up on one elbow and reached to the edge of the mat for the bottle of flat beer. He took a long sip, then went on.

"We cranked up'n took off for the beach area, where this camera cat was waitin'. It ain't more'n a dozen miles, and sure enough, he was standin' in the middle of a vacant lot, wavin' me in. The lot was a little tight, but I landed an' he invited us in for a drink while we talked about what he wanted us to do for his pictures."

Sales paused for breath and Ashdon found himself holding his own. He was propped up on an elbow, staring across the several feet that separated the low Japanese beds.

"I knew when we landed that the blades had cut off some stuff that was growin' over th' wall next door, but I didn't pay much attention. We had a drink, talked it over, then when I started up the machine, I musta chopped down some more flowers. The ole gal next door was on the phone, screamin' at the operations officer at El Toro about a crazy Marine cuttin' down her prize rose garden with a helicopter. He was tellin' her it couldn't be one of his, 'cause he didn't have a plane logged out."

"You hadn't checked out the ship?" Ashdon asked incredulously.

"Well," Sales defended, "with all this talk about a cover on *Life* an' the excitement, it sort of slipped my mind."

"Christ!" Ashdon offered in a show of sympathy.

"So, with this public information sergeant makin' like my co-pilot, I'm doin' all sortsa fancy passes up an' down the beach, while this guy's shootin' his pictures from the window. That was when the plane decided to catch fire."

"Oh, no!" Ashdon groaned.

"There was an open strip of beach there in front of those houses, so I set the 'copter down there, streamin' smoke an' cuttin' a few more roses that were hangin' over th' fence. Someone'd had sense enough to call the local fire department an' they had a truck there by the time I got on the ground, but by now this little ole flower fancier's back on the horn, readin' the numbers on my machine to the operations office. He finally had to admit he just might be short a plane and he asked that I get on th' phone."

Ashdon was trying hard not to laugh, maintaining with effort his frown of sympathetic understanding, but Sales seemed not to notice.

"I tried to explain t'the captain what'd happened an' how I'd just been tryin' to do my part for the Marine Corps' image, whatever that is," the pilot explained, a touch of self-pity in his tone. "He seemed almost understandin' till I explained how I couldn't get the chopper back in the air, an' they better get one of them low-boy trucks an' a crane t'lift it outa the sand so's we could haul it back to th' air station.

"An' durin' alla this, a coupla hundred people showed up to see what was on fire, then another thousand or so come along and blocked the street so traffic was backed up the whole forty miles to Los Angeles with th' Highway Patrol tryin' to untangle it. That was about th' time th' operations officer said th' commandin' general wanted t'see me th' minute I got back aboard th' station."

Ashdon shook his brown bottle and found that it was empty. "So what happened?"

"It was dark by th' time we got back to El Toro," Sales explained morosely. "We found th' Ole Man had left word we were to come directly t'his quarters. We went marchin' up there like it was to our own hangin'.

"He hadda party goin', so his aide told us t'go around to th' back door an' wait in th' kitchen. We was standin' there at attention, wonderin' how many years we'd get, when th' Cee Gee come in. He didn't say a word at first. Just walked over an' got down three glasses, then poured three fingers of bourbon in each of 'em. That was when he told us t'sit down an' handed us the booze. We all drank up, then he told us."

"I don't want to hear any excuses!" Sales mimicked in a world-weary tone. "I don't even want to know what happened. I wouldn't believe it anyhow. But I never want to see either of you bastards again!'"

"That's all that happened?"

"I'm in Korea, ain't I?" was Sales' disgruntled reply. "Come on. Let's finda beer for my hangover."

"I gotta find a phone, too," Ashdon reminded. "Gotta call that corporal and see whether his colonel decided on those supplies."

"Ain't you th' eager one," the pilot chided.

In the adjoining room, McCorkle was unaware of how much of the monologue he had overheard in his restless sleep. He came fully awake with a start that could have been caused by the sound of a sliding door, or it may simply have been the throbbing of his head.

For an instant, the bare white walls and the soft morning light caused him to think rather fuzzily that he was back in Hollywood and there had been a weekend party.

The stale taste of Asahi rice beer still clung to his mouth, and as he attempted to bring the molecules of his brain into some sort of align-ment, he silently cursed Ashdon and Sales. At the same time, he was undergoing some of the mental torment that has plagued drunks since the first grape was fermented.

Foremost was a feeling of failure. He had been sent here to accomplish a seemingly simple task, but if anything, he was further from getting the needed supplies than when he had landed in the antiquated old aircraft. There had been frustration in the runaround he had been accorded, but he had shown weakness in succumbing to that frustration so soon.

His other recriminations were vague, unrealistic as he attempted to piece together the evening, wondering how much of a fool he had been in company with the two enlisted men. And the girl with the gold tooth. What had happened to her?

In spite of the pain lancing through his temples, he sat up abruptly to glance at the rumpled but empty half of the thick mat, then mut-tered dejectedly, "There's that much to be thankful for." Lowering his head back to the pillow, he stared moodily at the blank ceiling. How was he going to obtain a promise of silence concerning this escapade without openly threatening the two sergeants?

Once clear of the theater and with Sales back in the borrowed uniform, there had been several more bars and more of the potent rice beer. As a result of his handling of the two military policemen, he had held the role of temporary hero. Worse, he had accepted the role, trying to live up to it in the eyes of the two sergeants. The so-briety he had regained on the icy roof had been short lived, and he soon had begun to look upon the girl's gold tooth as some sort of lucky talisman.

Remembering the girl, he rolled to the edge of the thick bed mat, reaching to where his uniform was neatly folded. He rummaged through the pockets until he found his wallet, then sighed in relief, as he found his money more or less intact.

As he started to stuff the folded leather back into his trousers pock-et, a white card fluttered to the floor. He picked it up and angled it toward the high window.

Emblazoned across the face of the card in glaring red was:

*DO NOT PATRONIZE THESE EVIL PIMPS!*

Beneath, in sedate wedding invitation script, he read:

*For Clazzy Girls, Great Fun, Excellent Liquor,*
*Come To The World Famed*
*ICHANIMISU HOTEL*


Beneath, in Japanese characters, was what he assumed to be the address. The lieutenant wrinkled his nose and stuffed the card beneath the thick pad. Then he rolled onto his back and shut his eyes, refusing to admit he had allowed the pair to lure him into a cat house!

Something had to be done, he realized. It may have been his current state of physical misery that suddenly had made his situation clear, but he knew that instead of leading, he was being led. The manner in which Ashdon had simply taken charge yesterday at COMNAVFE, leaving him to shift his feet in the background, made this obvious. Through his own reluctance, he had allowed things to get out of hand, but what puzzled him most was where he was to start if they were to be put right.

And for a moment, he thought of Major Lawrence, wondering if he ever had felt the same. A little sadly, he decided that the dead major probably had not. He had been secure enough that he had been able to roll with the punches, yet retaining the respect of the men beneath him.

As the officer opened his eyes and allowed them to adjust to the growing light, head still throbbing, he reviewed the chain of incidents since his arrival. The run-in with the chaplain; even the events leading up to incurring the animosity of Barrymore, not to mention the matter of the two MP's on the roof, had resulted from his efforts to act as a buffer between his own men and the brass.

He could rationalize the idea that, in each instance, he had been a victim of circumstances, but this was hardly true. He could simply have turned Sales over to the military police.

It had something to do with loyalty. Somewhere, back in the volumes he had absorbed about the Marine Corps and its leaders, there had been a statement concerning that illusive quality called Leadership: Loyalty operates in both directions; from the top down, as well as upward from the bottom. But he couldn't help wondering what degree of loyalty he could expect from Ashdon and Sales in seeing that word of this fiasco wasn't spread.

His thoughts were interrupted by a discrete tap at the paper panel and he pushed himself up on an elbow, frowning. "Yes?"

"Your bath is ready, Lieutenant-*san*," a soft, feminine voice replied, tone steeped in respect.

"What bath?"

"For your hangover. You'll feel much improved after," the voice promised. The rice paper panel squeaked in protest, then was pushed back and a head was poked cautiously into the room.

McCorkle had expected the girl with the gold tooth, but as he slowly sat up, he noted the black hair, brown eyes and her olive skin. She was dressed in the traditional kimono and *obi*, the wide padded belt that holds the gown in at the waist. Her bare feet were small and delicately formed, he noted in that initial glance.

"Come in," he invited, thinking of the card tucked beneath the sleeping pad. *Clazzy girls*, it had promised.

She took a tentative step into the room and extended a hand. It held one of the familiar brown quart bottles.

"*Biru*," she explained, "it will help your head."

"What do you know about my head?" He was suspicious, thinking of Ashdon and Sales. The girl suppressed a snicker.

"I saw you when you came in last night." She nodded for emphasis. "You have a bad head."

McCorkle wanted to ask whether the girl with the gold tooth had still been with him. Instead, he sighed an admission of defeat and accepted the bottle.

"They always told me any man who drinks before breakfast is on the way to acute alcoholism," he muttered, tipping up the glass neck. There was the bite of the amber liquid against his raw throat and he grimaced as he lowered the bottle to look up at the girl.

"Do you work here?" he asked, thinking of the inscribed promise on the business card. "This is the Ichanimisu Hotel, is it not?"

"I work for my father," she said gravely, her brown eyes upon his face. "He owns the hotel."

"And you're not one of those girls?" He waved a vague hand, glancing away, wondering why he had asked. "The ones mentioned on that card?"

"You want a girl?" she asked matter-of-factly, no change in her grave, searching expression.

McCorkle stared at her, trying to find something to criticize in the shoulder-length black hair. It was straight, but broken by a gentle curl at the ends. Her eyebrows were thin and precise above her soft, brown eyes. Pink tinged the olive of her skin and the shade seemed to deepen in the gentle sweep beneath her chin. Her mouth was small, delicately formed, the lips brightened by a touch of lipstick, but she wore no other make-up.

In spite of the fullness of the kimono, there was the valley of shadowed cleavage behind the plunging neckline, the gentle rise of a full bosom beneath the flowered cloth.

"A girl?" she repeated.

McCorkle shook his head, frowning. "No thanks." He had heard that the Japanese tended to look upon sex as a convenience, a natural biological necessity, but he had hardly expected such nonchalance. "What's your name?"

"Tomi," she replied simply. "You are Joe-*san*."

"How'd you know that?"

"The sergeants told me," she explained with the same directness. "They said I could call you that."

"They did, did they?" he grunted with irritation, tipping the bottle to his mouth. That matter of loyalty was in the front of his mind, again, but he was beginning to feel better. The beer was washing away some of his tenseness, soothing the ache in his head.

"Where are the sergeants?" he asked pointedly.

"In the bar. You don't like them?" she wanted to know, her tone taking on a troubled quality.

"It's something you might not understand," he explained, not certain that he understood himself. "It's a thing called discipline."

"I do understand," she insisted stiffly. "You are a lieutenant, they are enlisted, and never is the twain supposed to meet."

"Thank you, Rudyard Kipling," he grunted with a touch of sarcasm, wondering how he had gotten into this discussion and whether he could win.

"My name is Tomi and your bath is ready," she said with sudden formality, turning toward the open door. "This way, please."

As she disappeared through the opening, McCorkle struggled to his feet, gathering the silk sheet about his waist. Trailing its length in his wake, he followed her down the narrow hallway lined with closed doors. At the end of the corridor, she suddenly opened another door and waved him through.

The room was like a miniature of the swimming pool at the YMCA back home; no frills — no lockers either, in this case — just lots of concrete and the small pool filled with water. But judging from the steam rising in humid waves, hanging over its surface, it was obviously close to the boiling point.

He turned to glance at the girl, but she was closing the heavy door through which they had just come. "I must get towels," she said, as the panel swung shut.

There was another door and McCorkle pushed it open to look in. There was a smaller pool. Along the edge at intervals were cakes of soap, folded clothes beside them.

He turned back to the larger room, where the concrete walls and ceiling, painted a flat white, reflected the light upon the murky waters. Looking down at the surface, partially hidden by steam, there was no way for him to tell the depth, but at the end nearest him, concrete steps led downward, losing their shape in the depth.

McCorkle was inclined to make a strategic withdrawal to his bed, but the nerves still twitched at the back of his neck and there was a knot in his stomach. The hot water might relax these symptoms. Dropping the sheet, he stepped forward to gingerly stick a toe in the water, then withdraw it with a sharp intake of breath. The water was scalding!

"Soap first. In the other bath," the girl ordered behind him. McCorkle whirled, waving his arms in a vague effort to cover his nudity. She was in the doorway, kimono gone. Her olive toned figure now was covered only by a narrow halter holding her well developed breasts in check, while a short sarong surrounded full hips, but barely.

"The other tub," she repeated, taking a step toward him.

"Wh-what're you doing here?" McCorkle demanded, more embarrassed than belligerent. He took a step rearward, still trying to hide behind his spread hands.

He didn't hear her reply, for space suddenly opened and he shrilled a pained, startled cry, as he splashed into the steaming water.

An instant later, he broke water, sputtering and spitting spray. The water was boiling the flesh off his bones and he half waded, half swam toward the steps leading from the pool, shaking his head to clear the burning drops from his eyes.

The girl came gingerly down the steps, the water up to her knees. Then, with her next stride, it was above her waist, the sarong floating loosely about her.

"Get outa here," McCorkle snarled at her, realizing he was cornered. "You want to drown me?"

"Only to scrub your back," the girl announced. For emphasis, she reached to the edge of the pool and picked up a square of loose-woven terry cloth.

"I can wash my own back!" His voice climbed two octaves at the thought.

"Do not fight me, Joe-*san*," the girl ordered quietly. She spoke as though to quiet a troublesome infant, but she was advancing upon him slowly. "This is a service of the house."

"I know all about your services," he gulped, recalling the wording on the business card. "But I didn't come here to be seduced."

"That is not my function," she assured him coldly. "Just to scrub your back, wrong tub or not."

Retreating now, McCorkle took another step rearward, stumbled, and fought the water to regain his balance. When he righted himself, the girl was only inches away and he felt the rough, comforting surface of the wash cloth against his misused body. He surrendered, hoping that the blush that was enveloping his entire form would be mistaken as being caused by the heat.

"If it's inevitable," he muttered miserably, "relax and enjoy it."

"We are not thinking on the same plane," the girl told him primly, obviously familiar with the rest of the hoary phrase. "Turn around and let me wash your back."

Reluctantly, the officer turned, feeling the soap being applied gently to the tense area between his shoulder blades. As he looked up, he discovered Ashdon and Sales squatted at the edge of the pool, swathed in kimonos. Each had a fresh beer in hand and there was an amused, knowing grin on the pilot's face. Ashdon, however, showed concern.

"Hey, skipper," he called over the splashing, "I just talked t'that corporal. He says we ain't gonna get them supplies!"

# CHAPTER 11

THE GIRL washed McCorkle in spite of his struggle to keep open water between the two of them. In her brief cotton skirt and halter, she went about her labors in a brisk, business-like manner that bothered him even more than being stark, bare-assed naked in the same tub with her.

Rather confusedly, he pondered her deliberate disregard for his manhood and the resulting effect on his ego, but by the time Tomi was finished with scrubbing him down, the near-boiling water had sapped his strength so it was all he could do to drag himself up the stone steps and get the huge towel wrapped about his middle.

Sales and Ashdon had lost interest in the contest and had disappeared in search of more beer. At least, he didn't have to face them, he reflected with bitterness; not that he was likely to hear the last of this. As he staggered toward the door leading out of the bath, the girl came up from the water behind him.

"Go and lie down," she ordered shortly. "I will be there in a moment."

"Huh?" McCorkle paused in mid-stride to glance over his shoulder, sudden suspicion burdening his mind. It wasn't that he was virginal. It was more that being aided in the matter of sex was another blow to his ego. He was irritated at the idea of the two enlisted men deliberately setting him up as a target of seduction for their own amusement.

"Rubdown," the girl announced, not looking in his direction. Instead, she was rubbing her hair briskly with one of the towels. And in spite of his misgivings, McCorkle's interest began to rise. The girl's entire body shook with the effort of drying her hair, and the tiny halter across her bosom had slipped enough that he could see the pink flesh of a portion of her breasts, the dark shadow between.

"I'll come and give you a rubdown." the girl explained, still busy with her black hair, not bothering to look at him. "Good for your hangover."

"Yeah," he muttered, now resenting her objectivity. But as he turned back to the door, his stomach began to churn. The exertion and the hot water he had gulped inadvertantly during his initial plunge into the tub were telling their effects. Perspiring heavily, he found his room and threw himself onto the sleeping mat, drawing the sheet over him, then dragging deep breaths into his lungs.

The rice paper door was slid back and he rolled to his side, expecting the girl. It was Sales and Ashdon. The latter was still in the cotton kimono, but Sales was wearing the green uniform with the colonel's insignia.

"We goin' back to Chosin this mornin', skipper?" Sales asked with unusual formality, trying not to smile. "If you've been shot down on gettin' them supplies, there ain't much use in stayin' around here."

"We're going back," McCorkle agreed, sitting up and allowing the silk sheet to slip down to his lap.

"Well, I've gotta get this here uniform back to Colonel Ess-Ess. Meet with your approval if I meet you'n th' sarge at th' plane 'bout noon?"

"Sure. Fine," the officer said as Sales started to turn away. McCorkle stiffened, staring at the green blouse squared over the sergeant's shoulders. "Wait a minute!"

Sales paused, looking over his shoulder in question. McCorkle waved to his uniform.

"Whose uniform did you say that was?" he asked carefully.

"Ole Ess-Ess," Sales acknowledged. "Colonel Smith-Smythe. He's an ol' buddy o'mine."

McCorkle glanced at Ashdon for confirmation that this was the same officer in whose office they had been the day before, talking with his corporal. The sergeant nodded his head in reply.

"He was an old buddy," McCorkle told Sales, suddenly rising to his full height, still clutching the sheet about him and reaching for the kimono that lay beside his folded clothes. "You are going to get us those supplies, sergeant."

Sales was suddenly wary. Even in the short time he had known this youngster, this was unlike him. He took a step to the rear and glanced at the uniform in his hand. "Now wait a minute, looten-ant. I don't..."

"I'm certain I could still tell those MP's where to find a certain alcoholic exhibitionist," McCorkle cut in coldly. "The choice is yours."

Sales was suddenly miserable. Even his moustache seemed to droop. "You make it pretty plain that I ain't got no other choice," he half accused.

"Fine." McCorkle was ignoring Ashdon, who stared at him in puzzlement, and possibly in fear. This was a side he, too, had not seen before. He was plainly wondering whether he had created a Frankenstein. "Where's the telephone?" McCorkle asked.

The instrument was in the hotel's bar, and after five minutes of matching pidgin English with the operator, Sales was put through to Navy command headquarters and ultimately to the colonel's office. They had spent several minutes rehearsing his speech, but he was staring balefully at McCorkle as he spoke into the mouthpiece.

"Colonel, this is Sales...Yes, sir. Wanted to thank you f'r th' lend of th' uniform...No, sir. I can't very well bring it back right away...Seems there was some trouble." There was a long pause on Sales' part as he listened, features glum. It was plain that a friendship was being shredded.

"No, sir. I didn't lose it exackly. It's still in a dressin' room in some strip joint, but I was too damn drunk t' remember which one...Yes, sir. That's right. I don't remember, but Lootenant McCorkle does... Yes, sir."

The last words sounded almost relieved, and without explanation, he handed the receiver to the officer, who had been pacing back and forth, his self-confidence slowly subsiding.

"Ye-yes, sir," McCorkle stammered into the mouthpiece. His tone was not at all what he had intended it to be.

"What's that damned fool done now," a sharp voice grated in his ear. "And where the hell's my uniform?"

McCorkle took a deep breath, hesitated, then plunged, forcing himself to speak slowly, voice in a lower register than his panic decreed.

"The sergeant got pretty drunk and was doing a striptease in this joint, when I dragged him out just ahead of the Army MP's. We had to leave your uniform behind."

"Goddammit, that uniform has my name sewn in it," the voice

exploded, but in the next words there was the sound of worry. "What's going to happen if someone finds it in that stripper's dressing room?"

I wouldn't be able to say, sir," McCorkle stated properly, hesitating. Then he added, "They could think it was the colonel that was doing the striptease."

There was a strangled intake of breath, then Colonel Smith-Smythe, strangely subdued, asked, "Do you know where this place is?"

"Not exactly, sir," McCorkle replied truthfully. "I don't know the name of the place, but I might be able to find it."

"Then get there and get my uniform," the man ordered. "Now!"

"Colonel, I'm sorry, s-sir, but that doesn't coincide with my orders." McCorkle attempted to make his tone one of regret, but he was having a hard time controlling panic. This was going to be it. "We have to get back to Korea so that I can explain to the general about our supplies."

"What supplies?" the voice demanded to know, suspicious now.

"Photographic gear, sir. It's all listed in the re-request you received this morning." McCorkle was beginning to wish he had tried to be less brave.

"Wait one," came the order. Through the receiver, McCorkle could hear the frantic rustle of paper. He glanced at Ashdon and Sales, both of whom refused to meet his gaze. He wondered if it was because they didn't want to embarrass him, or whether they feared hanging from the same scaffold.

"You mean all of these glass jugs?" the voice accused finally.

"That is part of it, sir," McCorkle agreed. "W-we need them to store chemicals."

"Lieutenant, are you trying to blackmail me into giving you this gear?" The words came slowly, bluntly and without menace.

McCorkle was perspiring through the thin kimono. "N-no, sir. I am making a statement of fact. I-I will not have time to find y-your uniform. I am to report to the general."

"But you could find that soldier suit if that stuff was delivered to the airport say by noon?" The tone was cautious, though still heavy with accusation.

"I would do my best, sir."

"Do your best." There was surrender in the tone. "That stuff'll be there, but you have that uniform, or I'll have your ass!"

"Yes, sir." McCorkle gulped in relief. "Thank you, sir." But the phone went dead as the connection was broken. He slowly hung up the receiver, allowed his shoulders to slump and heaved a sigh. He felt as though he had just been through a third degree, but he turned to the two enlisted men.

"Get that uniform out to the plane right away," he ordered the pilot. "Give it to the colonel's man when you're sure all of those supplies are accounted for."

"Aye, sir." Sales started to turn away, then paused, staring at McCorkle with a strange sort of respect. "D'they teach you t'lie like that in OCS, lootenant?"

"No. It's a gift. Get moving!"

By the time Tomi came to his room, McCorkle had finished the remainder of the rice beer she had brought earlier and was stretched nude beneath the silk sheet. His hangover was gone and he felt a thrill of excitement over having achieved his mission. Yet there were misgivings. Inexperienced though he was, he realized that should he ever be ordered under Colonel Smith-Smythe's command, he would have to take corrective measures; like suicide.

"Feel better?" Tomi asked in her tone of professional sympathy. McCorkle lied by shaking his head, staring at the outlines of womanhood veiled by the kimono she wore.

"Turn on your stomach," she ordered in that same detached manner. "I will fix you."

He hesitated, still staring at her, then did as he had been told. There was a sudden draft as the sheet was jerked below his waist and he stiffened in reaction. An instant later, a compound, warm and soothing, was being poured along his spine. Then the girl's hands went to work, pounding, poking at the alcohol-loaded fibers of his body.

As she worked, McCorkle thought again of the ruse he had used to gain his ends and was suddenly doubtful. He realized that he had lied. What effect this was likely to have on Ashdon's opinion of him he could not be sure. Again, he thought of Major Lawrence, wondering whether he would have reacted the same in a similar situation. When he decided that the dead major might well have followed a similar course, some of the doubt left him. But not all.

By the time Tomi had finished, he was nearly asleep, but the sound of a tap on the frame of the rice paper door ended his relaxation. Sales, Ashdon at his shoulder, didn't wait but slid back the door.

"Everybody decent?" the pilot asked with a leer.

"What is it?" McCorkle snapped indignantly, reaching over his back to pull up the sheet, swinging his head to an awkward position and glaring at the pair.

"Coupla things, skipper," Sales declared. "First, I was just on th' phone to the airport, an' they ain't gonna have that turkey fixed till t'morrow. We gotta stay another night."

Feeling the warmth of the girl still seated beside him, her thigh pressed against his own, McCorkle didn't find this particularly disconcerting.

"And?" He managed to keep his voice on a formal note.

"Well," Sales stated slowly, "my flight suit's up there at Colonel Smith-Smythe's office. If I give him back his uniform at the plane like you ordered, what'll I wear? He looked down at his kimono. "This?"

"You stay here," McCorkle suggested, "and have Ashdon take the colonel's uniform to the airport. You can call the colonel's office first and have one of his men bring out your flight suit."

Sales shook his head sadly. "It ain't that easy. I already called and no one can find it. They think it was sent out for cleanin' or washin' by mistake."

No one said anything for a moment, each considering his individual plight. If Sales did not deliver the uniform, the colonel no doubt would hold up delivery of the supplies. If the pilot arrived at Haneda, ready to fly, in nothing more than a few yards of Japanese print, he'd no doubt be considered a psycho and hustled away from his aircraft in the direction of the nearest hospital.

"What're we gonna do, lootenant?" Ashdon asked, really seeking an answer.

"Surrender," McCorkle growled, but not believing it. There had to be a solution.

"May I suggest something?" Tomi asked shyly. All eyes turned upon her.

"Speak," Sales ordered sharply, but the girl seemed to ignore his tone.

"There is a tailor not far from here. He could make a new uniform."

"We don't have a week," McCorkle protested, but Sales waved a hand to silence him, staring at the girl.

"Wait, skipper. Some of these Nips are damned fast with a needle. What about it, Tomi? How long?"

The girl frowned, considered. "Three hours. Maybe a little longer."

"But what do they know about Marine uniforms?" McCorkle wanted to know. "They need a pattern."

Ashdon pointed a finger at the officer. "You're it, skipper. You're the pattern."

"No." McCorkle's voice was firm. "I'm not turning my uniform over to somebody I don't know. I don't want two of us running naked through Tokyo with the cops after us."

"But you could come along," Tomi explained. "Sergeant Sales could wait there so they could take the measurements, of course, and fit him properly. All they would have to do would be to look at your uniform and they'd get the idea."

McCorkle shook his head after considering for a moment. "They can't do it. They'll botch it."

"Then what're we gonna do?" Sales asked, for the first time appearing a trifle helpless.

McCorkle sat up, allowing the sheet to drop about his waist. "We're going to find that tailor." He looked at the girl, forgetting for the moment the dregs of his hangover.

"Where're my clothes?"

She motioned to the neatly folded stack beside his bed, trying not to laugh.

McCorkle pointed at Ashdon. "You find a cab and get on the way to the airport with that uniform."

Ashdon came to attention as a matter of reflex. "Aye, sir." He started to turn.

"Wait a minute. Don't turn that uniform over to anyone until you're certain all of those supplies are accounted for!"

"Yes, sir," the sergeant repeated and disappeared beyond Sales' drooping bulk. McCorkle ignored the pilot to glance at Tomi. "You can show us where this tailor is?"

She nodded vigorously, catching some of the excitement of his mood. *"Hai."*

"Then let's get another cab here by the time I get dressed." He glanced at Sales again, expression sardonic. "Think you can get low enough in the seat that the MP's won't spot you?"

Sales didn't even reply. Instead, he whirled and shut the door, his feet padding away down the corridor beyond.

"I'll help you dress, if you like." Tomi's manner was suddenly shy again and McCorkle scowled at her, trying to decide just where she fit into this situation.

"Out," he ordered. She seemed pleased at the order and rose to follow the pilot.

Twenty minutes later, fully dressed and clean shaven, McCorkle was led to the small lobby filled with Japanese curios. Waiting was a small, bald Japanese man wearing a kimono that seemed several sizes too large for him. Or it may have been, McCorkle considered, that the man within had shrunk instead.

The man's face was weathered and there were deep lines of care angling down from the corners of his mouth, heightening the impact of the hollow cheeks. But at the sight of Tomi, he smiled, showing several gold teeth. His dark eyes suddenly were no longer sad and he seemed to see only the girl.

Tomi spoke to him in Japanese, then turned to McCorkle, her shyness again seeming to take over.

"Lieutenant McCorkle," she said carefully, making certain to pronounce every syllable with care. "My father."

The officer couldn't help showing his surprise, but the older man seemed not to notice. Instead he bowed from the waist, then straightened.

"It is a pleasure, lieutenant," he said in perfect English, but the smile was gone from his eyes. He even appeared a little suspicious. "Tomi has told me of the sergeant's problem and your solution."

McCorkle started to protest, to tell the old man that it had been his daughter who had thought of the tailor and this instant uniform plan. But he decided against it.

"I can recommend him," the Japanese said. "He is an excellent craftsman. He made my own uniforms." There was a pause, then his tone was almost apologetic. "In the old days, of course."

"Were you in the Japanese Army, sir?"

"Yes, lieutenant, I was." There was a hint of nostalgia, but this was quickly brushed away with a wry smile. "But as you can tell by my approaching old age, that was a long time ago." He glanced at Tomi, the smile returning, then back to McCorkle, bowing once more. "There are some things I must attend to. Welcome to my humble establishment."

"My pleasure, sir." McCorkle started to thrust out his hand, but the old man took a step to the rear, bowed twice in quick, bobbing fashion, then turned to disappear into the dimness of a hallway, shuffling quietly.

McCorkle turned to look at the girl. She had changed to another kimono, this one of white silk, held about the waist with a scarlet *obi*. Her hair had been carefully combed and there was a trace of lipstick on her lips, but he could detect no other makeup.

"I wonder where Sales is?" McCorkle muttered uncomfortably. One of the diminutive Japanese taxicabs already was waiting outside the door, the driver lounging against its fender.

"Right here, lootenant!" Sales appeared from what obviously was the adjoining bar. Beneath his arm he had a cardboard box and from the obvious markings it contained quart bottles of beer.

"You're taking all that?" McCorkle's tone was more awed than disapproving.

"Aye, sir. Figger three quarts'n hour for four hours; it'll come out about right." The pilot still wore the kimono, his issue cordovan shoes showing beneath the hem. McCorkle was not up to arguing the mathematics of alcoholic consumption and simply waved him toward the door.

Once in the cramped confines of the cab, the three of them with the case of beer were hurtled through the narrow streets. Sales sat in front with the driver, hiding his Caucasian features as best he could with the case of beer. In the rear, McCorkle sat pressed against the window, staring straight ahead, wondering suddenly how all of this was going to come out. It seemed like a nightmare, but he knew it was real. Yet what else could he do? He had committed himself the previous night when he had not allowed the military police to take Sales in tow and usher him off to the nearest brig.

Tomi, sitting in the other corner, eyes lowered, seemed an entirely different girl from the one who had insisted upon washing his back. Indeed, she seemed a trifle frightened, but when McCorkle turned to frown, she looked up to smile at him.

"One question, sergeant," McCorkle said. "Do you have enough money to pay for this uniform?"

"If fifty bucks will cover it, I do," was Sales reply. In spite of the ample supply of beer on and within his lap, he seemed to have lost some of his usual brashness.

"I will talk to the tailor," Tomi volunteered quietly. "He is an old

104

family friend."

Minutes later, McCorkle paid the driver the amount specified by Tomi, while Sales, still attempting to hide behind his case of rice beer, sprinted across the narrow walkway and through the doorway of a shop. Tomi followed the sergeant, while McCorkle paused to look up and down the narrow street. The cab pulled away, the driver honking angrily at an old man on a bicycle, narrowly missing him, then turned a corner. The bike rider didn't even look around, seeming to take in stride the fact that he was a distinct traffic hazard.

McCorkle took in the narrow store fronts, the open doors of the shops, the strange array of signs and the Orientals of all ages who teemed the streets, carefully ignoring him. Half-way down the block was a theater and he had half turned before he paused to stare at the colorful three sheets that announced the current attractions. In spite of the fact that the artist had taken liberties and that the title and incidental credits were in Japanese, he recognized Clark Gable and Vivien Leigh. *Gone With The Wind.* But even more surprising was the companion feature, *Sands of Iwo Jima.* John Wayne's features were prominently displayed in Marine uniform, but the artist had given the star's eyes a pronounced slant. McCorkle wondered whether this was simply a way of getting even or if the Japanese version showed that their side had won.

Inside the shop, Tomi was in earnest conversation with a small Japanese man of about her father's age. This individual had white hair and thick glasses that threatened to fall off his nose as he constantly nodded over the girl's suggestions. Occasionally, he would turn to glance at Sergeant Sales, who stood self-consciously in the middle of the floor as though to hide behind the case of beer held protectively in his arms.

Behind the trio was a low railing and beyond that, fully a dozen Orientals, some of them women and one young boy who could have been no more than ten or twelve. All sat cross-legged on the floor, ignoring the new arrivals, bent over their sewing, needles glinting like fireflies in the dim light as they worked over a variety of garments. In a far corner, a wizened old woman hunched over an old-fashioned treadle sewing machine, its loose, worn rattlings sounding as though it might disintigrate at any moment.

Tomi turned to McCorkle, frowning. "He says he will make the uniform, but he has no khaki material for a shirt or tie."

I can handle that," the officer said. "I have extras." He glanced at

Sales' bulk. "It may be a tight squeeze, though."

"I'll shrink, sir," Sales promised.

"With a dozen quarts of beer inside you?"

Sales ignored the question, looking up at the ceiling.

"He wants you to stand over in the light," Tomi told McCorkle, "so he can sketch the uniform."

McCorkle moved to the spot she indicated, while the little Japanese tailor picked up a clipboard and began to draw rapidly. In less than ten minutes, he had developed a surprising likeness of the officer's uniform. Then it developed that there was a problem of buttons. He had none for a Marine uniform.

"We can get them at the Tokyo Post Exchange," McCorkle suggested, "if you show me how to get there." He had never been to the huge department-store-like installation, but had heard others mention it. It was often referred to as the Military Macy's.

"I shall," Tomi promised over the little tailor's shoulder. He had stepped in front of her with a small pocket ruler and was quickly measuring the distance of the pockets from the shoulder, the width of the belt and other necessities, jotting them on his sketch.

"Anyone for a beer?" Sales asked, his brashness suddenly returned. Since there were no chairs, he had removed a quart of beer and opened it, now sitting on the box as he held it up to the light for inspection.

"Stay sober enough to find your way back to the hotel," McCorkle instructed. Before the sergeant could frame a reply, the officer took the girl by the arm and started toward the door, but they were halted by Sales' panicked screech.

"What th' hell you want?"

They turned to see the sergeant, clutching the kimono about his lean body, while the little tailor danced about him. There was an air of indignation on the sergeant's battered features.

"He wants to measure you for the uniform," Tomi explained simply. "He can't do it with you standing on the box."

Sales hesitated for a moment, then gingerly descended, still clutching his beer as though to use the bottle as a club. As the tailor deftly looped a tape measure about the sergeant's waist, the latter wriggled uncomfortably, then started to laugh.

"Dammit," he gurgled, "that tickles. An' don't try t'get too damn familiar or I'll club yuh!"

# CHAPTER 12

"**S**HE CAN'T come in here, sir." If the burly Army MP was apologetic, his tone didn't show it. He was posted at the door of the multi-storied Tokyo Post Exchange and indicated Tomi with a disdainful wave of his hand. Then he expressed another thought.

"Unless she's a dependent, of course," his voice plainly indicated that he was certain she was not.

McCorkle, caught in the middle, could not help coloring as he glared at the military policeman, a corporal. He was about to demand an explanation, but Tomi tugged at his arm.

"You go in," she said quietly. "I will wait."

"You can't just stand here in the street," McCorkle declared, throwing a belligerent glance at the corporal, who had turned his attention to the street, his duty momentarily fulfilled.

"There is a place down the street," the girl said. "You can meet me there."

"A bar?" McCorkle, for reasons he didn't understand, didn't like the idea of the girl waiting alone in a bar for him. But she shook her head.

"I do not drink," she said simply. "It is what you call an ice cream parlor, I think."

"I'll walk you there," he insisted, but again, she shook her head, smiling.

"Get what you need," she suggested, "and we will walk together then." McCorkle wasn't certain what she meant by that statement, but he listened as she pointed down the thoroughfare, pointing out a sign a block away. That was where he was to meet her. As she hurried away, not looking back, McCorkle watched with an emotional mixture he did not recognize, partially resenting the admiring glances that she received from the other military personnel on the street. This tinge of jealousy he found disturbing as he turned to return the door sentry's salute and enter the huge service-controlled department store which catered to the thousands of American military families within the Tokyo area.

With the exception of the frequent signs warning of the court-martial penalty for indulging in black market activities, the installation might easily have been a major Los Angeles department store. The few Japanese who were involved in minor capacities were well dressed in the European style and presumably spoke excellent English. Most of the sales personnel, however, were Americans. The majority were women, the dependents of military men stationed in the area.

It took little time to find the military uniform section and to exchange some of the purple-toned occupation currency for the set of buttons he needed. Five minutes later, he was out the door and on the way down the street toward the sign Tomi had pointed out earlier. He was vaguely disturbed over the fact that she might have taken offense at the sentry's obvious insult and decided not to wait.

But inside, he found her seated alone at a table, spooning the remnants of a dish of vanilla ice cream. She looked up and smiled as she saw him, waving him to a chair.

"You found the buttons?" she asked, glancing at the paper bag he dropped on the table and slid onto the chair opposite her. "You would care for some ice cream?"

McCorkle shook his head, stomach reacting at the thought of diluting the beer that still remained within that cavity.

"You said something about walking," he reminded her as she scraped the bottom of the dish, spooning the last creamy bit to her mouth.

"We could go to the park," Tomi said, frowning. "Unless you would prefer to go to a bar?"

"I prefer the park," he said shortly. "And it'll be another three hours before Sales' uniform is done. What park?"

"Meiji Park. It is not far."

By the time the Japanese taxi driver had opened the door for them at the entrance to the park, McCorkle was certain that the girl's knowledge of geography had been learned from a Texan. Hurrying through the cluttered, heavily populated streets in the rear seat of the vehicle, it had seemed to him that they had driven for hours. However, his watch told him that the trip had taken less than thirty minutes.

But in his trip through the city, the knowledge that had come to him with his arrival at Haneda Airport was reinforced. The city was alive with uniforms. Not only were there hosts of American soldiers, sailors, Marines and airmen, but there were Australians, British, New Zealanders, Canadians, Turks and other uniforms that he failed to recognize.

Now, standing at the entrance to the park, McCorkle felt the sharpness of a still breeze, and noticed that the wide gravel walkway ahead was deserted. There was not another person in sight.

"Why did you want to come here?" he asked as the taxi pulled away and he took Tomi's arm.

"I come here sometimes to think," she explained shyly. "It is crowded on weekends, of course." Slowly, they began to walk along the path, neither saying anything. Ahead, a harsh sound came from the flanking spruces, then a large bird hurried across the pathway.

"Was that a peacock?" McCorkle asked, startled by the harshness. The girl nodded.

"There is a legend that what one has in one kind of beauty must be sacrificed in another," she explained. "The legend is about the peacock."

He glanced at the girl, trying not to show that he was inspecting her. If she noticed, she did not betray it. Instead, she looked straight ahead, as they moved down the pathway.

Tomi was becoming more and more of an enigma. She made no bones about the fact that her father owned a bordello, hiding behind the camouflage of a supposedly respectable hotel, and she had been equally matter of fact in admitting that she was a part of that operation. And as with the peacock, she could see the outward beauty, but could not help wondering about the other facets. While she appeared to take no part in the actual prostitution that he was certain was a part of her father's livelihood and her own, McCorkle found it hard to accept the fact that she was as pure as she seemed to appear. Yet she certainly was not to be compared with the pair that he and Ashdon had picked up at the dance hall the previous night. He shuddered at the recollection of the girl with the gold tooth and

Tomi glanced at him with concern.

"You are cold?" she asked. He shook his head.

"I'm not, but you must be." He glanced at her silk kimono, wondering what she wore beneath it.

"No." She smiled. "I enjoy it. There is something cleansing about the fresh air. I come as often as I can." McCorkle was still pondering the meaning of this as they came to the zoo and he began to inspect the various cages. A few Japanese school children, the girls in kimonos, the boys wearing the tight, dark-colored jackets and peaked hats with shiny visors of their standing, were giggling over the antics of monkeys and birds. But many of the cages were empty. Judging from the cleanliness of the floors, they had been empty for some time. McCorkle asked about it. Tomi nodded agreement.

"The war has only been over a few years," she reminded. "Toward the end, it was difficult enough to feed our people. Animals were an unnecessary luxury. Some were killed for their meat. The rest were killed simply to keep them from starving."

"You were hungry, Tomi?" There was more than curiosity in his tone. Pity, perhaps.

"Not often," she said softly, moving a step ahead of him along the wide spruce-flanked path. Then, directly ahead, McCorkle spotted the yellow stucco walls of a mountain-like structure.

"What's that?" he asked, pointing to it.

"The stadium. That is where your American soldiers compete in games."

As they moved through the trees, McCorkle could see the group of youngsters lined up on opposite sides, using a bundle of dirty rags for a football. At a signal, the make-shift ball was snapped and there ensued what appeared to be a ten-year-old's version of a sumo wrestling match. The ball carrier lost three yards.

"Football," Tomi explained unnecessarily, but McCorkle's eyes were upon the lettering above the doorway leading into the stadium. The painted black letters read:

### NILE KINNICK STADIUM

At this sight, an incident came rushing back through McCorkle's mind. He was thinking back to a cold day in 1939 when he had sat on a cold bench with other members of his grade school's Knothole Club. Below him, on the stadium floor, a smallish young man was generaling an underdog University of Iowa team to victory over powerful Minnesota.

"What is it, Joe-*san*?" the girl asked with concern. The officer shook his head and the vision disappeared. But the memory remained.

"Nothing," he murmured, then looked at her. "Do you know who Nile Kinnick was?"

She hesitated, puzzled at his strange behavior. "No. Did you know him?"

He shook his head again. "I only saw him once. He went down in a crash off a carrier in the last war. But where I come from he's still a hero."

"Because he crashed?"

"That's part of it, I guess, but more because of how he played football." McCorkle couldn't help smiling. "Back in Iowa, there's a saying that they have a good corn crop every year, and a good football team once every ten."

The football game had stopped in the area before the stadium and the dozen or so Japanese school boys were staring at them with open interest, talking among themselves in low tones. Suddenly, Tomi suppressed a giggle. McCorkle looked at her, disturbed that he didn't know what was being said.

"What is it?"

"They are talking about you," she explained, trying not to laugh. "They are wondering whether the round-eye knows how to play football."

"Tell them I do," he ordered indignantly. The idea that a horde of Japanese children should doubt the gridiron ability of any American disturbed him. The fact that he had been considered too light to play in college and lacked experience didn't enter into it at this point. In high school, he had not been allowed to go out for the team inasmuch as there was work to be done on the farm and suicidal sports played no part in that picture.

Tomi called to the boys, speaking in rapid Japanese. Suddenly, there was a mass shout of challenge from the group and one of the youngsters picked up the makeshift ball, hurling it toward McCorkle in a looping over-handed throw. He caught it and stood uncertainly as the entire group charged down upon him, screaming banzai challenges.

"You'd better run!" Tomi shouted in warning, no longer able to retain her laughter. She was jumping up and down, clapping her

111

hands in glee. Startled, McCorkle hesitated for a moment, then started to run, going straight toward the charging pack, his long legs driving upward like pistons, the bundle of rags cradled in his armpit as he had seen it done so many times from the grandstand.

Some of the youngsters reversed field, trying to cut him off, shouting warnings to one another as the Marine charged into their midst, sidestepping first one, dodging to avoid another would-be tackler. Then he felt something catch one of his feet as he was in mid-air and in instant later, the wind was knocked out of him as he thumped full length on the hard ground. Before he could roll over, he felt the weight of numerous small bodies landing atop him, grinding him into the thin grass.

There were still shouts of excitement in the shrill voices of the children, but beyond it, he could hear Tomi's excited voice, issuing stern orders in Japanese. Slowly, the boys began to disengage themselves. Finally, he was able to sit up and look about.

The youngsters surrounded him in a grinning circle, waiting to see his reaction. As he looked down, he saw that his uniform was covered with dust. Slowly he began to laugh, then one at a time, the others joined in. He glanced up at Tomi, who stood at the edge of the circle, staring at him with concern.

"How do you say 'very good?' 'Excellent?'" he asked.

"*Ichi-bon.* It means number one," she explained doubtfully.

He tossed the bundle of rags to one of the other lads, who could have been no more than twelve. "That's it," he declared. "*Ichi-bon.* You're all number one football players."

The youngsters caught his spirit and began to laugh, jostling each other, speaking in rapid, delighted syllables. One of the older boys held out his hand to help him up, but McCorkle shook his head, patting the ground beside him.

"Sit down," he ordered, and as the group dropped to their knees and buttocks, he glanced about the circle of small slanteyed faces. "Any of you know Nile Kinnick? Know what it means?"

There was a moment of silence, then one youngster raised his hand. "*Hai.* I know. Ame'can G.I." He spread his arms, flapping them up and down to indicate that the hero had been a pilot. "Killed *taksan* time in war."

Hours later, as McCorkle lay on the thick mat in the hotel, he could not help feeling some small satisfaction that the Japanese boys had known about Nile Kinnick. There was no reason why they should; there was no reason why they should even be interested, and there certainly was no reason why he should be feeling smug about it, but the feeling was there.

Tomi and he had left the park shortly before sundown and she had directed him to a small tea house not far from the hotel, where they had removed their shoes at the door, then had been led to a small room completely enclosed by the sliding rice paper doors. Here they had eaten, and he hadn't even been disturbed after the meal when she laughingly told him that he had just been eating octopus. He had washed it down with a quantity of rice wine, while Tomi had daintily concentrated upon her tea. Rather than themselves, the talk had been of the happenings of the day.

When they had stopped by the tailor shop, they had found it locked and neatly deposited upon the curb for pick-up was an empty case of quart beer bottles. Apparently, Sales had received his uniform and had returned with it to the hotel. This assumption had been found to be correct, for once in the doorway, they had heard the sergeant's loud laughter in the bar. While Tomi had drifted away, McCorkle had cautiously glanced past the doorway to find the pilot, still swathed in his kimono, standing at the bar, a drink before him and his hands upon the buttocks of the Japanese girls that flanked him on each side. A bit less greedy, perhaps, Ashdon was beyond, concentrating upon one girl, talking to her urgently in undertones. Not wanting to become further involved, McCorkle had found his room, had removed his uniform and crawled wearily between the cool silk sheets.

He was partially asleep, mind skipping over the events of the day, pausing now and then to ponder Tomi, when there was a gentle tap at his door. He sat up, rubbing his eyes.

"Yes?"

"You want *biru?* Tomi's voice called softly.

"I need a beer like I need my third head," he replied grumpily, then changed his mind. "But bring it in."

The panel slid back and the girl entered, a white-clad wraith in the near darkness. Silently, she padded across the room to kneel beside him on the sleeping mat.

"I am sorry. Were you asleep?" Her voice was still soft, almost caressing. McCorkle shook his head.

"No. I just didn't want to get tangled up with that pair in the bar.

**113**

Did Sales get the uniform?"

He could see the girl nod, smiling. "Yes. He is quite happy with it, but he wondered about the buttons."

"I'll give them to him in the morning." As he spoke, Tomi poured from one of the quart bottles and handed him the glass. McCorkle took a long sip, then lowered it to stare at the girl, who was still smiling.

"I enjoyed the day," she said. "Thank you."

McCorkle hunched his shoulders, wincing. "I did, too, but I may never be the same after the way those kids piled on me."

"Lie down," the girl ordered. "I will massage your back again. It is certain to help."

McCorkle gulped down the rest of the beer, then rolled over on his stomach, flattening himself on the mat. As before, the girl stripped back the sheet and began to gently knead his sore, tight muscles. McCorkle groaned and she paused, hand still on his back.

"It hurts." Her tone was positive but sympathetic.

"But it hurts good." She continued her work, hands gentle and searching out the tense areas.

"Joe-*san?*" Her voice was thoughtful.

"Yeah?"

"Today at the park. Why did you ask if I knew about Kinnick-*san?* You asked the boys, too. Why was it so important?"

McCorkle thought about it for a moment. Until now, it had not occurred to him that the incident had held importance. "I don't know," he said finally.

"Was it because it was something from home?" Tomi asked softly. "Because you are homesick?"

McCorkle snorted at the suggestion. "Marines aren't supposed to get homesick," he informed her. He started to roll over, but Tomi pushed him back.

"Don't get angry, Joe-*san.* It was only a thought."

McCorkle relaxed again, allowing her to continue to massage. But the thought had been implanted and he lay there, wondering whether she might not be right. Seeing the familiar name painted across the stadium had given him a thrill, realizing that here was a touch of home thousands of miles from the corn fields with which he was so familiar, yet which he had hoped to leave forever.

By the time Tomi was finished, he was nearly asleep. Her voice, close to his ear and wistful, jerked him back to reality.

"What is Korea like?" she wanted to know.

"It's a stinking hole," he told her forcefully, realizing for the first time; admitting it, at last, that it was just that. It had taken this brief return to civilization to silhouette the differences for him. "It's full of filth and smells and people who don't know about soap and water."

"Could that be because they don't have soap?" she asked softly.

He rolled on his back to look up. Her face was less than a foot from his own, as she knelt there Oriental fashion beside his bed. There was a touch of sadness in her eyes, an expression of deep but unsettled thought, and McCorkle frowned at her in the dim light.

"What's the matter?" he asked quietly. She shook her head, looking away. He reached to take her hand and found it small and warm in his palm.

"Tell me," he ordered, tone still gentle. "Was it something I said?"

"No," she said quietly, the inflection of bitterness almost hidden. "It is just that I ask all the Gee Eyes about Korea. They all answer the same as you. To all of them, it is dirty and miserable."

"But why should you care? Why do you ask them," he insisted, "if you keep getting the same answer?"

Tomi's eyes were pensive, hiding some deeper emotion. She hesitated, then shook her head, looking down at her hand in his. "It is nothing. I would like to hear someone speak well of the country. It is where I was born. My mother is buried there."

"You're not Korean." His tone was still insistent.

"No."

"I'm sorry," he said quietly. He had no particular reason for saying it, except that he really was sorry. "Maybe you can come over sometime and see the place."

The girl sighed, dropping her eyes, again, and her fingers balled into a small tight fist. She shook her head "It is not likely."

"How'd you come to be born there?" he asked, frowning his puzzlement.

"My father was an officer in the Imperial Japanese Army. He was stationed in Korea, when it belonged to Japan. That was before the war."

"Where did you learn to speak English?" he asked suddenly, realizing the wisdom of skirting the political issues. "You have hardly any accent."

"From the nuns," she told him without change of tone. "It is taught in their college there."

In defeat, McCorkle thought, Nippon was a strange country. A former Japanese officer ran a bordello; his daughter, who washed the backs of naked men, had been educated by nuns.

That was when he pushed himself up on one elbow and encircled her waist with one bare arm, pulling her down to him. She started in surprise, then surrendered as his lips found hers. For a moment, they clung together, then she cautiously pushed him away, staring at him searchingly, a tiny frown on her lips.

"You're not like the others," she said quietly. "Most of them have tried to get me in bed before they kiss me."

The next question was obvious, but McCorkle waited a long time before asking it. "But how many were successful?"

"Only one," she said quietly, looking down at her clenched hands. "He was a sergeant. In the Air Force. He was shot down in Chosin four months ago."

"I'm sorry," he said again, meaning it as before.

The girl looked up, frowning, shaking her head. "There is no need to be. Sorrow cannot bring him back."

He didn't know how long they just sat there, then he kissed her again. This time, her lips were parted and her tongue darted to meet his. His hands began to explore her body, slipping beneath the silk kimono. Instead of drawing away, she bent closer, the warmth of her body matching his own.

His brain was only half functioning amid the swirl of emotion, but McCorkle wondered why he was doing this. Was it simply biological or was it something more?

"I want you," he whispered in her ear, voice husky. She nodded.

"I know," she said simply.

McCorkle didn't wonder how Major Lawrence would handle this situation. He didn't have to.

# CHAPTER 13

The ancient torpedo bomber dropped onto the runway. It bounced erratically a time or two, sending McCorkle's stomach in the opposite direction before settling down.

"You can't never trust them Army engineers," the pilot grumbled through the earphones. "This damned strip's gotta hill in th' middle an' I can't never tell exactly where 'tis."

Sergeant Sales' tone was professionally soothing, but it only caused McCorkle added discomfort.

Before the flying sergeant could pull the battered old hulk off the runway and onto the metal matting that comprised the parking ramp, the officer had the door of the bomb bay open and was gulping in deep draughts of fresh air. As Sales taxied the plane about, then killed the engine, the lieutenant flung the door wide and leaped the three feet or so to the ground.

Behind him, Ashdon dismounted more leisurely. Both turned to wave their thanks to the pilot, but Sales' bass came over the dying whirr of the propeller, as he opened the heavy canopy.

"Any time you wanta go somewhere, lootenant, I can get this ole bird," he promised. "No one else wants t'fly her."

"I'll remember," McCorkle called back, his own promise less enthusiastic.

"Don't let anyone near her," Ashdon called to the pilot. "We'll send someone t'unload that gear soon's we can get some wheels." He turned to stare at McCorkle with grudging pride.

"Skipper," he offered with a touch of reverence, "we've got enough stuff in that plane to start our own studio. There's gear I didn't even know the Marine Corps had!"

"See if you can get Quillan to send down the jeep," McCorkle returned. After all, there was nothing like throwing a general's rank about and stooping to a bit of polite blackmail, but he took note that Ashdon avoided reference to either.

The sergeant threw a nonchalant salute and disappeared into the operations shack, where flights of all of the planes of the air wing were plotted. It was a low, squat structure of corregated metal, the red of rust showing through the thin protective coating of zinc.

McCorkle stared after the sergeant. On the trip from Haneda Airport, he had been strangely reserved, possibly realizing that he and Sales had overstepped the bounds of recognized discipline. The officer had been waiting for an opportunity to lower the boom, but Ashdon had not lowered his guard, totally ignoring the happenings of the past twenty-four hours. Instead, he had talked of inconsequential matters, asking the officer's opinion from time to time. Once aloft in the belly of the old plane, Ashdon had gone to sleep, leaving the officer to his frustrations over a chore undone.

Now, McCorkle glanced at his bleak surroundings, comparing them with the garish lights of the Tokyo night. Located as it was on the edge of the bay, the base more closely resembled a Cape Cod summer colony than an establishment devoted to the business of warfare. Sand dunes near the beach looked soft and inviting, and the scattered buildings, hastily thrown up from prefabricated sections, resembled rows of rental cottages. Staring up the length of the steel sectional matting upon which the planes took off and landed, McCorkle discovered that Sales had spoken the truth. There was a definite hump in the otherwise smooth surface. It was impossible to see the other end of the runway.

"Got troubles," Ashdon reported, coming out of the shack. "Quillan must be hungover. The phone's off the hook."

"We'll walk." McCorkle picked up his liberty bag. "Halloran can bring the jeep down to pick up the gear."

Ashdon shrugged and hoisted his own bag to his shoulder. There was the distinct clink of glass meeting glass and McCorkle glanced suspiciously at the seabag, then brushed aside his first reaction. There were some things, he told himself resignedly, that one had to learn to accept. Included was bootlegging across an international boundary.

As they trudged up the sandy roadway toward the sprawling pattern of tents and metal huts atop the low hill, he was troubled, wondering how much Ashdon suspected of his affair with Tomi. Lying there in the hotel room, both of them spent but happy, his arm had been about her, the musky odor of her hair in his nostrils. Even then, he wasn't certain whether he had seduced her or she had been the forward one. It was more satisfying to believe it had been a mutual need. Whatever, he had learned a great deal about her.

Tomi's father had been more than just an officer. He had been a Japanese general, but when the surrender had come, he had not committed *hari-kari* as he may have been expected to do. Instead, he had returned to Tokyo and his young daughter.

Shorn of his rank, he had been nearly destitute, but finally had taken over the hotel, depending largely upon looseness of American control and the demands of the occupation troops to keep his only child fed.

The Korean War, with its flood of fresh bodies, had been a boon and the added money had aided in financing Tomi's education. McCorkle could not help but feel a strange sympathy for one who would run a glorified house of ill repute so that his daughter could go to college in a country where daughters often were literally sold into bondage so that a favored son might be educated.

A portion of the girl's mask had slipped in those moments when she had talked of her childhood in Korea and the mother who had died there. It had dropped still further, while she lay there beside him on the sleeping mat, words coming softly to disguise her emotions. She still thought of her father as a general, but there must have been times when she found it difficult to retain this illusion.

"Skipper, you gotta do somethin'!" Sergeant Quillan was totally sober and McCorkle hardly had time to drop his bag before the master sergeant was outlining the tales of crisis.

"You was no sooner off the end of th' runway than that boy chaplain demanded we take a picture of him handin' out some ole clothes t'some orphans. Henry kicked him in th' shins."

"Jus' stamped on 'is foot a li'l," the Korean boy defended himself sullenly.

"Then your buddy Barrymore's screamin' around to know how we rate a jeep an' he hasta walk. Right this minute, he's in our vehicle, usin' our driver."

"What else?" McCorkle asked wearily.

Quillan hesitated. "They raided our still," he finally admitted miserably.

"What still?"

"That's what we kept askin', but they'd already found it."

"Won't need all them glass jugs now," Henry prophesied with evil satisfaction.

"Who turned you in?" the officer wanted to know, trying to grasp the full situation.

"Our own friendly, smilin' man of th' cloth," Quillan replied dourly. "He's th' only one I can figger."

"Why him?"

"He's th' only one on th' base that don't drink. He's got nothin' t'lose!"

McCorkle picked up his bag and turned to Ashdon, who stood with mouth agape. "Find me a Navy Photographic Manual, while I change clothes," the officer ordered.

"I ain't seen one since 1943," Ashdon protested.

"There's one around here somewhere," Quillan told him, as McCorkle disappeared into the rear of the tent. "It's part of the equipment."

McCorkle wearily removed his uniform, arranged the segments in a plastic bag and hung it from the tent frame. Quillan had asked for leadership, however subverted it might be, and the lieutenant stood there in his drawers, considering the alternatives. He was in the same position as he had been with Sales when the MP's were after him.

He could leave Quillan and the others to founder on the rocks of discipline, or he could lean over the edge of this precipice to try to help, placing himself in a similar position of jeopardy. In the outer office, he could hear the noisy search for the manual, as they rustled through the makeshift filing cases, jerked open boxes of old records, went through field desks.

"This it?" Henry's voice asked abruptly.

"Yeah," Quillan growled at him, "but why're the pages stuck t'gether?"

"Coffee," the Korean boy replied. "I set th' pot on it when it boils oveh."

When McCorkle reappeared in fresh dungarees, his field boots in his hand, Quillan extended the stained volume.

"Some th' worse for wear, sir," he apologized, but McCorkle glanced at Ashdon. Quillan's sudden air of respect was a bid for help, he was certain.

"Look through there and find something on uses for alcohol," he ordered, then turned to stare at the master sergeant, struck by a new thought. "Why aren't you in the brig?"

Quillan straightened indignantly. "Whoever heard of lockin' up a master sergeant? I'm a prisoner-at-large."

McCorkle was recalling his earlier promise to himself to set about straightening out the section, but that decision would have to be postponed. If this situation progressed, he might not have a section. "How much of that hooch have you got left?"

Quillan eyed him guardedly, suddenly suspicious. One could never tell about officers, especially the young ones with ambitions.

"I don't know, sir," he stated formally.

"How much?"

Quillan hesitated. "Maybe two gallons."

"Get over to that lab and pour it into a developer pan," McCorkle told him. "Throw in all the loose negatives you can find."

Quillan's expression was one of horror. "Our last two gallons?"

"I'm trying to keep your ass out of Portsmouth Naval Prison," McCorkle told him grimly. "Mine, too."

"But they can't touch you. Me either," Ashdon declared. "We weren't even here."

The officer glared at the tech sergeant. "There are some who believe that a commander is responsible for the actions of his men. I'm probably considered guilty simply by association."

Ashdon extended the thick official volume, marking a chapter with his finger. McCorkle opened to the passage, stared at it for a moment, then looked up to glare at Quillan.

"I told you what to do with that booze."

"I don't know whether my heart'll stand it," the other muttered.

"It'll take this better than a firing squad," the officer snarled at him. *"Move!"*

Quillan started for the door, face showing his surprise at this sudden transformation in his commanding officer.

"And don't try to drink all that stuff before I get there!" McCorkle called after him. "I'll have the general in tow!"

In spite of the position into which he was deliberately thrusting himself, McCorkle was pleased. In fact, as he re-read the passage in the photo manual, he had difficulty in not showing it. He realized that for the first time since his arrival he was in full command of his own men. In this moment of stress, rather than simply tolerating him as they had seemed to do in the past, they had turned to him, seeking guidance and leadership.

Whether this need would exist beyond this present crisis was a question about which he didn't even attempt to guess the answer. But for the moment, he was in command. It was a good feeling.

McCorkle's thoughts turned to Major Lawrence, pondering for an instant whether the dead officer would have handled the matter in a similar manner. Then he realized, with some surprise, that it no longer mattered. He was not Lawrence; he was not like him, and the situation had to be handled on his own. Trying to outguess the dead officer would not solve this problem.

McCorkle realized, too, in that moment that there had been a tinge of jealousy where Lawrence and his relationship with the enlisted men had been concerned. Now it no longer mattered. Whatever was going to happen was strictly upon his own shoulders.

Twenty minutes later, the photographic manual still in his hand, index finger marking a specific passage, McCorkle ducked under the flap of the tent that housed his unit's makeshift photo lab.

"Tenshun!" he bawled lustily.

Quillan, who had been bending over the white enameled developer tray, snapped rigidly to attention, turning to face the opening. McCorkle could hardly suppress a grin at this reaction to years of discipline. Ashdon also braced his shoulders and pulled in his chin and stomach as McCorkle stepped aside, clicking his heels in approved fashion. The general strode in, lifting the flap so that he did not have to bend. He scowled as he paused to glance about. The Chief-of-Staff was a step to the general's rear, but seemingly shared in the scowl.

"What's that odor?" the Chief demanded gruffly. He tilted his nose upward for a suspicious sniff, then cast McCorkle an accusing glance.

"Alcohol," the lieutenant replied firmly, his candor causing Quillan's double chin to tremble in apprehension. The general glanced at the two enlisted men, then at the pair of empty glass jugs on the dirt floor.

"At ease," the general growled, "before you fall down!"

As Quillan exhaled, allowing his shoulders to droop abruptly to half mast, the general took another step into the tent, surveying the master sergeant with open curiosity.

"Sergeant," he asked pointedly, "have you been drinking?"

"Not today, sir," was the staunch reply as Quillan automatically snapped back to attention. The general offered him a vague gesture and the master sergeant relaxed once more. The general waved again, this time to the pan filled with its dark brown liquid, the bent corners of photographic negatives showing here and there above its forbidding surface.

"Now what the hell is this all about?" he wanted to know. "That looks and smells like booze."

"This is what I was trying to explain, sir," McCorkle declared loudly. He extended his hand holding the manual, finger still marking the passage. His hand shook and for an instant some of his old uncertainty threatened to return.

"I—it's all..." He realized that he had stammered and paused to clear his throat, covering the lapse. "It's all right here in the manual, sir."

He took a precise step forward, remembering that much depended upon his performance. He flopped open the pages of the thick volume to the paragraphs which he had marked. Two worn pages fell out of the book and Ashdon stooped to recover them, then hid them self-consciously behind his back. This brought a glare from the Chief-of-Staff, but the general seemed interested in McCorkle's explanation.

"In such humid weather as we've experienced here, it is practically impossible to get a negative to dry. It sometimes takes days, and by that time, it's so covered with dust that it's ruined," McCorkle explained, attempting to ignore the general's shrewd, judging gaze. "So we use alcohol. We soak the negs in this stuff there in the pan. Then when we hang them up, they will dry in thirty minutes or so."

"Where do you get your alcohol?" the Chief wanted to know. "It's against orders for the Medical Section to release any for outside use unless I sign the order."

"We make it, sir," McCorkle replied. His tone was brave but he avoided the colonel's stare. There was a sharp intake of breath from Quillan; a gurgling sound suggesting that he might be strangling, but all eyes were upon the lieutenant.

"You make it," the general quoted, wanting to be certain. "Booze?"

McCorkle shook his head, trying not to appear defensive.

"Not booze, sir," he insisted. "Alcohol. We need it for this sort of work. So we make it."

The general thought about it, rubbing his chin. "What's it made out of?" McCorkle turned questioning eyes upon Quillan and the master sergeant came to attention out of force of habit. He was perspiring, and as he spoke he seemed to be having difficulty in finding his breath.

"Raisins, sir." His tone was suddenly apologetic. "Anything else we can lay hands on. It ain't fit t'drink, of course."

There was a painful silence. The Chief took a faltering step nearer the evil looking concoction and stood for a moment, staring into the brown ugly depths. His expression plainly told that he fully expected to see a pink whale rise to the surface and spout.

"If you need alcohol for a legitimate need, you could draw it," he suggested, disbelief still coloring his tone. "It'd certainly serve better than this stuff."

"That's the point, sir." McCorkle sought a note of sureness that didn't quite appear. "If I drew grain alcohol, there are those who would drink it."

This time there was an audible snort from Quillan, who was staring bug-eyed at his immediate superior.

"Would the colonel care to taste this stuff?" Ashdon asked, trying to back up McCorkle. The Chief-of-Staff's reply was a quick step to the rear. Before he could object vocally, there was a sound at the entrance and the chaplain pushed through the canvas flap. He stiffened, set his cap straight on his head, then faced the general, who had turned to glare at him.

"Sir," the chaplain stated formally, "I would like to prefer charge against this officer." He indicated McCorkle with a disdainful flip of his fingers. "And this man." His gesture toward Quillan was even more scornful.

The general glanced at the accused pair with professional interest. "For what, chaplain?"

"Dereliction of duty," the man of the cloth replied. "They wouldn't take my picture."

"They don't take mine very often either," the general half agreed, "but what is your specific complaint?"

"I have a shipment of clothing sent by a congregation in the States and I'm going to turn it over to an orphanage. When I asked for a photographer to take pictures, Sergeant Quillan refused."

"The sergeant's refusal was on my order," McCorkle put in coldly. He no longer stammered but failed to realize it. The ice in his tone was created by the chaplain's presence; were it not for him, none of them would be standing here, explaining the bogus need for alcohol. "As the general knows, we are short of film. We got some in Japan, but it won't last long."

He nodded to the churchman. "And we have shot the chaplain passing out his rags at least forty times. If the folks back home don't know he's a big man with the natives by now, any more is a waste of film."

"Wait a minute!" the chaplain howled in defense. "That's not..."

"Hold it!" the general roared and silence reigned. He stood for a moment, staring into the tray of liquor, then heaved a sigh. "Gawd," he muttered, "whatever happened to the wars where we fought the enemy instead of each other?

"Chaplain, I'll tell you how it's going to be. From now on, you take care of God and let McCorkle take care of the pictures!"

The chaplain looked uncomfortable. "What about their Korean boy? He kicked me. He belongs in an orphanage, not with a group of men like these." He paused to sniff suspiciously. "Someone's been drinking."

The general stirred dangerously. "Are you accusing me?"

"No, sir!" The youthful do-gooder snapped to automatic attention.

"As for that boy, he's in his formative years."

"But he's a delinquent," the other protested with an indignation he was unable to hide. "He says he's a spy!"

"He's a boy," the general insisted quietly, "and there is no boy who belongs in an orphanage if he has those who are interested in him."

"Yes, sir." The chaplain pouted his defeat. "Is that all, sir?"

"That is all, chaplain," the general agreed on a note of finality.

As the youthful chaplain's shoulders sagged and he moved uncertainly toward the entrance to the makeshift photo lab, McCorkle suddenly felt compassion for him. The man of the cloth, he realized, it coming as something of a revelation, was not too much different from himself.

There was little doubt that he was frightened, realizing that he lived in this small, exclusive world of men who were dedicated to warfare. As one Marine officer had once put it, "Our mission is to kill as many of the enemy as possible with as little cost to ourselves as is economical." This reasoning could hardly be understood by a new chaplain undoubtedly on his first assignment in the field. He would find it difficult to understand that most of these men were more interested in death and destruction of an opponent than in the saving of their own souls.

In almost any combat unit, the chaplain may be accepted without comment, but one rarely will find enthusiasm for his presence. He is viewed, instead, as a non-combatant who serves no useful function; he is dead wood that is tolerated only because the Department of the Navy and Marine Corps Headquarters have agreed that he shall be a part of the table of organization.

And because of his lack of popularity, McCorkle realized now, the chaplain had subconsciously attempted to hide behind his cross, clothing his own fears and knowledge of his inadequacies in the cloak of his station. In short, the man was insecure and was trying desperately not to show it.

At the tent flap, the chaplain turned uncertainly, glancing toward the gathering.

"There is one other matter, sir," he said, addressing the general on a note of sudden timidity.

"What now?" the general did not attempt to hide his growing annoyance.

"The Army MP's have Colonel Barrymore under arrest, sir."

There was a growl of disbelief from the Chief-of-Staff, a blasphemous curse from the general that caused the chaplain to retreat another step. To have the lowly Army arrest a Marine on his own ground was a challenge. In better days, such incidents had led to open warfare.

"They say he was driving a jeep that was stolen from the Army," the chaplain hastened to explain.

There was a roar of pain from the general. The pain was in that ambiguous area known as his *esprit de corps*, but this reaction sent the unnerved chaplain through the tent flap in terrified retreat.

There was a sound of apprehension from the Chief, who eyed McCorkle with ill-hidden belligerence. But the latter had his gaze upon Master Sergeant Quillan. Traces of a smile, sign of a job well done, tilted the sergeant's lips. There was no doubt as to who had squealed.

126

"Damn!" the general snarled at the group. "What the hell's happened to this Marine Corps? People can't even steal right any more!"

"Aye, sir," Quillan agreed properly, as it appeared no one else was going to.

The general cast him a curious glance, then his eyes narrowed in recollection. "Don't I know you, sergeant?"

"Yes, sir," Quillan agreed again. "Nicaragua, 1927. I was there when the general won the Medal of Honor."

"That's it," the general beamed, forgetting the Army and Colonel Barrymore. "Your name's Quillan."

"Right, sir."

"Good to see you again." The general thrust out his hand Quillan shook it with enthusiasm. "See that the lieutenant here keeps out of my brig, will you?"

"I'll do my best, sir." Under this newly assigned responsibility, Quillan stretched to his full height and attempted to suck in his belly. The Chief-of-Staff coughed nervously.

"Lieutenant Colonel Barrymore," he reminded the general with that right mixture of respect and mildness that helps one to become a colonel.

"Yeah," the general growled, then glanced about. "Dismissed."

Quillan and Ashdon lost no time in making for the opening. The Chief-of-Staff hesitated for a moment, glancing at the general, then stepped through the tent flap. McCorkle relaxed slightly as the general hesitated for a moment, then delicately extended an index finger and plunged it into the vat of brown liquid.

As he licked his finger, frowning thoughtfully, McCorkle came back to the position of attention, holding his breath.

"McCorkle!" the general growled severely as he turned to stare.

"Sir?"

"That booze needs more sugar!" There may even have been the hint of a smile in his eyes.

"Aye, sir!"

Then without another glance, the general stalked out. McCorkle stared after him, then slowly dipped his own finger into the raisin-jack, licking the digit experimentally.

# CHAPTER 14

"SERGEANT QUILLAN," McCorkle began carefully, "how the hell does one get to the front?"

"Sir?" The sergeant had heard the question perfectly, but had no ready answer. He and the lieutenant were alone in the tent, a position which Quillan found uncomfortable since the affair of the raisinjack. He liked others around as a buffer. McCorkle was too much the officer and gentleman to chew him out in front of the lesser ranking men.

"I've been here three months, and the only gunfire I've heard was that first night, when you were after that rat." There was a touch of bitterness in the officer's complaint. The master sergeant's brow wrinkled into a scowl.

"Well you might try goin' over the hill. Desertin'," he suggested. This approach had worked well for several members of the Marine guard section in San Diego who had arrived recently. They had simply walked away from their posts and stowed aboard outgoing troop transports. By the time they had been discovered, it had been too late to turn back. They had been reprimanded, unofficially forgiven and transferred to the front lines of the 1st Marine Division.

McCorkle shook his head. "There must be some way that's a little less spectacular."

"Then let it be known you're damn happy back here'n th' rear with th' gear. Some bastard's sure t'figger you're th' type that needs a little action."

The officer stared at him dubiously, not understanding. "Wouldn't it be easier to just volunteer?"

"Volunteer to get shot at an' they'll say you need a head-shrinker. But look at all these broad-assed administrators, all makin' sure they don't get no closer to th' front. Now if it looked like you was fixin' to nail down a plank and not move neither, they'd figger you was a threat to their own security. They'd getcha t' th' front." He paused, inspecting McCorkle curiously, seeing a side he had not discovered before. "You really wanta get shot at?"

McCorkle considered, finally heaving a sigh. "I don't think so, but when this is over, how am I going to explain what I was doing here? I can't tell people I spent the war trying to overlook the fact that you run a still."

Quillan stiffened at the mention of this illicit operation. It had been two weeks since the general's visit to the photo lab and McCorkle had made no mention of it. Instead, most of the command had been involved in keeping Barrymore from being dragged off bodily to an Army stockade.

When the smoke finally had cleared, Barrymore had remained free, but the contested jeep had been returned grudgingly to the Army. This had incensed Quillan and the others, but McCorkle had shrugged the matter away, refusing to become involved in any serious plot.

"Do what everyone else has to do," he finally had ordered with new authority. "When you need wheels for official business, call the motor pool."

"But we can't wait all day," Quillan protested realistically. "What if the general wants his picture took with some VIP like Syngman Rhee or Marilyn Monroe?"

"We only have to miss one shot that the general wants," McCorkle said without expression.

Quillan stared at him in red-eyed admiration. Until now, most of the junior officers he had encountered had fallen into precise, predictable categories. Either they were afraid of master sergeants and let the six-stripers call the shots, signing name, rank and serial number when called upon, or they were junior martinets who firmly believed that old sergeants were devoid of brains or they would all be colonels.

McCorkle had, in the beginning, fallen into the former category, but this no longer was true. He had been in command ever since the day of his return from Japan. The sergeant had pressed Ashdon for details of that trip, seeking a reason for the change, but the photographer had only shrugged. In his more sober moments, Quillan found that he was even a trifle fearful of the lieutenant and this change.

At this very moment, there was another crisis in the offing, but he had not told the young officer. The sergeant sighed and made the verbal plunge. "You hear about Henry?"

McCorkle looked up abruptly, scowling. "I haven't seen him all morning. Where is he?"

"Down at G-2. The intelligence pogues're interrogatin' him."

McCorkle straightened abruptly from his slouched position against the door frame. "Interrogating him about what?"

Quillan's tone was defensive. "They heard about that thing with th' dynamite, an' think maybe he really was tryin' t'blow us up. Handley musta tipped 'em off." He was wondering why he insisted upon defending the orphan; there were thousands of homeless waifs in the area. Grimly he thought back to other days in Shanghai, where he first had learned the code of the Orient. It was the custom in China that, if you saved a person's life, you were making yourself responsible for that life thereafter. Maybe he had come to believe it.

"That kid's been a disrupting influence ever since I've been here," McCorkle said, trying to sound realistic. "They're going to get him sooner or later."

Quillan stared at McCorkle coldly. "The orphanage, you mean?"

McCorkle glanced at him, then looked away. "What's the alternative? Transfer Handley?"

"You mean shanghai, don't you?"

McCorkle suddenly realized that he was being accused and he glared at the sergeant. Quillan shook his head, returning the stare.

"This is th' end of th' line, skipper. He's been shanghaied an' Korea's th' last place he can go. There ain't no other place t'send him."

Quillan realized that he might have McCorkle off balance and pressed his advantage. "You've been here long enough t'know th' score. All of us was shanghaied here f'r one cause or another. Hell, it's always been like that. Them guys that crossed th' Delaware in them leaky boats with Washin'ton was probably all outcasts; th' expendables."

McCorkle lowered himself into his canvas chair. He was scowling, yet intrigued with this philosophy.

"Th' Marine Corps ain't no different. When we're sent into action, everyone back home figgers th' first team's been committed an' we'll make th' whole world safe in th' next ten minutes.

"Maybe when a full Divvie or Wing goes, it's th' first team, but when th' replacements start t'flow in t'fill up the casualty holes, it changes. When th' word comes in a Stateside command that they need bodies f'r combat, it's the primma donnas, th' misfits, th' nonconformists that get weeded out. No one likes t'transfer a good soldier outa his outfit. They're hard come by. It's better t'send somebody else your troubles!"

Quillan ended his impassioned speech and sat staring at the officer, half-expecting the ass chewing he knew he rated. Instead, McCorkle frowned.

"How'd you get here?"

"I was shanghaied, too," Quillan admitted grumpily.

"I was livin' high off'n th' hog in New York City, Information Writer f'r th' recruitin' office. B'sides m'pay, I was drawin' extra quarters and subsistence allowance, an' there was this spot where I could buy booze wholesale. But I hadda try t'do my job too well." There was a tinge of bitterness in his tone.

"This rat race had just started, so I got this idea an' had a bunch of round carton covers printed up with big red letters: *Act Today — Be The First To Fight. Enlist Today, Korea Tomorrow! Join The Marines!*

"It sounded pretty good sober, but with a load of that cut-rate bourbon, I got upta th' top of th' Empire State Buildin' an' started sailin' them things out over th' city. I figgered I was gonna make th' whole town Marine conscious, an' I guess I musta.

"At least, it wasn't long b'fore the cops an' a batch of MP's showed up an' dragged me off t'the Tombs f'r breakin' some law against throwin' things offa the tops of buildin's. I was in there two days b'fore someone come t'bail me out.

"Then when I got t'th' office, that major that run th' place had m'orders cut, signed an' ready f'r delivery. They wanted t'get ridda me so bad, they flew me out here."

"A touching story," McCorkle sympathized, "but what's this got to do with Handley and Henry?"

Quillan squinted at the officer in speculation. "Well, I sorta figger they're good for each other."

It was obvious the sergeant had spent some thought on the subject, but didn't know exactly how to express it. He chose his words with care.

"After Handley seen his brother get killed and got transferred t'us, he wasn't worth a damn. All he did was mope around, an' every night, he'd lay there in his bunk an' cry till he went t'sleep."

"You should have turned him in to sickbay," McCorkle protested, and Quillan nodded agreement.

"That's how I figgered, too, but Major Lawrence didn't see it that way. He said it was better t'let him cry it out than get him aboard a hospital ship or back'n Japan, where some head-shrinker'd be askin' him whether he liked girls or why he hated his mother.

"Th' major was right. Handley's been okay ever since he learned t'hate. For a while, he acted like he didn't have no reason t'live, but as soon as he found Henry was always around f'r him t'hate, he perked up. Henry's good therapy f'r him."

McCorkle rose slowly from his chair. "Quillan, I know a psychology prof who'd love to hear your theories. He wouldn't believe them, but he'd love to hear them."

"You gonna shanghai either one of them?" Quillan was not certain how his case had been accepted.

"Not now," McCorkle told him grimly. "I need a vacation from this madhouse. I'm going to get to the front!"

# CHAPTER 15

**M**cCORKLE STOOD before the cracked mirror in the rear of the tent, critically inspecting the growth of hair that extended horizontally along his upper lip.

He dipped a finger into the can of melted wax and smoothed it along the strands, turning up the ends with a delicate twist. For a moment, the creation stood with magnificence. Then it began to droop abruptly. Frustrated, he pushed aside the wax and dropped to the edge of his bunk, growling over this defeat. What could Shamley and that crazy enlisted pilot use to produce that spike-like appearance of their own handlebars?

It wasn't the mustache alone. It was the whole setup. His written request to the Chief-of-Staff asking for an assignment at the front had been returned with disapproval and without reason. Like Gunner Schmake, he had been surrounded by a wall of paper. While others were fighting the war, he was battling an increasingly heavy load of white bond. The closest he had been to combat had been the night the military police had raided the burlesque house.

He shuddered at that recollection and twisted one end of his mustache back into position. Again facing the mirror, he watched glumly as it dropped back to a Fu Manchu angle.

And there was Barrymore. He had been shanghaied, although so blunt a term is hardly used in connection with the transfer of a staff grade officer. Instead, this is invariably described as a career guidance reassignment.

Whatever the term, Barrymore no longer was in the Operations Section. He had been transferred to Intelligence, where he had functioned for a short period as the Assistant Chief-of-Staff in charge of this unit. When he had been replaced by a bird-type colonel, the tarnished eagles of long service gracing his shoulders, it had become apparent that whatever adjusting Barrymore's career might be undergoing was in the wrong direction.

His demotion from Assistant Chief-of-Staff, G-2, had come after he had made a tour of nearby Pusan, a bumbling hive of humanity including several hundred thousand refugees. During the tour, a band of ragged, hungry orphans had virtually stripped the jeep he had been driving. The automotive parts would find their way into the black market and the children would eat for a day or so.

But during the trip, Barrymore had discovered that a certain Pusan fish market was using documents marked *Top Secret* for wrapping fish. This had been horrifying enough, but when he had discovered that these maps and plans apparently had come from his own section, he had raced the stripped vehicle back to Wing Headquarters to launch a full-scale investigation of this security leak.

This search had come tumbling down upon Barrymore's own head when it was learned that he personally had signed for all of the missing documents; if they had found their way into a fish market to serve as wrapping paper, it had happened since he had taken charge of the G-2 unit. That had been when the eagle colonel had quietly relieved him.

When one of McCorkle's photographers had missed a photo of General Ridgeway, commander of Far East Forces, arriving for a conference, McCorkle had been forced to explain that the motor pool had been unable to furnish a vehicle in time. A day or so later, when the information unit magically produced a jeep, this sudden acquisition had been officially ignored. What rankled Barrymore was the fact that, while unshaven sergeants and corporals motored about the area, suspicious brown jugs weighing down the vehicle, he was doomed to walk. Worse, investigations through his Intelligence channels had revealed that this was the same jeep that had been confiscated from him by the Army MP's at the time of his arrest.

The jeep long ago had been written off by the Army as "lost in combat," a catch-all phrase for lost equipment. To have the jeep suddenly reappear and negate all of the carefully juggled records had been too much for the Army supply system. They wanted only to be rid of it.

Through some unrevealed pipeline, Quillan had learned of this difficulty and had agreed to take the vehicle out of the Army supply system before its reappearance resulted in someone being jailed for falsifying records.

When Barrymore reported this to the Chief-of-Staff, the reception was cool. After all, the photographer would not have missed the picture of Ridgeway had it not been for the lieutenant colonel's piracy of the vehicle in the first place.

The general, the Chief informed him, still was piqued over not having his picture taken with General Ridgeway's arm about his shoulder. He might never get another chance and photos of that type could be invaluable to a career.

Some of these facts had been offered by Max Schmake, some had come from Quillan's pipeline, but most had been learned from Henry, who had been released after his interrogation, but McCorkle suspected that suspicion still rested upon him. In spite of this respite, he realized, too, that sooner or later things would have to come to a head over the boy. It was something he tried not to think about, but Barrymore's men had done the questioning. The lieutenant colonel's silence since the affair of the jeep was not necessarily a sign that McCorkle and his men were being ignored.

Quillan had agreed on this point and had ordered the photographers to break all of the bottles in the lab the moment anyone resembling an intelligence agent hove into sight. The psuedo chemicals, once free of the glass, might smell like raisinjack, he explained, but there would be no admissible evidence.

"'Ten'shun!" Quillan bawled in the outer office and there was the rustle of clothing, the leather squeak of combat boots, as the combined manpower came erect.

"At ease, men," the Chief-of-Staff growled. "Don't you people ever keep your phone on the hook?"

"Didn't know it was off, sir," Quillan lied. There was a fumbling sound, then the click of plastic against metal. "There we are."

The Chief's tone was still irritated. "It doesn't matter now. I'm here. Where's Lieutenant McCorkle?"

"Coming, sir!" McCorkle quickly wiped a towel across his drooping mustache. As he ducked through the curtained opening, the Chief was rocking back and forth on his heels, while the assorted members of the unit stood at attention in various degrees of dress. Corporal Handley stood naked from the waist down. His trousers were bunched in front of him, his ankles crossed coyly. There was a patch partially sewn across the weathered seat, needle and thread dangling from the fabric.

"Handley," McCorkle ordered sternly, "get your pants on."

"Aye, sir," the corporal acknowledged uncomfortably, then stood on one foot, trying despairingly to get his toes through the leg of the dungaree trousers. This was somewhat difficult inasmuch as he had sewn the leg closed.

"Sir?" McCorkle addressed the colonel inquiringly.

"I tried to call and finally walked down here," the Chief charged. He motioned to his flank. "This is Alan Dean."

At the summons, the boy stepped out of the shadow cast by the colonel. Even in the baggy khaki trousers, the field jacket and the familiar emblem of the United Nations Correspondent that graced his shoulder, he couldn't have been more than nineteen.

The Chief placed a fatherly hand on the youth's shoulder. "Al is out here for *Exploit* magazine," he explained, "and he's going to do some articles on our outfit."

"Welcome aboard," McCorkle greeted him, extending his hand. The boy, his black hair revealing a well rehearsed wave and side-burns, took it limply.

McCorkle and the enlisted men were staring at this new arrival with frank curiosity. Sergeant Shade's expression was disapproving, even hostile, at having someone younger than himself aboard.

"We need exposure in a national magazine," the Chief was explaining with enthusiasm. "Something to make the people back home realize we're fighting a war. Fighting it well." As he rocked back and forth on heel and toe, McCorkle realized suddenly that the Chief was slightly smashed.

"Yes, sir," the lieutenant agreed, covertly eyeing the youth.

"So, I'm turning Mister Dean over to your care. It'll be up to you to see that he gets whatever he needs in the way of cooperation. We're fraternity brothers, so I know he'll do a proper job for us." He turned slightly glazed eyes upon the youngster. "Right, brother?"

"I'll do my best, Ethan," Alan Dean agreed amiably.

McCorkle flinched at the youth's use of a first name for a staff officer and Quillan's brows elevated several degrees. The colonel only beamed.

"I know you will, son. You'll make us proud of you and we want you to be proud of us. Right, lieutenant?" He glared at McCorkle, daring him to take exception.

"R-right, sir."

"You can put Mister Dean up here, if he can stand this rathole." He glanced about, allowing his eyes to linger on Mister Truman's quote concerning the Corps' propaganda machine. His expression was proof that he was a Democrat and did not appreciate the humorous intent; but he also was a Marine who could not ignore the truth.

"Alan wants to fly a combat mission in one of our planes and he wants to go on a helicopter rescue mission up front." The colonel glanced at Dean for confirmation. The boy nodded enthusiastically and the Chief's gaze came back to McCorkle. "You'll see that he gets *whatever* he wants."

"A-aye, sir. Anything." McCorkle's voice sounded uncertain even to his own ears and he caught the grimace of contempt on Quillan's lips. Nursemaid to a teenager. What the hell kind of war was this?

"Alan is representing the press back home," the Chief offered in afterthought, but his tone suddenly was flat with threat. "Anything happens to him, McCorkle, it's your ass!"

"Aye, sir," the junior muttered in helpless resignation. "My ass."

"Goodnight, Alan," the Chief said. He lurched to the door, then looked back. "They don't treat you right there, just let me know. Okay, brother?" He offered a broad, meaningful wink, and McCorkle wondered whether this was some part of a secret fraternity ritual as Dean returned the wink with an equally grotesque smile.

The Chief-of-Staff passed into the night. There was a grunt followed by a curse, as he stumbled. An instant later, the garbled words of *White Star of Sigma Nu* drifted back on the damp night air.

Alan Dean was no more than five feet five inches and might have weighed 125 pounds. He looked skinnier in the over-size Army khaki and the U.S. Correspondent's patch sewed to his shoulder nearly encircled his scrawny arm. McCorkle cast a quick glance, an appeal for help, at Quillan, but the master sergeant was sullenly regarding the toes of his boots.

"Henry," McCorkle called and the Korean boy materialized from behind the stove, where he had sought wise refuge from Handley and his needle. "Get Major Lawrence's old bunk set up and put clean blankets on it for Mister Dean."

The boy glanced at Dean with open disdain. "Yuh mean I gotta sleep back there witha stinkin' civilian?" he spat.

"Just up and do as you're told," Quillan snarled at him.

"One moment, gentlemen."

Alan Dean's tone was soft and genteel, heavy with Ivy League training, as he stepped into the circle of light to glance about the array of hostile faces.

"Let's get a few things straight," he continued. "The Chief is a fraternity brother, but coming here with you was my idea, not his. Just know I'm not a headquarters spy."

"I'm a spy, too," Henry told him, showing traces of professional jealousy. "A damn good one."

"Get that bunk made up or you'll be spyin' from flat on your ass," Handley told him. Still half clad, he took a threatening step toward the Korean, but Henry retreated through the curtained doorway. Quillan cast Dean a condescending smile.

"You'll hafta excuse the kid, Mister Dean. He ain't been around civilians."

"I understand," the war correspondent acknowledged, then added brightly, "Is there a drink in the house?"

Quillan looked to the officer for instructions and the latter turned severely to the newcomer.

"How old are you, Mister Dean?" His tone was delicate.

"Nineteen," the other declared knowingly, "and if you can show me a law that says I'm too young to drink in this country, I'll abide by it."

"Henry!" Quillan glanced uneasily over his shoulder until the dried-up little face peered around the edge of the curtain.

"Henry, what's the legal drinkin' age in this country?" the master sergeant wanted to know.

"Hell, I don't know," the lad shrugged. "I'm a North Korean." He ducked back behind the curtain, as Alan Dean stared thoughtfully at McCorkle.

"The Chief-of-Staff did say something about treating me right, did he not?" the correspondent asked pointedly.

McCorkle exchanged stares with him, then surrendered. "Quillan, find him a drink. In fact, you'd better find us all a drink."

Quillan hesitated for a long moment, then nodded.

"Yes, sir," he declared emphatically. As he began pawing through his field desk, Ashdon and Shade began rounding up canteen cups.

Frantic now, Corporal Handley was trying to get into his pants.

As the boy reporter dropped to the edge of a bench fashioned from old rocket cases, McCorkle pulled up a canvas stool and sat down to face him.

"How did you get out here?"

"*Exploit* sent me," the lad offered with a guarded shrug.

Quillan had found two gallons of the mysterious looking brown liquid and half a pint was poured for each man. As Dean raised his cup, he paused with the rim just short of his lips. He frowned his disturbance.

"Did that kid say he was from *North* Korea?"

"That he did, sir," Quillan agreed expansively. The idea of a party always lightened his mood.

"He'll slit all our throats some night, too," Handley suggested bitterly. Dean was impressed with the threat.

"And you allow him to sleep here? In this tent?"

"He's harmless," Quillan grunted.

"Tell 'im I'm a spy," Henry called from beyond the dividing partition.

It was four o'clock in the morning before the party came to an unceremonious halt, and it ended then only because the raisinjack had run out and the latest batch wouldn't be cured for at least two more days.

Quillan, Dean and McCorkle were still on their feet, while the rest were strewn about the tent in various states of disarray. Shade was on the floor, snoring softly where he had fallen sometime in the night. Handley was propped up in a chair, one trouser still hanging loose as testimony that he had lost his battle with domesticity. Ashdon was slumped in a corner, a camera in his lap. He had gone to sleep after taking a dozen shots to commemorate the affair.

"Wanna know why I'm out here?" Dean asked abruptly, staring owlishly over the edge of his cup. There had been a reverent silence as this trio had nursed the final drops of Quillan's devil's brew.

"Wanna know whadda nineteen-year-old kid's doin' here?" This time he spoke positively, wagging his head loosely. "I'm dodgin' th' draft!"

Quillan belched unbecomingly. McCorkle leaned forward on his seat to stare at the youth and almost fell on his face. Dean smiled happily at the disruption he had created. He nodded sagely.

"Tha's right. I'm a daft roger."

**139**

"Draft dodger," McCorkle interpreted, but the correction went ignored.

"I was in college an' flunked out las' semester. Th' draft board was breathin' down m'neck. Tha's when m' ole man heard they couldn't draft a correspondent overseas. I got outa th' country jus' ahead of my call." He shook his head sadly. "Now I can't go back till this stinkin' mess is over."

He raised his head suddenly, offering a delicate sniff. His expression of self-pity gave way to gentle horror. The direction of the wind had changed. "Speakin' of stinks, wha's that?"

McCorkle thought back a million years or so to one who had asked the same question. And he offered the same answer.

"That's spring. Or maybe it's summer."

# CHAPTER 16

"**W**hen th' hell's Mac due back?" Sergeant Taylor demanded, stalking into the tent and halting to glare at Quillan. "He's gotta do somethin'."

"Mac who?" The top sergeant looked up from a well-worn copy of *War Aces* to return the glare.

"McCorkle."

"That's Lootenant McCorkle," Quillan returned icily.

"Now ain't we gettin' formal alluva sudden," Taylor sneered, but took a step backward as Quillan lurched to his feet, scowling at him. "Okay, okay. It's lootenant, but somebody's gotta do somethin' about this." He waved a sheet of mimeograph paper and shoved it into Quillan's grasp. The latter shoved it back.

"I've seen it," Quillan grumped at him. "Henry brought one."

"Well, what're we gonna do?" Taylor wanted to know, staring down at the paper. "This sorta thing's bad for morale. Not just ours. Everyone's."

"Morale's the chaplain's department," Quillan alibied.

"Hell, he wouldn't open his Book f'r this outfit it we was all standin' at the devil's doorway."

"I figger it that way, too," Quillan admitted, "an' I've been doin' some thinkin' about it. Can't tell when th' lootenant's gonna get back, so we'll hafta shift f'r ourselves. Round up th' rest of this crew and tell 'em to get their respective asses over here on th' double."

Taylor was mystified. "What're we gonna do?"

"We're gonna plan strategy," Quillan told him coldly.

"Whatever that means."

"Strategy's one of them big-time military words for connive, boy. Now move." As Taylor departed, Quillan turned back to the paper on his desk, shaking his head in an expression of disgust. The Old Corps had never been like this.

Ten minutes later, the rest of the writers and photographers who were not out on assignment were gathered about him. They were not exactly standing at attention, as they slouched about the various pieces of makeshift furniture or sat on the floor. Quillan looked over the group.

"Where's Alan Dean, boy reporter?" he wanted to know.

"This is internal bus'ness," Taylor replied. "We figgered it'd be better t'let him sleep."

Quillan hesitated, then nodded. He held aloft the piece of mimeograph paper. "Any of you seen this?" Some had, others had not. He began to read:

"To: Headquarters Squadron Personnel

"From: Acting Squadron Commander

"Subject: Uniformity Of Living Quarters

"1. During a recent inspection of the squadron living area by the undersigned, it was noted that tents and personal gear were in complete disarray, causing this camp to bear close resemblance to the wallow of a family of ill-bred swine. The below list of requirements has been established to govern the discrepancies noted.

"(1) Bunks in pyramidal tents will be arranged along tent walls, four men per tent.

"(2) All gear will be stored in packs or seabags and will not be left on bunk or floor.

"(3) Each Marine will be allowed nine nails in the wooden tent frame above his personal bunk. From left to right, these nails will hold:

"(A) Mess Gear. (Washed and clean at all times.)

"(B) Combat Pack (Complete with prescribed items to be carried into the field.)

"(C) Weapon. (Rifles and Carbines will be hung by the sling; pistols will not be hung by trigger guards or butt swivels and will be contained in proper holsters at all times.)

"(D) Towel. (Clean and folded at all times.)

"(E) Wash Cloth. (It has been noted that many individuals are using bits of supply parachute, handkerchiefs and miscellaneous rags. Standard cloths can be purchased through Marine Exchange facilities and will be displayed henceforth.)

"(F) Helmet. (When not in use, the steel helmet will hang completely assembled with liner and camouflage cover. The practice of using helmets for washing clothing, heating rations or breeding pollywogs for fishing bait will cease.)

"(4) The remaining nails are allowed for the personal convenience of the individual Marine. One may be used to hold a shaving mirror. Family portraits may be hung from these nails, but no pinup photos will be in evidence."

Quillan, showing evidences of thespic frustration, had read the entire order in a doomful tone. Now he looked up and down the circle of faces, scowling.

"What idiot wrote that?" someone wanted to know.

"Barrymore," Taylor put in. "They've made him acting squadron commander, while Colonel Hayes is in sickbay."

"Hell, don'tcha think Hayes'll cancel it when he gets out?"

"We don't know whether he's gonna get out," Quillan stated. "They're talkin' about sendin' him to Japan for hospitalization."

There was another long silence, while the Marines pondered the problem. They were quick to admit that they were members of a military establishment, but there were some conveniences that one should be able to expect in combat; some relaxation of the rules.

Quillan glanced at Sergeant Shamley, who was scowling darkly.

"That means all your pictures of naked broads've gotta come down," Quillan reminded him.

"Yeah. All 126 of 'em." There was a genuine note of concern in Shamley's voice. "What th' hell're we gonna do?"

"Dammit, he can't do this!" Corporal Handley announced in genuine frustration. "I'm a combat veteran. I've been shot at. Don't that give me some rights?"

"You read the order." It was a statement of fact from Quillan. But there was a dreamy note in his next question. "I wonder how many nails the general has over his bunk?"

"Hell, he's gotta closet over there'n Valhalla," Shamley muttered, referring to the enlisted men's designation for the general's plush quarters. "He don't need nails." He offered a deep sigh. "He prob'ly ain't even got any pin-up pictures."

143

"Not your kind, at least," Quillan agreed, nodding acceptance of this probability. "But what about the Chief-of-Staff. He lives in a tent. How many nails for him?"

"Rank has its privileges," Handley put in. "I'd figger him for about a thirteen-nail man. But what about Barrymore? How many nails you reckon he has over his bunk?"

"He don't need nails," Quillan sniffed. "His gear's all so damn full of starch it don't need t'be hung up. It just stands there by itself. He prob'ly hasta crack his dungarees with a hammer b'fore he can get 'em on!"

"There ain't no use arguin' amongst our own," Shamley put in fiercely. The fact that his nude photos were in jeopardy was approaching trauma. "We gotta figger somethin' fast."

"Th' Chief's gotta be th' answer," Quillan put in. "Chances are, he don't even know about this order."

"He must," the jeep driver argued. "He belongs t'this squadron."

"For administrative purposes only," Quillan pointed out. "He don't have nothin' to do with writin' th' minor orders."

"Okay, you're in charge," Taylor pointed out, irked over Quillan's earlier reminder of this point. "What's your solution?"

"Who in this outfit's th' only one that can get t'the Chief?" Quillan asked carefully.

"You're about to mention my name," Alan Dean announced somewhat grandly from the doorway. How much of the conversation he had heard was questionable, although he was still rubbing the sleep from his eyes.

"Somebody give Mister Dean a seat," Quillan ordered. The others turned to stare at him in a manner suggesting revolt, but Quillan waved to Shamley. "Let him have yours, Shifty."

Stifling a sneer, the sergeant stood and Dean slid onto his upturned ammo crate, glancing suspiciously about the group.

"To what do I owe this startling display of esteem?" he demanded cynically.

"You've been lookin' for a story that'd go over big in th' States an' I think we've found it for you," Quillan replied, tone suddenly soothing. It was enough to make the youngster still more suspicious.

"I find your consideration touching."

"Here," Quillan suggested, shoving the squadron order into his hand. "Read this, then I'll tell you about the story."

Dean read the paper, then handed it back to the master sergeant, expression one of bewilderment. "What story?"

Quillan shook his head in an indication that they didn't make correspondents like they used to in the Old Corps.

"It's a natural, kid. Can't you see a story about Nine Nail City. Maybe even about th' Chief bein' th' mayor. It could be a very funny piece."

Alan Dean considered for a long moment, eyes narrowing. "I think I'm being used."

Quillan thought about it for a moment, then nodded. "I agree. We want t'use you. Since you can get t'the Chief, you're th' only one that can make it work."

Dean was uncertain of his attitude. The fact that this group suddenly realized the importance of his position as a reporter for *Exploit* magazine did something for his ego, but it also strengthened his suspicions.

Quillan, trading upon this uncertainty, waved the paper at him. "Can't you see, this is nothing but the first step in creepin' militarism. If this thing's allowed t'stand, next there'll be an order against keepin' beer under our bunks. After that, they'll prob'ly ban booze entirely." He waved a vague hand. "After that, no tellin' what might happen. They might even insist we salute th' chaplain!"

"What's in it for me?" Dean demanded.

"Like I said, a story maybe. If not, you'll have the esteem of every man in Headquarters Squadron. Hundreds of friends." Quillan was laying it on thick, voice soft and enticing. While the others of the group were impressed with this display, Dean obviously wasn't buying it. Quillan heaved a sigh and offered a shrug.

"Okay, I promise you a whole gallon of our booze. A full gallon all your own. But you gotta help."

"I think that's bribery," Dean decided, eyes narrowed.

"It's bribery," Quillan admitted in defeat.

"Why didn't you say so. What do you have in mind?"

Without obvious signal, there was a sudden cheer from the group of Marines surrounding him and Dean could not help looking pleased.

Quillan rose suddenly, back in command, waving his hand at the others. "Okay. Everybody out. Al and me've gotta write th' script f'r this soap opera."

"Let me help," Handley said. "I used to write dramatic shows for radio."

"Not you. You're too goddamn honest," Quillan sneered. "This has to take a genuine con man." He glanced at Dean apologetically. "Beggin' your pardon."

Three hours later, Alan Dean and Quillan were in the Chief-of-Staff's office. Dean was lolling in a chair facing the colonel, while Quillan stood respectfully in the background, carrying the youth's camera bag. Dean waved airily in the sergeant's direction.

"I believe you've met Master Sergeant Quillan," he said and Quillan snapped to attention as the colonel cast him a dubious glance.

"I know who he is. But what was the purpose of this meeting?"

"Well, sir. I have this great idea for a story, and I brought Sergeant Quillan along so he could see that he was wrong. He feels that this is something that should be left alone. In fact, he doesn't feel it would reflect credit upon the military."

The Chief-of-Staff was suddenly all attention, sitting erect in his chair and wheeling closer to his desk.

"What's that?" he wanted to know, fumbling in his jacket pocket for a cigar.

"It has to do with this order," Dean explained, extending the slightly worn piece of mimeograph. The Chief-of-Staff accepted it and began to read it with a growing scowl, while Dean waited. After a moment the staff officer looked up.

"What do you have in mind?" he asked suspiciously.

"I've been around the base a bit this morning," Dean explained, leaning back and staring at the ceiling as though gathering his thoughts. In reality, it probably was because he did not dare to look the other in the eye.

"I've heard the men talking about this order and they're calling this base 'Nine Nail City.' It seems to me that there might be a good story, showing precisely how a military base is run. It is very much like a city, you know."

"It is?" the Chief muttered, a note of misery creeping into his tone. "I always felt it was run like a military base."

"You're missing the point," Dean declared. "The general is sort of like a mayor and one might say that the Chief-of-Staff functions as sort of a city manager." He paused to shake his head, suddenly frowning. "However, I'm a trifle puzzled on a point or two. I don't know exactly where Lieutenant Colonel Barrymore fits into this picture. I can't understand what position he could hold in a city administration where he could write an order that would tell all these people that they could have nine nails and they couldn't have pin-up pictures."

"What about a planning director, sir?" suggested Quillan rather formally from his corner near the door. Dean straightened in his chair, smiling his acceptance of an idea.

"Hey. That's not bad," he agreed enthusiastically. "Planning directors are in charge of telling people what they can do with their land." He turned his eyes to the Chief. "What do you think?"

"I've never known a planning director," the Chief said guardedly.

"You know," Dean explained. "He's the official who says you can't keep a horse in the backyard or build henhouses in residential areas."

The Chief shook his head, protesting innocence of such civilian entanglements, but Dean was frowning again.

"What else?" the Chief asked.

"There's one other fact I picked up this morning in talking to some of the enlisted men. One of them told me this base is exactly ten percent worse than the Japanese prison camp he was in."

"What?" The Chief-of-Staff was suddenly on his feet. He had nearly bitten his cigar in half, but didn't seem to notice that it now dangled at a dangerously limp angle between his teeth.

"That's what he explained," Dean went on innocently. Quillan was now at full attention, eyes boring a hole in the opposite wall. "This sergeant said that when he was a POW, they were allowed ten nails over their bunks. That was if they could find the nails."

The Chief of Staff suddenly exhaled and dropped limply into his chair. He closed his eyes for a moment, seeming to think, while Dean retained a respectful silence. Finally, he looked up. There was only one solution if he was to keep this entire command from becoming a laughing stock throughout the Far East.

"I must agree with Sergeant Quillan's view," the Chief said carefully, "but for quite another reason. Lieutenant Colonel Barrymore is no longer our planning director or whatever you called him. I'm certain his successor will change some of his orders."

"But if this nine-nail gimmick goes out, I won't have any story," Dean declared unhappily.

"Exactly."

Slowly Alan Dean got to his feet, shuffling them uncertainly. He heaved a sigh. "Well, it was a good idea, I thought. I want to thank you for your time, colonel."

"My pleasure, son." The Chief was suddenly expansive, aware that the heat was off. He came around his desk to clap the youth on the shoulder. "But there're plenty of stories around here. I'm certain Sergeant Quillan and his boys'll help you all they can, won't you, Quillan."

"That's our job, sir. To serve the press."

As they filed out, the Chief of Staff was right behind them. Max Schmake, the squat little adjutant, looked up as the colonel paused beside his desk, waiting until Dean and Quillan had disappeared into the corridor beyond.

"Max, get that two-toned idiot over here," the Chief ordered, a threatening rumble in his tone.

"Which one, sir?"

"Sorry. The three-toned one. Barrymore!"

# CHAPTER 17

**A**T WONSAN, North Korea, in the winter of 1950, the 3rd Army Division came ashore to take up positions left vacant by the 1st Marine Division. The 23,000 Leathernecks had marched northward toward the Yalu River and the waiting trap already laid by the Chinese People's Army.

Aboard one of the flat-bottomed L.S.T.'s carrying the Army troops and their gear was a former Japanese naval officer. Familiar with Wonsan Harbor, he had been hired to act as pilot in getting the vessel to the beach.

This elderly Japanese watched from the bridge as the bow ramp was dropped on the sand. A young second lieutenant drove a jeep out of the ship's innards and a superior gave him directions as to how to reach the rendezvous area. Nodding his understanding, the lieutenant and his driver sped away, followed by a string of trucks and tanks that erupted from the vessel's bowels.

Ten minutes later, he returned, the caravan in his wake. Crestfallen, the young officer asked renewed instructions. With these, he drove away, kicking up sand and snow in his wake, his wheeled entourage close behind.

It took him only eight minutes to return, visibly shaken at not being able to avoid the route that kept bringing him back to this starting point.

The former enemy on the bridge turned to an Army colonel on the operation staff, offering a polite bow.

"*Ah-so*, colonel-*san*. I know now how you won. You out-confused us!"

Now a similar situation existed. In only three days, Alan Dean

149

had disorganized McCorkle's section. And in that period, he had developed from a minor irritation to a full-fledged pain in the ass.

The disillusionment had started that first evening, when he had put so magnificent a dent in Quillan's jealously guarded cache of raisinjack. On the third night, when Dean had drunk Quillan under his own field desk, his actions obviously had been in poor taste. When he had finished off the last jug amid the horde of unconscious bodies, he had dealt a blow to the section. Morale was at an all-time low, animosity at a new high.

"It ain't fit for a kid that young to drink so much," Quillan growled the following morning. He raised his aching head from a steel helmet filled with ice water to glance at McCorkle. "There ain't no such thing as a natural-born drinker. It takes practice. It's took me thirty years of trainin'. Lookit me."

"I'd rather not," the officer muttered. On the edge of his bunk, he was trying to decide which boot to put on first. Whichever, he knew his head was going to fall off the instant he bent to pick it up.

"What's with this creep?"

McCorkle could only shrug. "He's a college boy. With his education, that makes him a potential second lieutenant, when he gets drafted. He could be your commanding officer."

"May the ghost of Smedley Butler strike me dead first," the master sergeant vowed. There was a touch of reverence in his mention of the Marine's World War I hero.

"Where is he now?" As he spoke, McCorkle plunged downward, slowly straightening, holding a boot aloft in the show of triumph.

"I don't know. Henry?"

"*Hai!*" the Korean answered, thrusting his head into the rear of the tent.

"Where's Little Lord Fauntleroy?" Quillan wanted to know.

"You mean that big drinkin' man?" the boy asked, grinning his evil.

"Go to hell!" Quillan snarled, grabbing for a heavy field boot.

"Quillan!" McCorkle shouted sternly, then added more bleakly, eyeing Henry, "Where is he?"

"Said he was goin' f'r chow," Henry replied. Quillan gagged at this mention of food and the boy turned quizzical eyes upon him.

"Somethin' wrong, sergeant?"

"No." Quillan straightened with effort, face still twisted with revulsion. "I jus' remembered Dean tryin' to sing." He looked at

McCorkle for conformation. "What was that he was killin'?"

"A college fraternity song," McCorkle explained, reaching for his other boot. Some of his confidence had returned with his initial success.

"Th' skipper maybe was one of them fraternity boys, hisself," Quillan looked warily at McCorkle. "Was you, sir?"

"Yeah," McCorkle nodded in recollection of his recent youth. "A long time ago."

The officer thought about it and couldn't think of a good reason why. "It's a good place to train for serious drinking, I guess."

This made sense to Quillan, who bristled suddenly. "I knew it. Somebody's run in a ringer on us!"

"A what?" McCorkle found it difficult to connect the master sergeant's rationalization with anything having to do with Greek letters.

"Like in horse races. You know. They enter some nag that couldn't run a trot to the feed stall, then when the loot's down, a fast nag that looks like the original's slipped in."

McCorkle shook his head. "Who would go to all the trouble to prove you're not the champion alcoholic of the entire Marine Corps?"

"I got enemies," Quillan declared darkly.

"Hi, ho, everybody," a cheerful voice called from beyond the curtain and the master sergeant straightened in a display of enlightenment.

"That's it," he growled softly. "He's the bastard son of Rudy Vallee!"

Alan Dean shoved Henry through the curtain and stood in the opening to glance about the gloom-shrouded cubicle. He had a thick manila-wrapped package beneath his arm.

"We have an assignment," he declared grandly, hoisting the envelope. "Just the kind of story I've wanted to do."

McCorkle eyed the thick packet with suspicion. "You're writing them pretty long this season."

"This is a flag," the boy explained, now a man with a mission. "The school children of Tustin, California, pooled their pennies to buy it."

"This is the kick that's replaced marijuana?" Quillan asked grumpily.

"This flag was flown out here aboard one of our transports and

**151**

they want us to raise it on the northernmost piece of soil held by the Marines. Then we're to return it and they'll fly it over their school."

"Peachy," Quillan agreed sarcastically, "but what's this *we* crap?"

Some of Dean's enthusiasm was replaced by stubborn calm. "I just had breakfast with Ethan. He was going to send the flag on up to the 1st Marines, but I talked him into letting us do the flag raising."

"There's somethin' you should know," the sergeant insisted with a kindliness born of desperation. "You can get killed up there." An admitted draft dodger being shot in combat didn't fit his view of The System at all.

McCorkle waved him to silence, sizing up Dean with thoughtful interest.

"What else did the Chief say?" McCorkle asked carefully.

"That you'd be glad to handle the details. If you have any questions, you're to call him. Otherwise, you're in charge." He started to tear the wrappings off the folded flag, but McCorkle was crowding past him, hangover cured by this promise of rescue from boredom.

"Top, I'm going down to G-2 and see where the most likely spot to raise the flag is. Round up Ashdon and Shade and tell them to get their motion picture gear together. Call Sales and see how soon he can get a plane for us."

"Ridin' with him's like rentin' a hearse to ride to somebody else's funeral!"

"He said he'd fly us any time we needed wings," McCorkle said briskly.

"Gung ho!" Quillan echoed thinly and heaved himself off his bunk.

"Gung who?"Dean asked with reportorial interest.

"Actshully, yuh mean Gung whom," Henry pointed out primly. Quillan glared at him.

"One thing I can't stand in the early mornin's a wise-ass junior spy," he growled.

The section was coming back to life as McCorkle strode out of the tent. Quillan was barking into the telephone, arousing other men of the unit from their hangovers. The officer was even feeling a bit more kindly toward Dean. Whatever the youthful correspondent might have in mind for the children of Tustin, California, this was a way of

**152**

getting to the front; a means of learning what this war was all about. And thinking back to the medal his father had held so dear, McCorkle could not help wondering whether he, himself, was not being a bit juvenile.

As he pushed through the door of the headquarters structure, he came face to face with Lieutenant Colonel Barrymore. The later lolled in the doorway of the Intelligence office, diligently manicuring his nails with a compact gold-plated set of nail clippers with attached file and other accessories.

McCorkle paused, watching the officer, wondering about Barrymore's preoccupation with his small, carefully kept hands. During their earlier meeting, McCorkle had noticed them and the fact that they were almost milk white and of the softness boasted about in detergent commercials.

Probably unknown to Barrymore, those hands had become something of a symbol and were largely responsible for his attitude toward life and his fellow man.

Barrymore had started life in a Pennsylvania coal mining town and in the era when most lads were either trying to win football scholarships or quitting high school to go to work in the coal mines, he had been studying, devoting his attention to higher mathematics. It was this knowledge that had enabled him to qualify for a college scholarship and later for the Navy's Pre-Flight Training Program. There he had done well, but when it had come to actual flying, his first realization of his handicap had come the first day he had appeared on a flight line at the Florida training field and his instructor had looked down at his pale hands and sneered.

"Hell, boy, you got hands like a woman!" the other had erupted. "You'll never be able to hold a stick with them!"

Just how deep the traumatic effect had been upon Barrymore not even the Naval flight surgeons suspected, but the accusation had undoubtedly set up some sort of a deep-seated homosexual panic within his thin body. It was a matter which he had constantly sought to smother, proving that he could fly and ending up near the top of his class. However, he never had been able to handle men, feeling no confidence in issuing orders he expected to be carried out. As a result, he eventually had assumed the veneer of super-nastiness. The fact that underlings shuddered before his superior gaze, shrank before the lash of his tongue he found pleasing. And he had worn this psychological disguise for so long that he had come to accept it

as the real Barrymore, hiding even more deeply from the under-
lying problems.

And during the years that this metamorphosis had taken place,
his original fear and hatred for the smallness and femininity of his
hands had changed, too. Eventually he had come to admire them,
lavishing care upon them much as might a concert pianist. He didn't
know why, or failed to admit the real reason, but he had come to be in
love with those ten carefully tended fingers and the constantly
buffed nails.

As he looked up, Barrymore saw McCorkle staring at him and he
returned the gaze with open distaste, snapping shut the gold clippers and depositing them in the pocket of his starched dungarees.

"What is it, McCorkle?" he half snarled.

"I'd like to look at your maps, sir," the younger officer stated formally, trying not to color under the hostile glare. "I have to find the
location of the northernmost position of the Division."

Barrymore offered a sniff of contempt. "That's classified information," was his cold reply. "Secret."

"I-I know," McCorkle grasped for words that might prove effec-
tive in the face of this negativism. "But the Chief-of-Staff wants
me to know."

The senior growled as he stepped grudgingly aside to allow the
lieutenant to enter his domain, "What's up?"

McCorkle sketched the plan to fly the banner as far north and as
close to enemy lines as possible, while Barrymore showed sullen
interest. He unveiled the huge map of the Korean peninsula that
extended from floor to ceiling, then pointed out an area designated
as the Punchbowl. The Marines had taken the area at great expense
and holding it had been costly.

A ragged line was sketched across the plastic covering with a
black grease pencil to indicate friendly lines. The colonel pointed to
this.

"That's as far north as you can get. We have an outpost out there
and about a hundred yards north, the enemy has an outpost." The
red line which extended downward almost touched the black, sup-
porting the explanation.

"From our outpost, you should be able to get your movies. We're
putting an air strike against the enemy installation tomorrow morning and the general's going to lead the strike." The colonel was smil-

ing thoughtfully, but McCorkle failed to notice.

"What's he going up there for, when he's supposed to be back here generaling?"

Barrymore shrugged. "He hasn't missed combat in any scrap since 1917. I guess he wants a perfect record."

McCorkle hesitated, knowing how the general felt, then asked, "Could I have a map of that area? I'm not familiar with it."

As the young officer departed, the map in his hand, Barrymore was still smiling, but there was a note of satisfaction in his tone as he hummed a snatch of a tune he didn't recognize.

Ashdon and Shade waited, gear packed and pistol belts weighted with .38 Smith & Wessons, spare cartridges and canteens. McCorkle noted with pride that they no longer resembled refugees from an alcoholic ward. They appeared efficient and warlike, serious about this assignment.

The officer spread the map on his desk, briefly explained the mission, then folded the classified paper into a small square. "Either of you familiar with the area?" he asked.

Ashdon nodded. "We both know it."

"Then let's go see it," the officer ordered, waving the pair toward the door. They filed out, packs slung over their backs, while Alan Dean brought up the rear, the flag under his arm. McCorkle turned to follow.

"Some people get all the action," Corporal Handley complained from a corner. He sat with one boot off, inspecting the hole in the sole. McCorkle looked at him.

"You want to go?"

Handley scowled and nodded toward the offending boot. "I couldn't walk far in this an' Supply ain't gonna have my size in for another week." He started to stuff a square of paper inside the footwear, covering the hole.

"You're forgettin' somethin', skipper," Quillan reminded. "A weapon."

McCorkle never had drawn a weapon from the Supply Section. He made the admission with embarrassment and Quillan nodded.

"That's one of th' things a feller don't think about back here. Take mine." He reached into the field desk and drew out the web pistol belt and black leather holster, the butt of the familiar forty-five protruding from it.

"You know how one of these things works, don't you, sir?"

"I know," the officer said shortly.

Alan Dean stuck his head through the doorway, coveting the automatic. "Can I have one of those?"

"There's a simple way," Quillan told him boldly. "Enlist!"

Dean's head disappeared and McCorkle followed him to where Halloran impatiently gunned the recently reclaimed jeep. Ashdon and Shade were settled in the rear seat.

"Off to the wars," Bob Shade commented cheerfully over the engine sounds.

"Finally," McCorkle muttered to himself, wondering briefly as to the true wisdom of this mission.

Half an hour later, the ancient torpedo bomber labored its way northward over the scattered rice paddies and the battle-scarred entrails of war. The hills below were barren, the greenery blasted away by artillery and bombs. Along the crest of each ridge he could make out the scattered foxholes and dugouts. They were caving in now under the frequent rains, but had been the semi-permanent homes for one side — or the other — only weeks earlier.

As the ancient warbird topped a hill, McCorkle glanced over the side of the cockpit to the ground several hundred feet below. There was a water-filled paddy with a single span of oxen in its center. The Korean farmer had paused and was looking skyward, shading his eyes against the sun. A few yards from him was a gigantic crater, memento of some past battle. Nothing grew now in the ragged hole and the farmer had sown his grain on all sides of it, ignoring this reminder of a war about which he knew so little.

"That's it up ahead," Sales' voice crackled in the earphones and McCorkle looked forward past the edge of the sergeant's head. Still several miles away, he could make out the pattern of perfectly aligned pyramidal tents and the dirt airstrip. At the edge of the crude runway stood a dozen or so of the unarmed observation planes used for artillery spotting. As he watched, one of them darted along the short strip, then lifted lazily into the air.

"You sure this is where you wanta get out?" Sales asked.

"There's another place?"

"It's fifteen miles to the front from here," the sergeant explained. "But there's another spot less'n three miles from th' lines. I drop you in there, you won't have near so far to walk."

"Let's try it," McCorkle told him.

"Aye, sir," the pilot said through the earphones, then the voice was replaced by static. McCorkle reached into the pocket of his jacket, searching for the map he had drawn from Barrymore, but it was not there. He tried his other pockets without success. He frowned for a moment, certain he had brought it with him. He hesitated, then lifted the microphone, pressing the switch on the side of the instrument.

"You people still down there, Ashdon?" he asked. The two sergeants and the civilian were in the converted bomb bay with their gear.

"Yes, sir," came the reply.

"You heard what Sales said about getting us closer to the lines?"

"I heard," was the wary reply. "But I don't think you're gonna like it."

Sales voice cut into the transmission. "Here we go," he called cheerfully.

The nose of the plane tilted down abruptly and McCorkle dropped the microphone, looking forward over the propeller. His stomach knotted in fear.

Directly ahead were acres and acres of trucks, vehicles of all sizes and descriptions parked row upon row; all of the rolling stock necessary to modern warfare.

And down the center of those rows was a narrow rutted road with a turning circle at its far end.

Men scattered in confusion to get away from the diving iron bird that threatened to destroy them. Abruptly, the old bomber flattened out into a glide and McCorkle could see the awed faces peering up from behind the trucks. He felt the shock of the wheels touching, then the plane bucked violently as the pilot fought the brakes and the controls. An instant later, Sales was in the turning circle, swinging the monster about.

"Everybody out!" Sales called through the earphones. "I gotta blow b'fore they get a make on me!"

Still shaken, McCorkle pushed back the plastic canopy and climbed over the side of the cockpit, angling his head against the air-hammer blast from the propeller. Below him, the door of the bomb bay opened and four rumpled figures tumbled out amid their packs and camera equipment.

A moment later, all four had reached the protective row of trucks as the bomber, engines roaring, lurched down the rutted roadway. As the wings bounced erratically, narrowly missing parked vehicles on each side, Marines again scattered, some diving for safety beneath the parked carriers. Only scant feet from a line of ammunition trucks at the far end, the plane suddenly lifted into the air. Then it gained momentum and sped away, the pilot flying close to the ground so that the outraged motor transport personnel could not read the identifying numerals on the undersides of the wings. As the aircraft disappeared behind a low hill, there was a surge toward the new arrivals.

A burly captain with a thick beard centered his glare upon Ashdon. Either he did not note McCorkle's rank or simply ignored it.

"You, again!" the captain snarled, waving vaguely after the departed plane. "And you still can't identify the idiot who flies that thing?"

Ashdon lied admirably. "Like before, captain, we was standin' in th' road, lookin' for a lift, when this plane dropped outa th' sky and he asked if we wanted a ride."

The captain sighed in defeat, staring at the photographer. "Okay. But tell that bastard I'm getting some machine guns. He even heads in this direction, we'll blow his tin ass clear out of the damned sky!"

Ashdon offered a formal salute. "I'll tell him, sir."

# CHAPTER 18

WO HOURS later, as they came out of a grove of splintered trees, they paused for breath. Shade pointed to the steep ridge above.

"That's it," he panted and McCorkle followed his gaze. Without the map, he knew he was hopelessly lost and had let the buck sergeant lead the way.

The hillside above them looked like an ant colony. There were deep paths up and down the steep terrain, while the network of trenches and bunkers on this reverse slope stretched just below the crest, extending in either direction as far as one could see.

"That should be George Company, 7th Marines," Shade explained knowingly.

"But it's so quiet," McCorkle said softly. There wasn't a sound. No shots; no artillery. Only an unnatural, waiting silence.

"It'll pick up after dark," Ashdon prophesied moodily. "They'll send out patrols and we'll send out some. They'll meet out'n that valley on th' other side. Then all hell'll break loose."

"What does a patrol do out there in the dark, infiltrate?" McCorkle's tone was careful. He did not want to expose the degree of his ignorance in the ways of war.

"It's a war of nerves. They're out there to see if we're out there, too. An' we have people out to see if they're there." Shade glanced at the officer. "Helluva way to lose sleep."

McCorkle stared up at the ragged, defaced hillside, where armed Marines moved along the trenches, careful to keep their silhouettes off the skyline.

"They're dug in to stay," he ventured.

"Been here all winter," Ashdon conceded, "but if you're gonna be in a spot for ten minutes, the brass wants holes dug. Next thing you know, you've dug 'em an empire."

Ashdon, familiar with the area, led them puffing up the narrow muddy trail to a young bearded captain in his mid-twenties. He had been a high school football coach in New Jersey before the Corps had recalled him to take advantage of his World War II experience. While McCorkle outlined the plan to film not only the next morning's air strike, but to raise the children's flag, the captain ran his fingers through the ragged mat on his face, scowling.

"Why me?" he asked bitterly. "Last week, they had that writer broad up here. What's her name?"

"Jane Whitlow?" Shade offered helpfully.

"I guess that's her. Nobody could take a crap for more'n six hours without her pokin' around. Then when she shoved off, every bastard on this whole damn hill was trying to get over a slit trench at the same time. If the gooks attacked then, they'd have caught every man in this outfit with his pants at half-mast!"

The captain heaved a frustrated sigh and McCorkle felt that old feeling of insecurity beginning to build within him. The other officer nodded. "You're here and it wouldn't do me any good to bitch to regiment. Have my gunnery sergeant draw you some rations and find a place to sack out." His eyes centered upon the two enlisted men.

"You bring any of that anti-freeze with you this time?"

Shade glanced at Ashdon for leadership. The cameraman nodded. "We got a few ounces."

The group had been standing waist deep in a trench, but now the company commander waved toward a burlap-shrouded doorway. He forgot for a moment to be professionally surly.

"Step into my office and we'll drink this thing over."

He dropped to hands and knees to enter the bunker, the others following. Inside, it was dark and the odor of musty earth assailed McCorkle's nostrils. The only light was from a kerosene lantern on a wooden box at the end of the low tunnel. On each side of the dugout were low wooden platforms covered with sleeping bags. The captain squatted on one of these and waved the others to seats.

"I'm Joe Shelley," he offered, eyes resting dubiously upon the correspondent patch that surrounded Dean's arm. When the teenager's role was explained, he said nothing. Instead, he poured a healthy shot of Ashdon's liquor into an empty ration can and gulped it down. McCorkle glanced down into his sergeant's open pack. The only

160

things it contained were another of the brown jugs and several pairs of socks used for protective padding.

Ashdon read his thoughts. "It's all I need, skipper. We ain't gonna make a career of this hole, are we?"

The lieutenant turned back to Shelley, manner uncertain. "Just where is this outpost?"

The captain turned to Ashdon. "You know where it is. Show it to the lieutenant." He glanced at the pack holding the pair of jugs. "I'll watch your safety sauce. See that it doesn't get boozenapped."

As they ducked out of the hole, McCorkle glanced curiously at his sergeant. "Safety sauce?"

"If you're popular in one of these outfits, th' troops'll take good care of you. Maybe even put a man with a tommy gun outside your hole at night so some gook don't get through th'barb wire an' drop a grenade in on you.

"Let it be known you're gonna leave some of that stuff when you take off, they make your sleep real peaceful."

Ashdon took the lead with Dean a step to his rear. Shade had remained with the captain to keep a check upon the officer's consumption.

In the rear, McCorkle raised his head a few inches to see over the trench and the crest of the hill. Not far away was a low blockhouse of logs and sandbags. Forward of the lines, it was low and ugly, small and insecure. Only eighty yards or so beyond was a pile of rocks and boulders at the nose of the hill. If Barrymore had been correct, the clustered boulders would be the enemy's own outpost infested with snipers.

Marines wearing healthy young beards, dirty faces and steel helmets were posted at intervals. They lolled there, watching the rock pile, rifles leveled across the parapet. One of them picked up a pair of field glasses to look out over the haze-wrapped valley to the high, rugged mountains that towered several miles away.

"May I look?" McCorkle asked and the boy, no more than eighteen and his beard only fuzz, turned to stare at him critically. He saw that the officer wore no helmet, noted the bar of rank twinkling on his utility cap.

"Rear echelon, huh?" The youth's tone was knowing. "Better git ridda that purty bar,'less yuh wanta pretty hole in yore head!"

McCorkle extended his hand stiffly and after hesitating, the boy handed him the binoculars. Raising them to his eyes, the officer focused them on the grotesque pile of rocks that was the empty out-post, then jerked with apprehension.

Two men huddled in a shallow cave at the base of a boulder. One, also holding binoculars, was staring back at him, while the other enemy soldier was hunched behind a machine gun, glaring intently through the sights. The gun was pointed at the lieutenant or his glinting silver bar.

McCorkle slapped the glasses into the hands of the surprised private, while a strange mixture of fear, surprise, even exhilaration, engulfed him. Without a word, he brushed aside the other Marine and hunched over the Garand rifle balanced over a sandbag.

"What the hell!" the private growled, but McCorkle was involved now in the war. He aligned the post front sight in the aperture, bringing both to center on one of the figures several hundred yards away. As he squeezed the trigger, the explosion ripped the silence and the rifle butt bucked against his shoulder. He triggered the weapon again, then fired a third round. That was when the private grabbed for the weapon, jerking the fourth shot wild.

"Tryin' t' start th' war up?" the lad demanded, snapping at his words. McCorkle had no chance to reply. There came the rattle of the oppos-ing machine gun and dirt was kicked into his face, the foul soil biting at his eyes.

Grabbed roughly, he was dragged down into the trench. He dug at his eyes with his knuckles, while an irate voice bellowed: "What god-damn stupid sonuvabitch fired those shots?" The enemy machine gun chattered again. Another automatic weapon, close by and deeper in tone, took up the chorus and rifle shots were being squeezed off by both sides.

McCorkle came to his knees, staring through blurred eyes. Marines, rifles in hand, were pouring out of their holes to fill the trenches like ants moving on a spilled bucket of honey. The private with the fuzzy beard hauled him to his feet, then shoved his head down to keep it below the level of the sandbags.

"Better find a hole," the boy suggested with weary kindliness, "an' just sit this one out." He turned, leaned into the rifle and began to fire toward the pile of rocks. The recoil drove his thin figure rearward with each shot, but he braced back into position to shoot again in a prac-ticed rhythm.

Ashdon and Dean crouched in the trench a dozen yards away. Dodging the legs of the riflemen braced against the forward wall of the trench, he scuttled through the loose dirt to join them. Ashdon stared at him in wonderment.

"You gotta phobia against peace and quiet?"

McCorkle gulped his shame, wanting to explain that he had seen an enemy soldier pointing a machine gun at him; this had been his reason for firing. Instead, he shrugged, trying to ignore the expression of disgust on his sergeant's face.

Alan Dean, checking his camera, grunted his satisfaction and started to rise.

"Where th' hell're you goin'?" Ashdon snarled, turning on him.

"To shoot the war!" The civilian raised his head and camera over the edge of the parapet, but McCorkle dived for his ankles. His action was prompted by the Chief-of-Staff's threat as to what he could expect should anything happen to the teenager.

The sergeant and lieutenant collided, each striking the photographer's calves at the same time. This brought a cry of outraged pain as the Ivy Leaguer came tumbling down, battling the pair.

"What're you doing?"

"Savin' your silly ass!" Ashdon shouted in return. He was atop Dean, who lay on his belly, face in the dirt. There was another squeal as the boy fought to get up.

Seeing that Ashdon was losing, McCorkle hurled himself on top of the mass of arms and legs. This put his head extremely close to the level of the sandbags, and each time that Dean was able to regain his knees, McCorkle was thrown upward into the war. Bullets pounded at the burlap sacks and showered sand into his face, refilling his tortured eyes. Desperately, he dug at the side of the trench with a toe, seeking leverage.

"Dammit, stay down!" he screeched in anger and terror.

"There's a crab down here! It's after my nose!" The muffled voice was a wail.

McCorkle shoved downward and there was a scream of horror and pain. The last was blotted out by several heavy explosions; enemy mortar shells. A dozen of the deadly explosions walked their way along the trench line, showering dirt upon the cringing Marines, while McCorkle fought even harder to keep his backside below the lip of the parapet.

When it was over, no one had been wounded except Dean, who sported a badly clawed nose.

"There was a crab," Ashdon said in surprise. "And thirty miles from salt water."

Dean sneered at him. "The nature lesson helps."

"All right," Shelley's voice interrupted, "which one of you rear echelon pogues done it?" He was hunched in the trench, hands on hips, glaring at the gathering.

Ashdon cast a glance at McCorkle, who hesitated, then nodded.

"I did," he admitted, waving vaguely toward the rock pile. "There's a man there with a machine gun and..."

Someone chuckled cynically and McCorkle glanced about, naked in his own misery and embarrassment.

"That man's been out there with that machine gun for months," Shelley told him. "But he's smart. He don't like us shooting at him any more than we like him to shoot at us.

"If we had a brig, I'd lock up your ass!" Shelley stated in grim disgust. "Do anything like that again and we'll build one!"

"Y-yes, sir," McCorkle gurgled.

Hours later, lying in the darkness of a bunker, he was unable to sleep. He had been unable to eat, too. Although he was surrounded by other dim forms, he was alone in his personal misery. He heaved a sigh.

For the rest of the afternoon and even as they had hunched on the reverse slope, picking at a can of cold rations with a plastic spoon, he had realized that men were looking at them. Some of them could not keep the pitying smiles off their lips. In short, he had made an ass of himself among seasoned Marines and the knowledge was painful.

He had spent the hours since darkness in going over the incident time after time, trying to clear his mind of rationalizations and determine the reason why he had grabbed the rifle and started firing at the enemy machine gunners. His first defense, of course, had been that they had been about to fire, but now he wasn't certain.

In spite of his formal military training, McCorkle never had paused to wonder before how it would feel to kill a man. Until now, warfare had been an impersonal thing in which one side was represented by a black line on a map, the other by a red mark. But he wondered now. Had he really wanted to kill the man with the machine gun?

Or was it the medal, the one his father had posted in the family living room for all to see? Was it the continuous brainwashing about the value of that medal to his father...the desire to prove himself equal as a soldier, perhaps with a medal of his own?

And the final question in McCorkle's mind was the one he liked least: Had his desire to see combat, his actions of this afternoon, even his enlistment, been a subconscious drive to prove to himself that he was not a coward?

As he lay there in the darkness, his self-imposed misery compounding itself, he felt vague rumblings in his stomach followed by the pressure of gas.

He had no answers for any of his questions, making the torment still worse. He heaved another sigh in the night, wishing there was someone to share his guilt.

A few moments later, the pressure against his stomach began to tell. It was time for a mission. Unhappily, he disengaged himself from his single blanket and began to pick his way amongst the snoring bodies that cluttered the dugout. At the entrance, he brushed aside the piece of tattered burlap that covered the low doorway and looked out. At first, all was silence. The blackness was a shroud, covering the activities of war. Then something stirred near him and he turned his head to see the Marine squatting near the entrance, a Thompson submachine gun cradled lovingly in his arms.

"What's up, Mac," the Marine rasped in a low tone.

"Where's the head?" McCorkle rasped back, the gasses starting to plague his intestinal tract. "I gotta go!"

"It ain't no place t'be at night," the Marine warned. "Better get back in there."

"They won't like me if I do. I have to go." He made his tone sound more urgent and the Marine waved a vague hand toward the lower extremities of the steep hill.

"There's a slit trench down there aways," the other told him. "It's marked with a piece of white cloth on a stick. But don't show no light or you won't hafta take a crap. Somebody'll oblige by shootin' your ass off!"

McCorkle pulled on his camouflage-covered helmet and stepped into the trench, starting to feel his way along it as he tried to recall the pattern in which these ditches had been laid out. He did have a recollection of the slit trench, a narrow octagonal hole in the ground which was designated by the white marker and knew its approximate location. At the same time, he was mentally whipping himself for not getting adequate directions earlier.

Moments later, he found a trench leading downward at right angles and decided that this must be the correct route. The head was not far off of this depression, he recalled. His eyes were becoming adjusted

**165**

to the murky blackness and he found the going easier, hesitating once as he was challenged by a Marine, then moving past after he had identified himself.

As the trench petered out, he spotted the white flag standing out in the darkness and made his way toward it, moving cautiously to avoid falling into the slit trench. His nose also helped, guiding him toward the odorous pit.

Locating the edge of the trench with his toe, he turned slowly, undid his belt and allowed his dungaree trousers to slide down over his hips, shivering as the cold night air struck his bare buttocks. He removed his helmet, setting it on the ground before him, then began to rummage in the liner for the small packet of toilet tissue that every Marine is supposed to carry. It was gone and for an instant he felt a small panic, while the gasses in his lower stomach continued to build, creating pain.

Rummaging through his pockets, he came across a folded sheet of paper and held it up, attempting to determine what it was, but it was only a large white square against the night. It would have to do.

An instant later, the pressure had been relieved and McCorkle crumpled the rough paper into a ball. But before he could proceed, there was a dull popping sound like the release of the cork in a champagne bottle. In the same moment, the entire terrain was flooded with light. McCorkle felt like an ant alone on a mountain of sugar as the aerial flare floated down overhead on its tiny parachute, illuminating the entire battlefield.

Suddenly there were excited shouts on the ridgeline above him. Then there came the firing of automatic weapons.

"Get th' sonuvabitch!" someone screamed. "He's comin' through th' wire." There was another string of machine gun fire, then a scream as the flare overhead began to die. In that instant of excitement, McCorkle had been frozen into immobility, recalling the similar situation when Henry had led him to the makeshift urinal and they had been attacked by a hidden sniper. Christ, he could only think, these gooks have an anal complex. Every time I drop my pants, the shooting starts!

Finished, he crumpled the wad of paper and dropped it into the slit trench, then slowly straightened and began to pull up his trousers, shaking against the cold and the unnerving experience.

There was another popping sound overhead, then another flare blossomed against the night. There was another burst of machine gun fire.

"Knock it off, goddammit," a voice shouted a command. "He's dead. You're shootin' at shadows."

"Shadows, hell!" someone called back indignantly. "That one hadda grenade in his hand!"

Before McCorkle could get his trousers beyond half mast, there was a sudden explosion and a blast fifty yards above him on the hill. Reacting, he dropped to the ground, clawing himself flat as he heard the segments of mortar shells whistling overhead. Moments later, several more of the mortar shells exploded in rapid succession, seeming to come closer. Frantically, his heart pumping, the concussion dulling his senses, McCorkle started to roll away, then found himself clawing madly at the soggy ground. He was poised on the edge of the slit trench, trying desperately to keep from plunging into its dubious depths.

Even as he fought to keep from falling into the mass of excrement, the odor welled up from the hole to nauseate him and he redoubled his efforts, thrusting out one long, skinny leg until it completely bridged the narrow pit, holding him in this suspended state.

He struggled to sit up, taking care to keep from slipping more. There were three more mortar shells, but he ignored them now, telling himself that this would prove an honorable wound, but one could never collect a Purple Heart for falling into a slit trench! In spite of the excitement that seemed to surround him, his thoughts were logical and there was a feeling of success that he had overcome panic in the face of this greater threat that was just below him.

He lay still for a moment, expecting more mortar shells, but they didn't come. There were other muffled shouts along the main line of resistance at the top of the hill, but he couldn't make out what was being said. After a moment, there was only silence. Taking a deep breath, concentrating upon his slightest move, he began to inch his way back from the slit trench, using his every faculty to maintain the thin edge of balance.

What seemed like hours later, as he slowly rose and pulled up his pants, he could feel the mud clinging to his buttocks, but it didn't seem important. He was weary, the sweat beneath his jacket leaving him cold and miserable. As he hitched his belt, he began the steep climb back up the hill. Detached, he wondered whether anyone had been hurt in the sudden attack.

But as he slid into the bunker and again found his blanket, he heaved a sigh and some of his earlier ghosts came back to haunt him. After the episode in which he had made a fool of himself he was thankful that no one had seen his escapade with the slit trench. The captain would probably have happily pushed him in, he reflected somewhat bitterly.

"Don't worry about it, skipper," a soft voice said, and McCorkle peered into the gloom to make out the features of the man from whom he had commandeered the rifle. He pushed himself up on an elbow, frowning at the private.

"Gook fever," the Marine offered knowingly. "We all get it th' first time we see one. Even Captain Shelley. Hell, you shoulda seen what *I* did."

"Knock it off an' go t'sleep," someone growled near the low entrance.

"Blow it out your ass," the boy snarled, but lowered his voice.

"I was forward observer for the eight-one mortars, an' damn good. But I got carried away with Luke th' Gook out there in them rocks. Let it get personal. That's why I'm in this hole, nursin' a rifle, 'stead of back there four hundred yards, livin' like a gent with th' resta th' mortar platoon."

"Why?" McCorkle tried to hide his interest but wanted to hear the rest of the story.

"I was up here spottin' targets but nothin' ever happened 'cept that damn gook'd scream at us every night."

"What kind of screams?"

"Same old crap like, "Merican, you die.' All night. Anyhow, I'm here lookin' through th' glasses one day when I see a sleepin' bag laid out on th' rocks t'air.

"That sorta pissed me off. It was like he was darin' me, so I gave the mortars the target an' called for white phosphorus. Three shells landed right on top of th' bag and made it into ashes. Yuh could hear that gook screamin' clear back to Seoul! Then for about a week, we had the damnedest war ever!"

"Harrison," said the voice with authority, "time for your watch."

"Hell," the Marine mourned, "jest when I was 'about t'talk myself t'sleep."

"Why'd you get thrown out of the mortar platoon?" McCorkle insisted, feeling it was important to his own problem that he know.

"I got blamed f'r startin' the whole battle." Harrison sat up and picked up his rifle. "When it was over, they figgered I had personal hate for ole Luke, so they put me up here, where I kin shoot at him all day long."

"But you weren't shooting today."

The Marine shrugged against the darkness. "Sometimes he shoots back."

# CHAPTER 19

**A** HAND ON his shoulder shook McCorkle from a restless slumber. Ashdon's soft voice announced, "Almost dawn, skipper. We better get out there, 'less you've changed your mind."

The officer sat up, stretching the kinks out of his spine. The ground beneath his blanket had been damp and now his clothing was clammy. He had noted the sergeant's tone, hopeful that this mission might be canceled.

Some of McCorkle's earlier shame and guilt came flooding back, but there was a note of stubbornness in his voice. "We're going."

"I'll get Shade an' that kid," the sergeant said dubiously in the darkness.

"Let them sleep," McCorkle ordered in a fierce whisper. "I don't want Dean to get shot and two of us will be plenty."

"It's supposed to be his mission. What happens if he squeals to the Chief?"

"Let's get out of here." McCorkle patted his hip to be certain the borrowed automatic was still there. "What do you want me to carry?"

"Just th' tripod. I'll lead off."

The night was cold, damp and perpetual odor of the rice paddies engulfed them as they pushed through the burlap that covered the low entrance. Behind them, in the bunker, someone groaned in his sleep.

The gray of false dawn was in the East and McCorkle eyed it uneasily, then stumbled into the trench after his sergeant. They moved slowly to avoid the extended legs of the sentries stationed at intervals along the cut.

The excavation became more shallow and branched toward the

low silhouette of the outpost eighty yards away. Ashdon went on his hands and knees, half crawling, while he hugged his camera bag to his chest. McCorkle followed suit, making as small a target of himself as possible in the coming light.

As they neared the lone bunker, a figure suddenly rose, black against the sky, rifle leveled.

"Halt!" the figure hissed. "Th' password!"

"I don't have it." McCorkle was suddenly aware of this oversight. He had neglected to ask.

"You'd better find it, buster," the figure threatened. There was an ominous metallic click as the safety on the rifle was released.

"Put down that rifle b'fore I take it away from you," Ashdon snarled. There was an instant's hesitation before the figure slumped, the muzzle of the weapon dropping. McCorkle, who had been holding his breath, exhaled.

"Pass, friends," the sentry muttered and stepped back, allowing them to scuttle into the bunker.

Several heavy sleepers in the sandbagged structure matched snoring techniques, and the odor, if possible, was worse than the rice paddies. It had been a long stretch between showers for this outfit.

"Who is it?" a voice asked from the far side of the dugout.

"The press," Ashdon replied in a hushed tone. "We're goin' out forward t'shoot movies of th' air strike. How far out's that shell hole they mentioned?"

"'Bout fifty yards. Maybe half-way t'Luke's Castle."

"Try not t'shoot us if you hear us movin' around, huh?"

"There was somebody out there a bit ago," the voice warned. "Think I hit 'im. Let me know."

"Sure," Ashdon sneered. "I'll send a carrier pigeon."

Again in the open, McCorkle whispered, "Are you sure you know where that hole is?" He was nervous, frightened. This was no longer a game; no longer an experiment in fear, and he realized he was putting his life in the sergeant's hands.

"About," Ashdon replied. "We sorta keep crawlin' till we fall into it."

"What happens if we miss it?"

"There's gonna be some mighty su'prised gooks when we drop in on 'em!" The sergeant dropped to his knees and began to crawl. McCorkle gave him a start of several yards, then followed, cradling the folded camera tripod in his elbows. Pushing himself forward with the

**171**

pressure of his toes in the earth and a swiveling motion of his hips, he was breathing heavily before he had gone a dozen yards. He was sweating, too, his wet dungaree jacket cold against his back. The false dawn had died for the moment and, staring into the blackness, he could see no sign of Ashdon. Panic building in his throat, forming a lump, he halted, listening, but the sound of his own labored breathing covered any other sound. Then he heard the click of metal against a rock.

There was a sharp outcry from somewhere ahead and he froze, ducking his head to press his face into the sour earth. The shout in an Oriental tongue was repeated, then a shot was fired. His stomach shrank to half its normal size as the bullet cracked, parting the air overhead. Then there was an answering shot and a curse from a Marine in the outpost to the rear.

After that, all was quiet.

McCorkle lay listening to the beat of his heart, cold sweat rolling down his forehead and cheeks. Back at headquarters, this had seemed a simple matter, but the bullet snapping spitefully over his head had suddenly made it seem considerably more complicated.

Prostrate in the dirt, he fought with the panic that sought to choke him. He wanted to turn back now, use what was left of the night to seek safety, but he knew he could not. One of his men was somewhere there ahead, and he had come to lead, not to run. His recollection of the events of the afternoon and the pitying stares of the enlisted men made up his mind for him.

He began to edge forward, moving inch by inch now, trying to avoid making noise. He paused once to listen, but could not hear Ashdon. He raised his head a fraction, making out the lines of the towering pile of rocks against the thinning night. He had to be nearly there.

Then he froze, shocked with the realization that he could have passed Ashdon in the darkness. The sergeant could be behind him, waiting.

He jerked in fear and apprehension at the sound of a low hiss a few feet in front of him, then realized it was the cameraman. He shoved the tripod in front of him, using it as a locater, then let it slip over the edge of the hole. It clattered against a rock and brought a sharp gasp of fear from Ashdon. He burrowed into the ground, awaiting a hail of bullets from the enemy outpost, but it didn't come. Snaking head first into the shallow depression, he landed in a heap, the lever of the tripod gouging his kidneys.

Ashdon hurriedly set up the tripod, leveling it by instinct while McCorkle shrank against the face of the hole, each metallic click being magnified in his ears. As the sergeant screwed the sixteen millimeter camera onto the tripod head, the true dawn was coming. From where McCorkle sat, the pile of boulders and rocks, less than sixty yards away, looked castle high, accentuated by his low angle.

Ashdon dropped to the dirt beside him, rubbing a grimy hand across his chin. "Nothin' t'do now but wait for them planes."

But McCorkle was even more disturbed, glancing about with a scowl. "We're here, but it's getting light. How in hell are we going to get back?"

Ashdon shrugged, suppressing a twisted grin. "I don't know, lootenant. I just take orders."

Nerves tight, McCorkle verged on eruption, but thought better of it. "Then get your shots as fast as you can. While they still have their heads down from those explosions, we'll have to haul ass!" The sergeant nodded agreement to this order, face showing no emotion. McCorkle didn't know whether it was logical or not, but he knew he wasn't going to spend the entire day in this hole, awaiting another night. He shuddered at the thought.

He was the first to hear the foreign sounds and glanced skyward. Darkness was being stripped from the landscape like a cloak and the sun was rising at the far end of the valley, turning the low, misty clouds a dirty yellow. He squinted, trying to make out the shapes, then he saw them; eight planes flying in tight formation. And to the rear, he could hear the forward air controller talking into his radio.

"Oxbow, this is Homemaker. You are over target area now. Repeat. Oxbow, this is Homemaker. You are over target area. I will mark target with white phosphorus. Repeat. Will mark with double-ewe pee."

McCorkle wondered whether the voice was loud enough to carry to the Reds hidden deep in the rocks and boulders. He glanced at Ashdon. "All set?"

There was a sudden grimness in the nod, as the other made a final adjustment of the camera. It was set up so that only a portion of the turret was visible over the edge of the hole, yet it could be tilted upward to follow the planes in their diving attacks, track the bombs as they fell and still catch the explosions upon the objective.

Ashdon leaned back in the hole, pulling the canteen from his belt. He twisted off the lid and extended it toward the officer.

"Coffee?"

McCorkle shook his head, wondering where Ashdon had conned it. The longer he was with this group, the more convinced he became they could steal the general's stars if they could devise a practical use for them.

The sergeant tilted back his head and took a long gulp. Lowering the container, he offered a grimace of distaste.

"Gawd, they musta used rice-paddie water." He paused to look at the officer. "Skipper, just why th' hell're we out here?"

He caught McCorkle offguard. "Huh?"

"What're we doin' out here like this, askin' t'get our asses clobbered?" The sergeant's tone was low but insistent.

"Duty," McCorkle replied shortly, knowing this was a lie. But he could hardly admit to the sergeant that for months he had nursed a secret desire to get into combat. Even less could he explain his reasons for this compulsion, when he wasn't certain of them in his own mind.

"Tell me about this duty thing." Ashdon sunk lower in the hole, staring at his superior with what could have been a chiding expression.

Like most of the breed, McCorkle had been made aware of the fact that, when the Korean War had broken out, the Marine Corps already had been slashed to the bone, every unit skeletonized. When General MacArthur had asked for a Marine Division and a Marine Air Wing to help in the defense of the Pusan Perimeter, all that could be mustered was a reinforced regiment and a single air group. The lieutenant drew upon this now for support.

"You're here to help impress the American public with the importance of the Corps," he stated, wanting to believe this reason was more important for their being here than his own. "The life of the Marine 'Corps is only as long as the column inches we get in the papers and the time we can get on television and movie screens. People are always talking about unifying the services, and we'll be the first to go."

"That's why we're out here, waitin' to get our balls shot off?" Ashdon was having difficulty in fitting his present situation into the Big Picture.

"As long as we can do something like this to convince the people that the Marine Corps serves a function, the politicians will be afraid to abolish us."

"I guess I'm s'posed t'be convinced," Ashdon replied doubtfully, reaching for his canteen. The move was interrupted by an explosion, then the air was filled with smoke, while burning white particles atop the pile of rocks marked the enemy outpost.

"That's th' double-ewe pee," Ashdon noted, staring critically over the lip of the hole. "Right on target."

He sat up abruptly, reaching for the camera and tilting the lense upward. Overhead, the dull hum of engines turned to a laboring roar and the first plane nosed into its dive, seeming to come straight toward the hole where the two Marines crouched. Beneath the belly of the aircraft was a strange, angular device.

Ashdon was following the plane through the view finder, while film measured its way through the internal sprockets. Suddenly there was a sound as though a hundred skyrockets had been launched from a single fuse. The mechanism slung beneath the Corsair's fuselage suddenly flashed ahead of the plane. It wobbled at first, uncertain of its path, then streaked downward, a trail of sparks and burning gases in its wake.

The sergeant stiffened, then raised his head, forgetting the camera. Suddenly, he dived for the bottom of the hole, scratching dirt with his nails.

*"Duck!"* he screamed. "Tiny Tim!"

McCorkle, frozen, was staring open-mouthed at the approaching rocket as Ashdon grabbed him unceremoniously by the lapels and jerked him face down in the hard clay.

An explosion jarred the earth, and even in the protective hole, the concussion battered at their eardrums, seeming to compress their brains. McCorkle lay there, feeling those angry snakes of raw fear writhing through his guts, constricting his stomach.

Rocks and dirt began to shower upon them. One chunk of granite caught the officer in the back near his spine and pain laced through assorted nerves and muscles.

As the rattle of stones and gravel died, there came the same hissing sound of another rocket, this one closer. He rolled on his side to see it arc downward, coming directly toward the hole. He rolled back onto his face, protecting his head with both arms, compressing his body into as small a form as possible, while childhood prayers coursed through his mind.

At the second explosion, the bottom of the shell hole seemed to rise up and slap him. The force of the blast hurled Ashdon on top of him and the two rolled about, while rocks and dirt rained upon them.

"Kheerist!" the sergeant gasped. "That was behind us!" He raised his head enough to peer through the dust toward the Marine lines. McCorkle looked, too. A part of the friendly outpost had been blasted away by the rocket, shattering logs, ripping open sandbags.

And amid this debris was Sergeant Shade dramatically raising a flag into position atop a gnarled pole, while Alan Dean was directing him into a posture faintly reminiscent of the legendary Iwo Jima flag raising.

"Get under cover, you stupid bastards!" McCorkle screamed at them above the sounds of another diving aircraft. If either heard, the order went ignored. Instead, Shade posed proudly with the banner, pretending to raise it atop the blasted bunker. Beneath him, Marines were pouring from the bombed structure, seeking the dubious sanctuary of the main line of resistance.

Suddenly, Shade saw the plane diving upon him and scrambled headlong off the low roof, trying heroically to keep the flag from touching the dirt. As another huge explosion beneath the crest of the hill obscured his view, McCorkle threw himself flat in the hole, pressing against Ashdon's trembling form.

As the roar of the blast rolled off between the hills, Ashdon glanced at his leader. "Did Barrymore tell you they'd be shootin' fourteen-inch rockets? This war surplus crap?"

McCorkle's own thoughts were paralleling those of the sergeant. He paused to scowl, then shook his head.

"Lootenant," the sergeant stated slowly, unscrewing the camera from the tripod. "You ain't healthy t'be around. Not if that colonel's tryin' t'get you killed!"

McCorkle's thoughts were interrupted by a new sound, a series of low, rapid explosions. Overhead, the planes were scattered, but there were black puffs of smoke appearing near one of them. Red golf balls were streaking through the sky to cause the explosions. Anti-aircraft.

Behind them, the frantic air controller's cries penetrated the haze of battle. "Call it off!" the unseen officer was shouting. "Cool it! Those damned rockets can't be trusted!"

"Helluva time t'decide," Ashdon growled. "Rockets eight'r nine years old, an' we sit out here while they experiment!"

"Did you get any pictures?" McCorkle asked. Ashdon looked at him reproachfully.

"I don't mean t'sound disrespectful, sir, but're you some kinda nut?"

Apparently the planes overhead had received the air controller's message. They were reformed and headed south in tight formation. All but one. This one was far to the rear, smoke streaming from its dark silhouette.

There was another explosion, again to the rear, but this one had a different kind of sound. It was only a few yards away. The world whirled crazily and McCorkle closed his eyes. Saliva thickened in his mouth and he knew he was going to vomit, but Ashdon didn't give him time. The sergeant nudged him.

"Time t'git or them mortars'll be in this hole with us!"

McCorkle didn't move, didn't open his eyes, then he felt the weight of a hand stinging his cheek. He opened his lids to stare into Ashdon's twisted angry face. "C'mon. Move or you'll get us both killed!"

Somehow, he was on his feet, running toward the badly damaged bunker, which still was obscured by smoke and dust. At any moment, he expected to feel the white knife of hot shrapnel tearing through his skin. There was another blast, further away, in the Marine's main line of resistance and he stopped in his tracks to look about wildly. Ashdon gave him a vicious shove from behind and he almost fell, then he was running agin, seeking the looming protection of the outpost bunker.

Then they were in the trench at the rear of the bunker, the entrance to which was partially clogged by broken sandbags and twisted timber. Dust still hung in the air, obscuring the opening. McCorkle and Ashdon leaned against the dirt wall, their breath coming in wracking gasps. The saliva was hot in McCorkle's mouth and he bent to heave, tasting the bile in his mouth, but nothing happened. Ashdon put a sympathetic hand on the officer's shoulder.

"It's always this way the first time," he said softly, as McCorkle straightened. The officer stared into his eyes in puzzlement, seeking the anger of a moment before. There was only understanding.

"Shade?" McCorkle asked thickly. "And that idiot? What happened to them?"

Ashdon shook his head, glancing toward the main line of resistance, which still vibrated with rifle and machine gun fire.

"I dunno," he admitted. "I was too busy to see what was goin' on. They may've made it back there." He kicked one of the exploded sandbags. "At least neither of them's here."

McCorkle glanced about nervously. "This is no place to stop," he

suggested, expecting more mortar shells. "We'd better check inside."
Ashdon nodded dutifully and ducked through the bunker's shattered
doorway, the officer a scant yard behind him. The inner darkness was
a curtain at first, the only light coming hazily through the rectangular
slit in the wall facing the enemy outpost. After a moment, McCorkle
could see that this was manned by a single Marine, who was firing
through it toward the pile of rocks that had been the target for the aircraft. Other Marines were scattered about the bunker, some lying flat,
seemingly unconcerned, others sitting, holding their heads. Some had
their hands over their ears, eyes closed, still suffering the effects of
shock from the explosion. A few were standing, seemingly expectant,
awaiting orders with their rifles in their hands.

The outpost commander stood in the middle of the dirt floor, peering through the dust. He glanced at the two newcomers, then ignored
them. He was barely recognizable beneath the thick coating of dust
across his features. In one corner, a Navy hospital corpsman was
wrapping a compress bandage about a Marine's arm, the dungaree
jacket rolled to the man's shoulder.

"Lucky," the platoon leader muttered. "He's the only one hit. How
is it? Bad?"

The Marine, face also coated with dirt, looked up to grin. He had licked the dirt away from his lips and they gave him the grotesque
appearance of a skinny Jolson, framing his white teeth.

"Hell, I ain't hurt," the youngster declared. "Not even enough t'get
sent back t'the rear with th' beer."

"Don't play hero," the commander snapped at him, still concentrating on the corpsman. The latter looked up, nodding.

"He ain't even got enough of a cut t'get infected," the Navy man
opined. "At least any place 'cept this hole."

The platoon leader heaved a sigh and turned his attention to
McCorkle and Ashdon. He was probably sneering behind the dirt. It
was difficult to tell.

"Well, I hope you two got what you came for. I'm Rockwood."

McCorkle shrugged, trying to ignore the sarcasm in the other
officer's voice. "I don't know."

"I know." Ashdon stated tentatively, glancing from one to the other,
then concentrating on McCorkle, expression one of pained embarrassment. "An' you ain't gonna like it, skipper."

"What're you talking about?" McCorkle's tone was edgy, some of
the tenseness and excitement of the past few minutes starting to catch

up with him.

"I dropped the camera." Ashdon waved a hand vaguely in the direction of the enemy outpost. "It's out there."

McCorkle stared at him, mouth open. He could feel disgust welling up inside of him, mixed with anger.

"You mean I got all my pretty sandbags torn up for nothing?" Lieutenant Rockwood wanted to know.

Ashdon started to turn, shoulders hunched against the disapproval of the two officers. "I'll go and get it," he muttered miserably.

"Wait," McCorkle ordered sharply and Ashdon turned back to regard his senior with the wistful expression of one hoping for a reprieve, but doubting the likelihood.

"Where is it?"

Ashdon shook his head, eyes on the floor. "I dunno exackly. 'Bout half way out, I think."

McCorkle turned to glance at the outpost commander. "You have any glasses?" He didn't reply. Instead, walked to a corner, kicked amid a pile of blankets and other gear, then bent to pick up a set of binoculars. Stepping back, he dangled them by the strap in front of McCorkle, eyeing him doubtfully.

The latter took the glasses and moved to the viewing port, where the private still stood with his rifle, standing clear of the opening, looking through it at a cautious angle. He glanced up in surprise as McCorkle joined him, taking the same care, then began to view the area through the artillery spotting glasses. The first thing he picked up from his slightly higher vantage point was the shell hole he and the sergeant had used for cover. There were other newer holes surrounding it. Slowly, he swept the area, moving the glasses along the finger of land, seeking any indication of the camera. Most of the chromium parts of the mechanism had long since been painted black by Ashdon and the others so as to avoid glare or reflection. That made it doubly difficult and he wasn't certain that he really had spotted it. It looked like a large black rock among the other bits of broken boulder. He leaned forward, trying to get a better look.

"Better watch it," the private warned, but he was too late. There was the crack of a bullet and the wood which formed the frame of the viewing port splintered. McCorkle reacted, whirling away, pressing his body against the wall.

"I should've warned you, Mac," Rockwood chided. "They get sort of touchy after they get a few of them Air Farce tactics your flyboys pull."

McCorkle ignored him, turning to Ashdon to nod. "It's out there," he declared.

"I'll get it," Ashdon stated again, obviously wanting to be told to forget it.

"I'll get it," McCorkle corrected him shortly. "You get back to the trenches and find Shade and that kid."

Ashdon shook his head staunchly. "I'm th' one that dropped it," he reminded.

"Don't argue," McCorkle ordered. "This was all my idea. I'm responsible."

"I've heard about you Hollywood types," the commander declared. "Why not hand wrestle to see which one gets his ass shot off? Or you could decide to wait till night."

"Anything could happen to that camera by then," McCorkle said, "with all the stuff that's flying around here. I'm going after it."

"Don't go out there, Mac." It was an order.

"Don't tell me what to do. I'm senior to you," McCorkle told him stiffly. It caused the other to laugh again, shaking his head.

"You know what they say about lieutenants pulling numbers on each other, Mac," he reminded. "It's like whores arguing over seniority."

There was no way for McCorkle to explain to the officer that this was something he had to do. Having been stuck here in this bunker day after day, watching his men hacked down one at a time by snipers, he was certain to be cynical. But this was McCorkle's first combat assignment. He had been sent here to take motion pictures of the air strike and those pictures were still in the camera out there on that hilltop. He couldn't just walk away and leave them there.

Then, too, there was the matter of Ashdon. He had been pondering the fact that the sergeant had seen him make a fool of himself during the interlude in Japan. Ashdon had said no more about the matter and McCorkle was certain the cameraman had been discreet enough not to mention it to any of the other members of the section. But there still was something he had to prove to the sergeant.

McCorkle realized that the reasons for these feelings were something he didn't fully understand himself; they were little more than vague, semi-formed convictions that he could not attempt to explain to someone else without looking like an idiot. Particularly not with an entire platoon looking on.

"Okay. You're going, but at least let's try getting something going in your favor." He turned to a corporal who sat against the wall, a field telephone between his outstretched legs.

"See if you can raise that mortar section and tell them I want all the smoke they can spare on Luke's Castle," the leader ordered.

"What color?" the corporal asked, looking up to stare through his glasses.

"I'd prefer deep purple. It goes with my mood, but we'll take any-thing we can get. And all we can get, but tell them we want it fast." He glanced at his watch. "Starting in about three minutes."

The corporal began cranking the telephone and after a moment began to talk, cupping his hand over the mouthpiece, his words only a murmur. Rockwood turned back to McCorkle.

"If you've got to do this, Mac, I suggest you run, don't walk. When that smoke hits them, it'll confuse them for a few seconds if we're lucky. They may not start shooting and if they do, they may not know where to shoot. At least, they won't be able to see you. But if they start shooting, don't stop to shoot back. I don't feel heroic enough to come out there to get you." He waved his hands about the bunker. "And I won't send one of my men in for you, either. They have troubles of their own."

McCorkle stared at him, hearing the troubled sympathy in his voice. "Anything else?"

"Yeah. We may get another mortar barrage as soon as they get the smoke out of their eyes."

McCorkle nodded his understanding and turned to move toward the door, but it was blocked by Ashdon. There was a stubborn hard-ness to the sergeant's chin.

"I'm going with you, skipper," he declared almost beligerently.

"I'll make a better deal than that," McCorkle told him, trying to sound amused but doubting that it came off. "If anything happens, come after me and the camera."

Ashdon hesitated, then nodded. "Okay." McCorkle knew that he meant it.

The sergeant was at his shoulder as the two of them edged through the door of the bunker, hugging the shattered wall of sandbags, peer-ing around the corner of the structure toward the pile of rocks that pro-tected the enemy outpost. McCorkle was perspiring, his dungarees dark with the product of his own nervous fear. In spite of this, he felt cold and knew he was on the verge of shaking.

"I still think this is crazy, skipper," the sergeant insisted. McCorkle replied without taking his eyes off of the pile of boulders and the spire of solid rock that loomed cathedral-like above it.

"You offered to go," he pointed out.

"That's diff'rent," Ashdon insisted. Nothing more was said. The two stood there, McCorkle counting the seconds silently, waiting for the smoke shells to land. Suddenly there was the flat, angry crack of a bullet overhead and both of them ducked.

"They know somethin's up," Ashdon worried. McCorkle didn't reply. Instead, he was attempting to assess his own feelings. He was suddenly calm, peering around the corner of the protective bunker, trying to spot the lost camera. Finally he spotted a square of blackness. That had to be it.

Suddenly, without warning, there was a dull, muffled explosion and the enemy outpost was enveloped in a puff of smoke. An instant later, there was another puff of smoke. The first had been white, but this one was a strange shade of orange.

"Go!" Ashdon ordered. McCorkle hesitated, though. There was sudden frantic firing from the enemy position and he heard several bullets snap past, not knowing how close they had come.

Then he launched himself forward, running a zig-zag line as he had been taught years earlier back at Quantico, keeping low, presenting as small a target as possible. Even as he ran, he knew he should be frightened, but suddenly his goal — a small black box out there forty yards between the outposts — was more important that fear. As he ran, his eyes were on the ground, but he realized that more mortar shells were falling upon the enemy position, making the veil of smoke even thicker for his protection. The outpost commander was keeping his word.

He could still hear firing coming from the rock pile in sporadic bursts, but behind him, the Marine line seemed to have accepted the challenge, firing back.

He made the distance more rapidly than he had expected, dropping to one knee as he almost stepped on the camera. He scooped it up without even looking toward the enemy outpost, then whirled and ran back toward the friendly bunker. Ashdon was fully exposed now, frantically waving him on and shouting over the gunfire. A moment later, he was in the shallow trench beside Ashdon, who had dropped to his knees. McCorkle couldn't help grinning as he flicked the camera to the sergeant, who stuffed it inside his dungaree jacket.

"We better haul ass," the sergeant muttered. "They'll be slamming some stuff of their own in here an' it won't be mortars."

Half crawling, Ashdon led the way down the shallow trench connecting the outpost with the main line of resistance. An instant later, he dropped to his belly as mortar shells crashed to their rear. McCorkle dropped behind him, pushing his face into the dirt. In a moment, there was a lull and Ashdon moved forward, the lieutenant behind him. Almost on top of each other, they broke into the connecting trench where Marines were firing from its position. The two of them sprawled there, panting, half laughing for a moment before McCorkle sobered abruptly. There had been a moment of relief, close to hysteria, but suddenly it was over.

"Shade?" he asked thickly. "What happened to him?"

Ashdon jerked his head to indicate the main trench line. "They got him up there. He's hit."

Leading the way, McCorkle dodged along the narrow ditch to where a Navy hospital corpsman was bending over the white-faced boyish sergeant. A part of Shade's dungaree jacket had been cut away and the corpsman was applying a compress bandage.

Shade looked up and smiled weakly. "Shrapnel," he explained between clenched teeth. "But by damn, I'll get one medal outa this clambake!"

"You did fine," McCorkle told him soberly, then looked beyond to where the bearded captain, Shelley, and another corpsman knelt beside another body. But this one showed no signs of life. Half of his head had been shot away. Nonetheless, McCorkle recognized him as Harrison, the boy who had talked to him in the bunker. Shelley's helmet was missing and he was crying as he knelt beside the lifeless body, tears silently rolling down his weathered cheeks to become lost in the tangle of his dirty beard.

Suddenly the exhilaration of success was gone. McCorkle's earlier feeling of guilt came flooding back, a dark veil of sin over his conscience. Shade would be unharmed had they stayed in the rear; Harrison might still be alive. He recalled the lecture on duty he had delivered to Ashdon out there in the darkness and realized that it would have meant nothing to this boy who had died for his own peculiar interpretation of duty. The boy on the ground had carried on his own personal feud with Luke the Gook, pursuing what he felt was his own duty; but Luke had won.

Shelley was looking at him, accusation mixed with his sorrow.

"McCorkle," he said, "get this goddamn crew outa here. Don't ever bring them back. You ain't gonna have a chance to get any more of my people hurt."

"Captain, I..." McCorkle suddenly realized there was nothing he could say. Shelley didn't wait for an explanation. Still helmetless, he rose and lumbered away down the trench while the hospital corpsman covered the dead boy's face.

"Look at me," a voice whispered behind him and McCorkle half turned, looking past Ashdon's shoulder to see Alan Dean's dust-covered outline. There was blood on his nose, where the cuts caused by the irate crab had been opened.

"I'm wounded," the draft dodger whined. McCorkle stared at him through slitted eyes. He wanted to vomit again, but knew he wouldn't. Not now. That part was over.

"I ought to get a medal," Dean wailed. "A Purple Heart, at least."

McCorkle's words were slow and distinct, colored with his own bitterness. Even Captain Shelley paused in his grief, looking back over his shoulder in sudden surprise.

"Kid, *shut your friggin mouth!*"

# CHAPTER 20

T HE TERM "head" in Naval parlance does not necessarily refer to a segment of the human anatomy, nor does it generally indicate a leader. To be blunt, it means toilet.

There is a theory among the lower echelons of the Marine Corps that wars are not won on the fields of battle, but in the heads. Whenever a general officer is seen rushing toward the outhouse bearing the stars of his rank, it is generally conceded that the war is about to pick up; that the general is removing himself to plan strategy. There is even one theory among more art-minded Leathernecks that Rodin's famed nude sculpture, *The Thinker,* actually is a statue of an early Marine general, who has found a hollow stump on which to relieve himself while plotting the plan of battle.

Possibly Henry thought of himself as a future general; whatever his reasoning, he had a decided penchant for two things having to do with officers.

He always had managed to sneak into the outdoor movie and occupy a seat in the Officer's Section until the night there had been run a reissue of *Frankenstein.* Initial sight of the Karloff monster had sent the lad screaming into the night. He had not ventured outside the Informational Services tent after sundown since that evening.

His other vice was sneaking into the Officer's Head at any time he felt the urge. He had been verbally banished on numerous occasions, but he always returned to the crude shed when it was empty. And this threatened to be his downfall.

He had been quietly sitting over one of the holes in the board seat, when the door had been flung open and a squat, bristling man with a single star of a brigadier general had stood glaring down at him.

"What're you doing here, boy?" the surprised general asked in a manner not designed to increase Allied understanding.

"I'm thinkin', suh," the boy replied, staring owlishly at the star.

"Don't you indigents have your own head?"

"In-what?"

"Indigents," the general explained impatiently. "Koreans."

"I'm a North Korean," the boy replied, as though this should clear all facets of misunderstanding.

General Sloop took a step closer, his frown clouding into a scowl. "What's that you have there?"

The boy glanced down at the section of map he clutched in his hand. If he understood the meaning of the words, *Top Secret*, stamped across the white border, he was unimpressed.

"My head papah," he said matter-of-factly. "Them officer pogues're too cheap to leave any, so I hafta use this rough stuff. Plays hell with m'ass, too."

General Sloop pulled himself to his full height. "Do you know who I am, boy?"

Henry shrugged. He long ago had learned that a display of ignorance could nullify many sins. "No, suh!"

"I am Inspector General of the Marine Corps!" the brigadier bellowed.

Henry shook his head, displaying his puzzlement. "Is this whatcha do? Inspec' th' heads?"

"Out!" The general's wrath was verging on hysteria.

"Now?" There was disbelief in Henry's tone. "I gotta at least wipe m'..."

"*Out!*" The general grabbed the front of the boy's baggy dungarees and lifted him bodily off the holed plank. "The map! Where'd you get it?"

"Lemme down!" the boy screeched indignantly, kicking his legs, the oversized trousers ballooning about his ankles. "Wha' kinda horseshit's this?"

"Where'd you get that map?" The brigadier was still holding him by the blouse, but trying desperately to protect his groin from Henry's lashing legs.

"In a trash barrel!" Then realization dawned; here was an opportunity to do a service to humanity. "Tha' Barrymore man was burnin' papahs an' this blew away. Somebody else stuck it in th' trash." If it was a lie, he told it well. The general released him and he landed in a heap, entangled in his trouser legs and bruised pride.

"Barrymore?" the Inspector General panted, trying to straighten his rumpled uniform into a semblance of generalship. With another scowl, he turned and charged through the doorway. Brave Dave Sloop was off to war; his own personal campaign against slovenliness.

It had long been his theory that efficiency is the keynote of victory in battle and he had been a hard master while in charge of troops. Yet those men invariably won the campaigns to which they were committed. Now that he had become commander of a desk in Marine Corps headquarters, he attacked all problems with this same theory.

The general had come by the nickname, Brave Dave, honestly. In World War II he had led his troops at Tarawa and Iwo Jima with a professional dedication that ultimately had earned him his star of rank. At times, enlisted men are inclined to display their feelings of irony or bitterness by tagging unlikely but descriptive names upon their seniors, but in other instances, these titles are applied with affection.

The latter was the case with General Sloop. He was respected for feats past. He also was feared, particularly by the incompetent who had been able to cloak their faults. In keeping with this formula, Lieutenant Colonel Barrymore should have been afraid of Brave Dave. And he was.

Sloop reported the colonel's apparent dereliction of duty to the commanding general. He also made the recommendation that all Korean orphans be banished from the Officers' Head, even if it required sending them to orphanages. Then he charged off in the direction of the 1st Marine Division to put matters right in that segment of the war.

What transpired between the general and Barrymore was unreported, but the latter was reassigned from the Intelligence Section and was designated as the Post Police Officer.

This is a far less important position than it may sound. The term "police" as a military-rooted verb, means *clean-up*, Barrymore had assigned to him one sergeant, one corporal and fifty Korean laborers. His function was to see that the heads were burned out regularly; that all loose paper about the base was picked up and destroyed; that arrangements were made for sanitary disposal of garbage, and that the rocks lining the path before the general's quarters were kept whitewashed.

This had transpired while McCorkle was at the front and he learned the circumstances from Henry, Quillan and others upon his return. There also was a persistent rumor that the general was giving consideration to the recommendation that all orphans be banished from the base. After all, the Inspector General's recommendations would go back to Washington with him. Ultimately, there would be demands from Henderson Hall as to what action had been taken.

"What th' hell's that?" Quillan demanded, staring at Ashdon. The cameraman sat at a field desk, stacks of packaged film before him, but he was holding a round, circular object to his eye, staring speculatively through the irregular hole. Slowly he lowered it, staring at the object curiously.

"I think it's a doughnut," he decided. "At least, that's what I bought it for."

"But what're yuh doin' with it?" Quillan wanted to know, properly intrigued. This perhaps was brought on by the fact that it hardly resembled a doughnut.

"I don't know," Ashdon shrugged. "I ain't d'cided yet whether t' frame it or send it t'my congressman an' complain about war profiteerin'."

"Where'd you get it?" McCorkle asked, equally intrigued. Ashdon cast him a baleful look.

"From th' Red Cross in Seoul, when we was tryin' t'get back down from th' front." Rather than risk the chance of Sales being shot down in the motor transport parking lot, they had gone by truck from the front lines to Seoul, where they eventually had been able to find a plane returning to their base.

"An' they prob'ly begged th' makin's from some mess hall, too," Ashdon charged, "then had th' guts t'charge me for it."

"I doubt that," McCorkle charged. "After all, what does the Red Cross do with all our donations? I'm sure they can afford the materials for a few doughnuts."

"Wanna try t'bite through it?" Ashdon asked, extending the hollow circle, but the officer waved it away.

"That's a curious outfit," Quillan stated, seemingly agreeing with Ashdon's point of view. "They've sure enough screwed up th' Marine Corps."

McCorkle glared at the master sergeant, his expression daring the other to explain. Quillan pretended not to notice as he smothered a yawn, then continued.

"Yes, sir. Back in the days b'fore World War Deuce, th' Corps had a reputation for takin' care of its own, but th' Red Cross has sure loused that up.

"Why, when I was at th' Marine Barracks at Eighth an' Eye in Dee See, if some peon found himself sudden like tossed in th' brig f'r what seemed like no reason, he could figger it was f'r his own good.

"An' it seemed like it was always th' same. Some broad had always busted into th' Ole Man's office and allowed as how she was with child an' it was one of his men that done it. Th' Ole Man'd try t'get her calmed down, alla th' time sayin' that all of us was of excellent moral character and wouldn't do nothin' like run around and sleep with some unwed lass."

Quillan paused, yawning again, while he considered his choice of words. Aware that he had a full audience, in spite of McCorkle's expression of doubt, he went on.

"But th' Ole Man finally would call in th' first sergeant an' have him take down everything this broad knew about th' guy she said was th' one. Then they'd tell her to come back for th' sunset parade at th' barracks an' she'd have a chance t'pick th' guy outa formation. That'd shut her up an' get her outa th' office.

"But she'd no sooner be outa th' door than the top'd be on th' phone, roundin' th' culprit up. After that, there'd be a father an' son talk. If th' kid allowed that he might be th' right one, they'd ask if he wanted t'marry her. When he said he didn't, they'd tell him t'pack his gear and turn in his bedroll. After that, he'd be marched off t'the brig."

"What did that solve?" Ashdon asked impatiently. "An' what's it got t'do with th' Red Cross?" He held aloft his memento, twirling it about his finger.

"Well, that evenin', when this gal would show up for th' parade, th' first sergeant'd hold th' troops b'fore they was dismissed and she'd be led through th' ranks t'look f'r him. When it turned out he wasn't there at all, she'd shed a few tears and tell about how she'd been tricked an' he musta give her a wrong name. Then she'd shove off.

"Meantime, this Marine'd be kept in th' brig without charges till th' Ole Man heard of some Navy ship what was headed in th' general direction of China, the Philippines, or even th' South Pole.

That took care of his problem an', at th' same time, the Corps was gettin' a volunteer for overseas duty.

"But all that went t'hell in th' last war. The Marine Corps got up t'half a million men an' that started all sortsa problems. Up till then, we was considered justa 'nother branch of th' Navy and senators an' congressmen didn't give us much time. Hell, some of 'em didn't even know there was a Marine Corps!

"Then all of a sudden, some of them started gettin' nasty letters from pregnant ladies. They was complainin' about this thing of their lovers bein' whisked right out from under their weddin' vows in favor of combat. An' by that time, th' Red Cross'd got into th' act, complainin' that there was gonna be a population explosion of bastard kids if somethin' wasn't done.

"Then things went from bad t'worse, when some of them pregnant pretties wouldn't be able t'identify th' right man, so they'd just pick at random th' one they figgered to make th' best husband. With some Red Cross director on one side an' an armed guard on th' other, he'd be hauled kickin' an' screamin' his innocence in front of th' chaplain. Sort of a military shotgun weddin'."

"What's all this got to do with Henry?" McCorkle asked, wondering how this conversation had gotten started.

"Sounds like we better keep him clear of th' Red Cross," Ashdon suggested, staring through the ring in his doughnut again, "or they'll be sure t'do whatever's best for him."

"An' we gotta watch John-Ethel-Lionel," Quillan prophesied. "After him tryin' t'get you an' th' skipper killed, he must have it in for this outfit." He glanced at McCorkle, seeking support. "What're we gonna do t'protect Henry, skipper?"

"Hell, what're we gonna do to protect us from Henry?" Corporal Handley wanted to know, but he went ignored.

McCorkle had been pondering this. Also, he had slowly come to understand, partially at least, the affection felt by all but Handley for the wizened little Korean. Almost everywhere that Marines are found, they adopt two things — stray dogs and stray children. In Korea, where the general populace considers even the most bastardly mongrel a delicacy to be fattened then eaten with relish, there was a startling shortage of adult dogs.

This left only stray children of which the war had created a ready supply. Henry was only one of a hundred or so in this camp, all of them earning their keep by working as houseboys and errand runners.

But there were further complications. McCorkle had not found the map he had drawn from Barrymore prior to the foray to the front. He had been certain he had left it on his desk, but in spite of a quiet search, had not been able to find it. He had asked Quillan whether he had seen it and there had been other subtle questions without results. Meantime, there had been two calls from the Intelligence Section, asking him to return it to their files. McCorkle had been able to put off these demands.

There had been a visible change in his attitude since the return from the front lines. Quillan and the others had noted it and discussed it among themselves. The young officer had gained stature. He was more quiet than ever, but there was a new strength about him that had not been there before. While he did not seem particularly forceful in giving an order, there was a maturity to his manner that had not been there before. People moved more rapidly when he spoke to them.

McCorkle, himself, was not especially aware of this quality. If anything, he felt more withdrawn than before. The events that had taken place on the hilltop battle line still crowded into his thoughts in spite of his efforts to keep from thinking about them. He had been unable to rationalize away the thought that he was directly responsible for what had happened to Shade and the other Marine. It was particularly bad at night, when he would awaken from a sound sleep, recalling the mortar barrage and the dead Marine.

It was for this reason that he rather welcomed Quillan's challenge as to what was to be done about Henry. There was the possibility that the boy might have taken the missing map to the Officers' Head with him to use as toilet paper. And there was still another possibility, which he was forced to consider.

Intelligence still was concerned over the fact that there had been enemy anti-aircraft in the area of the Communist emplacement. There had been no such weapon during earlier air strikes upon the outpost. Thinking was that the enemy might have known of the plan.

Whatever the reasoning, one of the Marine Corsairs had been so badly shot up that the pilot had been forced to crash land the craft, suffering injuries. This fact made the missing map even more important.

"Did you tell General Sloop you're a spy?" McCorkle asked the boy, who hid behind the stove, still attempting to regain his dignity.

"There wasn't no time," the boy growled. "Th' ole man was so mad, he didn' even gimme a chance t'wipe m'ass!"

"Ask the kid about your missing map. In fact, ask him where he was the night you went to the front."

McCorkle glanced at Handley, but the radioman was glaring accusingly at Henry. The officer was disturbed, but there was more to it than simply the corporal's animosity toward the boy. With Handley's statement, the matter of the map was now public property in spite of his own efforts to keep the matter quiet.

"You better haul yur tail down t'Supply an' see if them new boots come in," Quillan ordered the corporal.

Handley glanced at him, offering a knowing shrug. "It's a long walk just to change the subject. Besides, I was there yesterday."

"Check again. Now!" There was no doubting Quillan's tone nor his scowl. The corporal rose, hitching up his trousers, and made for the door. He paused to look back at the officer, then at the Korean boy.

Sergeant Shade was still aboard the hospital ship in Inchon Harbor, where he had been flown by helicopter from the front. News concerning his condition was garbled, but one report was that he might lose the wounded arm. Now, as McCorkle sat staring covertly at Henry, Handley's accusation was still in his ears. He remembered the night that the boy had sat there in the dark, crying against his shoulder and he realized that he never had kept his promise to replace the dead dog.

And he recalled Ashdon's vague suggestion that Henry's family might have been bombed by American planes. That would certainly be enough to cause the boy to seek revenge.

"Henry," he asked quietly, "where were you the night we went to the front?"

"Here," the boy replied sullenly, looking around the stove.

"Don't lie," Quillan ordered. "And stand up when an officer speaks to you."

Slowly the boy rose to his feet, glancing at the other Marines. Quillan was scowling at him, while Ashdon watched with reserved curiosity, not certain of the significance of the questioning. Jane had stopped typing and was glancing uncomfortably from face to face.

"Where were you?" McCorkle asked again. His tone was firm,

demanding an answer.

"He was in th' village," Quillan cut in. "Said he wanted t'go down for Korean chow. That our stuff was gettin' too hard on his guts."

McCorkle's eyes were still on the boy, who had dropped his own gaze to center on his feet. The officer knew that he was about to destroy something; the unspoken rapport that had been between them since that dark night in the tent. "Did you have that map when you went to the village?"

The boy shook his head, not looking up. "Don' know nothin' about no map." The words were muttered but stubborn.

"Speak up!" Quillan ordered. McCorkle glanced at the master sergeant, jerking his head in a negative signal.

"You'd better get over t'the other tent an' get them bunks made up," Quillan told the boy. Henry hesitated, then began to shuffle toward the door. Several feet from McCorkle, he looked up, staring the officer in the face. His own features were devoid of expression.

"Don' know nothin' 'bout no map," he repeated dully. Then he was through the door, the panel slamming in his wake. As McCorkle stared after the boy, there was doubt and confusion in his mind. He had expected Henry's expression to be one of hurt, one of betrayal. It had been neither, and the officer didn't know how to interpret this.

"What're you gonna do, skipper?" Quillan asked anxiously. McCorkle shook his head, knowing he was going to have to admit to upper echelon that the map was missing and that it was his responsibility. If Henry had indeed smuggled the map to a spy, the entire chain of events on the hill would have been his fault.

Quillan leaned forward, extending a canteen cup. The officer sniffed the contents, then shook his head morosely. "I'm still recovering from that coming-out party we had up front."

"Comin' out party?" Quillan asked. Any mention of festivities aroused his interest.

"Comin' out alive," Ashdon told him, looking up from this work. "That bastard, Barrymore, had to be tryin' to get us killed."

"He can't do much now," Quillan commented, "'less one of us is sittin' on th' head when he decided to burn it out."

McCorkle ignored the exchange, still pondering the problem of the Korean boy and the missing map. But he was watching as Ashdon carefully packed the raw color film in cartons, then labeled each. Bending closer, he read the address as the cameraman tossed the bundle onto Quillan's desk for the daily mail run.

"Where are you sending that?" McCorkle's tone already was disapproving.

"Kodak in Hawaii. We'll have it back in a coupla weeks."

"It's supposed to be sent to Washington."

"You've been readin' that Navy Photo Manual again," Ashdon accused.

McCorkle tried to sound stern but succeeded only in appearing puzzled. "You send it to Hawaii to be developed, it comes back here, then you ship it off to Dee Cee?"

"We look at it in between. It's good for my ego," Ashdon explained. "Send it to Headquarters an' we don't even see reports on how it turned out. This way, I run it off an' can at least tell whether th' cameras're still workin'."

McCorkle was trying to believe the logic of what he was being told, but a picture of a bearded captain weeping silently over the lifeless body of a boy rose up to block his realization.

"We were out in that hole getting shot at for no good reason? We let them drop that stuff around us for a few feet of film that might never be seen?"

Ashdon shrugged. "No one I know's ever seen any of the stuff we've shot in the newsreels or television. Not legally, at least."

"What about illegally?" the officer asked cautiously.

"Major Lawrence made a deal with th' Tokyo office of *News of th' Day* an' a couple other newsreel outfits. We shot what they wanted, turned it over to 'em, an' they replaced th' raw stock. Worked great for a time."

"What happened?"

"Some clown in th' news outfit's home office wrote th' Commandant of th' Marine Corps a letter of thanks. Even sent him a print of some close air support stuff I'd shot. Next thing, th' roof fell in. All sortsa letters outa Washington, an' th' major tryin' t'explain to th' general that he wasn't really underminin' th' System. He was doin' his best t'get us exposure in spite of it."

McCorkle stared at the sergeant. "Why didn't you tell me this, when I was lecturing you out there in that hole about the life of the Corps being only as long as its publicity?"

Ashdon shook his head, looking away. "Didn't seem a fit time t'disillusion you, sir."

The devil's brew in Quillan's cup was starting to take hold. The master sergeant wavered on his stool, regarding the officer with admiration. "Skipper, anyone ever tell you you'd make a helluva'n enlisted man?"

McCorkle returned the stare, not certain whether he should approve. A discreet knock delayed any decision. "Come in."

The door squeaked open and Sales stepped in. He paused to look knowingly at Quillan. "Got any more of that stuff, Top?"

"Ain't you just been t'Japan?" Quillan demanded with a touch of belligerence.

"An' I brought a su'prise," Sales retorted with an air of superiority.

"Bubonic plague we don't need," the master sergeant grumbled, but handed the cup to the pilot. Sales tilted it, took several gulps, then lowered the container to stare critically into its depths.

"A little green, ain't it?" he wanted to know.

"We hadda bury it b'fore it was done t'keep Brave Dave an' his Snoop Patrol from findin' it."

"What about this su'prise?" Ashdon asked.

Sales looked over his shoulder toward the door, "Tomi-*san*," he called in a bored tone.

McCorkle sat bolt upright, staring, as a figure stepped in, bundled up in old dungarees. A faded utility cap was pulled down over her ears, but there was no denying the swell of the bosom beneath the green jacket.

"Tomi!" McCorkle yelped. The girl paused to look at him in the dimming light. Then she smiled and pulled off the cap, allowing her dark hair to tumble down over her shoulders.

"Hello, Joe-*san*," she said easily.

"How the hell'd you get here?" McCorkle didn't need an answer. His eyes were upon the flying sergeant. "How drunk were you to dream up this stunt?"

"Pretty drunk," Sales admitted agreeably, smoothing the spikes of his mustache. "But even after I sobered up, it seemed a good idea."

"She's Japanese!" Jane accused suddenly from behind her typewriter. She rose abruptly, nearly dumping the machine into Quillan's lap. "What are you doing in my country? We don't like Japanese!"

Unruffled, Tomi smiled. "It's my country, too," she explained softly. "I was born here. I wanted to see it."

"She's a stinkin' spy!" charged Henry. He was framed in the doorway, watching the girl. "A stinkin' Jap spy!"

Then the three Orientals lapsed into the rattling syllables of mixed

Japanese and Korean, while the Marines looked on uncomfortably. McCorkle stepped between them.

"Hold it!" he ordered, glaring at Jane. "What did you say to her?"

"She wanted to know if I thought you have sexy eyes," Tomi replied indignantly.

"Do you?" Jane demanded, not troubling to hide her belligerence.

"Yes," the Japanese girl stated with a boldness enhanced by the simplicity of the word. She was staring at McCorkle, who was attempting to hide his pain. Quillan began to chuckle, then remembered his twenty-odd years of honorable service as the officer turned on him. He scowled instead.

"You'll have to go back, Tomi. Tonight," the officer told the girl as kindly as he could. He looked at Sergeant Sales: "Wind up that plane and get her back to Tokyo."

The sergeant shrugged, enjoying the consternation he had created. "Can't skipper. That ole turkey broke down again. Won't be fixed for two, three days."

"But where can she stay?" McCorkle demanded, his uneasiness growing more evident.

"Here. She's a correspondent." Sales nudged the girl. "Show him your press card."

The girl fumbled in a pocket and produced a rectangular bit of red pasteboard bearing printed Oriental characters. She held it out for McCorkle's inspection.

"What's it say?" he asked suspiciously.

"That I'm a United Nations Correspondent."

"She's a spy!" Henry spat balefully.

Quillan leaned closer to look at the card, then glared at Sales. "Thassa ticket t' th' Nichigeki Burlesque!"

"Prove it!" Tomi demanded coldly. Before anyone could get closer to the card, she tucked it back into her pocket.

"Who are you writing for?" McCorkle demanded over Henry's gurgles of indignation.

"My college newspaper," the girl replied. "Where do I sleep?"

McCorkle ignored the question to rummage through his desk until he came up with a small packet of toilet paper of the type issued with C-rations in the field. He turned to the door.

"Where to, lootenant?" Quillan wanted to know.

"To the head. To think!"

As the door closed behind the officer, Sales reached for Quillan's canteen cup.

"Now there's a romantic exit," he offered with ironic thoughtfulness.

# CHAPTER 21

**A**S PARTIES GO, this one was a sort of negative success, McCorkle reflected. He lay in a corner, staring through the haze of smoke and alcohol fumes that were in more or less equal parts. Everyone had consumed too much of Quillan's raisinjack; there had been three fights, and Alan Dean was bemoaning the irritations the true artist must undergo from unsympathetic editors.

The lad had not been quite the same since he had cabled *Exploit* to describe in glowing terms the flag raising he had recorded for posterity. A day later, the editors had reported that if they wanted flag raising photos, they'd use the one Joe Rosenthal had shot a war earlier at Iwo Jima; not a cheap copy.

Quillan was probably the first horizontal bartender in history, pouring ample shots from his prone position beside a Korean wench. Shamley was amusing another girl by proving he could kiss her without tickling her with his mustache and Halloran was displaying his lack of imagination by getting quietly drunk. Corporal Handley had been invited, but had refused, silently sneering at the willingness of the others to fraternize.

The party had been blackmail, the only circumstance under which Jane would agree to house Tomi until the old torpedo bomber could be repaired. McCorkle had pointed out to her all of the legal technicalities, including the fact that it was against regulations for members of the command to fraternize with indigenous personnel and more illegal to venture past the main gate after sundown.

Jane had countered that it was also illegal to smuggle aliens — particularly Japanese — into Korea. As a result of Nippon's conrol and exploitation of this Land of the Morning Calm prior to World War II, Japanese nationals were hardly welcome.

"Okay," McCorkle finally had agreed in frustration. "We have a party."

"But if you got any ideas about seducin' the lootenant," Quillan warned the Korean girl, "forget 'em."

"Quillan," McCorkle warned softly. He could feel Tomi's eyes upon him and wondered what she might be thinking. It disturbed him, too, that she cared.

"Th' last time she threw one of these brawls, we didn't find Major Lawrence for three days," Quillan explained gruffly.

"It will be a number one party," Jane beamed. *"Ichi-bon.* But I must invite more girls."

"Beat it," Quillan ordered sourly. "We'll be along as soon as it's dark."

McCorkle had attempted to talk Dean into remaining behind with Handley and Henry. The corporal had shown increasing bitterness toward the Korean boy since Shade had been wounded, but Dean had refused to accept the role of buffer.

"If th' Chief-of-Staff gets wind of this, we'll know who t'thank," Quillan warned.

Dean glared at the master sergeant with a show of hurt. "You think I'm a stool pigeon?"

Quillan nodded his frankness. "T'be blunt, yes."

"If I told Ethan what I know about this outfit, you'd all be in the brig," Dean declared.

"That's what's botherin' me."

"Ethan and I are not speaking." The boy fingered his scabbed nose. Quillan noted the gesture and grinned.

"'Cause he wouldn't give you a Purple Heart? Hell, I've been cut worse'n that just openin' a beer can!"

"But you got the Purple Heart for that," the correspondent accused.

"There's a rule that military awards don't go to civilians 'cept in unusual and heroic circumstances. There ain't nothin' heroic 'bout gettin' bit on th' beak by a crab."

Dean looked from Quillan to Ashdon, frustration shading his features. "You guys bother me," he said grumpily. "After being brainwashed all my life, you're tearing down all my idols. You'll tell me next that the Marines really do assign a photographer to every squad, like the Army says."

"We're spread thinner'n that," Ashdon said, "but we move fast. After all, the brass knows the life of th' Corps is only as long as our column inches."

McCorkle stared at Ashdon, wondering what had prompted the sergeant to quote from his own ill-timed lecture, and he recalled for the thousandth time the tragic results of that exploit. He twisted uncomfortably, waiting for Ashdon to turn accusing eyes upon him. Instead, the sergeant went on.

"Publicity's a matter of survival. Back in World War Deuce, there was a little outfit called th' Army Air Corps. They gave a commission t' every writer an' professional liar they could find. Look who's got alla th' defense budget now."

"He's right," Quillan agreed bitterly. "Up there at 5th Air Force in Seoul, they got twenty officers doin' propaganda work. None of 'em are carried as information specialists, 'cause that'd be askin' f'r a congressional investigation. Th' colonel in charge's carried as a special assistant t'th' commandin' general. They got one writer listed as a bombadier, but he ain't been no closer t' combat than th' officer's club."

Now, stretched out on the thin Korean sleeping mat, McCorkle stared through the smoke at Ashdon.

The cameraman, like all the others, was horizontal on his own mat, an arm wrapped loosely about the hips of a buxom Korean girl. As he muttered to her, she giggled, looking away in pretended embarrassment. Somewhere, Jane had rounded up kimonos for the entire group, insisting they shed their outer garments and don the loose robes.

McCorkle pulled the thin silk more closely about him. Quillan was the only man in the room without a girl and McCorkle wondered whether he was married. He was surprised to find that he didn't know the answer.

"I have a yen for you," the feminine voice whispered in his ear.

"Huh?" He turned on his elbow to look at the Japanese girl beside him. Even with the smoke and odor of stale alcohol, he could smell the spice of her hair and the warm cleanness of her body. She extended her hand. Between her fingers was a Japanese bank note.

"A *yen* for your thoughts," she insisted, smiling strangely.

McCorkle shook his head. "I was just wondering what I'm doing here. Why any of us are here in the middle of a rice paddy. Whether we're really proving anything."

The girl searched his face, frowning her sympathy. "The war isn't going well for your side?"

He offered the suggestion of a shrug. "From this far back, one can never be sure there really is a war."

"But you were at the front," the girl replied. "Sales-*san* told me about it. How you could have been killed."

"Someone was killed. For what? A few feet of film that no one is likely to see." He tried to keep the hopelessness out of his tone, starting to look away, but the girl's hand came up to his downturned mouth, soft fingertips caressing his lips.

"But it is your job," she argued softly. "That you do it well is surely enough."

She was closer now. Glancing against his will, McCorkle saw the deep valley of darkness shadowing her breasts. He wondered whether she wore anything beneath the almost transparent silk of her kimono.

McCorkle gathered the girl in his arms, feeling the fullness of her bosom against his chest as he held her. Clumsily, his lips found hers, soft and wanting, warm with passion.

"Lights out!" Quillan's voice called and the kerosene lamp was extinguished suddenly. The master sergeant's laughter rolled across the heavy darkness. "Keerist, lootenant. I was beginnin' t' think you was backwards!"

As McCorkle ground his lips against the girl's mouth, his hand found the opening at the top of her loose robe and his fingers edged it downward. Suddenly she wiggled, trying to pull away.

"No," she whispered, words warm and damp against his ear. "Not now. Not here."

A thunderous rapping at the door caused McCorkle to jerk away from the girl. The lamp was turned up suddenly and all eyes were on the heavy wooden slab, the most sturdy part of the mud-walled hut.

"Who is it?" Jane called loudly.

"Military Police," a gruff voice replied. "Open up!"

"It's a raid!" McCorkle rasped under his breath. "Everybody move out!"

He was on his feet, grabbing frantically for his dungarees and boots, which he had rolled into a tight bundle. The other men were rising, reaching for their scattered clothing, then melting into the darkness toward the rear of the room. McCorkle, clutching his uniform, bent to kiss the Japanese girl. Her arms went about his neck and he could feel her trembling as he reluctantly pulled away.

"What is it?" the girl asked with concern.

"Just play it dumb and pretend you're Korean," he whispered hoarsely. "Don't even admit you speak English!"

"Joe-*san!*" The girl's tone was pleading, but her frightened cry was buried beneath renewed pounding upon the door.

"Keep your brassard on, copper," Jane screamed nastily. "We are gettin' dressed." None of the girls had moved, McCorkle noted as the lamp was turned up. They even seemed bored, as though this was old business with them.

McCorkle was behind Halloran, who resembled an out-of-uniform scarecrow, his skinny shins showing beneath the kimono. They moved through another room in darkness, then the officer saw starlight through an open door. Cold air swept across his face and thinly cloaked body.

As he broke through this rear door, he heard a shout somewhere to his right. That was enough to drive him into a stumbling run, dodging clumps of brush that rose in his path. It was at least two hundred yards to the hole in the fence, but he made it in record time.

As he paused beside the wire, he glanced about for sign of the others, but there was only the night. Somewhere to the rear, he heard a police whistle. The shrilling note spurred him to pull apart the strands of wire, starting to crawl through.

"Halt!" a voice called. Awkwardly balanced half-way through the wire, McCorkle suddenly was bathed in the glare from a flashlight.

"Awright, come through there slow an' easy."

Gingerly, he edged between the barbs, then straighted to his full height, squinting against the light.

"Well," a familiar voice intoned, heavy with sarcasm, "Mister McCorkle, I believe." Even with the blinding glare in his eyes, the officer recognized the voice of Lieutenant Colonel Barrymore. An instant later, the colonel, wearing a pistol and the brassard of the Air Wing's staff duty officer, stepped into the light. He halted before McCorkle, looking him over triumphantly.

"Would it be out of place to ask what you're doing here?" the colonel asked with victorious amusement.

McCorkle gulped, looking down at the fluttering folds of the gown framing his bare legs.

"I was on my way to the showers," he muttered uncomfortably.

# CHAPTER 22

"**W**HERE'S ALL that crap I've heard about loyalty?" Alan Dean snarled, as he peeled off the torn, dirty kimono. "Invite me to a party, then leave me to the wolves. A hellish way to treat a guest!"

"Boy, why don't you drop dead?" Halloran rasped from a corner of the tent, where he sat with bare legs immersed in a tub of near boiling water. "At least, you ain't got no scars."

Dean hurled the tattered robe into a corner, then glared balefully at the jeep driver. He had crept into the tent only moments before. Outside, dawn was breaking and he had spent most of the dark hours lying in a rice paddy, while military policemen had methodically searched the surrounding levees. Dean was in no mood to be treated as a teenager, but he sneezed at that moment to ruin his attempt at dignity.

"Why don't you go tell your buddy, Ethan, how we led you astray?" Halloran asked sarcastically, reaching for a pail and pouring more water over his feet. He paused, bucket in mid-air, to stare suspiciously at the youth. "Or did you tip him off in th' first place?"

"You're accusing me?" Dean demanded in genuine rage. Standing nude, except for muddy socks, he was a bit ridiculous.

"Knock it off, both of you," Quillan growled from his field desk, where he was nursing the last dregs of the bootleg raisinjack. He had had sufficient foresight to take with him a partially full jug in fleeing the hut. Now he glared at Halloran, wrinkling his nose in disgust, then rose and walked across the tent. He poured half the contents of the brown bottle into the water in which the driver's feet were submerged.

"What th' hell!" Halloran demanded indignantly.

"It's an improvement over th' way you smell now." Quillan shook his head. "I don't know about you, boy. You kin find your way around that paddy in th' dark like you had radar. Then you get over-confident once you're inside th' fence an' fall in a garbage pit!"

"It wasn't th' fallin' in that was tough. It was th' gettin' out." The driver had showered three times under Quillan's personal supervision but the odor of decay still clung to him. The master sergeant took a final gulp from the jug, then poured the rest of the alcoholic mixture into the water. "Good f'r athlete's foot, too," he proclaimed.

"Henry!" he called and the Korean appeared from the rear of the tent, rubbing sleep from his eyes. "You seen th' lootenant?"

"Lootenant, hava-no." He shook his head, stifling a yawn. "He didn' come back."

"Where's Handley?"

Henry offered a shrug. "He left when I hit th' sack. Said he wouldn' sleep wi' no gook."

Quillan waved a hand to the torn, mud-splattered kimonos scattered about the office floor.

"Take these things out an' bury 'em," the master sergeant ordered. "An' don't get caught!"

Henry started to gather up the silk robes, wrinkling his nose at the one that had been in the garbage pit and that which Dean had dragged through a recently fertilized rice paddy.

"Tole yuh that broad was trouble," the boy muttered darkly. "Screwed up th' whole outfit. Like where'sa lootenant?"

"McCorkle's a big boy," Quillan defended sternly. "He kin take care of himself in th' clinches."

Halloran stared dreamily into the water. "Wouldn' mind clinchin' with her m'self."

All eyes turned to the door as it swung open. McCorkle paused in the entrance. He was hatless and his dungarees were dark with perspiration. He needed a shave and his eyes were red from sleeplessness and hangover.

"Where is Sales?" the officer asked thickly, sinking limply into the chair before his desk.

"Should be takin' off any minute," Quillan said. "He bummed some green brew offa me a coupla hours ago. Needed it t' bribe th' mechanics t' work all night on that plane.

"We have to get her out of here." The others knew he was referring to Tomi. "Every cop on this base is looking for her."

"That's where Sales is goin'," Quillan soothed. "Back t' Japan an' she'll be with him. If th' lootenant'd care t' step outside, he'll be able t' see 'em take off any minute."

McCorkle shook his head. "The lieutenant can't. The lieutenant is confined to quarters."

"What?" The chorus was unanimous. Even Alan Dean sounded surprised.

"You got caught?" The master sergeant's tone was both wary and accusing.

"Half-way through the wire," McCorkle confessed glumly. "And Barrymore was the duty officer."

"What's he gonna do?" Ashdon wanted to know.

"He mentioned a general court-martial," McCorkle stated with bitterness. "He is researching the proper charges and I'm not to move from this tent until he has all of the charges lined up." He glanced about the circle of grim faces. "He brought up another matter, too. About a missing map."

The death of the man on the hill, Shade's wounds and the fact that enemy anti-aircraft had shot up a plane added to the seriousness of the missing map. All were aware of the seriousness with which rear echelon soldiers consider their paper warfare.

"Jeez," Halloran declared, "of all th' nights t'go over th' fence we pick one when Barrymore's got th' duty."

"How'd you get Tomi aboard that plane?" McCorkle asked.

"She was afraid one of them MP's recognized her from th' hotel," Quillan explained. "So she took off an' found that hole in th' wire where Jane told her it was. She found Sales' plane and got in th' bomb bay. She was sleepin' there when some mech found her. He was all f'r draggin' her off t' th' brig till she said Sales was her friend.

"Jack bribed 'em with my booze t'do a rush fix on th' plane, while she hid inside."

The sound of a laboring aircraft engine permeated the canvas walls of the tent. There was a tense silence as the engine missed several beats, then leveled into an uneven drone that slowly dissolved with distance.

"You should feel honored, skipper," Quillan said with a touch of admiration. "Tomi's heard enough about that wreck since she's known this mob t' realize it's downright dangerous. She musta wanted t'see you bad."

McCorkle wriggled uncomfortably in his chair, then slumped down to hide behind his hangover. He hoped the others didn't notice his blush or the pleased expression in his eyes.

"At least we don't have to worry about Barrymore laying hands on her," he said. "That MP must have remembered her, though. They spent half the night accusing me of starting a white slavery ring."

"What'd you tell 'em?" Ashdon was unable to hide the uneasiness in his tone.

"I kept insisting I simply got lost on my way to the showers," McCorkle explained with an air of innocence. "Dark of the moon and all that."

"Hell, you was two miles from th' officers' showers," Quillan charged unbelievingly. "What'd Barrymore say t' that?"

"It sort of caught him off guard," McCorkle couldn't help a smile at his recollection of the lieutenant colonel's frustration at being confronted with such an excuse.

The field telephone rang at his elbow, but he made no immediate effort to pick it up, but stared at it with hostility. As it trilled again with a long, insistent jangle, he shrugged his surrender.

"McCorkle," he acknowledged into the mouthpiece, then sat listening, finally nodding grimly. "Okay, Gunner. I'll be right there."

He replaced the instrument in its horsehide case, turning to the others. "Schmake says the Chief wants to see me."

Quillan stared at the driver. "Bring the jeep around. No man should hafta walk t'his own court-martial."

"Th' general oughta be th' one t'give you th' word," Ashdon ventured. "When they buck the dirty work t'th' second team, it's bad."

"He can't see th' general," Henry announced from the doorway. "He's in heck."

"He's what?" McCorkle asked with a scowl.

"In heck," the Korean insisted, waving his hands in frustration.

There was a general gasp of disbelief and Quillan rose to tower over the child. "In hack? Under arrest?"

"In heck," the boy agreed proudly.

"Why? What'd he do?"

"Guess that Air Force gen'ral at Seoul got mad when he flew that mission on Luke th' Gook. Says our general's tryin' t'get more publicity'n him."

McCorkle looked at Quillan dubiously. "Can an Air Force general lock up a Marine general?"

It was Quillan's turn to show frustration. "In this goddamn war, anything's possible.

"B'sides, by th' Book, the Ole Man ain't got no business up there, askin' to get his ass shot off. When you get that many stars, you're s'posed t'stick t' generalin'."

Ten minutes later, McCorkle, shaven and wearing clean dungarees, drew up before the sheet metal headquarters and clambered from the jeep. He paused to shake his head, closing his eyes against the rush of pain. His belt buckle was polished to a bright finish as were the silver bars at his collar and on his cap. His face was shiny, too, beneath a glaze of cold perspiration.

"You okay, skipper?" The driver was watching him with concern.

McCorkle straightened and heaved a painful sigh. "If I get out of this, I may lock up Quillan's ass for poisoning the officer-in-charge. What's he put in that stuff?"

Halloran considered the question before replying. "I don't think its s'much what he puts in it. It's more what he does over it while th' stuff's fermentin'."

"What things?"

The driver shrugged, not wanting to display his full ignorance. "A batcha ole voodoo words. Stuff he picked up'n Haiti'r one of them other black magic countries. He says recitin' 'em gives th' stuff more kick."

McCorkle shook his head in a lack of comprehension and turned slowly toward the door.

"Want I should wait, lootenant?" Halloran asked, the first time he had not been in a rush to be away. McCorkle offered him a long suffering look.

"No. Go tell Quillan to make a voodoo doll that looks like Barrymore and push some pins through it!" he ordered bitterly.

"Aye, sir!" The driver straightened behind the steering wheel to cast the officer a precise military salute. McCorkle returned the gesture and watched as the vehicle pulled away amid screeching tires and clashing gears. This was the first time, too, that any of his organization ever had saluted him, McCorkle realized. Did it mean that an officer had no stature with his troops until his military record was about to be tarred and feathered? Until he was about to be ridden out of camp on the *Uniform Code of Military Justice?*

The corridor was dark with shadows and McCorkle halted a few steps inside, blinking to adjust his eyes to the dimness after the brightness.

"Son," Max Schmake half sneered from his office doorway, "you just don't use good sense." McCorkle blinked again, not certain the warrant officer was addressing him.

"With Barrymore hot after your ass, you hafta go over the fence to play footsies with the native broads?"

"But it wasn't like that at all," McCorkle said defensively.

"That bit about the showers?" Schmake shook his head with professional disdain. "It'll never sell." Then he pondered the possibilities. "But it shows originality. Where else could you be headed in a kimono?"

"What about the Chief-of-Staff?" McCorkle's hangover and the lack of sleep were catching up with him and he only wanted this interview ended, regardless of outcome.

Schmake motioned toward a chair. "I'll check if he's ready t'see you."

McCorkle eased into the chair, allowing his chin to sink against his chest. Against the dark screen of his eyelids, he could picture Tomi's lithe form, see the dark shadow of cleavage in the vee of her kimono, and recalled the promise in her voice.

But there was a darker shadow hovering in the background and his eyes snapped open. He had noted that Corporal Handley had not been in the tent that morning. If someone had tipped off the military police concerning Jane's party, it had to be the radio correspondent. He had refused to attend the off limits party, using his hatred of Koreans as an excuse. But would that hatred encompass the entire unit?

"Okay, son." As McCorkle rocked to his feet, the warrant officer was staring at him shrewdly. "You feel okay?"

"Just tired," McCorkle muttered. "It was a helluva night."

"Had yourself quite a time, didn't you, McCorkle?" the Chief asked with dull sarcasm. He was standing at his window, chewing belligerently at his cigar.

"I don't know, sir. I don't remember a good share of it." McCorkle was stiffly at attention, eyes boring a hole in the wall behind the colonel's desk.

"Come now," the colonel condescended. "I'll admit it's dark as a coal digger's ass around here, but how could anybody stray *two miles* from the showers?"

McCorkle shook his head stubbornly, not allowing his gaze to stray from the spot on the wall. "I don't know, sir."

The colonel stared at him for a moment, pondering the fact that this lieutenant no longer seemed to fear him. There wasn't a trace of stammer in his carefully chosen words. Then he tried to fight back a grin as he turned back to the window, chewing even harder on the cigar.

"We have a saying in the Corps that some of you youngsters should heed," he said slowly, then began to recite:

"A Marine never gets drunk, and if he gets drunk, he never staggers. If he staggers, he never falls, and if he falls, he never passes out. And if he passes out, he at least has the professional pride to fall face down in the gutter, so no one can tell he's a Marine."

"Yes, sir," McCorkle agreed humbly. The Chief turned to cast an inquiring glance at Schmake.

"Where the hell's Barrymore? He's preferring the charges."

"Colonel Barrymore was told to be here, sir," the Marine gunner announced. "I'll check." He did an abrupt about face and retreated into his own office, quietly closing the door between. McCorkle glanced at the door on the opposite side of the room.

"Will the general be here?" he asked.

A pained expression crossed the Chief's face as though he had been stabbed. "The general," he declared with unnecessary formality, "is indisposed." He shook his head.

"I don't know what to think about you, McCorkle. When you were assigned to take over that bunch of rabble rousers, I told the general they'd get you locked up in thirty days."

"Yes, sir," McCorkle agreed for no reason other than it seemed expected.

"But you've done a better job of getting work out of them than anyone yet. That's why I'm sorry to see this happen." The colonel's demeanor suddenly changed and he squinted at the lieutenant.

"What about the Japanese girl?" he rasped.

"The what?" McCorkle snapped to renewed attention, his surprise genuine.

"Where are you hiding her?" the Chief demanded. "We know she's here."

"Could I plead the Fifth Amendment?" McCorkle asked with

delicacy.

"There's no such provision in the Marine Corps Manual," Schmake prompted as he reentered. McCorkle glanced at him, then turned back to the Chief-of-Staff with a shake of his head.

"I don't know where she is," he declared truthfully, then added with a touch of diplomacy: "If there is a she."

The colonel paced back and forth behind the desk, not looking at the lieutenant. "Do you realize what complications this could create? The Koreans still consider the Japs their enemy. Any Japanese national caught here would no doubt be considered a spy."

"It could prove embarrassing to the general, if she was being harbored here on the base," McCorkle agreed, staring straight ahead.

Either the Chief-of-Staff had not considered this facet or had sought to ignore it. Now he halted, glaring at the younger officer in frustration. "That's the trouble with this Marine Corps. Too damned many smart-ass junior officers!"

"Yes, sir," the lieutenant agreed matter-of-factly.

"And there's that map that G-2 says was checked out to you. It's never been turned in."

"No, sir." No matter how delicately put, it was an admission of guilt. "I seem to have misplaced it."

"A *Secret* map loose in your place and that North Korean sleeping there. Do you consider that very smart?"

"If that map is missing, the responsibility is mine, not his." He was perspiring again and his clenched hands felt clammy but he had been able to keep his voice level.

"Max," the colonel demanded, "where the hell is Barrymore?"

"In sickbay," the warrant officer reported. "He turned in a few minutes ago with a pain in his gut. They think it's an ulcer."

For a moment it meant only relief, then McCorkle stifled a groan, vaguely recalling his final instructions to Halloran. There was the possibility his words had been taken seriously and that Quillan was hidden somewhere in the dark, muttering strange African rites over a likeness of the victim, vengefully pushing pins into the figure.

The colonel turned upon him, scowling. "This can wait, but get rid of that Korean kid. Clear off this base. Into an orphanage."

# CHAPTER 23

"**A**RE YOU deliberately disobeying a direct order?" McCorkle demanded, staring into Quillan's red face. The master sergeant was completely sober and it was a painful experience. But it was not so painful as the position in which he now found himself.

"Lootenant," he asked slowly, "are you gonna put it that way? Are you gonna order me t'tell th' kid he hasta go to an orphanage?"

McCorkle continued to stare at Quillan for a moment, then glanced at the others. All of the troops were there at his order. Now they appeared shocked by the news, and all of them averted their eyes beneath his scrutiny. Even Handley looked down, nervously picking at a loose thread in his dungaree trousers.

"Somebody has to tell him," McCorkle muttered, realizing he was losing control of the situation. "I thought one of you might be able to tell him better than I. Make it sound good."

"What's so good about goin' to an orphanage?" Ashdon asked. He had raised his eyes and was frowning at the officer with an expression that barely avoided open hostility. McCorkle had no reply and turned again to Quillan.

"What about Jane?"

Quillan shook his head. "That'd be like havin' your mother explain why she hasta drown you in th' well."

"Okay." He offered a sigh, expressing some of his misery. "I'll tell him."

"We might take this place apart again an' try t'find that damn map," Sergeant Shamley suggested. "That might do his case some good."

"That'd be th' fifth time we've looked," Quillan reminded. "It just ain't here."

"Get that chaplain and see what arrangements he can make with one of the orphanages," McCorkle ordered. "That, at least is his department."

Halloran spoke up. "He left yesterday for R 'n R in Japan. Five days."

Quillan's expression brightened as he glanced at McCorkle. "That gives us some time."

"Time for what?" the officer asked glumly. "The Chief gave an order. He didn't leave much room for negotiation."

"We'll figger somethin'."

McCorkle shuddered. Quillan had sworn he had had nothing to do with Barrymore's sudden seizure. In fact, he would not admit he knew anything about voodoo rites. The officer also was inclined to blame the sergeant for his current situation. Had Barrymore not been stricken and held in sickbay, he might have had the matter of discipline settled for better or worse. As it was, he had been placed in hack — official arrest in quarters — until such time as the lieutenant colonel recovered sufficiently to press charges. Under such arrest, McCorkle was honor bound not to set foot outside the tent, except for three trips to chow each day.

"You're in good company, at least," Quillan had declared. "Th' general ain't been outa his quarters since th' day he shot them rockets. He's doin' ten days in hack, too."

This failed to impress McCorkle, who had spent two days wearing the boards raw in the rear of the tent. His constant nervous pacing had reached such proportions that Jane had started to type in rhythm with his steps. This was playing hell with her accuracy; whenever his footsteps faltered, so did her flying fingers.

McCorkle glanced at his wristwatch, seeming to concentrate upon the dial for a moment, scowling.

"I'm going to chow," he announced finally, glancing about. "Keep quiet about this when Jane and Henry get back." The others nodded their understanding, then he slammed the door behind him in an unconscious show of frustration.

Quillan bent over his desk, shuffling papers, pretending to search for something. The others glanced at each other, then away quickly, frowning over their own thoughts. The tent was enclosed in an uneasy silence.

Slowly Handley bent over and began to unlace his boots, pulling them off one at a time to glare at the holes in the soles.

"Another week and there won't be anything left even to cover with paper," he muttered bitterly. "The whole damn sole will be gone an' I'll be walkin' on my feet!"

"We all got problems, Corporal," Quillan growled at him. "If you gotta bitch, go talk t'that boy chaplain. That's what he's here for." Then he added an afterthought. "I guess."

Handley started to speak, then shut his mouth, compressing his lips into a tight line. Sitting there in his stockinged feet, he picked up one of the boots again and shoved his hand into it, feeling for the mass of soggy paper that covered the hole. He drew it out, staring at the mass of damp, mud-soaked pulp, then tossed it into the can at Quillan's elbow.

He reached to a nearby chair and picked up a copy of *Stars & Stripes,* scanning the headline to assure himself that it was several days old, then folded it carefully several times, holding it to the sole to assure himself that it would fit. Then he stuffed it down the throat of the boot, carefully fitting it into the interior. Satisfied, he held up the piece of foot gear to stare into it, nodding his head in a show of gloomy satisfaction.

"As long as *Stars & Stripes* is still in business, I guess I am," he muttered.

He dropped the boot, then bent over to pick up its mate, inspecting the sole with the same masochistic care he had shown the first. Finally, he reached into the interior and extracted another piece of damp, wadded paper. He started to toss this, too, into the can next to Quillan's desk, then paused to look at it more carefully. After a moment, he placed the boot between his knees and began to unfold the paper. A quick glance was enough to satisfy him and he quickly compressed it back into the shapeless wad, stuffing it into the pocket of his dungaree jacket. Another glance about told him that no one had noticed.

Thoughtfully, he picked up an other section of newspaper and began to shape it as an insert for his worn, battered boot. His movements were slow and thorough, but his mind obviously was not on what he was doing. A frown tugged at the corners of his mouth.

"The skipper says not to say anything t' Henry," Sergeant Taylor said suddenly, staring at Quillan, "but he's gonna hafta be prepared for it."

"It'll come in time," Quillan murmured, pretending to concentrate upon the papers in front of him. "Let th' lootenant worry about th' administrative matters. That's why we've got him."

"Gettin' rid of that damn kid'll be th' best thing that's ever happened to this outfit," Handley said suddenly, dropping the boot carelessly beside the other one. There was a harsh note of urgency in his tone and the other Marines looked up, their faces reflecting varying degrees of surprise at the sudden outburst. The frown still tugged at the corners of the corporal's mouth and it deepened in a show of stubbornness.

"I don't see you volunteerin' t'deliver th' bad news," Halloran sneered at him.

"I'll be happy to do it," Handley blustered with the trace of a sneer. "In fact, I'll laugh all th' way to that orphanage if you want me to take him."

"That'll be th' chaplain's job," Halloran said disgustedly. He looked for a moment as though he might spit in one of Handley's boots and the radioman kicked them beneath the stool where he sat.

"Shut up!" Quillan ordered angrily, banging a fist on his desk. "McCorkle's about t'get his ass locked up an' you two're arguin' like a coupla school girls!"

"Henry's important!" Taylor argued hotly. He glanced at Handley with open hostility. "T'some of us, at least."

"First things first," Quillan ordered sternly.

"Where'd you hear that the lieutenant was in trouble?" Handley asked thoughtfully, his sneer gone now.

"Henry," Quillan answered. "He says they're figgerin' out all sortsa things t'charge him with."

"Henry!" Handley snorted. "That figures, too."

"He ain't never been wrong yet," Halloran spoke up, defending the boy. "We get more straight scoop outa him than anyone else around this Boy Scout camp."

"That's right," the radioman agreed hotly, "and how much of the dope he gets d'you think he's passin' onto the line crossers."

"Hell, he don't even know what a line crosser is!"

"In about three seconds I'm gonna be crossin' some lines myself," Quillan warned darkly. "It'll be that line about a master sergeant knockin' a peon on his goddamn ass." He glared from one to the other. "I'm lookin' at both of you, so shut up."

"What was that ole sayin' about givin' a man a choice of a medal or a court-martial?" Taylor asked thoughtfully. His tone was delicate as though this was a forbidden subject, but Quillan didn't take it so.

"It's happened a few times," the master sergeant acknowledged. "Like that kid, Muldoon, with th' Searchlight Platoon."

The others, with the exception of Handley, nodded. His lips were compressed in a tight, unyielding line. The exploits of Corporal Muldoon had become legend all along the Korean battle line; he lived as a monument to inefficiency and blind luck. As a result he was revered by enlisted men wherever his name and tale were told.

This was the case with Muldoon. Except for an occasional curious glance at the daily headlines, he knew little of what was happening on some far-off peninsula called Korea. After all, he was an electrician; lead man on the lights that cut the night skies in front of Grauman's Chinese Theatre each time there was a major studio preview. This gave him stature in the trade and a degree of fame.

Understandably, he panicked when he unexpectedly received that official looking document headed: *Greetings.* Before he could recover, he found himself learning what one does with a rifle on the drill field at the Marine Corps Recruit Depot at San Diego. No sooner had he been able to memorize his serial number and the digits on his rifle, than he was being flown to Korea to help fill the ranks of the wound-depleted 1st Marine Division.

The Armed Forces have gained a negative renown for pounding square pegs into round holes, but just this once, the correct niche was found for the right man, more out of desperation than any degree of efficiency. It had been decided that the 1st Provisional Searchlight Platoon should be formed, and when a new, experimental organization is ordained in any army, the personnel experts burn the late candles to uncover those who might know anything about this new facet of warfare.

Some private first class had ruffled through Muldoon's service record and discovered the notation concerning his civilian experience in front of Grauman's Chinese. He had been assigned immediately to the new outfit.

The Searchlight Platoon had been specifically commissioned to discourage night infiltrations through the lines by the Reds. Stationed several miles behind the main line of resistance, the search-lighters used gas-powered generators hooked in tandem to illuminate their huge glaring charges. The beams bouncing off the low hanging clouds over the front lines bathed No Man's Land with an eerie, unreal glow, lighting up the possible routes of approach. Result was that the Marines didn't sleep well because of all of this light. They also shot hell out of anything that moved — and a lot of things that didn't — out there between the lines.

On the night that he gained fame, Muldoon was at Division Headquarters in the rear, repairing an unserviceable searchlight. He had mistakenly shorted the huge globe and it suddenly directed its glaring beam straight upward into the night.

At that precise moment, a pilot of a Marine night fighter squadron was headed northward to attack enemy supply lines and the beam caught his plane full in its glare. Surprised and confused, the pilot released his bomb load and all hell broke loose below.

One of the bombs hit the headquarters area power plant, plunging the array of tents into blackness. Another hit the enlisted men's head, hurling excrement over part of the camp and half burying the hallowed ground of the chaplain's tent. Half a dozen Marines broke legs or arms as they sought their foxholes, discharging weapons at each other. And three minutes later, certain his headquarters had been invaded, the Division commander was screaming for a helicopter to take him to the rear, where he could command and not have to worry about possibly being buried beneath a ton or so of human manure.

When the lights came on again, Muldoon was the goat. Even his paid-up card in the Los Angeles local of the electrical workers union failed to make any impression.

He was promptly brigged and ordered to stand by for court-martial. The military lawyers were thumbing through their volumes, trying desperately to find some parallel to this situation in the *Uniform Code of Military Justice*, when word came suddenly from the upper echelons that Muldoon was to be released.

One of the bombs had landed atop the hill overlooking the Division commander's quarters. On that hill had been a three-man Chinese suicide team with demolitions and automatic rifles. It was clear that their purpose had been to assassinate the commander and throw local morale into low gear. Through his shorted connection, Muldoon had inadvertently saved his commander's life. Everyone agreed it was better to have to clean a little human feces out of the chapel than to bury the Old Man. The commander, of course, was the first to agree with this logic.

Instead of being shorn of his stripes and drummed out of the camp, Muldoon was promoted to sergeant, awarded the Bronze Star Medal, then sent to Pusan — some three hundred miles from the Division and its commander — for duty. Put in charge of a military theatre, he soon found a searchlight, renamed the place Grauman's Korean Theatre and found himself back at the same old stand.

"Ever hear of a man that's just been decorated also bein' court-martialed?" Quillan wanted to know.

Ashdon looked up from a reel of film, considered for a moment, then shook his head. "Not that I remember."

Quillan frowned thoughtfully. "That th' stuff you an' th' skipper shot at th' front? How's it look?"

Ashdon grimaced his disgust. "Only got one good shot. That first plane t'come in. Looks like that rocket was right on target."

Quillan bounced to his feet. "Find a projector an' come with me!"

The cameraman stared at him, scowling. "Come where?"

"Th' general was flyin' that first plane. He'd like t'see how well he did."

Ashdon was dubious, still scowling. "If he's really locked up for pullin' that stunt, that'd be rubbin' salt in th' wound."

Quillan's tone was suddenly condescending. "Look, I've known th' Ole Man since he was a shavetail lootenant an' won that li'l blue ribbon with all th' stars on it. He may be sorry he's locked up, but he ain't a damn bit sorry he flew that mission. Come on!"

The general's quarters had been erected on a picturesque hilltop overlooking the bay. Although it was constructed primarily of corrugated sheet metal, California's ranch-style architecture had been carefully copied. As it had been built with Air Force rather than Marine Corps funds, the general had not been hesitant about asking for the best. Had it been Marine Corps money, he no doubt would have had someone erect a tent and dig a slit trench behind it. Here, according to popular rumor, there was even an American-made toilet that flushed.

As Quillan and Ashdon dismounted from the jeep, dragging out the cased movie projector, Halloran stared at the front of the house, charmed by the chintz curtains at the windows.

"Maybe you shoulda called first," he suggested. His foot was nervously heavy on the gas pedal, in a hurry to be away from Officers' Country.

"No need t'wait for us," Quillan told him with a show of confidence. "We'll call when we wanta be picked up." As the pair moved toward the door, Halloran spun the wheels and threw up a cloud of red dust that hid the sergeants from view.

"What're we doin' this for?" Ashdon wanted to know. "We oughta be figgerin' somethin' f'r Henry."

"Some of it might rub off."

There was no bell, so Quillan knocked delicately upon the wooden panel, while the other sergeant flinched uneasily with each echoing rap of knuckles. The door was flung open to frame a huge Negro sergeant.

"What'cha all want, Top?" he asked grumpily.

"Master Sergeant Quillan," he announced on a formal note. "I'm here t'show th' general some movies."

"He's got his own movie machine," the Negro declared loftily.

"But he ain't got this film," Quillan told the general's cook. "This here's somethin' he'll want to see."

The Negro shook his head. "Not now. He's indisposed."

"Who is it, Willie?" the general called from the inner dimness. Before the cook could turn, Quillan announced himself in loud, clear tones.

"Master Sergeant Quillan, sir. Late of Marine Aircraft Squadrons, Nicaragua." His bass reverberated off the inner walls. An instant later, the general's bold, squinting face loomed over the cook's shoulder.

"Quillan?" There was a curious intonation in his tone, a sound that was two parts loneliness, one part foreboding. "Are you sober?"

"Mostly, sir." Quillan waved at Ashdon. The latter was attempting to hide behind the projector, although it hung from his hand at knee level. "We just got in some pictures of that air strike. Thought th' general might liketa see 'em."

The frown in the general's eyes deepened to a scowl and his face began to get red. Noting the danger signs, Sergeant Ashdon began to retreat, the projector banging noisily against his knees.

"Let them in," the general ordered abruptly and turned away. The cook cast his back a surprised, disapproving glance, then stepped out of the doorway. Quillan motioned Ashdon into the room.

As they followed the general through what was obviously a parlor,

Quillan gauged the array of bottles in the liquor cabinet and licked his lips covetously. The general saw the look and nodded to the colored cook.

"Willie, fix us a drink."

Ashdon had been studying the voluminous folds of the cotton kimono that shrouded the general's squat figure. Across the shoulders were several Japanese characters and the sergeant's lips slowly but silently spelled out their proper pronunciation. The general cast him an inquiring look, then glanced at the projector.

"Well, set that thing up and let's see what you have," he ordered with the trace of a smile.

"Aye, sir." But as he began to uncoil an extension cord, Ashdon could not resist another glance at the Japanese characters on the coarse cloth.

Among the Japanese, it is often the custom for one to have his profession or job stenciled or embroidered into the fabric of his favorite robe as a bowling team in this country carries the name of a sponsor or club across the backs of members' tournament shirts.

But in view of the delicacy of this mission, Ashdon decided, this was certainly not the time to ask the general whether he was aware he was advertising himself as the local garbage collector.

# CHAPTER 24

**P**EDRO ARMANDO Guillermo Ramon Mendoze-Mendez had been living quietly in the Puerto Rican ghetto of New York City, secure in the thought that the United States was truly the Land of Opportunity.

After all, on his native Caribbean island, when one was out of work, one was out of work. He either could go fishing and hope to catch enough to stave off starvation or he could attempt to borrow enough money from relatives to catch a plane to New York. There he could invariably live with other relatives until he learned the ropes of city living.

It had been a glorious but short period of high living that had come to a startling halt the day he had signed his name to the paper a tall, friendly man in a blue uniform had thrust before him.

Pedro made no secret of the fact that he still did not wholly understand the circumstance that had taken him from a nice warm, overcrowded tenement to the dubious climes of Korea in a scant six months. To him, recruit training in a mosquito-infested swamp called Parris Island, then combat training on the West Coast were only parts of a bad dream from which he still sought escape.

He had been assigned as a cook, but in keeping with Latin culinary tastes, he held to the belief that everything should be well seasoned. It was not until the morning he had sprinkled cayenne pepper in the oatmeal served the Chief-of-Staff that it was decided the Personnel Section had made a gross error.

Just how it had come about that he finally was made the barber at Wing headquarters never had been made completely clear. It may have been based upon the theory that one can recover from a poor tonsorial effort, while this is less likely in the instance of explosive cooking.

Whatever the reasoning, it had become possible to tell when a VIP, a politician or a movie star was expected aboard. In these instances, everyone from the Chief-of-Staff down would surrender to Pedro's undisciplined clippers, then attempt to pass it off as a battle wound if the visitor stared too closely at the tonsorial havoc wrought by the erratic Latin. There had even been one instance when Pedro had drunk a bit too much of the native brandy and had appropriated the Chief-of-Staff's jeep for a flying midnight visit to a house of ill repute in the nearby village.

He had been apprehended and had promptly been locked up. But there were complications. He was the only barber in Wing Headquarters, so everyone had been forced to visit him in the brig for the following thirty days if they wanted their hair cut. Needless to say, during this period he did not have his heart in his work and the effect was worse than usual. Or it may simply have been revenge.

On this particular morning, McCorkle had noticed in the Officers' Mess that all of the high ranking had that clipped look. Several would have been hard pressed to determine even for themselves precisely where their respective hairlines began, making it evident that Pedro was still expressing his hurt over being locked up.

McCorkle had sat alone in the mess, being ignored by the other officers. Since he was under official arrest, awaiting disciplinary action, he was considered contaminated. It was not good for one's career to appear too friendly toward one who was under the cloud of discipline. The only person who had even nodded to him had been Max Schmake. The little warrant officer had paused with his chow tray long enough to ask how he had enjoyed his breakfast.

"What're they doing?" McCorkle had asked with a degree of irritation. "Trying to fatten me up for the kill?"

Schmake, still standing, eyed him speculatively. "You're pretty bitter, ain't yuh, boy?"

McCorkle shook his head, dropping his eyes. "No. Confused. I'd like to know what's going on. If I'm to be court-martialed, I'd like to know it."

"These things take time," Schmake had explained thoughtfully. It was enough to make McCorkle look up abruptly, conscious of his own misery and uncertainty.

"Then I am being court-martialed?"

Schmake shook his head. "That ain't my department, son. Besides, you know I couldn't tell yuh nothin' either way." Without awaiting a reply, he had drifted on, finding a seat several yards away. Although the conversation had been carried on in undertones, most of the other officers in the mess had paused in their eating, curiously observing the exchange between the pair. As McCorkle glanced toward them, they hurriedly dropped their eyes, concentrating upon their food. It appeared that everyone on the staff knew what was happening except himself, he reflected bitterly. Listlessly, he dug at a bowl of watery oatmeal with an iron spoon.

In the tent that housed the Information Section, Handley was pacing the floor, glancing at Quillan from time to time, scowling.

"What th' hell's th' matter with you?" the master sergeant finally demanded, leaning back in his chair to stare at the corporal. Handley paused to stare at him.

"What'd the general say when you showed him that film?"

Quillan shrugged. "He didn't say nothin' in particular. Just wanted t'know why th' skipper's under arrest."

"He didn't know?"

The master sergeant shrugged again. "Hell, he's under arrest himself. He prob'ly don't know half of what's goin' on around here."

"What'd you tell him?" Handley wanted to know.

"I told him I didn't know none of th' details," Quillan explained. "Wouldn't do, would it, t'have him knowin' we was all over the fence that night." He added, "All but you."

Handley thought about it, then shook his head. "I don't know." He thought for a moment, then glanced toward the door. "Where in hell's that goddamn kid?"

"Henry?" Quillan asked, surprised. "What's th' matter? Yuh in such a mood yuh need somebody t'kick."

Handley started to reply, then thought better of it. He crossed the room and slumped into one of the makeshift chairs, starting to tinker with his tape recorder.

When McCorkle arrived, he paused in the outer office to glance about, shaking his head.

"I don't get it," he declared. "Have any of you heard about any VIPs coming in?"

"No, sir. None," Quillan stated. "What's up?"

"Everybody's got a fresh haircut?" His tone was troubled. "Is that a requirement to attend an official hanging?"

"Maybe they just needed cutting," Quillan suggested, voice soothing, but McCorkle refused to accept it.

"Every colonel in the wing?" McCorkle's tone was openly doubtful, but he also realized the fallacies of his own thinking. In the days during which he had been under arrest and confined to the tent, worrying had become the only recreational outlet left that afforded any degree of novelty.

"It's th' general," Henry ventured from the curtained entrance to the rear room. He undoubtedly had overheard Handley questioning his whereabouts and now he glanced toward the corporal with practiced wariness before venturing into the office. "This is th' day th' general gets outa heck."

"Hack," the officer corrected automatically, his mind still on his own problems.

Quillan agreed with the boy. "With th' Ole Man comin' back t'his office, everyone must be out t'make a good impression."

The junior officer also realized that the matter of the missing map also was coming to a head. His negligence probably would be included in the charges to be brought against him.

And by now there was a vague, unfounded dread that had come to him during the night. He had experienced a dream, reliving the events on the front lines, again seeing the dead lad, his head half torn off by shell fire and Sergeant Shade sitting in the trench, gritting his teeth against the pain.

In the midst of this dream, McCorkle had come suddenly awake, swinging up to sit on the edge of his bunk, shaking and sweating, thankful that the only sound was Quillan's snoring in the bunk across the room and Henry's measured breathing from his own bed.

The moment was past, but that vague feeling persisted as he sat there and he attempted to focus his attention upon its meaning.

Then, as he reviewed the events on the mountain top, it had come to him. That night at the slit trench, when he had attempted to relieve himself, he had carried no head paper. Instead, he had found a wad of paper crumpled up in his pocket and had started to use this just as the mortar barrage had started and had left him virtually stranded across the slit trench, battling to keep from falling in.

Sitting there, shaking with the cold, McCorkle had attempted to decide whether that piece of paper could possibly have been the missing map. It had been dark and he had not been able to see what the paper really was. But had he taken the map along to the front?

He didn't know, but the longer he thought about it, the more convinced he became that the classified map was now at the bottom of that slit trench, no doubt covered by now with the excreta of several hundred Marines.

How did you explain that at a court-martial?

"He's back, skipper."

McCorkle's musings were interrupted by Shamley, who was framed in the doorway, nervously fingering his mustache.

*"Who's back?"*

"The chaplain. Came in on the mornin' courier plane."

McCorkle flinched at this news. Since he had agreed to break the news to Henry of the Chief-of-Staff's decision concerning the orphanage, he had purposely ignored the matter, trying not to think about it. Now his reprieve had run out.

He looked about the circle of faces. The eyes of the other Marines were upon him, some sad, others simply wondering. Jane had stopped typing and was watching him from beneath lowered lashes and he wondered whether she had learned of the situation.

"Henry." His voice was higher pitched than he meant it to be. The small gnome-like face peered inquiringly from behind the stove.

"Henry, come in the back room. I have to talk to you." He turned toward the curtained doorway, shoulders drooping, as Henry shuffled slowly to his feet.

"It's about time," Handley muttered from a corner. "He's been a long time on the gravy train."

"Shut up!" Quillan snarled at him.

"You're all too soft," the corporal said. McCorkle halted and turned to glare coldly.

"Handley," he grated, "if I hear another goddamn word out of you, I'll personally staple your mouth shut with your teeth!"

The corporal opened his mouth to argue, then saw the officer's expression. His mouth snapped shut, lips making a tight, angry line. McCorkle held the blanket aside for Henry, then looked back to the men, jerking his head toward the door. One at a time, they began to file out. Jane started to resume her typing, but Quillan took her firmly by an elbow and lifted her off her chair, guiding her toward the door, while she looked up at him in puzzlement. McCorkle dropped the blanket and turned to the boy, motioning him to his own bunk.

"Sit down, Henry. We have to talk."

The boy was tense, uncomfortable, as he slowly edged onto the bunk, watching the officer with flat, expressionless eyes. McCorkle sat down beside him, wondering how to start. In ignoring the fact that this moment had to come, he had rehearsed no speech.

"Henry, you're getting to be quite a boy. One day soon, you'll be big enough, old enough to make your own way." He paused, reviewing this choice of words to conclude that he was off to a poor start.

"Every man in this outfit loves you, Henry, but there are some things over which we have no control. Sometimes, we have to carry out orders that we don't understand or don't like. You understand that, don't you?"

The boy stared up at him, nodding slowly. "Yes, suh."

"There was a lot of trouble up front. One man was killed, then Shade was wounded. There was even one of our planes shot up." The boy said nothing, continuing to stare with that expression that was no expression at all. "Some of the headquarters people started to ask questions about that missing map."

"I'm going to th' orphanage." It was a statement of fact rather than a question. The boy made it quietly, but it stunned McCorkle. There was a long moment before he could bring himself to nod. There was a lump in his throat that he couldn't quite control.

"I can't help it, Henry. None of us can." He put a hand on the boy's shoulder, feeling the thin form. "Try to understand."

The boy nodded solemnly, then lowered his eyes. "I unnerstan'. Ohders." His tone was devoid of emotion, too.

McCorkle's grip tightened on the boy's shoulder. "That's right. Orders." Maybe it wasn't going to be as bad as he had thought Henry seemed to understand. To realize there was nothing any of them could do. Then the boy looked up at him.

The expression of sullenness was gone. In its place was grief. Grief marked by the tears, which the boy fought to hold back.

"I unnerstan'," he maintained stubbornly in spite of his quivering lower lip.

The officer's arm went about the boy, holding him close, and he could feel the shuddering sobs as the boy buried his face against his shoulder, allowing the dam of emotions to flood over. And in that moment McCorkle remembered a similar incident, the night in the dark when Henry had cried against his shoulder. He also remembered his promise to get the Korean boy a new dog, and cursed himself for forgetting that pledge amid the press of his own problems.

"I'm sorry, Henry. I'm sorry." He said it over and over, gently rocking the child, realizing how futile his words must sound. How pointless they were even to his own ears.

In the outer office, the telephone rang but McCorkle ignored it. The instrument continued to jangle until the door slammed loudly. Then he heard Quillan's hoarse mutterings. An instant later, the curtain was thrown back and the master sergeant's head protruded into the cubicle. He scowled, hesitating as he took in the situation.

"Gunner Schmake," he explained softly. "Th' general wants t'see you in his office at eleven hundred sharp. That's thirty minutes."

McCorkle didn't answer. Instead, he glanced down at the child still clinging to him, his tears soaking through the dungaree jacket. His own problems seemed less important now.

Quillan advanced slowly into the tent and touched the officer lightly on the shoulder.

"I'll take over, skipper." He paused, frowning his sorrow. "I'm sorry it hadda be you."

As McCorkle slowly rose, Quillan slipped into his place on the edge of the bunk, enveloping the Korean in his huge arms, whispering to him with a tenderness that might have been embarrassing under lesser circumstances. Looking away, McCorkle covertly ground a knuckle into his own eye. It came away damp.

Possessed suddenly by a feeling of emptiness, he pushed into the outer office and glanced about. The place was still deserted, depressing in its unusual silence.

Suddenly he turned and launched a clenched fist at the thin board wall that divided the tent. With the sound of splintering wood, his hand went through the pine partition.

As he stared down at his bleeding knuckles, he muttered, "The stupid, frigging bastards." But he didn't know whether he was referring to the high brass, the war that had done this to a child, or himself.

# CHAPTER 25

**H**andley stood at the doorway, holding open the panel to stare out across the rice paddy below the base. He stood there for several minutes, deep in thought, until Quillan's growl caused him to turn.

"Huh?" he asked uncomprehendingly.

"I said shut that goddamn door b'fore every fly in Korea finds its way in here." Quillan ordered roughly. The master sergeant was sober, which may have accounted for part of his seeming anger, but there was undoubtedly another reason. No one was certain exactly what had happened between himself and Henry there in the rear of the tent after McCorkle had broken the news to the boy that he was to be sent to the orphanage, but it certainly had not helped his temper. Now he sat at his desk, shuffling papers with quick, abrupt movements that gave away his mood. Handley stepped back and allowed the door to slam shut. The two of them were alone in the makeshift office, but each had, for the past ten minutes, seemed intent upon pretending the other was not there.

"What about McCorkle?" Handley demanded suddenly, ignoring Quillan's eyes as the other looked up.

"Lootenant McCorkle," Quillan corrected firmly. "What about him?"

"What's going to happen to him?" the corporal insisted.

"Who knows?" Quillan shrugged. "There's been papers made up t'recommend him f'r a general court-martial."

"Henry tell you that?" Handley demanded again, his tone suddenly harsh.

"No, Henry didn't tell me that," Quillan mimicked, showing a note of disgust.

"What're the charges?" Handley asked, scowling. Quillan shook his head, returning the scowl.

"How th' hell should I know? D'I look like a legal officer t'you?"

Handley's answer was truthful. "No."

"What're yuh hangin' 'round here for?" Quillan made no effort to hide his irritation. "You got them new boots, so why ain't yuh headed f'r the front?"

Handley hesitated. "I have as much right as anyone else to stick around and find out what happens to the skipper, don't I?"

The master sergeant couldn't hide his surprise. "You mean it's possible yuh give a damn about somebody besides yourself?" Before Handley could answer, he went on. "Or is it just that you're so lousy miserable that yuh enjoy other people's problems?"

Handley ignored the question. Instead, he thrust his hands into his dungaree pockets and began to pace the floor.

"Goddammit," Quillan snarled. "Yo're as nervous as a virgin at a stop light. Sit down!"

Handley stopped in mid-pace, face twisted with an expression of concern that caused the master sergeant to pause, staring at him. There was a scowl on Quillan's face, but it slowly softened as he digested the hurt and confusion that showed in the young corporal's expression.

"What is it, boy?" Quillan asked quietly, the harshness gone from his tone.

Handley shook his head, showing a degree of stubbornness, but it didn't quite come off. "I don't know. Maybe nothing," he muttered.

"Somethin' been buggin' yuh bad, boy," Quillan insisted, some of his own hardness returning. "Better find out what th' hell it is."

"Where's Henry?" Handley wanted to know abruptly. "I'd better talk to him."

"No need," Quillan declared, some of the nastiness coming back into both tone and expression. "He's bein' shanghaied, so there's no need t'pick on him. In fact, that oughta cheer yuh up some. Make your day complete."

"It doesn't make my day complete," Handley declared on a defensive note. "And he has to do something for me." The last was almost on a note of pleading. Quillan only shook his head, his lip starting to curl.

"Henry's been detached from this outfit. He don't hafta run no errands here no more, so get your ass outa my sight an' do your own dirty work!" He started to rise, but Handley, still defensive, was backing toward the door.

"Then, where's the lieutenant?" he asked, still pleading with voice and eyes. "It's important."

Quillan was on the point of lowering the boom on the corporal, but hesitated, then heaved a sigh. He shook his head. "I wish t'hell I could figger you college boys out, Handley.

"Th' skipper said he was gonna get a fast haircut b'fore he reported to'th' general." He glanced at his wristwatch. "In fact, he's prob'ly in th' general's office right now, gettin' a pound of flesh cut outa his ass by Barrymore an' Company."

Handley didn't reply. Instead, he turned and half ran through the door. As it slammed behind him, Quillan shook his head, muttering an oath, then dropped back into his chair.

Five minutes before the designated hour, McCorkle stood in Max Schmake's office, his cap in hand. The little warrant officer looked up from the never diminishing stack of official paper and his eyes widened.

"What'n hell happened to you?" he wanted to know. There was reason for the query. McCorkle's head was clipped to the scalp, the skin showing pink and baby-like through the pore-level stubble.

The officer shrugged. "I thought the condemned man always had his head shaved before being executed." He made an effort to make the speech sound nonchalant, but he could not hide the heaviness of defeat in his tone.

Schmake judged him narrowly, the wonder still in his eyes. His attitude was reflected in the puzzled shake of his head. "You got some mighty strange bumps on your skull, son. Wonder what one of them head fellers'd have t'say about 'em."

"A phrenologist? He'd probably tell me I'd been beaten about the head as a child or I wouldn't have been fool enough to volunteer for this outfit!"

Bitterness crept into McCorkle's tone in spite of the fact that he stood with head lowered, seeming to stare at the cap held in his hands. He had crumpled the headpiece into a shapeless ball, but now straightened it. His tone was ignored by Schmake who ruffled the stack of papers to come up with a formal-looking document. He glanced at his wristwatch, then laid aside the paper. McCorkle craned his neck to get a look at the closely spaced typing, but all he could see was his name centered near the top of the page in black capital letters. He ran a nervous hand over his prickly scalp. He tried to edge closer without appearing obvious, but the warrant officer gave him a knowing glance, then piled some other papers atop the document. He glanced at his watch.

"A couple of more minutes," he offered noncommittally. "The general's waitin' for some other officers."

How many people does it take for a hanging? McCorkle pondered hopelessly. His question was answered a moment later as several members of the staff, all colonels and lieutenant colonels, entered Schmake's office and paused. One of the colonels glanced at his watch, then to Schmake.

"It's about time," he commented as the warrant officer rose. McCorkle had automatically come to attention, but had not failed to notice that Colonel Barrymore was near the end of the line. Schmake motioned toward the door.

"Right on through to the general's office," he said. "He's waiting for you."

There were several curious glances cast in the lieutenant's direction, while others simply ignored his presence. There was the hint of a wolfish grin on Barrymore's lips as he looked McCorkle up and down, then followed the others through the Chief-of-Staff's office, closing the door behind him.

Schmake glanced at his watch again. "It's time," he announced. He gathered up the papers and motioned the lieutenant to the door to the Chief's office. McCorkle opened it and glanced about. The room was empty, but on the opposite side was the door leading into the general's sanctum. The rectangular slab of wood looked suddenly foreboding. Feet dragging, McCorkle started the last infamous mile across the floor, Schmake close at his heels.

"Lieutenant."

McCorkle stopped and turned, while Schmake almost ran him down. Handley was standing in the open doorway through which they had just passed.

"I have to see you for a minute, skipper," Handley stated nervously, turning his hat in his hand, half hiding some object beneath the cover. In spite of his nervous appearance, there was a note of concern and insistence in his tone.

"Not now," Schmake declared brusquely. "The general's waiting."

"It's important, sir," Handley pleaded, ignoring the warrant officer and appealing to McCorkle with his eyes.

"What is it?" McCorkle wanted to know, but Schmake was trying to shove him toward the door. The lieutenant planted his feet abruptly, glaring at the warrant officer. "This is one of my men," he explained.

"You don't keep th' general waitin', son," the warrant officer declared with exasperation. "Your boy'll keep."

"I won't either," Handley stated firmly, taking a step into the Chief-of-Staff's office.

"You askin' t'get locked up, boy?" Schmake demanded of the radio correspondent. "Git outa here!"

"At ease, Gunner,' McCorkle ordered coldly and the warrant officer blinked in surprise. "What is it, Handley?"

"Dammit, you'd keep th' coroner waitin'," Schmake grumbled, but McCorkle ignored him. His curious gaze was upon the corporal as Handley self-consciously withdrew his hand from behind his dungaree cap and extended a dirty, torn mud-encrusted lump. Gingerly, McCorkle accepted it, then stared at Handley for explanation.

"I found it in my boot, sir," the corporal apologized. "I been usin' it all this time since it turned up missing to cover one of them holes. I didn't know what it was till I started to change the paper."

McCorkle looked down at the wad of paper and started to open it. It was the missing map. Schmake teetered nervously back and forth on heel and toe, glancing from one to the other, but the lieutenant was gazing shrewdly at Handley.

"But you've had new boots for three days," he pointed out thoughtfully. The corporal nodded, looking down at his cap.

"I know," he admitted slowly. "At first, I figgered if I just hung onto it, Henry'd be blamed and they'd get rid of him."

"That's what happened," McCorkle pointed out.

Handley looked up and there was misery in his eyes. He nodded. "I know. But now I don't want you an' th' kid to take th' rap for it."

"You're a little late," McCorkle told him, but there was no accusation in his voice.

"Maybe it'll help some in there." The pleading tone was back in Handley's voice, seeking forgiveness, as he jerked his head toward the door. "In there, I mean."

"It might. Thank you." McCorkle started to turn toward the door, but the corporal reached out to grip his elbow.

"Th' general ain't gonna like this," Schmake warned balefully, but again he went ignored by both the officer and the corporal.

"This is th' Fourth of July, skipper," Handley was saying, excitement, desperation suddenly creeping into his voice. "Remember how Shade was going to show Henry how we celebrate it back in the States?"

McCorkle nodded, recalling the incident with the captured case of Chinese dynamite.

"I'd like to show him." Handley allowed his gaze to drop in sudden embarrassment. "Maybe if I talk to him right, tell him I was wrong, he'll let me."

McCorkle hesitated, recalling Quillan's philosophy that there are some men who need to hate in order to exist in warfare. The recollection now bothered him. Had finding the map in his own possession caused the radio correspondent to realize the error in his thinking or would he simply transfer his hatred to another target? There was no way of knowing the answer, but McCorkle came to another realization in that brief moment. He couldn't ask. Some philosophies are meant to remain private.

"Go ahead."

"Aye, sir." The corporal snapped to attention, sudden relief showing in his face. A brief smile now coated his embarrassment.

"Dammit, boy, I'm beginnin' to think we've got the wrong man for the chaplain," Schmake muttered as he reached for the knob on the general's door. He couldn't open it for a moment, because McCorkle was still in the way. The lieutenant turned to him, eyeing him thoughtfully.

"Like I told you, Gunner, he's one of my men," he said simply.

The general was behind his desk, a grim smile on his lips, face bleached and white from the ten days of forced abstinence from the elements. McCorkle paused, surveying the others in the room. Lined up with the Chief-of-Staff, all facing the general, were colonels, lieutenant colonels, majors. Near the end of the rank stood Barrymore, a sickly but nonetheless wolfish smile curving his lips.

Schmake took his place at an angle from the general and glanced at the young officer. "Lieutenant McCorkle! Front and center!"

Stepping forward to plant himself deliberately before the general's desk, McCorkle heard the drone of Schmake's uninspired monotone reading from the document. There were vague phrases mentioning Hill Eight-Eight-Nine and a meaningless date, but the officer was confusedly wondering about this panel of high-ranking officers assembled to his rear.

Was he a special case? Never before had he been involved in the court-martial of an officer, but he could not imagine a situation wherein all members of the court stood at attention, while charges were read. The lump of sodden paper was still in his hand and he squeezed it until some of the absorbed perspiration channeled between his fingers to drip on the floor, but he failed to notice.

"...and gallant devotion to duty throughout reflect the higher credit upon First Lieutenant McCorkle and the United States Naval Service," Schmake intoned religiously.

McCorkle's ears caught the final words and his eyes swiveled to the adjutant. The other lowered the citation, frowning at it.

Pain lanced his chest and McCorkle winced. "Ouch!" he snapped, then turned to find himself face to face with the general.

"Sorry," the wing commander murmured, taking a bit more care in pinning on the medallion. McCorkle glanced down to see the Bronze Star dangling above his jacket pocket. Then the general was pumping his hand.

"Congratulations, Mac," he was saying with a grin. "A magnificent job."

"Thank you, sir." McCorkle didn't have the slightest idea what the general meant. Then the other members of the staff were crowding about, slapping him on the shoulder, offering their praises. Returning his thanks, he was glancing about for Barrymore, but the colonel had fled.

As the others began to drift toward the door, McCorkle started to follow. He glanced down at the medal, pride beginning to replace his confusion. He'd have to read the citation, he reminded himself, to learn the reason.

"Lieutenant McCorkle," the general said behind him, "would you remain for a moment?"

As the door was shut, cutting off the mutter of voices, the general chuckled and waved to a chair. "At ease, Mac. Sit down."

McCorkle took the indicated seat, balancing uncomfortably on the edge of the chair. The wet wad of paper still was clutched in his hand. He held it up to view.

"Here's that missing map, sir," he volunteered uncertainly.

"What missing map?" The general was concentrating on lighting a cigar.

"It's unimportant. I'll take it up with the Chief-of-Staff." McCorkle sat back in the chair slowly, allowing himself to relax.

"Those were excellent movies you took of the attack on that enemy outpost."

"I didn't know the general had seen them." Nor had he known the developed film had been returned from the Honolulu processing plant. "Tech Sergeant Ashdon had more to do with it than I, sir."

The general nodded agreement. "He'll be awarded the Bronze Star, too, at a formation of troops. Good for morale if they see one of their own being decorated.

"In your case," the general added with some delicacy, "it was important that we present you with your medal right away. I hope you don't mind the informality."

McCorkle still didn't understand, but it seemed logical that he shouldn't mind. The general settled back in his chair, admiring the ash on his cigar.

"The Marine Corps wants a public relations man assigned to Tokyo. One who can get news of our activities placed with the news services and magazine writers. So far, we're lumped together with the Air Force and the Army. In fact, we've all but lost our identity."

The general rose, extending his hand again, and McCorkle realized he was being dismissed.

"I know you'll do a job for us in Tokyo and my thanks for what you've accomplished here."

"Not at all, sir."

In the adjutant's office, Schmake stared at him sourly. "Mac, you amaze me."

"How so?" McCorkle started to unpin the medal from his chest.

"You screw up Barrymore's plans for you and get decorated along with it. You could fall in a slit trench and come out smellin' like some of that there Canal Number Five."

"Circumstances," McCorkle defended.

"Then you get shanghaied from a rice paddy to paradise," Schmake marveled, shaking his head.

"Shanghaied?" McCorkle glanced up with a scowl.

The gunner raised an eyebrow. "You don't think you're bein' sent to Tokyo out of reward? You've screwed up Th' System t'where they're scared of you. Son, you're dangerous an' somethin' hadda be done t'get rid of you."

McCorkle straightened, taking a deep breath. He recalled a similar situation and a man whose first name he had never known.

"Gunner," he declared coldly, "I am a first lieutenant in the United States Marine Corps. As a first lieutenant, I outrank you. Ever call me son again, and I'll have your ass!"

Schmake stared at him, thunderstruck. "I'll be goddamned," he gurgled finally. "Another Lawrence!"

Before McCorkle could frame any reply, there was a loud rolling explosion that almost knocked him off his feet. The glass in the office window rattled dangerously and books toppled from Schmake's field desk. The warrant officer dived for cover beneath his chair.

As McCorkle recovered his balance, the adjoining door burst open and the Chief-of-Staff, hair awry and cigar broken at its center, burst in the room.

"What in creeping Christ was that?" he demanded, looking about wildly.

"A lesson in Fourth of July fireworks for a Korean orphan," McCorkle replied boldly. "It's a matter I'd like to discuss with you, sir."

# CHAPTER 26

THE PARTING festivities could have been termed a mixture of sentiment and culture. Henry, holding a small brown and white puppy between his knees, had attempted to play the *Marine Hymn* on an Oriental nose flute after which Jane, in high, cracked tones, had rendered *Auld Lang Syne*. Luckily, there had been no vote to determine which had been the worse performance.

McCorkle's final order had been for Quillan and the others to find a dog for Henry in fulfillment of a nearly forgotten promise. Just where the canine had been procured was a mystery better ignored, McCorkle had decided. The likelihood that the mongrel would ultimately end up as stew in a local household also went undiscussed by mutual agreement.

There had been several other moments of tenderness during the bon voyage celebration. Sergeant Shamley had painstakenly written down his formula for mustache wax, which consisted of unequal parts of beeswax, used crankcase oil and cordovan shoe polish. Corporal Handley had recorded the entire event on tape, taking special pains with Henry's efforts on the nose flute, then had presented the spool to McCorkle.

Although still confined to the hospital ship, Sergeant Shade had sent, suitably framed, the battered razor blade he had used since the day McCorkle had ordered him to shave. An accompanying note boasted that the sergeant's beard had progressed so that he now required a new blade at least every three months. Halloran had performed the unheard of task of washing the jeep for McCorkle's final trip to the airstrip.

Occupied with his pup, Henry appeared to have given up serious spying. He was less sullen and there had even been tears in the lad's eyes as Halloran had driven McCorkle away in the jeep. Not trusting his own emotions, the officer had waved at the boy in an airy gesture, then had turned his attention to the view through the dirty windshield, blinking away the beads of moisture that insisted upon forming on his own lids.

At least for the moment, McCorkle reflected, the Korean boy's future seemed secure. The general had not heard of the plan to ban the orphans from the base and had cancelled it when it had been brought to his attention. The chaplain had been instructed to limit his efforts to the military population and to stay out of civilian affairs, including the orphan problem.

What would happen when there came a change of command, when there was a new commanding general, of course, could not be foretold, but McCorkle had even taken some steps to alleviate that eventuality.

His relief had been flown in from Japan, and as he had looked the new arrival up and down, trying not to appear embarrassed by the formal greeting of Second Lieutenant Keefer O. Whitcock, McCorkle could not help but recall that initial meeting with Major Lawrence. In the arrival of this green youngster, he could not help but feel the superiority he was certain Lawrence had felt over him. There also had been some misgivings about turning over his outfit to this bright-eyed junior officer who was only a few weeks out of the Basic School at Quantico.

The various members of the unit had been introduced to Whitcock and it was obvious that he viewed them with displeasure. Henry had been the last to be introduced.

"You're his thirty-eighth father," McCorkle had decreed with a touch of cruelty.

"M-me?" the surprised second lieutenant had stammered. "B-but I'm not even married?" But before the youngster could protest further, McCorkle had embarked upon the same lecture he had received from Lawrence concerning each new arrival's responsibility for the orphan lad. As this had gone on, Whitcock had glanced about as though seeking some escape, seeming to wilt beneath the amused glances from Quillan and the others. McCorkle had ended the monologue by pointing to Corporal Handley, who had donned clean dungarees for the occasion.

"And he's in charge of citizenship," McCorkle had explained. He wasn't certain whether the radioman's chest had swelled a trifle, but the latter had cast a glance toward Henry, almost smiling.

"What kind of a citizen?" Whitcock had asked sullenly. "He's a Korean."

"I'm a goddam Marine!" Henry had spat at him with open hostility.

But now, there was one minor matter that plagued McCorkle. Neither Quillan nor Ashdon had been present for the final farewells. When he had asked about them, Shamley had volunteered that the two were in conference with Lieutenant Whitcock.

"Indoctrination," Shamley explained confidentially. "They don't want to have as much trouble with him as we had with you to start.

"But there's one advantage," he added. "He's younger. Maybe he ain't had the same amount of brainwashin' you'd had."

"Thanks," McCorkle had muttered, trying not to sound sardonic.

Deposited at the airstrip, McCorkle had returned the driver's salute.

"I get over t'Japan, yuh kin buy me a beer, skipper," Halloran had suggested.

"My pleasure." McCorkle suddenly realized his disappointment at Quillan and Ashdon not being on hand for his departure was unimportant. It was not as though he were going back to the States, he told himself. There would be plenty of opportunity to see them.

Climbing the metal ladder to the cabin of the R4D, an over-age twin-engine transport, he had strapped himself into the canvas-covered bucket seat which was slung between two sections of pipe.

With a touch of nostalgia, he stared through the tiny square window toward a bank of dark clouds that hung on the horizon.

There was the screech of protesting metal and the door was flung open for Quillan and Ashdon to swoop into the transport's cabin. McCorkle, alone until now, stared at them in surprise.

"Did I forget something?" he asked warily.

"Yes, sir. Us," Ashdon replied briskly. He was carrying his seabag, while Quillan had a small liberty bag. Both had shed their weathered dungarees in favor of carefully pressed worsted uniforms. The officer surveyed the pair with suspicion, awaiting a fuller explanation, as they stowed their gear beneath the seats then dropped onto the taut canvas opposite him.

"Th' general decided you'd prob'ly need help," Ashdon explained. "So I agreed t' extend my tour another three months t' see that you stay outa trouble."

"Thanks," McCorkle growled, recalling the complications of his last trip to Tokyo. Then he turned his questioning gaze upon the master sergeant. "What's your excuse?"

"Th' general's so damned proud of that film yuh shot of him in that bombin' run that he wants t' see if we can get it on teevee or maybe th' newsreels," he explained grandly.

"But that film is supposed to be forwarded to Washington," McCorkle protested.

"Lootenant," Quillan said gently, "S'far as I'm concerned, the general's two numbers junior to God. If he wants t' be on teevee, he's gonna be!"

McCorkle heaved a sigh, staring through several pairs of legs as more Marines came aboard and milled about to select seats. After all, the unit here no longer was his responsibility.

"Ashdon," he intoned, "if you're going to work for me at COM-NAVFE, there'll be none of that happy horseshit of the past. We're going to work. Playing will be incidental."

The door of the plane clanged shut with a metallic crash.

"Never fear!" the familiar voice boomed from behind the finely honed spike mustache. "Sales is here!" He saw McCorkle and offered a languid salute, winking, "Welcome aboard, hero!"

"Sergeant!" Ashdon and Quillan jerked erect, pained at the recognition of a new but familiar voice.

Lieutenant Colonel J.E.L. Barrymore sat far forward in the cabin. He was scowling darkly at Sales.

"Me, sir?" the pilot asked in surprise.

"Are you to fly this machine?" Barrymore asked, tone surly.

"I'm going to do my best, sir."

"I am a sick man," the colonel stated irritably. "Do you understand?"

"We'll ride like a feather," Sales promised. "When we hit Haneda, I'm goin' home. This'll be the easiest, safest ride of the colonel's life."

"See that it is," Barrymore ordered, openly disappointed that his words had to sound so anti-climactic.

"What's he doin' on this plane?" Quillan demanded under his breath. Ashdon shrugged, looking covertly toward the lieutenant colonel.

"Henry says he's bein' sent to a hospital f'r his ulcer."

"I thought you weren't allowed in Japan." McCorkle was staring at Quillan. "That old business with the police."

"I'm goin' incognito," the master sergeant said, as though the term should be self-explanatory.

McCorkle slowly slumped back against the seat, dropping his chin against his chest, but he was watching Barrymore through his lowered lashes. Then there was the familiar sound of magnetoes turning over the engines, then one of them roared into life. An instant later, the second engine caught. Barrymore brought his gaze to bear upon the slumped figure. His brows arched in recognition.

"McCorkle!" His tone was scarcely softened by the roar of engines. The lieutenant looked up slowly, sighing in surrender.

"Come here, lieutenant," Barrymore ordered, motioning to an empty seat beside him.

The plane was lumbering down the runway as McCorkle unlashed his safety belt and rose, lurching against the inertia of the moving craft. Fighting to maintain his balance, he moved up the aisle, stepping over the outthrust feet, sitting down in the canvas seat beside the colonel.

"What are you doing here?" Barrymore was staring at him as though he suspected desertion.

"I'm being reassigned, sir." McCorkle did his best not to sound too triumphant. "To COMNAVFE as the Marine Information Representative."

Barrymore raised his eyes as though seeking heavenly interference. His face still was drawn and pale beneath his suntan.

"Sorry to hear the colonel has been ill." McCorkle tried to sound as though he meant it. The colonel seemed to ignore him. His eyes were focused upon the opposite bulkhead of the aircraft as he chewed his lip for a moment.

"McCorkle, I don't agree with the way you do things," he stated carefully, "but you do get results." He nodded to indicate Quillan and Ashdon. "And from all reports, you were able to control those outcasts up to a point." His tone was grudging and the lieutenant waited for him to continue.

"I'll make a deal with you," Barrymore said abruptly, no longer able to keep the self-pity out of his tone. "If we ever again turn up in the same outfit, the last man to report should immediately request transfer!"

McCorkle considered, as the wheels of the old transport lifted off the runway and the craft began to climb. Ashdon brushed past and entered the pilot's compartment.

"It would solve problems for both of us," the lieutenant agreed.

The compartment door opened and Sales stepped out, grinning down at McCorkle.

"Tomi'll meet you at th' airport, lootenant. I just radioed a friend. He's passin' th' word to her!"

"Tomi!" Barrymore glared triumphantly at Sales, then at McCorkle. "That Japanese girl you were hiding!"

The aircraft lurched drunkenly, bouncing McCorkle from his unsecured seat. The plane seemed to stand on its left wing and Sales grabbed for support.

"Who's flying this thing?" McCorkle screeched at him.

"Take it easy," was the unperturbed reply. "Ashdon's got her."

"He's no pilot," McCorkle insisted in panic. Barrymore was trying desperately to catch his breath.

"Sure he is," Sales said amiably. "Taught him m'self. This here's his fourth lesson."

"Get in there before he kills us!" the lieutenant ordered as the plane nosed down in a power dive. Even over the laboring engines, the scream of air through the rigging invaded the cabin. Sales turned and slammed the door behind him.

McCorkle stared through the small square window opposite his seat. At wing level was the American flag that fluttered over the Rice Paddy Pentagon. The pole, he knew, was no more than thirty feet tall. Barrymore saw it, too, and let out a wail of fear.

The plane started to climb and McCorkle turned to look out the window to his rear. A short, squat figure stood bare-headed at the foot of the pole. Even at the growing distance, he could see that the Chief-of-Staff had both fists clenched, waving them wildly above his head in threat.

Barrymore, face green, was fumbling with his safety belt.

"You've gone too far," he grated. "I'm radioing to have all of you arrested the minute we touch down."

With a jerk, his belt separated and the colonel rose unsteadily to his feet, taking a step toward the pilot's compartment. Suddenly, though, he gasped, bending almost double to clutch his stomach as he toppled back into the seat. He groaned his misery, face twisted in agony. Gently, McCorkle replaced the safety straps across his lap and cinched them down.

Quillan had a crude doll fashioned from a crumpled brown paper sack. He muttered strange, nearly silent words to this image, then poked it unmercifully with a ball-point pen. Beside McCorkle, the lieutenant colonel loosed another groan.

"Quillan, knock that off!" McCorkle roared over the engines. The master sergeant reluctantly lowered the makeshift voodoo doll, sighing his disgust at the lieutenant's sudden leniency. McCorkle patted Barrymore sympathetically on the shoulder.

"I'll radio. For an ambulance to meet us at the airport." He paused before rising, turning to look through the window, again. The Korean peninsula was disappearing behind the plane, being blotted out in the early morning mists. He smiled with expectation. Ahead, Tomi would be waiting.

Sales was in the pilot's seat, while Ashdon leaned back in the co-pilot's position, headphones over his cap. Sales looked up expectantly, then shook his head.

"Eight more months'll make twenty years, then they kin have this outfit," he declared critically. "Gonna go back t'Carolina an fo'get th' Barrymores. Gonna catch me a barefoot gal an' settle down on a chicken ranch. Ever catch a kid of mine steppin' off on his left foot, I'll kick his ass clear up where it chokes 'im."

McCorkle digested this bitterness for a moment, then spoke slowly. "You don't really feel that way."

The pilot looked up at him sheepishly, shook his head, again. "No. Reckon I don't." He was frowning over his thoughts. "Ain't nothin' wrong with th' Corps. Just a few bastards in it."

"Amen," McCorkle intoned quietly and without rancor.